F.

Central Support Unit
Catherine Street Dumfries DG1 1JB
tel: 01387 253820 fax: 01387 260294
e-mail: libs&i@dumgal.gov.uk

Dumfries and Galloway
L I B R A R I E S
Information and Archives

UK

CUSTOMER
SERVICE
EXCELLENCE
The Government Standard

24 HOUR LOAN RENEWAL ON OUR WEBSITE - WWW.DUMGAL.GOV.UK/LIA

THE ENGLISH GIRL

Also written by Daniel Silva

The Unlikely Spy (1996)

THE MICHAEL OSBOURNE SERIES
The Mark of the Assassin (1998)
The Marching Season (1999)

THE GABRIEL ALLON SERIES
The Kill Artist (2001)
The English Assassin (2002)
The Confessor (2003)
A Death in Vienna (2004)
Prince of Fire (2005)
The Messenger (2006)
The Secret Servant (2007)
Moscow Rules (2008)
The Defector (2009)
The Rembrandt Affair (2010)
Portrait of a Spy (2011)
The Fallen Angel (2012)

DANIEL SILVA

The English Girl

HarperCollins*Publishers*

HarperCollins Publishers

Hammersmith, London W6 8JB

www.harpercollins.co.uk

Published by HarperCollins Publishers 2013

Once again, for my wife, Jamie,

and my children, Lily and Nicholas

He who lives an immoral life dies an immoral death.

—CORSICAN PROVERB

PART ONE

THE HOSTAGE

PIANA, CORSICA

THEY CAME FOR HER IN late August, on the island of Corsica. The precise time would never be determined—some point between sunset and noon the following day was the best any of her housemates could do. Sunset was when they saw her for the last time, streaking down the drive of the villa on a red motor scooter, a gauzy cotton skirt fluttering about her suntanned thighs. Noon was when they realized her bed was empty except for a trashy half-read paperback novel that smelled of coconut oil and faintly of rum. Another twenty-four hours would elapse before they got around to calling the gendarmes. It had been that kind of summer, and Madeline was that kind of girl.

They had arrived on Corsica a fortnight earlier, four pretty girls and two earnest boys, all faithful servants of the British government or the political party that was running it these days. They had a single car, a communal Renault hatchback large enough to accommodate five uncomfortably, and the red motor scooter which was exclusively Madeline's and which she rode with a recklessness bordering on suicidal. Their ocher-colored villa stood at the western fringe of the village on a cliff overlooking the sea. It was tidy and compact, the sort of place estate agents always described as "charming." But it had a swimming pool and a walled garden filled with rosemary bushes and pepper trees; and within hours of alighting there they had settled into the blissful state of sunburned semi-nudity to which British tourists aspire, no matter where their travels take them.

Though Madeline was the youngest of the group, she was their unofficial leader, a burden she accepted without protest. It was Madeline who had managed the rental of the villa, and Madeline who arranged the long lunches, the late dinners, and the day trips into the wild Corsican interior, always leading the way along the treacherous roads on her motor scooter. Not once did she bother to consult a map. Her encyclopedic knowledge of the island's geography, history, culture, and cuisine had been acquired during a period of intense study and preparation conducted in the weeks leading up to the journey. Madeline, it seemed, had left nothing to chance. But then she rarely did.

She had come to the Party's Millbank headquarters two years earlier, after graduating from the University of Edinburgh with degrees in economics and social policy. Despite her second-tier education—most of her colleagues were products of elite public schools and Oxbridge—she rose quickly through a series of clerical posts before being promoted to director of community outreach. Her job, as she often described it, was to forage for votes among classes of Britons who had no business supporting the Party, its platform, or its candidates. The post, all agreed, was but a way station along a journey to better things. Madeline's future was bright—"solar flare bright," in the words of Pauline, who had watched her younger colleague's ascent with no small amount of envy. According to the rumor mill, Madeline had been taken under the wing of someone high in the Party. Someone close to the prime minister. Perhaps even the prime minister himself. With her television good looks, keen intellect, and boundless energy, Madeline was being groomed for a safe seat in Parliament and a ministry of her own. It was only a matter of time. Or so they said.

Which made it all the more odd that, at twenty-seven years of age, Madeline Hart remained romantically unattached. When asked to explain the barren state of her love life, she would declare she was too busy for a man. Fiona, a slightly wicked dark-haired beauty from the Cabinet Office, found the explanation dubious. More to the point, she believed Madeline was being deceitful—deceitfulness being one of Fiona's most redeeming qualities, thus her interest in Party politics. To support her theory, she would point out that Madeline, while loquacious on almost every subject imaginable, was unusually guarded when it came to her personal life. Yes, said Fiona, she was willing to toss out the occasional harmless tidbit about her troubled childhood—the dreary council house in Essex, the father whose face she could scarcely recall, the alcoholic brother who'd never worked a day in his life—but everything else she kept hidden behind a moat and walls of stone. "Our Madeline could be an ax murderer or a high-priced tart," said Fiona, "and none of us would be the wiser." But Alison, a Home Office underling with a much-broken heart, had another theory. "The poor lamb's in love," she declared one afternoon as she watched Madeline rising goddess-like from the sea in the tiny cove beneath the villa. "The trouble is, the man in question isn't returning the favor."

"Why ever not?" asked Fiona drowsily from beneath the brim of an enormous sun visor.

"Maybe he's in no position to."

"Married?"

"But of course."

"Bastard."

"You've never?"

"Had an affair with a married man?"

"Yes."

"Just twice, but I'm considering a third."

"You're going to burn in hell, Fi."

"I certainly hope so."

It was then, on the afternoon of the seventh day, and upon the thinnest of evidence, that the three girls and two boys staying with Madeline Hart in the rented villa at the edge of Piana took it upon themselves to find her a lover. And not just any lover, said Pauline. He had to be appropriate in age, fine in appearance and breeding, and stable in his finances and mental health, with no skeletons in his closet and no other women in his bed. Fiona, the most experienced when it came to matters of the heart, declared it a mission impossible. "He doesn't exist," she explained with the weariness of a woman who had spent much time looking for him. "And if he does, he's either married or so infatuated with himself he won't have the time of day for poor Madeline."

Despite her misgivings, Fiona threw herself headlong into the challenge, if for no other reason than it would add a hint of intrigue to the holiday. Fortunately, she had no shortage of potential targets, for it seemed half the population of southeast England had abandoned their sodden isle for the sun of Corsica. There was the colony of City financiers who had rented grandly at the northern end of the Golfe de Porto. And the band of artists who were living like Gypsies in a hill town in the Castagniccia. And the troupe of actors who had taken up residence on the beach at Campomoro. And the delegation of opposition politicians who were plotting a return to power from a villa atop the cliffs of Bonifacio. Using the Cabinet Office as her calling card, Fiona quickly arranged a series of impromptu social encounters. And on each occasion—be it a dinner party, a hike into the mountains, or a boozy afternoon on the beach—she snared the most eligible male present and deposited him at Madeline's side. None, however, managed to scale her walls, not even the young actor who had just completed a successful run as the lead in the West End's most popular musical of the season.

"She's obviously got it bad," Fiona conceded as they headed back to the villa late one evening, with Madeline leading the way through the darkness on her red motor scooter.

"Who do you reckon he is?" asked Alison.

"Dunno," Fiona drawled enviously. "But he must be someone quite special."

It was at this point, with slightly more than a week remaining until their planned return to London, that Madeline began spending significant amounts of time alone. She would leave the villa early each morning, usually before the others had risen, and return in late afternoon. When asked about her whereabouts, she was transparently vague, and at dinner she was often sullen or preoccupied. Alison naturally feared the worst, that Madeline's lover, whoever he was, had sent notice that her services were no longer required. But the following day, upon returning to the villa from a shopping excursion, Fiona and Pauline happily declared that Alison was mistaken. It seemed that Madeline's lover had come to Corsica. And Fiona had the pictures to prove it.

The sighting had occurred at ten minutes past two, at Les Palmiers, on the Quai Adolphe Landry in Calvi. Madeline had been seated at a table along the edge of the harbor, her head turned slightly toward the sea, as though unaware of the man in the chair opposite. Large dark glasses concealed her eyes. A straw sun hat with an elaborate black bow shadowed her flawless face. Pauline had tried to approach the table, but Fiona, sensing the strained intimacy of the scene, had suggested a hasty retreat instead. She had paused long enough to surreptitiously snap the first incriminating photograph on her mobile phone. Madeline had appeared unaware of the intrusion, but not the man. At the instant Fiona pressed the camera button, his head had turned sharply, as if alerted by some animal instinct that his image was being electronically captured.

After fleeing to a nearby brasserie, Fiona and Pauline carefully examined the man in the photograph. His hair was gray-blond, windblown, and boyishly full. It fell onto his forehead and framed an angular face dominated by a small, rather cruel-looking mouth. The clothing was vaguely maritime: white trousers, a blue-striped oxford cloth shirt, a large diver's wristwatch, canvas loafers with soles that would leave no marks on the deck of a ship. That was the kind of man he was, they decided. A man who never left marks.

They assumed he was British, though he could have been German or Scandinavian or perhaps, thought Pauline, a descendant of Polish nobility. Money was clearly not an issue, as evidenced by the pricey bottle of champagne sweating in the silver ice bucket anchored to the side of the table. His fortune was earned rather than inherited, they decided, and not altogether clean. He was a gambler. He had Swiss bank accounts. He traveled to dangerous places. Mainly, he was discreet. His affairs, like his canvas boat shoes, left no marks.

But it was the image of Madeline that intrigued them most. She was no longer the girl they knew from London, or even the girl with whom they had been sharing a villa for the past two weeks. It seemed she had adopted an entirely different demeanor. She was an actress in another movie. The other woman. Now, hunched over the mobile phone like a pair of schoolgirls, Fiona and Pauline wrote the dialogue and added flesh and bones to the characters. In their version of the story, the affair had begun innocently enough with a chance encounter in an exclusive New Bond Street shop. The flirtation had been long, the consummation meticulously planned. But the ending of the story temporarily eluded them, for in real life it had yet to be written. Both agreed it would be tragic. "That's the way stories like this *always* end," Fiona said from experience. "Girl meets boy. Girl falls in love with boy. Girl gets hurt and does her very best to destroy boy."

Fiona would snap two more photographs of Madeline and her lover that afternoon. One showed them walking along the quay through brilliant sunlight, their knuckles furtively touching. The second showed them parting without so much as a kiss. The man then climbed into a Zodiac dinghy and headed out into the harbor. Madeline mounted her red motor scooter and started back toward the villa. By the time she arrived, she was no longer in possession of the sun hat with the elaborate black bow. That night, while recounting the events of her afternoon, she made no mention of a visit to Calvi, or of a luncheon with a prosperous-looking man at Les Palmiers. Fiona thought it a rather impressive performance. "Our Madeline is an extraordinarily good liar," she told Pauline. "Perhaps her future is as bright as they say. Who knows? She might even be prime minister someday."

That night, the four pretty girls and two earnest boys staying in the rented villa planned to dine in the nearby town of Porto. Madeline made the reservation in her schoolgirl French and even imposed on the proprietor to set aside his finest table, the one on the terrace overlooking the rocky sweep of the bay. It was assumed they would travel to the restaurant in their usual caravan, but shortly before seven Madeline announced she was going to Calvi to have a drink with an old friend from Edinburgh. "I'll meet you at the restaurant," she shouted over her shoulder as she sped down the drive. "And for heaven's sake, try to be on time for a change." And then she was gone. No one thought it odd when she failed to appear for dinner that night. Nor were they alarmed when they woke to find her bed unoccupied. It had been that kind of summer, and Madeline was that kind of girl.

CORSICA-LONDON

THE FRENCH NATIONAL POLICE OFFICIALLY declared Madeline Hart missing at 2:00 p.m. on the final Friday of August. After three days of searching, they had found no trace of her except for the red motor scooter, which was discovered, headlamp smashed, in an isolated ravine near Monte Cinto. By week's end, the police had all but given up hope of finding her alive. In public they insisted the case remained first and foremost a search for a missing British tourist. Privately, however, they were already looking for her killer.

There were no potential suspects or persons of interest other than the man with whom she had lunched at Les Palmiers on the afternoon before her disappearance. But, like Madeline, it seemed he had vanished from the face of the earth. Was he a secret lover, as Fiona and the others suspected, or had their acquaintance been recently made on Corsica? Was he British? Was he French? Or, as one frustrated detective put it, was he a space alien from another galaxy who had been turned into particles and beamed back to the mother ship? The waitress at Les Palmiers was of little help. She recalled that he spoke English to the girl in the sun hat but had ordered in perfect French. The bill he had paid in cash—crisp, clean notes that he dealt onto the table like a high-stakes gambler—and he had tipped well, which was rare these days in Europe, what with the economic crisis and all. What she remembered most about him were his hands. Very little hair, no sunspots or scars, clean nails. He obviously took good care of his nails. She liked that in a man.

His photograph, which was shown discreetly around the island's better watering holes and eating establishments, elicited little more than an apathetic shrug. It seemed no one had laid eyes on him. And if they had, they couldn't recall his face. He was like every other poseur who washed ashore in Corsica each summer: a good tan, expensive sunglasses, a golden hunk of Swiss-made ego on his wrist. He was a nothing with a credit card and a pretty girl on the other side of the table. He was the forgotten man.

To the shopkeepers and restaurateurs of Corsica, perhaps, but not to the French police. They ran his image through every criminal database they had in their arsenal, and then they ran it through a few more. And when each search produced nothing so much as a glimmer of a match, they debated whether to release a photo to the press. There were some, especially in the higher ranks, who argued against such a move. After all, they said, it was possible the poor fellow was guilty of nothing more than marital infidelity, hardly a crime in France. But when another seventy-two hours passed with no progress to speak of, they came to the conclusion they had no choice but to ask the public for help. Two carefully cropped photographs were released to the press—one of the man seated at Les Palmiers, the other of him walking along the quay—and by nightfall, investigators were inundated with hundreds of tips. They quickly weeded out the quacks and cranks and focused their resources on only those leads that were remotely plausible. But not one bore fruit. One week after the disappearance of Madeline Hart, their only suspect was still a man without a name or even a country.

Though the police had no promising leads, they had no shortage of theories. One group of detectives thought the man from Les Palmiers was a psychotic predator who had lured Madeline into a trap. Another group wrote him off as someone who had simply been in the wrong place at the wrong time. He was married, according to this theory, and thus in no position to step forward to cooperate with police. As for Madeline's fate, they argued, it was probably a robbery gone wrong—a young woman riding a motorbike alone, she would have been a tempting target. Eventually, the body would turn up. The sea would spit it out, a hiker would stumble across it in the hills, a farmer would unearth it while plowing his field. That was the way it was on the island. Corsica always gave up its dead.

In Britain, the failures of the police were an occasion to bash the French. But for the most part, even the newspapers sympathetic to the opposition treated Madeline's disappearance as though it were a national tragedy. Her remarkable rise from a council house in Essex was chronicled in detail, and numerous Party luminaries issued statements about a promising career cut short. Her tearful mother and shiftless brother gave a single television interview and then disappeared from public view. The same was true of her holiday mates from Corsica. Upon their return to Britain, they appeared jointly at a news conference at Heathrow Airport, watched over by a team of Party press aides. Afterward, they refused all other interview requests, including those that came with lucrative payments. Absent from the coverage was any trace of scandal. There were no stories about heavy holiday drinking, sexual antics, or public disturbances, only the usual drivel about the dangers faced by young women traveling in foreign countries. At Party headquarters, the press team quietly congratulated themselves on their skillful handling of the affair, while the political staff noticed a marked spike in the prime minister's approval numbers. Behind closed doors, they called it "the Madeline effect."

Gradually, the stories about her fate moved from the front pages to the interior sections, and by the end of September she was gone from the papers entirely. It was autumn and therefore time to return to the business of government. The challenges facing Britain were enormous: an economy in recession, a euro zone on life support, a laundry list of unaddressed social ills that were tearing at the fabric of life in the United Kingdom. Hanging over it all was the prospect of an election. The prime minister had dropped numerous hints he intended to call one before the end of the year. He was well aware of the political perils of turning back now; Jonathan Lancaster was Britain's current head of government because his predecessor had failed to call an election after months of public flirtation. Lancaster, then leader of the opposition, had called him "the Hamlet from Number Ten," and the mortal wound was struck.

Which explained why Simon Hewitt, the prime minister's director of communications, had not been sleeping well of late. The pattern of his insomnia never varied. Exhausted by the crushing daily grind of his job, he would fall asleep quickly, usually with a file propped on his chest, only to awaken after two or three hours. Once conscious, his mind would begin to race. After four years in government, he seemed incapable of focusing on anything but the negative. Such was the lot of a Downing Street press aide. In Simon Hewitt's world, there were no triumphs, only disasters and near disasters. Like earthquakes, they ranged in severity from tiny tremors that were scarcely felt to seismic upheavals capable of toppling buildings and upending lives. Hewitt was expected to predict the coming calamity and, if possible, contain the damage. Lately, he had come to realize his job was impossible. In his darkest moments, this gave him a small measure of comfort.

He had once been a man to be reckoned with in his own right. As chief political columnist for the *Times*, Hewitt had been one of the most influential people in Whitehall. With but a few words of his trademark razor-edged prose, he could doom a government policy, along with the political career of the minister who had crafted it. Hewitt's power had been so immense that no government would ever introduce an important initiative without first running it by him. And no politician dreaming of a brighter future would ever think about standing for a party leadership post without first securing Hewitt's backing. One such politician had been Jonathan Lancaster, a former City lawyer from a safe seat in the London suburbs. At first, Hewitt didn't think much of Lancaster; he was too polished, too good-looking, and too privileged to take seriously. But with time, Hewitt had come to regard Lancaster as a gifted man of ideas who wanted to remake his moribund political party and then remake his country. Even more surprising, Hewitt discovered he actually *liked* Lancaster, never a good sign. And as their relationship progressed, they spent less time gossiping about Whitehall political machinations and more time discussing how to repair Britain's broken society. On election night, when Lancaster was swept to victory with the largest parliamentary majority in a generation, Hewitt was one of the first people he telephoned. "Simon," he had said in that seductive voice of his. "I need you, Simon. I can't do this alone." Hewitt had then written glowingly of Lancaster's prospects for success, knowing full well that in a few days' time he would be working for him at Downing Street.

Now Hewitt opened his eyes slowly and stared contemptuously

at the clock on his bedside table. It glowed 3:42, as if mocking him. Next to it were his three mobile devices, all fully charged for the media onslaught of the coming day. He wished he could so easily recharge his own batteries, but at this point no amount of sleep or tropical sunlight could repair the damage he had inflicted on his middle-aged body. He looked at Emma. As usual, she was sleeping soundly. Once, he might have pondered some lecherous way of waking her, but not now; their marital bed had become a frozen hearth. For a brief time, Emma had been seduced by the glamour of Hewitt's job at Downing Street, but she had come to resent his slavish devotion to Lancaster. She saw the prime minister almost as a sexual rival and her hatred of him had reached an irrational fervor. "You're twice the man he is, Simon," she'd informed him last night before bestowing a loveless kiss on his sagging cheek. "And yet, for some reason, you feel the need to play the role of his handmaiden. Perhaps someday you'll tell me why."

Hewitt knew that sleep wouldn't come again, not now, so he lay awake in bed and listened to the sequence of sounds that signaled the commencement of his day. The thud of the morning newspapers on his doorstep. The gurgle of the automatic coffeemaker. The purr of a government sedan in the street beneath his window. Rising carefully so as not to wake Emma, he pulled on his dressing gown and padded downstairs to the kitchen. The coffeemaker was hissing angrily. Hewitt prepared a cup, black for the sake of his expanding waistline, and carried it into the entrance hall. A blast of wet wind greeted him as he opened the door. The pile of newspapers was covered in plastic and lying on the welcome mat, next to a clay pot of dead geraniums. Stooping, he saw something else: a manila envelope, eight by ten, no markings, tightly sealed. Hewitt knew instantly it had not come from Downing Street; no one on his staff would dare to leave even the most trivial document outside his door. Therefore, it had to be something unsolicited. It was not unusual; his old colleagues in the press knew his Hampstead address and were forever leaving parcels for him. Small gifts for a well-timed leak. Angry rants over a perceived slight. A naughty rumor that was too sensitive to transmit via e-mail. Hewitt made a point of keeping up with the latest Whitehall gossip. As a former reporter, he knew that what was said behind a man's back was oftentimes much more important than what was written about him on the front pages.

He prodded the envelope with his toe to make certain it contained no wiring or batteries, then placed it atop the newspapers and returned to the kitchen. After switching on the television and lowering the volume to a whisper, he removed the papers from the plastic wrapper and quickly scanned the front pages. They were dominated by Lancaster's proposal to make British industry more competitive by lowering tax rates. The *Guardian* and the *Independent* were predictably appalled, but thanks to Hewitt's efforts most of the coverage was positive. The other news from Whitehall was mercifully benign. No earthquakes. Not even a tremor.

After working his way through the so-called quality broadsheets, Hewitt quickly read the tabloids, which he regarded as a better barometer of British public opinion than any poll. Then, after refilling his coffee cup, he opened the anonymous envelope. Inside were three items: a DVD, a single sheet of A4 paper, and a photograph.

"Shit," said Hewitt softly. "Shit, shit, shit."

What transpired next would later be the source of much speculation and, for Simon Hewitt, a former political journalist who surely should have known better, no small amount of recrimination. Because instead of contacting London's Metropolitan Police, as required by

British law, Hewitt carried the envelope and its contents to his office at 12 Downing Street, located just two doors down from the prime minister's official residence at Number Ten. After conducting his usual eight o'clock staff meeting, during which no mention was made of the items, he showed them to Jeremy Fallon, Lancaster's chief of staff and political consigliere. Fallon was the most powerful chief of staff in British history. His official responsibilities included strategic planning and policy coordination across the various departments of government, which empowered him to poke his nose into any matter he pleased. In the press, he was often referred to as "Lancaster's brain," which Fallon rather liked and Lancaster privately resented.

Fallon's reaction differed only in his choice of an expletive. His first instinct was to bring the material to Lancaster at once, but because it was a Wednesday he waited until Lancaster had survived the weekly gladiatorial death match known as Prime Minister's Questions. At no point during the meeting did Lancaster, Hewitt, or Jeremy Fallon suggest handing the material over to the proper authorities. What was required, they agreed, was a person of discretion and skill who, above all else, could be trusted to protect the prime minister's interests. Fallon and Hewitt asked Lancaster for the names of potential candidates, and he gave them only one. There was a family connection and, more important, an unpaid debt. Personal loyalty counted for much at times like these, said the prime minister, but leverage was far more practical.

Hence the quiet summons to Downing Street of Graham Seymour, the longtime deputy director of the British Security Service, otherwise known as MI5. Much later, Seymour would describe the encounter—conducted in the Study Room beneath a glowering portrait of Baroness Thatcher—as the most difficult of his career. He agreed to help the prime minister without hesitation because that was what a man like Graham Seymour did under circumstances such as these. Still, he made it clear that, were his involvement in the matter ever to become public, he would destroy those responsible.

Which left only the identity of the operative who would conduct the search. Like Lancaster before him, Graham Seymour had only one candidate. He did not share the name with the prime minister. Instead, using funds from one of MI5's many secret operational accounts, he booked a seat on that evening's British Airways flight to Tel Aviv. As the plane eased from the gate, he considered how best to make his approach. Personal loyalty counted for much at times like these, he thought, but leverage was far more practical.

3

JERUSALEM

I N THE HEART OF JERUSALEM, not far from the Ben Yehuda Mall, was a quiet, leafy lane known as Narkiss Street. The apartment house at Number Sixteen was small, just three stories in height, and was partially concealed behind a sturdy limestone wall and a towering eucalyptus tree growing in the front garden. The uppermost flat differed from the others in the building only in that it had once been owned by the secret intelligence service of the State of Israel. It had a spacious sitting room, a tidy kitchen filled with modern appliances, a formal dining room, and two bedrooms. The smaller of the two bedrooms, the one meant for a child, had been painstakingly converted into a professional artist's studio. But Gabriel still preferred to work in the sitting room, where the cool breeze from the open French doors carried away the stench of his solvents.

At the moment, he was using a carefully calibrated solution of acetone, alcohol, and distilled water, first taught to him in Venice by the master art restorer Umberto Conti. The mixture was strong enough to dissolve the surface contaminants and the old varnish but would do no harm to the artist's original brushwork. Now he dipped a hand-fashioned cotton swab into the solution and twirled it gently over the upturned breast of Susanna. Her gaze was averted and she seemed only vaguely aware of the two lecherous village elders watching her bathe from beyond her garden wall. Gabriel, who was unusually protective of women, wished he could intervene and spare her the trauma of what was to come—the false accusations, the trial, the death sentence. Instead, he worked the cotton swab gently over the surface of her breast and watched as her yellowed skin turned a luminous white.

When the swab became soiled, Gabriel placed it in an airtight flask to trap the fumes. As he prepared another, his eyes moved slowly over the surface of the painting. At present, it was attributed only to a follower of Titian. But the painting's current owner, the renowned London art dealer Julian Isherwood, believed it had come from the studio of Jacopo Bassano. Gabriel concurred—indeed, now that he had exposed some of the brushwork, he saw evidence of the master himself, especially in the figure of Susanna. Gabriel knew Bassano's style well; he had studied his paintings extensively while serving his apprenticeship and had once spent several months in Zurich restoring an important Bassano for a private collector. On the final night of his stay, he had killed a man named Ali Abdel Hamidi in a wet alleyway near the river. Hamidi, a Palestinian master terrorist with much Israeli blood on his hands, had been posing as a playwright, and Gabriel had given him a death worthy of his literary pretensions.

Gabriel dipped the new swab into the solvent mixture, but before he could resume work he heard the familiar rumble of a heavy car engine in the street. He stepped onto the terrace to confirm his suspicions and then opened the front door an inch. A moment later Ari

Shamron was perched atop a wooden stool at Gabriel's side. He wore khaki trousers, a white oxford cloth shirt, and a leather jacket with an unrepaired tear in the left shoulder. His ugly spectacles shone with the light of Gabriel's halogen work lamps. His face, with its deep cracks and fissures, was set in an expression of profound distaste.

"I could smell those chemicals the instant I stepped out of the car," Shamron said. "I can only imagine the damage they've done to your body after all these years."

"Rest assured it's nothing compared to the damage you've done," Gabriel replied. "I'm surprised I can still hold a paintbrush."

Gabriel placed the moistened swab against the flesh of Susanna and twirled it gently. Shamron frowned at his stainless steel wristwatch, as though it were no longer keeping proper time.

"Something wrong?" asked Gabriel.

"I'm just wondering how long it's going to take you to offer me a cup of coffee."

"You know where everything is. You practically live here now."

Shamron muttered something in Polish about the ingratitude of children. Then he nudged himself off the stool and, leaning heavily on his cane, made his way into the kitchen. He managed to fill the teakettle with tap water but appeared perplexed by the various buttons and dials on the stove. Ari Shamron had twice served as the director of Israel's secret intelligence service and before that had been one of its most decorated field officers. But now, in old age, he seemed incapable of the most basic of household tasks. Coffeemakers, blenders, toasters: these were a mystery to him. Gilah, his long-suffering wife, often joked that the great Ari Shamron, if left to his own devices, would find a way to starve in a kitchen filled with food.

Gabriel ignited the stove and then resumed his work. Shamron stood in the French doors, smoking. The stench of his Turkish tobacco soon overwhelmed the pungent odor of the solvent.

"Must you?" asked Gabriel.

"I must," said Shamron.

"What are you doing in Jerusalem?"

"The prime minister wanted a word."

"Really?"

Shamron glared at Gabriel through a cloud of blue-gray smoke. "Why are you surprised the prime minister would want to see me?"

"Because—"

"I am old and irrelevant?" Shamron asked, cutting him off.

"You are unreasonable, impatient, and at times irrational. But you have never been irrelevant."

Shamron nodded in agreement. Age had given him the ability to at least see his own shortcomings, even if it had robbed him of the time needed to remedy them.

"How is he?" asked Gabriel.

"As you might imagine."

"What did you talk about?"

"Our conversation was wide ranging and frank."

"Does that mean you yelled at each other?"

"I've only yelled at one prime minister."

"Who?" asked Gabriel, genuinely curious.

"Golda," answered Shamron. "It was the day after Munich. I told her we had to change our tactics, that we had to terrorize the terrorists. I gave her a list of names, men who had to die. Golda wanted none of it."

"So you yelled at her?"

"It was not one of my finer moments."

"What did she do?"

"She yelled back, of course. But eventually she came around to my way of thinking. After that, I put together another list of names, the names of the young men I needed to carry out the operation.

23

All of them agreed without hesitation." Shamron paused, and then added, "All but one."

Gabriel silently placed the soiled swab into the airtight flask. It trapped the noxious fumes of the solvent but not the memory of his first encounter with the man they called the Memuneh, the one in charge. It had taken place just a few hundred yards from where he stood now, on the campus of the Bezalel Academy of Arts and Design. Gabriel had just left a lecture on the paintings of Viktor Frankel, the noted German Expressionist who also happened to be his maternal grandfather. Shamron was waiting for him at the edge of a sunbaked courtyard, a small iron bar of a man with hideous spectacles and teeth like a steel trap. As usual, he was well prepared. He knew that Gabriel had been raised on a dreary agricultural settlement in the Valley of Jezreel and that he had a passionate hatred of farming. He knew that Gabriel's mother, a gifted artist in her own right, had managed to survive the death camp at Birkenau but was no match for the cancer that ravaged her body. He knew, too, that Gabriel's first language was German and that it remained the language of his dreams. It was all in the file he was holding in his nicotine-stained fingers. "The operation will be called Wrath of God," he had said that day. "It's not about justice. It's about vengeance, pure and simple—vengeance for the eleven innocent lives lost at Munich." Gabriel had told Shamron to find someone else. "I don't want someone else," Shamron had responded. "I want you."

For the next three years, Gabriel and the other Wrath of God operatives stalked their prey across Europe and the Middle East. Armed with a .22-caliber Beretta, a soft-spoken weapon suitable for killing at close range, Gabriel personally assassinated six members of Black September. Whenever possible he shot them eleven times, one bullet for each Israeli butchered in Munich. When he finally returned home, his temples were the color of ash and his face was that of a man twenty years his senior. No longer able to produce original work, he went to Venice to study the craft of restoration. Then, when he was rested, he went back to work for Shamron. In the years that followed, he carried out some of the most fabled operations in the history of Israeli intelligence. Now, after many years of restless wandering, he had finally returned to Jerusalem. No one was more pleased by this than Shamron, who loved Gabriel as a son and treated the apartment on Narkiss Street as though it were his own. Once, Gabriel might have chafed under the pressure of Shamron's constant presence, but no more. The great Ari Shamron was eternal, but the vessel in which his spirit resided would not last forever.

Nothing had done more damage to Shamron's health than his relentless smoking. It was a habit he acquired as a young man in eastern Poland, and it had grown worse after he had come to Palestine, where he fought in the war that led to Israel's independence. Now, as he described his meeting with the prime minister, he flicked open his old Zippo lighter and used it to ignite another one of his foul-smelling cigarettes.

"The prime minister is on edge, more so than usual. I suppose he has a right to be. The great Arab Awakening has plunged the entire region into chaos. And the Iranians are growing closer to realizing their nuclear dreams. At some point soon, they will enter a zone of immunity, making it impossible for us to act militarily without the help of the Americans." Shamron closed his lighter with a snap and looked at Gabriel, who had resumed work on the painting. "Are you listening to me?"

"I'm hanging on your every word."

"Prove it."

Gabriel repeated Shamron's last statement verbatim. Shamron

smiled. He regarded Gabriel's flawless memory as one of his finest accomplishments. He twirled the Zippo lighter in his fingertips. Two turns to the right, two turns to the left.

"The problem is that the American president refuses to lay down any hard-and-fast red lines. He says he will not allow the Iranians to build nuclear weapons. But that declaration is meaningless if the Iranians have the *capability* to build them in a short period of time."

"Like the Japanese."

"The Japanese aren't ruled by apocalyptic Shia mullahs," Shamron said. "If the American president isn't careful, his two most important foreign policy achievements will be a nuclear Iran and the restoration of the Islamic caliphate."

"Welcome to the post-American world, Ari."

"Which is why I think we're foolish to leave our security in their hands. But that's not the prime minister's only problem," Shamron added. "The generals aren't sure they can destroy enough of the program to make a military strike effective. And King Saul Boulevard, under the tutelage of your friend Uzi Navot, is telling the prime minister that a unilateral war with the Persians would be a catastrophe of biblical proportions."

King Saul Boulevard was the address of Israel's secret intelligence service. It had a long and deliberately misleading name that had very little to do with the true nature of its work. Even retired agents like Gabriel and Shamron referred to it as "the Office" and nothing else.

"Uzi is the one who sees the raw intelligence every day," said Gabriel.

"I see it, too. Not all of it," Shamron added hastily, "but enough to convince me that Uzi's calculations about how much time we have might be flawed."

"Math was never Uzi's strong suit. But when he was in the field, he never made mistakes."

"That's because he rarely put himself in a position where it was possible to make a mistake." Shamron lapsed into silence and watched the wind moving in the eucalyptus tree beyond the balustrade of Gabriel's terrace. "I've always said that a career without controversy is not a proper career at all. I've had my share, and so have you."

"And I have the scars to prove it."

"And the accolades, too," Shamron said. "The prime minister is concerned the Office is too cautious when it comes to Iran. Yes, we've inserted viruses into their computers and eliminated a handful of their scientists, but nothing has gone boom lately. The prime minister would like Uzi to produce another Operation Masterpiece."

Masterpiece was the code name for a joint Israeli, American, and British operation that resulted in the destruction of four secret Iranian enrichment facilities. It had occurred on Uzi Navot's watch, but within the corridors of King Saul Boulevard, it was regarded as one of Gabriel's finest hours.

"Opportunities like Masterpiece don't come along every day, Ari."

"That's true," Shamron conceded. "But I've always believed that most opportunities are earned rather than bestowed. And so does the prime minister."

"Has he lost confidence in Uzi?"

"Not yet. But he wanted to know whether I'd lost mine."

"What did you say?"

"What choice did I have? I was the one who recommended him for the job."

"So you gave him your blessing?"

"It was conditional."

"How so?"

"I reminded the prime minister that the person I *really* wanted in the job wasn't interested." Shamron shook his head slowly. "You are the only man in the history of the Office who has turned down a chance to be the director."

"There's a first for everything, Ari."

"Does that mean you might reconsider?"

"Is that why you're here?"

"I thought you might enjoy the pleasure of my company," Shamron countered. "And the prime minister and I were wondering whether you might be willing to do a bit of outreach to one of our closest allies."

"Which one?"

"Graham Seymour dropped into town unannounced. He'd like a word."

Gabriel turned to face Shamron. "A word about what?" he asked after a moment.

"He wouldn't say, but apparently it's urgent." Shamron walked over to the easel and squinted at the pristine patch of canvas where Gabriel had been working. "It looks new again."

"That's the point."

"Is there any chance you could do the same for me?"

"Sorry, Ari," said Gabriel, touching Shamron's deeply crevassed cheek, "but I'm afraid you're beyond repair."

4

KING DAVID HOTEL, JERUSALEM

O N THE AFTERNOON OF JULY 22, 1946, the extremist Zionist group known as the Irgun detonated a large bomb in the King David Hotel, headquarters of all British military and civilian forces in Palestine. The attack, a reprisal for the arrest of several hundred Jewish fighters, killed ninety-one people, including twenty-eight British subjects who had ignored a telephone warning to evacuate the hotel. Though universally condemned, the bombing would quickly prove to be one of the most effective acts of political violence ever committed. Within two years, the British had retreated from Palestine, and the modern State of Israel, once an almost unimaginable Zionist dream, was a reality.

Among those fortunate enough to survive the bombing was a young British intelligence officer named Arthur Seymour, a veteran of the wartime Double Cross program who had recently been transferred to Palestine to spy on the Jewish underground. Seymour should have been in his office at the time of the attack but was running a few minutes late after meeting with an informant in the Old City. He heard the detonation as he was passing through the Jaffa Gate and watched in horror as part of the hotel collapsed. The image would haunt Seymour for the remainder of his life and shape the course of his career. Virulently anti-Israeli and fluent in Arabic, he developed uncomfortably close ties to many of Israel's enemies. He was a regular guest of Egyptian president Gamal Abdel Nasser and an early admirer of a young Palestinian revolutionary named Yasir Arafat.

Despite his pro-Arab sympathies, the Office regarded Arthur Seymour as one of MI6's most capable officers in the Middle East. And so it came as something of a surprise when Seymour's only son, Graham, chose a career at MI5 rather than the more glamorous Secret Intelligence Service. Seymour the Younger, as he was known early in his career, served first in counterintelligence, working against the KGB in London. Then, after the fall of the Berlin Wall and the rise in Islamic fanaticism, he was promoted to chief of counterterrorism. Now, as MI5's deputy director, he had been forced to rely on his expertise in both disciplines. There were more Russian spies plying their trade in London these days than at the height of the Cold War. And thanks to mistakes by successive British governments, the United Kingdom was now home to several thousand Islamic militants from the Arab world and Asia. Seymour referred to London as "Kandahar on the Thames." Privately, he worried that his country was sliding closer to the edge of a civilizational abyss.

Though Graham Seymour had inherited his father's passion for pure espionage, he shared none of his disdain for the State of Israel. Indeed, under his guidance, MI5 had forged close ties with the Office and, in particular, with Gabriel Allon. The two men regarded themselves as members of a secret brotherhood who did the unpleasant chores no one else was willing to do and worried about the consequences later. They had fought for one another, bled for one another, and in some cases killed for one another. They were as close as two spies from opposing services could be, which meant they distrusted each other only a little.

"Is there anyone in this hotel who doesn't know who you are?" Seymour asked, shaking Gabriel's outstretched hand as though it belonged to someone he was meeting for the first time.

"The girl at reception asked if I was here for the Greenberg bar mitzvah."

Seymour gave a discreet smile. With his pewter-colored locks and sturdy jaw, he looked the archetype of the British colonial baron, a man who decided important matters and never poured his own tea.

"Inside or out?" asked Gabriel.

"Out," said Seymour.

They sat down at a table outside on the terrace, Gabriel facing the hotel, Seymour the walls of the Old City. It was a few minutes after eleven, the lull between breakfast and lunch. Gabriel drank only coffee but Seymour ordered lavishly. His wife was an enthusiastic but dreadful cook. For Seymour, airline food was a treat, and a hotel brunch, even from the kitchen of the King David, was an occasion to be savored. So, too, it seemed, was the view of the Old City.

"You might find this hard to believe," he said between bites of his omelet, "but this is the first time I've ever set foot in your country."

"I know," Gabriel replied. "It's all in your file."

"Interesting reading?"

"I'm sure it's nothing compared to what your service has on me."

"How could it be? I am but a humble servant of Her Majesty's Security Service. You, on the other hand, are a legend. After all," Seymour added, lowering his voice, "how many intelligence officers can say they spared the world an apocalypse?"

Gabriel glanced over his shoulder and stared at the golden Dome of the Rock, Islam's third-holiest shrine, sparkling in the crystalline Jerusalem sunlight. Five months earlier, in a secret chamber 167 feet beneath the surface of the Temple Mount, he had discovered a massive bomb that, had it detonated, would have brought down the entire plateau. He had also discovered twenty-two pillars from Solomon's Temple of Jerusalem, thus proving beyond doubt that the ancient Jewish sanctuary, described in Kings and Chronicles, had in fact existed. Though Gabriel's name never appeared in the press coverage of the momentous discovery, his involvement in the affair was well known in certain circles of the Western intelligence community. It was also known that his closest friend, the noted biblical archaeologist and Office operative Eli Lavon, had nearly died trying to save the pillars from destruction.

"You're damn lucky that bomb didn't go off," Seymour said. "If it had, several million Muslims would have been on your borders in a matter of hours. After that . . ." Seymour's voice trailed off.

"It would have been lights out on the enterprise known as the State of Israel," Gabriel said, finishing Seymour's thought for him. "Which is exactly what the Iranians and their friends in Hezbollah wanted to happen."

"I can't imagine what it must have been like when you saw those pillars for the first time."

"To be honest, Graham, I didn't have time to enjoy the moment. I was too busy trying to keep Eli alive."

"How is he?"

"He spent two months in the hospital, but he looks almost as good as new. He's actually back at work."

"For the Office?"

Gabriel shook his head. "He's digging in the Western Wall Tunnel again. I can arrange a private tour if you like. In fact, if you're interested, I can show you the secret passage that leads directly into the Temple Mount."

"I'm not sure my government would approve." Seymour lapsed into silence while a waiter refilled their coffee cups. Then, when they were alone again, he said, "So the rumor is true after all."

"Which rumor is that?"

"The one about the prodigal son finally returning home. It's funny," he added, smiling sadly, "but I always assumed you'd spend the rest of your life walking the cliffs of Cornwall."

"It's beautiful there, Graham. But England is your home, not mine."

"Sometimes even I don't feel at home there any longer," Seymour said. "Helen and I recently purchased a villa in Portugal. Soon I'll be an exile, like you used to be."

"*How* soon?" asked Gabriel.

"Nothing's imminent," Seymour answered. "But eventually all good things must end."

"You've had a great career, Graham."

"Have I? It's difficult to measure success in the security business, isn't it? We're judged on things that *don't* happen—the secrets that *aren't* stolen, the buildings that *don't* explode. It can be a profoundly unsatisfying way of earning a living."

"What are you going to do in Portugal?"

"Helen will attempt to poison me with her exotic cooking, and I will paint dreadful watercolor landscapes."

"I never knew you painted."

"For good reason." Seymour frowned at the view as though it was far beyond the reach of his brush and palette. "My father would be spinning in his grave if he knew I was here."

"So why *are* you here?"

"I was wondering whether you might be willing to find something for a friend of mine."

"Does the friend have a name?"

Seymour made no reply. Instead, he opened his attaché case and withdrew an eight-by-ten photograph, which he handed to Gabriel. It showed an attractive young woman staring directly into the camera, holding a three-day-old copy of the *International Herald Tribune*.

"Madeline Hart?" asked Gabriel.

Seymour nodded. Then he handed Gabriel a sheet of A4 paper. On it was a single sentence composed in a plain sans serif typeface:

You have seven days, or the girl dies.

"Shit," said Gabriel softly.

"I'm afraid it gets better."

———

Coincidentally, the management of the King David had placed Graham Seymour, the only son of Arthur Seymour, in the same wing of the hotel that had been destroyed in 1946. In fact, Seymour's room was just down the hall from the one his father had used as an office during the waning days of the British Mandate in Palestine. Arriving, they found the DO NOT DISTURB sign still hanging from the latch, along with a sack containing the *Jerusalem Post* and *Haaretz*. Seymour led Gabriel inside. Then, satisfied the room had not been entered in his absence, he inserted a DVD into his notebook computer and clicked PLAY. A few seconds later Madeline Hart, missing British subject and employee of Britain's governing party, appeared on the screen.

"I made love to Prime Minister Jonathan Lancaster for the first time at the Party conference in Manchester in October 2012 . . ."

5

KING DAVID HOTEL, JERUSALEM

THE VIDEO WAS SEVEN MINUTES and twelve seconds in length. Throughout, Madeline's gaze remained fixed on a point slightly to the camera's left, as if she were responding to questions posed by a television interviewer. She appeared frightened and fatigued as, reluctantly, she described how she had met the prime minister during one of his visits to the Party's Millbank headquarters. Lancaster had expressed admiration for Madeline's work and on two occasions invited her to Downing Street to personally brief him. It was at the end of the second visit when he admitted that his interest in Madeline was more than professional. Their first sexual encounter had been a hurried affair in a Manchester hotel room. After that, Madeline had been spirited into the Downing Street residence by an old friend of the prime minister, always when Diana Lancaster was away from London.

"And now," said Seymour gloomily as the computer screen turned to black, "the prime minister of the United Kingdom of Great Britain and Northern Ireland is being punished for his sins with a crude attempt at blackmail."

"There's nothing crude about it, Graham. Whoever's behind this knew the prime minister was involved in an extramarital affair. And then they managed to make his lover disappear without a trace from Corsica. They're obviously extremely sophisticated."

Seymour ejected the disk from the computer but said nothing.

"Who else knows?"

Seymour explained how the three items—the photograph, the note, and the DVD—had been left the previous morning on Simon Hewitt's doorstep. And how Hewitt had transported them to Downing Street, where he showed them to Jeremy Fallon. And how Hewitt and Fallon had then confronted Lancaster in his office at Number Ten. Gabriel, a recent resident of the United Kingdom, knew the cast of characters well. Hewitt, Fallon, Lancaster: the holy trinity of British politics. Hewitt was the spin doctor, Fallon the master schemer and strategist, and Lancaster the raw political talent.

"Why did Lancaster choose you?" asked Gabriel.

"Our fathers worked together in the intelligence service."

"Surely there's more to it than that."

"There is," Seymour admitted. "His name is Siddiq Hussein."

"I'm afraid it doesn't ring a bell."

"That's not surprising," Seymour said. "Because, thanks to me, Siddiq disappeared down a black hole several years ago, never to be seen or heard from again."

"Who was he?"

"Siddiq Hussein was a Pakistani-born resident of Tower Hamlets in East London. He popped up on our radar screens after the bombings in 2007 when we finally came to our senses and started pulling Islamic radicals off the streets. You remember those days," Seymour said bitterly. "The days when the leftists and the media insisted we do something about the terrorists in our midst."

"Go on, Graham."

"Siddiq was hanging around with known extremists at the East London Mosque, and his mobile phone number kept appearing in all the wrong places. I gave a copy of his file to Scotland Yard, but the Counterterrorism Command said there wasn't enough evidence to move against him. Then Siddiq did something that gave me a chance to take care of the problem on my own."

"What was that?"

"He booked an airline ticket to Pakistan."

"Big mistake."

"Fatal, actually," said Seymour darkly.

"What happened?"

"We followed him to Heathrow and made sure he boarded his flight to Karachi. Then I placed a quiet call to an old friend in Langley, Virginia. I believe you know him well."

"Adrian Carter."

Seymour nodded. Adrian Carter was the director of the CIA's National Clandestine Service. He oversaw the Agency's global war on terror, including its once-secret programs to detain and interrogate high-value operatives.

"Carter's team watched Siddiq in Karachi for three days," Seymour continued. "Then they threw a bag over his head and put him on the first black flight out of the country."

"Where did they take him?"

"Kabul."

"The Salt Pit?"

Seymour nodded slowly.

"How long did he last?"

"That depends on whom you ask. According to the Agency's account of the events, Siddiq was found dead in his cell ten days after arriving in Kabul. His family alleged in a lawsuit that he died while being tortured."

"What does this have to do with the prime minister?"

"When the lawyers representing Siddiq's family asked for all MI5 documents related to his case, Lancaster's government refused to release them on grounds it would damage British national security. He saved my career."

"And now you're going to repay that debt by trying to save his neck?" When Seymour made no reply, Gabriel said, "This is going to end badly, Graham. And when it does, your name will feature prominently in the inevitable inquest."

"I've made it clear that, if that happens, I'll take everyone down with me, including Lancaster."

"I never had you figured for the naive type, Graham."

"I'm anything but."

"So walk away. Go back to London and tell your prime minister to go before the cameras with his wife at his side and make a public appeal for the kidnappers to release the girl."

"It's too late for that. Besides," Seymour added, "perhaps I'm a bit old-fashioned, but I don't like it when people try to blackmail the leader of my country."

"Does the leader of your country know you're in Jerusalem?"

"Surely you jest."

"Why me?"

"Because if MI5 or the intelligence service tries to find her, it will leak, just the way Siddiq Hussein leaked. You're also damn good at finding things," Seymour added quietly. "Ancient pillars, stolen Rembrandts, secret Iranian enrichment facilities."

"Sorry, Graham, but—"

"And because you owe Lancaster, too," Seymour said, cutting him off.

"Me?"

"Who do you think allowed you to take refuge in Cornwall under a false name when no other country would have you? And who do you think allowed you to recruit a British journalist when you needed to penetrate Iran's nuclear supply chain?"

"I didn't realize we were keeping score, Graham."

"We're not," said Seymour. "But if we were, you would surely be trailing in the match."

The two men lapsed into an uncomfortable silence, as though embarrassed by the tone of the exchange. Seymour looked at the ceiling, Gabriel at the note.

You have seven days, or the girl dies . . .

"Rather vague, don't you think?"

"But highly effective," said Seymour. "It certainly got Lancaster's attention."

"No demands?"

Seymour shook his head. "Obviously, they want to name their price at the last minute. And they want Lancaster to be so desperate to save his political hide, he'll agree to pay it."

"How much is your prime minister worth these days?"

"The last time I had a peek at his bank accounts," Seymour said facetiously, "he had upward of a hundred million."

"Pounds?"

Seymour nodded. "Jonathan Lancaster made millions in the City, inherited millions from his family, and married millions in the form of Diana Baldwin. He's a perfect target, a man with more money than he needs and a great deal to lose. Diana and the children live within the security bubble of Number Ten, which means it would be almost impossible for a kidnapper to get them. But Lancaster's mistress . . ." Seymour's voice trailed off. Then he added, "A mistress is an altogether different matter."

"I don't suppose Lancaster has mentioned any of this to his wife?"

Seymour made a gesture with his hands to indicate he wasn't privy to the inner workings of the Lancaster marriage.

"Have you ever worked a kidnapping case, Graham?"

"Not since Northern Ireland. And those were all IRA-related."

"Political kidnappings are different from criminal kidnappings," Gabriel said. "Your average political kidnapper is a rational fellow. He wants comrades released from prison or a policy changed, so he grabs an important politician or a busload of schoolchildren and holds them hostage until his demands are met. But a criminal wants only money. And if you pay him, it makes him want *more* money. So he keeps asking for money until he thinks there's none left."

"Then I suppose that leaves us only one option."

"What's that?"

"Find the girl."

Gabriel walked to the window and stared across the valley toward the Temple Mount; and for an instant he was back in a secret cavern 167 feet beneath the surface, holding Eli Lavon as his blood pumped into the heart of the holy mountain. During the long nights Gabriel had spent next to Lavon's hospital bed, he had vowed to never again set foot on the secret battlefield. But now an old friend had risen from the depths of his tangled past to request a favor. And once more Gabriel was struggling to find the words to send him away empty-handed. As the only child of Holocaust survivors, it was not in his nature to disappoint others. He made accommodations for them, but he rarely told them no.

"Even if I'm able to find her," he said after a moment, "the kidnappers will still have the video of her confessing an affair with the prime minister."

"But that video will have a rather different impact if the English rose is safely back on English soil."

"Unless the English rose decides to tell the truth."

"She's a Party loyalist. She wouldn't dare."

"You have no idea what they've done to her," Gabriel responded. "She could be an entirely different person by now."

"True," said Seymour. "But we're getting ahead of ourselves. This conversation is meaningless unless you and your service undertake an operation to find Madeline Hart on my behalf."

"I don't have the authority to place my service at your disposal, Graham. It's Uzi's decision to make, not mine."

"Uzi's already given his approval," Seymour said flatly. "So has Shamron."

Gabriel glared at Seymour in disapproval but said nothing.

"Do you really think Ari Shamron would have let me within a mile of you without knowing why I was in town?" Seymour asked. "He's very protective of you."

"He has a funny way of showing it. But I'm afraid there's one person in Israel who's more powerful than Shamron, at least when it comes to me."

"Your wife?"

Gabriel nodded.

"We have seven days, or the girl dies."

"Six days," said Gabriel. "The girl could be anywhere in the world, and we don't have a single clue."

"That's not entirely true."

Seymour reached into his briefcase and produced two Interpol photographs of the man with whom Madeline Hart had lunched on the afternoon of her disappearance. The man whose shoes left no marks. The forgotten man.

"Who is he?" asked Gabriel.

"Good question," said Seymour. "But if you can find him, I suspect you'll find Madeline Hart."

6

ISRAEL MUSEUM, JERUSALEM

G ABRIEL TOOK A SINGLE ITEM from Graham Seymour, the photograph of a captive Madeline Hart, and carried it westward across Jerusalem, to the Israel Museum. After leaving his car in the staff parking lot, a privilege only recently granted to him, he made his way through the soaring glass entrance hall to the room that housed the museum's collection of European art. In one corner hung nine Impressionist paintings that had once been in the possession of a Swiss banker named Augustus Rolfe. A placard described the long journey the paintings had taken from Paris to this spot—how they had been looted by the Nazis in 1940, and how they were later transferred to Rolfe in exchange for services rendered to German intelligence. The placard made no mention of the fact that Gabriel and Rolfe's daughter, the renowned violinist Anna Rolfe, had discovered the paintings in a Zurich bank vault—or

that a consortium of Swiss businessmen had hired a professional assassin from Corsica to kill them both.

In the adjoining gallery hung works by Israeli artists. There were
three canvases by Gabriel's mother, including a haunting depic-
tion of the death march from Auschwitz in January 1945 that she
had painted from memory. Gabriel spent several moments admiring her draftsmanship and brushwork before heading outside into
the sculpture garden. At the far end stood the beehive-shaped Shrine
of the Book, repository of the Dead Sea Scrolls. Next to it was the
museum's newest structure, a modern glass-and-steel building, sixty
cubits long, twenty cubits wide, and thirty cubits high. For now, it
was cloaked in an opaque construction tarpaulin that rendered its
contents, the twenty-two pillars of Solomon's Temple, invisible to
the outside world.

There were well-armed security men standing along both sides of
the building and at its entrance, which faced east, as had Solomon's
original Temple. It was just one element of the exhibit that had made
it arguably the most controversial curatorial project the world had
ever known. Israel's ultra-Orthodox haredim had denounced the exhibit as an affront to God that would ultimately lead to the destruction of the Jewish state, while in Arab East Jerusalem the keepers of
the Dome of the Rock declared the pillars an elaborate hoax. "There
was never an actual Temple on the Temple Mount," the grand mufti
of Jerusalem wrote in an op-ed published in the *New York Times*,
"and no museum exhibit will ever change that fact."

Despite the fierce religious and political battles raging around the
exhibit, it had progressed with remarkable speed. Within a few weeks
of Gabriel's discovery, architectural plans had been approved, funds
raised, and ground broken. Much of the credit belonged to the project's
Italian-born director and chief designer. In public she was referred to

by her maiden name, which was Chiara Zolli. But all those associated with the project knew that her real name was Chiara Allon.

The pillars were arranged in the same manner in which Gabriel had found them, in two straight columns separated by approximately twenty feet. One, the tallest, was blackened by fire—the fire the Babylonians had set the night they brought low the Temple that the ancient Jews regarded as the dwelling place of God on earth. It was the pillar Eli Lavon had clung to as he was near death, and it was there that Gabriel found Chiara. She was holding a clipboard in one hand and with the other was gesturing toward the glass ceiling. She wore faded jeans, flat-soled sandals, and a sleeveless white pullover that clung tightly to the curves of her body. Her bare arms were very dark from the Jerusalem sun; her riotous long hair was full of golden highlights. She looked astonishingly beautiful, thought Gabriel, and far too young to be the wife of a battered wreck like him.

Overhead two technicians were making adjustments to the exhibit's lighting while Chiara supervised from below. She spoke to them in Hebrew, with a distinct Italian accent. The daughter of the chief rabbi of Venice, she had spent her childhood in the insular world of the ancient ghetto, leaving just long enough to earn a master's degree in Roman history from the University of Padua. She returned to Venice after graduation and took a job at the small Jewish museum in the Campo del Ghetto Nuovo, and there she might have remained forever had an Office talent spotter not noticed her during a visit to Israel. The talent spotter introduced himself in a Tel Aviv coffeehouse and asked Chiara whether she was interested in doing more for the Jewish people than working in a museum in a dying ghetto.

After spending a year in the Office's secretive training program, Chiara returned to Venice, this time as an undercover agent of Israeli intelligence. Among her first assignments was to covertly watch the back of a wayward Office assassin named Gabriel Allon, who had come to Venice to restore Bellini's San Zaccaria altarpiece. She revealed herself to him a short time later in Rome, after an incident involving gunplay and the Italian police. Trapped alone with Chiara in a safe flat, Gabriel had wanted desperately to touch her. He had waited until the case was resolved and they had returned to Venice. There, in a canal house in Cannaregio, they made love for the first time, in a bed prepared with fresh linen. It was like making love to a figure painted by the hand of Veronese.

Now the figure turned her head and, noticing Gabriel's presence for the first time, smiled. Her eyes, wide and oriental in shape, were the color of caramel and flecked with gold, a combination that Gabriel had never been able to accurately reproduce on canvas. It had been many months since Chiara had agreed to sit for him; the exhibit had left her with little time for anything else. It was a distinct change in the pattern of their marriage. Usually, it was Gabriel who was consumed by a project, be it a painting or an operation, but now the roles were reversed. Chiara, a natural organizer who was meticulous in all things, had thrived under the intense pressure of the exhibit. But secretly Gabriel was looking forward to the day he could have her back.

She walked to the next pillar and examined the way the light was falling across it. "I called the apartment a few minutes ago," she said, "but there was no answer."

"I was having brunch with Graham Seymour at the King David."

"How lovely," she said sardonically. Then, still studying the pillar, she asked, "What's in the envelope?"

"A job offer."

"Who's the artist?"

"Unknown."

"And the subject matter?"

"A girl named Madeline Hart."

Gabriel returned to the sculpture garden and sat on a bench over-looking the tan hills of West Jerusalem. A few minutes later Chiara joined him. A soft autumnal wind moved in her hair. She brushed a stray tendril from her face and then crossed one long leg over the other so that her sandal dangled from her suntanned toes. Suddenly, the last thing Gabriel wanted to do was to leave Jerusalem and go looking for a girl he didn't know.

"Let's try this again," she said at last. "What's in the envelope?"

"A photograph."

"What kind of photograph?"

"Proof of life."

Chiara held out her hand. Gabriel hesitated.

"Are you sure?"

When Chiara nodded, Gabriel surrendered the envelope and watched as she lifted the flap and removed the print. As she examined the image, a shadow fell across her face. It was the shadow of a Russian arms dealer named Ivan Kharkov. Gabriel had taken everything from Ivan: his business, his money, his wife and children. Then Ivan had retaliated by taking Chiara. The operation to rescue her was the bloodiest of Gabriel's long career. Afterward, he had killed eleven of Ivan's operatives in retaliation. Then, on a quiet street in Saint-Tropez, he had killed Ivan, too. Yet even in death, Ivan remained a part of their lives. The ketamine injections his men had given Chiara had caused her to lose the child she was carrying. Untreated, the miscarriage had damaged her ability to conceive. Privately, she had all but given up hope she would ever become pregnant again.

She returned the photograph to the envelope and the envelope to Gabriel. Then she listened intently as he described how the case had ended up in Graham Seymour's lap, then in his.

"So the British prime minister is forcing Graham Seymour to do his dirty work for him," she said when Gabriel had finished, "and Graham is doing the same to you."

"He's been a good friend."

Chiara's face was expressionless. Her eyes, usually a reliable window into her thoughts, were concealed behind sunglasses.

"What do you suppose they want?" she asked after a moment.

"Money," said Gabriel. "They always want money."

"Almost always," responded Chiara. "But sometimes they want things that are impossible to surrender."

She removed her sunglasses and hung them from the front of her shirt. "How long do you have before they kill her?" she asked. And when Gabriel answered, she shook her head slowly. "It can't be done," she said. "You can't possibly find her in that amount of time."

"Look at the building behind you. Then tell me if you still feel the same way."

Chiara looked at nothing other than Gabriel's face. "The French police have been searching for Madeline Hart for over a month. What makes you think you can find her?"

"Maybe they haven't been looking in the right place—or talking to the right people."

"Where would you start?"

"I've always believed the best place to begin an investigation is the scene of the crime."

Chiara removed her sunglasses from the front of her shirt and absently polished the lenses against her jeans. Gabriel knew it was a bad sign. Chiara always cleaned things when she was annoyed.

"You'll scratch them if you don't stop," he said.

"They're filthy," she replied distantly.

"Maybe you should get a case instead of just throwing them into your purse."

She made no response.

"You surprise me, Chiara."

"Why?"

"Because you know better than anyone that Madeline Hart is in hell. And she's going to stay in hell until someone brings her out."

"I just wish it could be someone else."

"There is no one else."

"No one like you." She examined the lenses of her sunglasses and frowned.

"What's wrong?"

"They're scratched."

"I told you you'd scratch them."

"You're always right, darling."

She slipped on the glasses and looked across the city. "I assume Shamron and Uzi have given their blessing?"

"Graham went to them before talking to me."

"How clever of him." She uncrossed her legs and rose. "I should be getting back. We don't have much time left before the opening."

"You've done a magnificent job, Chiara."

"Flattery will get you nowhere."

"It was worth a try."

"When will I see you again?"

"I only have seven days to find her."

"Six," she corrected him. "Six days or the girl dies."

She leaned down and kissed his lips softly. Then she turned and walked across the sun-bleached garden, her hips swinging gently, as if to music only she could hear. Gabriel watched until she disappeared into the tarpaulin-covered building. Suddenly, the last thing he wanted to do was to leave Jerusalem and go looking for a girl he didn't know.

Gabriel returned to the King David Hotel to collect the rest of the dossier from Graham Seymour—the demand note that contained no demand, the DVD of Madeline's confession, and the two photographs of the man from Les Palmiers in Calvi. In addition, he requested a copy of Madeline's Party personnel file, deliverable to an address in Nice.

"How did it go with Chiara?" asked Seymour.

"At this moment, my marriage might be in worse shape than Lancaster's."

"Is there anything I can do?"

"Leave town as quickly as possible. And don't mention my name to your prime minister or anyone else at Downing Street."

"How do I contact you?"

"I'll send up a flare when I have news. Until then, I don't exist."

It was with those words that Gabriel took his leave. Returning to Narkiss Street, he found, resting on the coffee table in plain sight, a money belt containing two hundred thousand dollars. Next to it was a ticket for the 4:00 p.m. flight to Paris. It had been booked under the name Johannes Klemp, one of his favorite aliases. Entering the bedroom, Gabriel packed a small overnight bag with Herr Klemp's trendy German clothing, setting aside one outfit, a black suit and black pullover, for the plane ride. Then, standing before the bathroom mirror, he made a few subtle alterations to his own appearance—a bit of silver for his hair, a pair of rimless German spectacles, a pair of brown contact lenses to conceal his distinctive green eyes. Within a few minutes he scarcely recognized the face staring back at him. He was no longer Gabriel Allon, Israel's avenging angel. He was Johannes Klemp of Munich, a man permanently ready to take offense, a small man with a chip balanced precariously on his insignificant shoulder.

After dressing in Herr Klemp's black suit and dousing himself with Herr Klemp's appalling cologne, he sat down at Chiara's dressing table and opened her jewelry case. One item seemed curiously out of place. It was a strand of leather hung with a piece of red coral shaped like a hand. He removed it and slipped it into his pocket. Then, for reasons not known to him, he hung it round his neck and concealed it beneath Herr Klemp's pullover.

Downstairs an Office sedan was idling in the street. Gabriel tossed his bag onto the backseat and climbed in after it. Then he glanced at his wristwatch, not at the time but at the date. It was September 27. It had once been his favorite day of the year.

"What's your name?" he asked of the driver.

"Lior."

"Where are you from, Lior?"

"Beersheba."

"It was a good place to be a kid?"

"There are worse places."

"How old are you?"

"I'm twenty-five."

Twenty-five, thought Gabriel. Why did it have to be twenty-five? He looked at his wristwatch again. Not at the time. The date.

"What were your instructions?" he asked of the driver, who just happened to be twenty-five.

"I was told to take you to Ben Gurion."

"Anything else?"

"They said you might want to make a stop along the way."

"Who said that? Was it Uzi?"

"No," replied the driver, shaking his head. "It was the Old Man."

So, thought Gabriel. He remembered. He glanced at his watch again. *The date . . .*

"Well?" asked the driver.

"Take me to the airport," replied Gabriel.

"No stops?"

"Just one."

The driver slipped the car into gear and eased slowly from the curb, as though he were joining a funeral procession. He didn't bother to ask where they were going. It was the twenty-seventh of September. And Shamron remembered.

―――――――――

They drove to the Garden of Gethsemane and then followed the narrow, winding path up the slope of the Mount of Olives. Gabriel entered the cemetery alone and walked through the sea of headstones, until he arrived at the grave of Daniel Allon, born September 27, 1988, died January 13, 1991. Died on a snowy night in the First District of Vienna, in a blue Mercedes automobile that was blown to bits by a bomb. The bomb had been planted by a Palestinian master terrorist named Tariq al-Hourani, on the direct orders of Yasir Arafat. Gabriel had not been the target; that would have been too lenient. Tariq and Arafat had wanted to punish him by forcing him to watch the death of his wife and child, so that he would spend the rest of his life grieving, like the Palestinians. Only one element of the plot had failed. Leah had survived the inferno. She lived now in a psychiatric hospital atop Mount Herzl, trapped in a prison of memory and a body destroyed by fire. Afflicted with a combination of post-traumatic stress syndrome and psychotic depression, she relived the bombing constantly. Occasionally, however, she experienced flashes of lucidity. During one such interlude, she had granted Gabriel permission to marry Chiara. *Look at me, Gabriel. There's nothing left of me. Nothing but a memory.*

Gabriel glanced at his wristwatch again. Not the date but the time.

There was time for one last good-bye. One final torrent of tears. One final apology for failing to search the car for a bomb before allowing Leah to start the engine. Then he staggered from the garden of stone, on the day that used to be his favorite of the year, and climbed into the back of an Office sedan that was driven by a boy of twenty-five.

The boy had the good sense not to speak a word during the journey to the airport. Gabriel entered the terminal like a normal traveler but then went to a room reserved for Office personnel, where he waited for his flight to be called. As he settled into his first-class seat, he felt a wholly unprofessional urge to phone Chiara. Instead, using techniques taught to him in his youth by Shamron, he walled her from his thoughts. For now, there was no Chiara. Or Daniel. Or Leah. There was only Madeline Hart, the kidnapped mistress of British prime minister Jonathan Lancaster. As the plane rose into the darkening sky, she appeared to Gabriel, in oil on canvas, as Susanna bathing in her garden. And leering at her over the wall was a man with an angular face and a small, cruel mouth. The man without a name or country. The forgotten man.

7

CORSICA

THE CORSICANS SAY THAT, WHEN approaching their island by boat, they can smell its unique scrubland vegetation long before they glimpse its rugged coastline rising from the sea. Gabriel experienced no such revelation of Corsica, for he journeyed to the island by air, arriving on the morning's first flight from Orly. It was only when he was behind the wheel of a rented Peugeot, heading south from the airport at Ajaccio, that he caught his first whiff of gorse, briar, rockrose, and rosemary spilling down from the hills. The Corsicans called it the *macchia*. They cooked with it, heated their homes with it, and took refuge in it in times of war and vendetta. According to Corsican legend, a hunted man could take to the *macchia* and, if he wished, remain undetected there forever. Gabriel knew just such a man. It was why he wore a red coral hand on a strand of leather around his neck.

After a half hour of driving, Gabriel left the coast road and headed inland. The scent of the *macchia* grew stronger, as did the walls surrounding the small hill towns. Corsica, like the ancient land of Israel, had been invaded many times—indeed, after the fall of the Roman Empire, the Vandals had plundered Corsica so mercilessly that most of the island's inhabitants fled the coasts and retreated into the safety of the mountains. Even now, the fear of outsiders remained intense. In one isolated village, an old woman pointed at Gabriel with her index and little fingers in order to ward off the effects of the *occhju*, the evil eye.

Beyond the village, the road was little more than a single-lane track bordered on both sides by thick walls of *macchia*. After a mile he came to the entrance of a private estate. The gate was open but in the breach stood an off-road vehicle occupied by a pair of security guards. Gabriel switched off the engine and, placing his hands atop the steering wheel, waited for the men to approach. Eventually, one climbed out and came slowly over. He had a gun in one hand and another shoved into the waistband of his trousers. With only a movement of his thick eyebrows, he inquired about the purpose of Gabriel's visit.

"I wish to see the don," Gabriel said in French.

"The don is a very busy man," the guard replied in the Corsican dialect.

Gabriel removed the talisman from his neck and handed it over. The Corsican smiled.

"I'll see what I can do."

It had never taken much to spark a blood feud on the island of Corsica. An insult. An accusation of cheating in the marketplace. The dissolution of an engagement. The pregnancy of an unmarried woman. After the initial spark, unrest inevitably followed. An ox would be killed, a prized olive tree would topple, a cottage would burn. Then the murders would start. And on it would go, sometimes for a generation or more, until the aggrieved parties had settled their differences or given up the fight in exhaustion.

Most Corsican men were more than willing to do their killing themselves. But there were some who needed others to do their blood work for them: notables who were too squeamish to get their hands dirty, or who were unwilling to risk arrest or exile; women who could not kill for themselves or had no male kin to do the deed on their behalf. People like these relied on professional killers known as *taddunaghiu*. Usually, they turned to the Orsati clan.

The Orsatis had fine land with many olive trees, and their oil was regarded as the sweetest in all of Corsica. But they did more than produce olive oil. No one knew how many Corsicans had died at the hands of Orsati assassins down through the ages, least of all the Orsatis themselves, but local lore placed the number in the thousands. It might have been significantly higher were it not for the clan's rigorous vetting process. The Orsatis operated by a strict code. They refused to carry out a killing unless satisfied the party before them had indeed been wronged and blood vengeance was required.

That changed, however, with Don Anton Orsati. By the time he gained control of the family, the French authorities had managed to eradicate feuding and the vendetta in all but the most isolated pockets of the island, leaving few Corsicans with the need for the services of his *taddunaghiu*. With local demand in steep decline, Orsati had been left with no choice but to look for opportunities elsewhere, namely, across the water in mainland Europe. He now accepted almost every job offer that crossed his desk, no matter how distasteful, and his killers were regarded as the most reliable and professional on the Continent. In fact, Gabriel was one of only two people ever to survive an Orsati family contract.

Though Orsati descended from a family of Corsican notables, in appearance he was indistinguishable from the *paesanu* who guarded the entrance to his estate. Entering the don's large office, Gabriel found him seated at his desk wearing a bleached white shirt, loose-fitting trousers of pale cotton, and a pair of dusty sandals that looked as though they had been purchased at the local outdoor market. He was staring down at an old-fashioned ledger, his heavy face set in a frown. Gabriel could only wonder at the source of the don's displeasure. Long ago, Orsati had merged his two businesses into a single seamless enterprise. His modern-day *taddunaghiu* were all employees of the Orsati Olive Oil Company, and the murders they carried out were booked as orders for product.

Rising, Orsati extended a granite hand toward Gabriel without a trace of apprehension. "It is an honor to meet you, Monsieur Allon," he said in French. "Frankly, I expected to see you long ago. You have a reputation for dealing harshly with your enemies."

"My enemies were the Swiss bankers who hired you to kill me, Don Orsati. Besides," Gabriel added, "instead of giving me a bullet in the head, your assassin gave me that."

Gabriel nodded toward the talisman, which was lying on Orsati's desk next to the ledger. The don frowned. Then he picked up the charm by the leather strand and allowed the red coral hand to sway back and forth like the weight of a clock.

"It was a reckless thing to do," the don said at last.

"Leaving the talisman behind or letting me live?"

Orsati smiled noncommittally. "We have an old saying here in Corsica. *I solda un vènini micca cantendu*: Money doesn't come from singing. It comes from work. And around here, work means fulfilling contracts, even when they are taken out on famous violinists and Israeli intelligence officers."

"So you returned the money to the men who retained you?"

"They were Swiss bankers. Money was the last thing they needed." Orsati closed the ledger and laid the talisman on the cover. "As you might expect, I've been keeping a close eye on you over the years. You've been a very busy man since our paths crossed. In fact, some of your best work has been done on my turf."

"This is my first visit to Corsica," Gabriel demurred.

"I was referring to the south of France," Orsati replied. "You killed that Saudi terrorist Zizi al-Bakari in the Old Port of Cannes. And then there was that bit of unpleasantness with Ivan Kharkov in Saint-Tropez a few years ago."

"It was my understanding Ivan was killed by other Russians," Gabriel said evasively.

"*You* killed Ivan, Allon. And you killed him because he took your wife."

Gabriel was silent. Again the Corsican smiled, this time with the assurance of a man who knew he was right. "The *macchia* has no eyes," he said, "but it sees all."

"That's why I'm here."

"I assumed that was the case. After all, a man such as you surely has no need of a professional killer. You do that quite well all on your own."

Gabriel withdrew a bundle of cash from his coat pocket and placed it on Orsati's ledger of death, next to the talisman. The don ignored it.

"How can I help you, Allon?"

"I need some information."

"About?"

Without a word, Gabriel laid the photograph of Madeline Hart next to the money.

"The English girl?"

"You don't seem surprised, Don Orsati."

The Corsican said nothing.

"Do you know where she is?"

"No," Orsati answered. "But I have a good idea who took her."

Gabriel held up the photo of the man from Les Palmiers. Orsati nodded once.

"Who is he?" asked Gabriel.

"I don't know. I met him only once."

"Where?"

"It was in this office, a week before the English girl vanished. He sat in the very same chair where you're sitting now," Orsati added. "But he had more money than you, Allon. Much more."

8

CORSICA

I T WAS LUNCHTIME, DON ORSATI'S favorite time of the day. They adjourned to the terrace outside his office and sat at a table laid with mounds of Corsican bread, cheese, vegetables, and sausage. The sun was bright, and through a gap in the laricio pine Gabriel could glimpse the sea shimmering blue-green in the distance. The savor of the *macchia* was everywhere. It hung on the cool air and rose from the food; even Orsati seemed to radiate it. He dumped several inches of bloodred wine into Gabriel's glass and then set about hacking off several slices of the dense Corsican sausage. Gabriel didn't inquire about the source of the meat. As Shamron liked to say, sometimes it was better not to ask.

"I'm glad we didn't kill you," Orsati said, raising his wineglass a fraction of an inch.

"I can assure you, Don Orsati, the feeling is mutual."

"More sausage?"

"Please."

Orsati carved off two more thick slabs and deposited them on Gabriel's plate. Then he slipped on a pair of half-moon reading glasses and examined the photograph of the man from Les Palmiers. "He looks different in this picture," he said after a moment, "but it's definitely him."

"What's different?"

"The way he's wearing his hair. When he came to see me, it was oiled and combed close to the scalp. It was subtle," Orsati added, "but very effective."

"Did he have a name?"

"He called himself Paul."

"Last name?"

"For all I know, that *was* his last name."

"What language did our friend Paul speak?"

"French."

"Local?"

"No, he had an accent."

"What kind?"

"I couldn't place it," the don said, furrowing his heavy brow. "It was as if he learned his French from a tape recorder. It was perfect. But at the same time it wasn't quite right."

"I assume he didn't find your name in the telephone book."

"No, Allon, he had a reference."

"What sort of reference?"

"A name."

"Someone who hired you in the past."

"That's the usual kind."

"What kind of job was it?"

"The kind where two men enter a room and only one man comes

out. And don't bother asking me the name of the reference," Orsati added quickly. "We're talking about my business."

With a slight inclination of his head, Gabriel indicated he had no desire to pursue the matter further, at least for the moment. Then he asked the don why the man had come to see him.

"Advice," answered Orsati.

"About what?"

"He told me he had some product to move. He said he needed someone with a fast boat. Someone who knew the local waters and could move at night. Someone who knew how to keep his mouth shut."

"Product?"

"This might surprise you, but he didn't go into specifics."

"You assumed he was a smuggler," said Gabriel, more a statement of fact than a question.

"Corsica is a major transit point for heroin moving from the Middle East into Europe. For the record," the don added quickly, "the Orsatis do not deal in narcotics, though, on occasion, we have been known to eliminate prominent members of the trade."

"For a fee, of course."

"The bigger the player, the bigger the fee."

"Were you able to accommodate him?"

"Of course," the don said. Then, lowering his voice, he added, "Sometimes we have to move things at night ourselves, Allon."

"Things like dead bodies?"

The don shrugged. "They are an unfortunate byproduct of our business," he said philosophically. "Usually, we try to leave them where they fall. But sometimes the clients pay a bit extra to make them disappear forever. Our preferred method is to put them into concrete coffins and send them to the bottom of the sea. Only God knows how many are down there."

"How much did Paul pay?"

"A hundred thousand."

"What was the split?"

"Half for me, half for the man with the boat."

"Only half?"

"He's lucky I gave him that much."

"And when you heard the English girl had gone missing?"

"Obviously, I was suspicious. And when I saw Paul's picture in the newspapers . . ." The don's voice trailed off. "Let's just say I wasn't pleased. The last thing I need is trouble. It's bad for business."

"You draw the line at kidnapping young women?"

"I suspect you do, too."

Gabriel said nothing.

"I meant no offense," the don said genuinely.

"None taken, Don Orsati."

The don loaded his plate with roasted peppers and eggplant and doused them in Orsati olive oil. Gabriel drank some of the wine, paid a compliment to the don, and then asked for the name of the man with the fast boat who knew the local waters. He did so as if it were the furthest thing from his thoughts.

"We're getting into sensitive territory," replied Orsati. "I do business with these people all the time. If they ever find out I betrayed them to someone like you, things would get messy, Allon."

"I can assure you, Don Orsati, they will never know how I obtained the information."

Orsati appeared unconvinced. "Why is this girl so important that the great Gabriel Allon is looking for her?"

"Let's just say she has powerful friends."

"Friends?" Orsati shook his head skeptically. "If you're involved, there's more to it than that."

"You are very wise, Don Orsati."

"The *macchia* has no eyes," the don said cryptically.

"I need his name," Gabriel said quietly. "He'll never know where I got it."

Orsati picked up his glass of the bloodred wine and lifted it to the sun. "If I were you," he said after a moment, "I'd talk to a man named Marcel Lacroix. He might know something about where the girl went after she left Corsica."

"Where can I find him?"

"Marseilles," replied Orsati. "He keeps his boat in the Old Port."

"Which side?"

"The south, opposite the art gallery."

"What's the boat called?"

"Moondance."

"Nice," said Gabriel.

"I can assure you there's nothing nice about Marcel Lacroix or the men he works for. You need to watch your step in Marseilles."

"This might come as a surprise to you, Don Orsati, but I've done this a time or two before."

"That's true. But you should have been dead a long time ago." Orsati handed Gabriel the talisman. "Put it around your neck. It wards off more than just the evil eye."

"Actually," replied Gabriel, "I was wondering whether you had something a bit more powerful."

"Like what?"

"A gun."

The don smiled. "I have something better than a gun."

———

Gabriel followed the road until it turned to dirt, and then he followed it a little farther. The old goat was waiting exactly where Don Orsati had said it would be, just before the sharp left-hand turn, in the shade of three ancient olive trees. As Gabriel approached, it rose from its resting place and stood in the center of the narrow track, its chin raised defiantly, as if daring Gabriel to attempt to pass. It had the markings of a palomino and a red beard. Like Gabriel, it was scarred from old battles.

He inched the car forward, hoping the goat would surrender its position without a fight, but the beast stood its ground. Gabriel looked at the gun Don Orsati had given to him. A Beretta 9mm, it was lying on the front passenger seat, fully loaded. One shot between the goat's battered horns was all it would take to end the standoff, but it was not possible; the goat, like the three ancient olive trees, belonged to Don Casabianca. And if Gabriel so much as touched one hair on its wretched head, there would be a feud, and blood would be spilled.

Gabriel tapped the car horn twice, but the goat did not budge. Then, sighing heavily, he climbed out and attempted to reason with the beast—first in French, then Italian, and then, exasperated, in Hebrew. The goat responded by lowering its head and aiming it like a battering ram toward Gabriel's midsection. But Gabriel, who believed the best defense was a good offense, charged first, flailing his arms and shouting like a madman. Surprised, the goat gave ground instantly and vanished through a gap in the *macchia*.

Gabriel quickly started back toward the open car door but stopped when he heard a sound, like the cackling of a mockingbird, in the distance. Turning, he looked up toward the ocher-colored villa anchored to the side of the next hill. Standing on the terrace was a blond-haired man dressed entirely in white. And though Gabriel could not be certain, it appeared the man was laughing uncontrollably.

9

CORSICA

THE MAN AWAITING GABRIEL IN the villa was not a Corsican—at least he had not been born one. His real name was Christopher Keller, and he had been raised in a solidly upper-middle-class home in the posh London district of Kensington. On Corsica, however, only Don Orsati and a handful of his men were aware of these facts. To the rest of the island, Keller was known simply as the Englishman.

The story of Christopher Keller's journey from Kensington to the island of Corsica was one of the more intriguing Gabriel had ever heard, which was saying something in itself. The only son of two Harley Street physicians, Keller had made it clear at an early age that he had no intention of following in his parents' footsteps. Obsessed with history, especially military history, he wanted to become a soldier. His parents forbade him to enter the military, and for a time he acceded to their wishes. He enrolled at Cambridge and began reading history and Oriental languages. He was a brilliant student, but in his second year he grew restless and one night vanished without a trace. A few days later he surfaced at his father's Kensington home, hair cut to the scalp, dressed in an olive-drab uniform. He had enlisted in the British army.

After completing his basic training, Keller joined an infantry unit, but his intellect, physical prowess, and lone-wolf attitude quickly captured the attention of the elite Special Air Service. Within days of his arrival at the Regiment's headquarters at Hereford, it became clear Keller had found his true calling. His scores in the "killing house," an infamous facility where recruits practice close-quarters combat and hostage rescue, were the highest ever recorded, while the instructors in the unarmed combat course wrote that they had never seen a man who possessed such an instinctual knack for the taking of human life. His training culminated with a forty-mile march across the windswept moorland known as the Brecon Beacons, an endurance test that had left men dead. Laden with a fifty-five-pound rucksack and a ten-pound assault rifle, Keller broke the course record by thirty minutes, a mark that stands to this day.

Initially, he was assigned to a Sabre squadron specializing in mobile desert warfare, but his career soon took another turn when a man from military intelligence came calling. The man was looking for a unique brand of soldier capable of performing close observation and other special tasks in Northern Ireland. He said he was impressed by Keller's linguistic skills and his ability to improvise and think on his feet. Was Keller interested? That same night Keller packed his kit and moved from Hereford to a secret base in the Scottish Highlands.

During his training, Keller displayed yet another remarkable gift. For years the British security and intelligence forces had struggled with the myriad of accents in Northern Ireland. In Ulster the opposing communities could identify each other by the sound of a voice, and the way a man uttered a few simple phrases could mean the difference between life and an appalling death. Keller developed the ability to mimic the intonations perfectly. He could even shift accents at a moment's notice—a Catholic from Armagh one minute, a Protestant from Belfast's Shankill Road the next, then a Catholic from the Ballymurphy housing estates. He operated in Belfast for more than a year, tracking known members of the IRA, picking up bits of useful gossip from the surrounding community. The nature of his work meant that he would sometimes go several weeks without contacting his control officers.

His assignment in Northern Ireland came to an abrupt end late one night when he was kidnapped in West Belfast and driven to a remote farmhouse in County Armagh. There he was accused of being a British spy. Keller knew the situation was hopeless, so he decided to fight his way out. By the time he left the farmhouse, four hardened terrorists from the Provisional Irish Republican Army were dead. Two had been virtually cut to pieces.

Keller returned to Hereford for what he thought would be a long rest and a stint as an instructor. But his stay ended in August 1990, when Saddam Hussein invaded Kuwait. Keller quickly rejoined his old Sabre unit and by January 1991 was in the western desert of Iraq, searching out the Scud missile launchers that were raining terror on Tel Aviv. On the night of January 28, Keller and his team located a launcher about one hundred miles northwest of Baghdad and radioed the coordinates to their commanders in Saudi Arabia. Ninety minutes later a formation of Coalition fighter-bombers streaked low over the desert. But in a disastrous case of friendly fire, the aircraft attacked the SAS squadron instead of the Scud site. British officials concluded the entire unit was lost, including Keller. His obituaries made no mention of his intelligence work in Northern Ireland, or of the four IRA fighters he had butchered in the farmhouse in County Armagh.

What British military officials did not realize, however, was that Keller had survived the incident without a scratch. His first instinct was to radio his base and request an extraction. Instead, enraged by the incompetence of his superiors, he started walking. Concealed beneath the robe and headdress of a desert Arab, and highly trained in the art of clandestine movement, Keller made his way through the Coalition forces and slipped undetected into Syria. From there, he hiked westward across Turkey, Greece, and Italy until he finally washed ashore in Corsica, where he fell into the waiting arms of Don Orsati. The don gave Keller a villa and a woman to help heal his many wounds. Then, when Keller was rested, the don gave him work. With his northern European looks and SAS training, Keller was able to fulfill contracts that were far beyond the capabilities of Orsati's Corsican-born *taddunaghiu*. One such contract had borne the names Anna Rolfe and Gabriel Allon. For reasons of conscience, Keller had been unable to carry it out, but professional pride had compelled him to leave behind the talisman—the talisman that Gabriel now held in the palm of his hand.

Remarkably, the two men had met once before, many years earlier, when Keller and several other SAS officers had come to Israel for training in the techniques of counterterrorism. On the final day of their stay, Gabriel had reluctantly agreed to deliver a classified lecture on one of his most daring operations—the 1988 assassination of Abu Jihad, the PLO's second-in-command, at his villa in Tunis. Keller had sat in the front row, hanging on Gabriel's every word; and afterward, during a group photo session, he had positioned himself at Gabriel's side. Gabriel had worn sunglasses and a hat to shield his identity, but Keller had stared directly into the camera. It was one of the last photographs ever taken of him.

Now, as Gabriel alighted from his rented car, the man who had once spared his life was standing in the open doorway of his Corsican hideaway. He was taller than Gabriel by a chiseled head and much thicker through the chest and shoulders. Twenty years in the Corsican sun had done much to alter his appearance. His skin was now the color of saddle leather, and his cropped hair was bleached from the sea. Only his blue eyes seemed to have remained unchanged. They were the same eyes that had watched Gabriel so intently as he had recounted the death of Abu Jihad. And the same eyes that had once granted him mercy on a rainy night in Venice, in another lifetime.

"I'd offer you lunch," Keller said in his clipped English accent, "but I hear you've already dined at Chez Orsati."

When Keller extended his hand toward Gabriel, the muscles of his arm coiled and bunched beneath his white pullover. Gabriel hesitated for an instant before finally grasping it. Everything about Christopher Keller, from his hatchet-like hands to his powerful spring-loaded legs, seemed to have been expressly designed for the purpose of killing.

"How much did the don tell you?" asked Gabriel.

"Enough to know that you have no business approaching a man like Marcel Lacroix without backup."

"I take it you know him?"

"He gave me a ride once."

"Before or after?"

"Both," said Keller. "Lacroix did a stretch in the French army. He's also spent time in some of the toughest prisons in the country."

"Am I supposed to be impressed?"

" 'If you know your enemies and know yourself, you can win a hundred battles without a single loss.' "

"Sun Tzu," said Gabriel.

"You cited that passage during your lecture in Tel Aviv."

"So you were listening after all."

Gabriel slipped past Keller and entered the large great room of the villa. The furnishings were rustic and, like Keller, covered in white fabric. Piles of books stood on every flat surface, and on the walls hung several quality paintings, including lesser works by Cézanne, Matisse, and Monet.

"No security system?" asked Gabriel, looking around the room.

"None needed."

Gabriel walked over to the Cézanne, a landscape painted in the hills near Aix-en-Provence, and ran his fingertip gently over the surface.

"You've done very well for yourself, Keller."

"It pays the bills."

Gabriel said nothing.

"You disapprove of the way I earn my living?"

"You kill people for money."

"So do you."

"I kill for my country," replied Gabriel. "And only as a last resort."

"Is that why you blew Ivan Kharkov's brains all over that street in Saint-Tropez? For your country?"

Gabriel turned from the Cézanne and stared directly into Keller's eyes. Any other man would have wilted under the intensity of Gabriel's gaze, but not Keller. His powerful arms were folded casually across his chest, and one corner of his mouth was lifted into a half smile.

"Maybe this isn't such a good idea after all," said Gabriel.

"I know the players and I know the terrain. You'd be a fool not to use me."

Gabriel made no reply. Keller was right; he was the perfect guide to the French criminal underground. And his physical and tactical skills would surely prove valuable before this affair was over.

"I can't pay you," said Gabriel.

"I don't need money," replied Keller, looking around the beautiful villa. "But I do need you to answer a few questions before we leave."

"We have five days to find her, or she dies."

"Five days is an eternity for men like us."

"I'm listening."

"Who are you working for?"

"The British prime minister."

"I didn't realize you were on speaking terms."

"I was retained by someone inside British intelligence."

"On the prime minister's behalf?"

Gabriel nodded.

"What's the prime minister's connection to this girl?"

"Use your imagination."

"My goodness."

"Goodness has very little to do with this."

"Who's the prime minister's friend inside British intelligence?"

Gabriel hesitated and then answered the question truthfully. Keller smiled.

"You know him?" asked Gabriel.

"I worked with Graham in Northern Ireland. He's a pro's pro. But like everyone else in England," Keller added quickly, "Graham Seymour thinks I'm dead. Which means he can never know that I'm working with you."

"You have my word."

"There's something else I want."

Keller held out his hand. Gabriel surrendered the talisman.

"I'm surprised you kept it," Keller said.

"It has sentimental value."

Keller slipped the talisman around his neck. "Let's go," he said, smiling. "I know where we can get you another."

The *signadora* lived in a crooked house in the center of the village, not far from the church. Keller arrived without an appointment, but the old woman did not seem surprised to see him. She wore a black frock and a black scarf over her tinder-dry hair. With a worried smile, she touched Keller's cheek softly. Then, fingering the heavy cross around her neck, she turned her gaze toward Gabriel. Her task was to care for those afflicted with the evil eye. It was obvious she feared Keller had brought the very incarnation of the evil one into her home.

"Who is this man?" she asked.

"A friend," replied Keller.

"Is he a believer?"

"Not like us."

"Tell me his name, Christopher—his *real* name."

"His name is Gabriel."

"Like the archangel?"

"Yes," said Keller.

She studied Gabriel's face carefully. "He is an Israelite, yes?"

When Keller nodded his head, the old woman gave a mild frown of disapproval. Doctrinally, she regarded the Jews as heretics, but personally she had no quarrel with them. She opened the front of Keller's shirt and touched the talisman hanging around his neck.

"Isn't this the one you lost several years ago?"

"Yes."

"Where did you find it?"

"In the bottom of a very crowded drawer."

The *signadora* shook her head reproachfully. "You're lying to me, Christopher," she said. "When will you learn that I can always tell when you're lying?"

Keller smiled but said nothing. The old woman released her hold on the talisman and again touched Keller's cheek.

"You're leaving the island, Christopher?"

"Tonight."

The *signadora* did not ask why; she knew exactly what Keller did for a living. In fact, she had once hired a young *taddunaghiu* named Anton Orsati to avenge the murder of her husband.

With a movement of her hand, she invited Keller and Gabriel to sit at the small wooden table in her parlor. Before them she placed a plate filled with water and a vessel of olive oil. Keller dipped his fore-finger in the oil; then he held it over the plate and allowed three drops to fall onto the water. By the laws of physics, the oil should have gathered into a single gobbet. Instead, it shattered into a thousand droplets and soon there was no trace of it.

"The evil has returned, Christopher."

"I'm afraid it's an occupational hazard."

"Don't make jokes, my dearest. The danger is very real."

"What do you see?"

She gazed intently into the liquid, as if in a trance. After a moment she asked quietly, "Are you looking for the English girl?"

Keller nodded, then asked, "Is she alive?"

"Yes," the old woman answered. "She's alive."

"Where is she?"

"It is not in my power to tell you that."

"Will we find her?"

"When she is dead," the old woman said. "Then you will know the truth."

"What can you see?"

She closed her eyes. "Water . . . mountains . . . an old enemy . . ."

"Of mine?"

"No." She opened her eyes and looked directly at Gabriel. "Of his."

Without another word, she took hold of the Englishman's hand and prayed. After a moment she began to weep, a sign the evil had passed from Keller's body into hers. Then she closed her eyes and appeared to be sleeping. When she awoke she instructed Keller to repeat the trial of the oil and the water. This time the oil coalesced into a single drop.

"The evil is gone from your soul, Christopher." Then, turning to Gabriel, she said, "Now him."

"I'm not a believer," said Gabriel.

"Please," the old woman said. "If not for you, for Christopher."

Reluctantly, Gabriel dipped his forefinger into the oil and allowed three drops to fall onto the surface of the water. When the oil shattered into a thousand pieces, the woman closed her eyes and began to tremble.

"What do you see?" asked Keller.

"Fire," she said softly. "I see fire."

There was a five o'clock ferry from Ajaccio. Gabriel eased his Peugeot into the car deck at half past four and then watched, ten minutes later, as Keller came aboard behind the wheel of a battered Renault hatchback. Their compartments were on the same deck, directly across the corridor. Gabriel's was the size of a prison cell and equally inviting. He left his bag on the cot-size bed and headed upstairs to the bar. By the time he arrived, Keller was seated at a table near the window, a glass of beer raised to his lips, a cigarette smoldering in the ashtray. Gabriel shook his head slowly. Forty-eight hours earlier, he had been standing before a canvas in Jerusalem. Now he was searching for a woman he did not know, accompanied by a man who had once accepted a contract to kill him.

He ordered black coffee from the barman and stepped outside onto the aft deck. The ferry was beyond the outer reaches of the harbor and the evening air was suddenly cold. Gabriel turned up the collar of his coat and wrapped his hands around the cardboard coffee cup for warmth. The eastern stars shone brightly in the cloudless sky, and the sea, turquoise a moment earlier, was the color of India ink. Gabriel thought he could smell the *macchia* on the wind. Then, a moment later, he heard the voice of the *signadora*. When she is dead, the old woman was saying. Then you will know the truth.

10

MARSEILLES

WHEN GABRIEL AND KELLER ARRIVED in Marseilles early the next morning, *Moondance*, forty-two feet of seagoing smuggling power, was tied up in its usual slip in the Old Port. Its owner, however, was nowhere to be seen. Keller established a static observation post on the north side, Gabriel on the east, outside a pizzeria that inexplicably bore the name of a trendy Manhattan neighborhood. They moved to new positions at the top and bottom of each hour, but by late afternoon there was still no sign of Lacroix. Finally, anxious over the prospect of a lost day, Gabriel walked around the perimeter of the harbor, past the fishmongers at their metal tables, and joined Keller in the Renault. The weather was deteriorating: heavy rain, a cold mistral howling out of the hills. Keller flipped the wipers every few seconds to keep the windshield clear. The defroster panted weakly against the fogged glass.

"Are you sure he doesn't keep an apartment in town?" asked Gabriel.

"He lives on the boat."

"What about a woman?"

"He has several, but none can tolerate his presence for long." Keller wiped the windshield with the back of his hand. "Maybe we should get a hotel room."

"It's a bit soon for that, don't you think? After all, we've only just met."

"Do you always make stupid wisecracks during operations?"

"It's a cultural affliction."

"Stupid wisecracks or operations?"

"Both."

Keller dug a paper napkin from the glove box and did his best to rectify the mess he had made of the windshield. "My grandmother was Jewish," he said casually, as though admitting that his grandmother had enjoyed playing bridge.

"Congratulations."

"Another wisecrack?"

"What am I supposed to say?"

"You don't find it interesting that I have a Jewish ancestor?"

"In my experience, most Europeans have a Jewish relative hidden somewhere in the woodpile."

"Mine was hidden in plain sight."

"Where was she born?"

"Germany."

"She came to Britain during the war?"

"Right before," said Keller. "She was taken in by a distant uncle who no longer considered himself Jewish. He gave her a proper Christian name and sent her to church. My mother didn't know she had a Jewish past until she was in her mid-thirties."

"I hate to be the bearer of bad news," Gabriel said, "but in my book, you're Jewish."

"To be honest with you, I've always felt a little Jewish."

"You have an aversion to shellfish and German opera?"

"I was speaking in a spiritual sense."

"You're a professional assassin, Keller."

"That doesn't mean that I don't believe in God," Keller protested. "In fact, I suspect I know more about your history and scripture than you do."

"So why are you hanging around with that crazy mystic?"

"She isn't crazy."

"Don't tell me you believe all that nonsense."

"How did she know we were looking for the girl?"

"I suppose the don must have told her."

"No," Keller said, shaking his head. "She saw it. She sees every-thing."

"Like the water and the mountains?"

"Yes."

"We're in the south of France, Keller. I see water and mountains, too. In fact, I see them almost everywhere I look."

"She obviously made you nervous with that talk about an old en-emy."

"I don't get nervous," said Gabriel. "As for old enemies, I can't seem to walk out my front door without running into one."

"Then perhaps you should move your front door."

"Is that a Corsican proverb?"

"Just a friendly piece of advice."

"We're not exactly friends yet."

Keller shrugged his square shoulders to convey indifference, in-jury, or something in between. "What did you do with the talisman she gave you?" he asked after a sulky silence.

Gabriel patted the front of his shirt to indicate that the talisman, which was identical to Keller's, was hanging around his neck.

"If you don't believe," asked Keller, "why are you wearing it?"

"I like the way it accents my outfit."

"Whatever you do, don't ever take it off. It keeps the evil at bay."

"I have a few people in my life I'd like to keep at bay."

"Like Ari Shamron?"

Gabriel managed to hide his surprise. "How do you know about Shamron?" he asked.

"I met him when I came to Israel to train. Besides," Keller added quickly, "everyone in the trade knows about Shamron. And everyone knows he wanted you to be the chief instead of Uzi Navot."

"You shouldn't believe everything you read in the papers, Keller."

"I have good sources," said Keller. "And they tell me the job was yours for the taking but you turned it down."

"You might find this hard to believe," said Gabriel, staring wearily through the rain-spattered glass, "but I'm really not in the mood to take a stroll down memory lane with you."

"I was just trying to help pass the time."

"Perhaps we should enjoy a comfortable silence."

"Another wisecrack?"

"You'd understand if you were Jewish."

"Technically, I am Jewish."

"Who do you prefer? Puccini or Wagner?"

"Wagner, of course."

"Then you can't possibly be Jewish."

Keller lit a cigarette and waved out the match. A gust of wind hurled rain against the windshield, obscuring the view of the harbor. Gabriel lowered his own window a few inches to vent Keller's smoke.

"Maybe you're right," he said. "Maybe we should get a hotel room after all."

"I don't think that's going to be necessary."

"Why not?"

Keller flipped the wipers and pointed through the glass.

"Because Marcel Lacroix is headed our way."

He wore a black tracksuit and neon-green trainers, and carried a Puma sports bag over one shoulder. Obviously, he had spent a good portion of the afternoon at the gym. Not that he needed it; Lacroix was at least six-foot-two and weighed well over two hundred pounds. His dark hair was oiled and pulled back into a short ponytail. He had studs in both ears and Chinese characters tattooed on the side of his thick neck, evidence he was a student of the Asian martial arts. His eyes never stopped moving, though they failed to register the two men seated in the battered Renault hatchback with fogged windows. Watching him, Gabriel sighed heavily. Lacroix would surely be a worthy opponent, especially within the tight confines of *Moondance*. Regardless of what anyone said, size mattered.

"No wisecracks?" asked Keller.

"I'm working on one."

"Why don't you let me handle it?"

"Somehow I don't think that's a good idea."

"Why not?"

"Because he knows you work for the don. And if you show up and start asking questions about Madeline Hart, he'll know the don betrayed him, which will be detrimental to the don's interests."

"Let me worry about the don's interests."

"Is that why you're here, Keller?"

"I'm here to make sure you don't end up in a cement coffin at the bottom of the Mediterranean."

"There are worse places to be buried."

"Jewish law doesn't permit burial at sea."

Keller fell silent as Lacroix stepped onto the dock and started toward *Moondance*. Gabriel looked at the way the fabric of his tracksuit was falling across the small of the Frenchman's back. Then he looked at the way the gym bag was hanging over his shoulder.

"What do you think?" asked Keller.

"I think he's carrying his gun in the bag."

"You noticed that, too?"

"I notice everything."

"How are you going to handle it?"

"As quietly as possible."

"What do you want me to do?"

"Wait here," said Gabriel, opening the car door. "And try not to kill anyone while I'm gone."

The Office had a simple doctrine regarding the proper operational use of concealed firearms. It had been given by God to Ari Shamron—at least that was how the story went—and Shamron in turn had given it to all those who went secretly into the night to carry out his wishes. Though it appeared nowhere in written form, every field officer could recite it as easily as they could recite the Shabbat blessing of the candles. An Office agent draws his weapon for one reason and one reason only. He does not wave it around like a gangster or make idle threats. He draws his gun in order to fire it—and he does not stop firing it until the person at whom it is pointed is no longer among the living. Amen.

It was with Shamron's admonition ringing in his ears that Gabriel walked the final steps toward *Moondance*. He hesitated before boarding; even a man with a build as slender as his would cause the boat to list slightly. Therefore, speed and an appearance of outward confidence were critical.

Gabriel cast one last glance over his right shoulder and saw Keller eyeing him warily through the driver's-side window of the Renault. Then he climbed aboard *Moondance* and made his way quickly across the aft deck toward the doorway of the main cabin. Lacroix was on his feet in the passageway by the time Gabriel arrived. In the cramped quarters of the boat, the Frenchman seemed even larger than he had appeared on the street.

"What the fuck are you doing on my boat?" he asked quickly.

"I'm sorry," Gabriel said, raising his palms in a placatory gesture. "I was told you would be expecting me."

"Told by whom?"

"Paul, of course. Didn't he tell you I was coming to see you?"

"Paul?"

"Yes, Paul," said Gabriel assuredly. "The man who hired you to deliver the package from Corsica to the mainland. He said you were the best he'd ever seen. He said that if I ever needed someone to transport valuable goods, you were the person to handle the job."

On the Frenchman's face, Gabriel saw several competing reactions: confusion, apprehension, and, of course, greed. In the end, greed emerged victorious. He stepped aside and with a movement of his eyes invited Gabriel to enter. Gabriel took two languid steps forward while scanning the interior of the cabin for Lacroix's gym bag. It was lying on a tabletop next to a bottle of Pernod.

"Do you mind?" asked Gabriel, nodding toward the open door. "It's not the sort of thing I want your neighbors to hear."

Lacroix hesitated for a moment. Then he walked over to the door and closed it. Gabriel positioned himself next to the table where the gym bag lay.

"What kind of job is it?" asked Lacroix, turning around.

"A very simple one. In fact, it will only take a few minutes."

"How much?"

"What do you mean?" asked Gabriel, feigning bewilderment.

"How much money are you offering?" asked Lacroix, rubbing his first two fingers against his thumb.

"I'm offering you something much more valuable than money."

"What's that?"

"Your life," said Gabriel. "You see, Marcel, you're going to tell me what your friend Paul did with the English girl. And if you don't, I'm going to cut you to pieces and use you as chum."

The Israeli martial arts discipline known as Krav Maga is not known for its gracefulness, but then it was not designed with aesthetics in mind. Its sole purpose is to incapacitate or kill an adversary as quickly as possible. Unlike many Eastern disciplines, it does not frown upon the use of heavy objects to ward off an attacker of superior size and strength. In fact, instructors encourage their students to use whatever objects they have at their disposal to defend themselves. David did not grapple with Goliath, they are fond of saying. David hit Goliath with a rock. And only then did he cut off his head.

Gabriel chose not a rock but the bottle of Pernod, which he seized by the neck and hurled, daggerlike, toward the charging figure of Marcel Lacroix. Fittingly, it struck him in the center of the forehead, opening a deep horizontal gash just above the ridge of his heavy brow. Unlike Goliath, who instantly toppled onto his face, Lacroix managed to remain on his feet, though just barely. Gabriel lunged forward and drove a knee into the Frenchman's unprotected groin. From there, he worked his way violently upward, pummeling Lacroix's midsection before breaking his jaw with a well-placed elbow. A second elbow, delivered to the temple, put Lacroix on the floor. Gabriel reached down and touched the side of the Frenchman's neck to make certain he still had a pulse. Then, looking up, he saw Keller standing in the doorway, smiling. "Very impressive," he said. "The Pernod was a lovely touch."

11

OFF MARSEILLES

T HE RAIN DIED AT SUNSET but the mistral blew without remorse long after dark. It sang in the riggings of the boats huddled in the Old Port and chased round the decks of *Moondance* as Keller guided it expertly out to sea. Gabriel remained by his side on the flying bridge until they were clear of the harbor. Then he headed downstairs to the main salon where Marcel Lacroix lay facedown on the floor, bound, gagged, and blinded by silver duct tape. Gabriel rolled the Frenchman onto his back and tore away the blinding layer of tape with a single rough movement. Lacroix had regained consciousness; in his eyes there was no sign of fear, only rage. Keller had been right. The Frenchman did not frighten easily.

Gabriel reapplied the duct tape blindfold and commenced a thorough search of the entire craft, beginning in the main salon and concluding in Lacroix's stateroom. It produced a cache of illegal narcotics, approximately sixty thousand euros in cash, false passports and French driver's permits in four different names, a hundred stolen credit cards, nine disposable cellular phones, an elaborate collection of print and electronic pornography, and a receipt with a telephone number scrawled on the back. The receipt was from a place called Bar du Haut on boulevard Jean Jaurès in Rognac, a working-class town north of Marseilles, not far from the airport. Gabriel had passed through it once in another lifetime. That was the kind of town Rognac was, a way station on a road to somewhere else.

Gabriel checked the date on the receipt. Then he searched the calling histories of the nine cell phones for the number written on the back. He found it on three of the phones. In fact, Lacroix had called it twice that morning using two different devices.

Gabriel slipped the cell phones, the receipt, and the cash into a nylon rucksack and returned to the main salon. Once again he tore the duct tape from Lacroix's eyes, but this time he removed the gag as well. Lacroix's face was now heavily distorted from the swelling caused by the broken jaw. Gabriel squeezed it tightly as he stared into the Frenchman's eyes.

"I'm going to ask you a few questions, Marcel. You have one chance to tell me the truth. Do you understand?" Gabriel asked, squeezing a little harder. "One chance."

Lacroix made no response other than to groan in pain.

"One chance," Gabriel said again, holding up his index finger to emphasize the point. "Are you listening?"

Lacroix said nothing.

"I'll take that as a yes," said Gabriel. "Now, Marcel, I want you to tell me the names of the men who are holding the girl. And then I want you to tell me where I can find them."

"I don't know anything about a girl."

"You're lying, Marcel."

"No, I swear—"

Before Lacroix could utter another word, Gabriel silenced him by sealing his mouth once again. Next he wrapped several feet of additional tape around the Frenchman's head until only his nostrils were visible. Belowdecks he retrieved a length of nylon rope from a storage cabinet. Then he headed back upstairs to the flying bridge. Keller was clutching the wheel with both hands and squinting through the window at the turbulent seas.

"How's it going down there?" he asked.

"Surprisingly, I wasn't able to persuade him to cooperate."

"What's the rope for?"

"Additional persuasion."

"Anything I can do to help?"

"Reduce speed and put us on autopilot."

Keller did as instructed and followed Gabriel down to the main salon. There they found Lacroix in obvious distress, his chest heaving as he struggled for air through the duct tape helmet. Gabriel rolled him onto his stomach and fed the nylon line through the bindings at his feet and ankles. After securing the line with a tight knot, he dragged Lacroix onto the afterdeck as though he were a freshly harpooned whale. Then, with Keller's help, he lowered him onto the swim step and rolled him overboard. Lacroix struck the black water with a heavy thud and began to thrash wildly in an attempt to keep his head above the surface. Gabriel watched him for a moment and then scanned the horizon in all directions. Not a single light was visible. It seemed they were the last three men on earth.

"How will you know when he's had enough?" asked Keller as he watched Lacroix fighting for his life.

"When he starts to sink," replied Gabriel calmly.

"Remind me never to get on your bad side."

"Don't ever get on my bad side."

After forty-five seconds in the water, Lacroix went suddenly still. Gabriel and Keller hauled him quickly back on board and removed the duct tape from his mouth. For the next several minutes the Frenchman was unable to speak as he alternately gasped for air and coughed seawater from his lungs. When the retching finally stopped, Gabriel took hold of his broken jaw and squeezed.

"You might not realize it at this moment," he said, "but this is your lucky day, Marcel. Now, let's try this again. Tell me where I can find the girl."

"I don't know."

"You're lying to me, Marcel."

"No," Lacroix said, shaking his head violently from side to side. "I'm telling you the truth. I have no idea where she is."

"But you know one of the men who's holding her. In fact, you had drinks with him at a bar in Rognac a week after she disappeared. And you've been in contact with him ever since."

Lacroix was silent. Gabriel squeezed the broken jaw harder.

"His name, Marcel. Tell me his name."

"Brossard," Lacroix gasped through the pain. "His name is René Brossard."

Gabriel looked at Keller, who nodded his head.

"Very good," he said to Lacroix, releasing his grip. "Now keep talking. And don't even think about lying to me. If you do, you'll go back in the water. But the next time it will be forever."

12

OFF MARSEILLES

THERE WERE TWO OPPOSING SWIVEL chairs on the afterdeck. Gabriel secured Lacroix to the one on the starboard side and then lowered himself into the other. Lacroix remained blindfolded, his tracksuit sodden from his brief swim in the ocean. Shivering violently, he pleaded for a change of clothing or a blanket. Then, after receiving no answer, he recounted a warm evening in mid-August when a man had appeared unannounced on *Moondance*, just as Gabriel had earlier that afternoon.

"Paul?" asked Gabriel.

"Yes, Paul."

"Had you ever met him before?"

"No, but I'd seen him around."

"Where?"

"Cannes."

"When?"

"The film festival."

"This year?"

"Yes, in May."

"You went to the Cannes Film Festival?"

"I wasn't on the guest list, if that's what you're asking. I was working."

"What kind of work?"

"What do you think?"

"Stealing from the movie stars and the beautiful people?"

"It's one of our busiest weeks of the year, a real boon to the local economy. The people from Hollywood are total idiots. We rob them blind every time they come here, and they never even seem to notice."

"What was Paul doing?"

"He was hanging out with the beautiful people. I think I actually saw him going into the hall a couple of times to see the films."

"You think?"

"He always looks different."

"He was running scams from the inside at Cannes?"

"You'd have to ask him. We didn't discuss it when he came to see me. We only talked about the job."

"He wanted to hire you and your boat to move the girl from Corsica to the mainland."

"No," said Lacroix, shaking his head vehemently. "He never said a word about a girl."

"What *did* he say?"

"That he wanted me to deliver a package."

"You didn't ask what the package was?"

"No."

"Is that the way you always operate?"

"It depends."

"On what?"

"On how much money is on the table."

"How much was there?"

"Fifty thousand."

"Is that good?"

"Very."

"Did he mention where he got your name?"

"He got it from the don."

"Who's the don?"

"Don Orsati, the Corsican."

"What kind of work does the don do?"

"He's got his fingers into all kinds of rackets," answered Lacroix, "but mainly he kills people. Occasionally, I give one of his men a lift. And sometimes I help make things disappear."

The purpose of Gabriel's line of inquiry was twofold. It allowed him to test the veracity of Lacroix's responses while at the same time covering his own tracks. Lacroix was now under the impression Gabriel had never had the pleasure of making the acquaintance of a Corsican killer named Orsati. And, at least for the moment, he was answering Gabriel's questions truthfully.

"Did Paul tell you when the job was supposed to go down?"

"No," Lacroix answered, shaking his head. "He told me he would give me twenty-four hours' notice, that I would probably hear from him in a week, ten days at most."

"How was he going to contact you?"

"By phone."

"Do you still have the phone you used?"

Lacroix nodded and then recited the number associated with the device.

"He called as planned?"

"On the eighth day."

"What did he say?"

"He wanted me to pick him up the next morning at the cove just south of the Capo di Feno."

"What time?"

"Three a.m."

"How was the pickup supposed to work?"

"He wanted me to leave a dinghy on the beach and wait for him offshore."

Gabriel looked up toward the flying bridge where Keller stood watching the proceedings. The Englishman nodded, as if to say there was indeed a suitable cove on the Capo di Feno and that the scenario as described by Lacroix was entirely plausible.

"When did you arrive on Corsica?" asked Gabriel.

"A few minutes after midnight."

"You were alone?"

"Yes."

"Are you sure?"

"Yes, I swear."

"What time did you leave the dinghy on the beach?"

"Two."

"How did you get back to *Moondance*?"

"I walked," quipped Lacroix, "just like Jesus."

Gabriel reached out and ripped the stud from Lacroix's right ear.

"It was just a joke," gasped the Frenchman as blood flowed from his ruined lobe.

"If I were you," replied Gabriel, "I wouldn't be making jokes about the Lord at a time like this. In fact, I would be doing everything I could to get on his good side."

Gabriel glanced up toward the flying bridge again and saw Keller trying to suppress a smile. Then he asked Lacroix to describe the events that followed. Paul, the Frenchman said, had arrived right on schedule, at three o'clock sharp. Lacroix had seen a single vehicle, a small four-wheel-drive, bumping down the steep track from the cliff tops to the cove with only its parking lamps burning. Then he had heard the throb of the dinghy's outboard echoing back at him across the water. Then, when the dinghy nudged against the stern of *Moondance*, he had seen the girl.

"Paul was with her?" asked Gabriel.

"Yes."

"Anyone else?"

"No, only Paul."

"She was conscious?"

"Barely."

"What was she wearing?"

"White dress, black hood over her head."

"You saw her face?"

"Never."

"Any injuries?"

"Her knees were bloody and she had scratches all over her arms. Bruises, too."

"Restraints?"

"Her hands."

"Front or back?"

"Back."

"What kind of restraints?"

"Flex-cuffs, very professional."

"Go on."

"Paul laid the girl on a couch in the main salon and gave her a shot of something to keep her quiet. Then he came up to the bridge and told me where he wanted me to go."

"Where was it?"

"The tidal creek just west of Saintes-Maries-de-la-Mer. There's a small marina. I've used it before. It's an excellent spot. Paul had obviously done his homework."

Another glance at Keller. Another nod.

"Did you go straight across?"

"No," Lacroix answered. "That would have brought us ashore in broad daylight. We spent the entire day at sea. Then we went in around eleven that night."

"Paul kept the girl in the salon the entire time?"

"He took her to the head once, but otherwise . . ."

"Otherwise what?"

"She got the needle."

"Ketamine?"

"I'm not a doctor."

"Really."

"You asked me a question, I gave you an answer."

"Did he take her ashore in the dinghy?"

"No. I went straight into the marina. It's the kind of place where you can park a car right next to your slip. Paul had one waiting. A black Mercedes."

"What kind of Mercedes?"

"E-Class."

"Registration?"

"French."

"Unoccupied?"

"No. There were two men. One was leaning against the hood as we came in. The other one was behind the wheel."

"Did you know the one leaning against the hood?"

"I'd never seen him before."

"But that wasn't true of the one behind the wheel, was it, Marcel?"

"No," Lacroix answered. "The one behind the wheel was René Brossard."

René Brossard was a foot soldier in an up-and-coming Marseilles crime family with international connections. He specialized in muscle work—debt collection, enforcement, security. In his spare time, he worked as a bouncer in a nightclub near the Old Port, mainly because he liked the girls who came there. Lacroix knew him from the neighborhood. He also knew his phone number.

"When did you call him?" asked Gabriel.

"A few days after I read the first story in the newspaper about the English girl who vanished while on holiday in Corsica. I put two and two together and realized she was the girl I'd dropped at the marina in Saintes-Maries-de-la-Mer."

"You're something of a math genius?"

"I can add," Lacroix quipped.

"You realized that Paul stood to get a lot of ransom money from someone, and you wanted a piece of the action."

"He misled me about the kind of job it was," said Lacroix. "I would have never agreed to take part in a high-profile kidnapping for a mere fifty thousand."

"How much were you after?"

"I try not to make a habit of negotiating with myself."

"Wise man," said Gabriel. Then he asked Lacroix how long Brossard waited to return his call.

"Two days."

"How much detail did you go into on the phone?"

"Enough to make it clear what I was after. Brossard called me back a few hours later and told me to come to Bar du Haut the next afternoon at four."

"That was a very foolish thing to do, Marcel."

"Why?"

"Because Paul might have been there instead of Brossard. And he might have put a bullet between your eyes for having the temerity to ask for more money."

"I can look after myself."

"If that were true," said Gabriel, "you wouldn't be taped to a chair on your own boat. But you were telling me about your conversation with René Brossard."

"He told me Paul wanted to be reasonable. After that, we entered into a period of negotiations."

"Negotiations?"

"Over the price of my settlement. Paul made an offer, I made a counteroffer. We went back and forth several times."

"All by phone?"

Lacroix nodded.

"What's Brossard's role in the operation?"

"He's staying in the house where they're keeping the girl."

"Is Paul there with him?"

"I never asked."

"How many others are there?"

"I don't know. All I know is that another woman is also staying there so they look like a family."

"Has Brossard ever mentioned the English girl?"

"He said she's alive."

"That's all?"

"That's all."

"What's the current state of your negotiations with Paul and Brossard?"

"We reached an agreement this morning."

"How much were you able to chisel out of them?"

"Another hundred thousand."

"When are you supposed to take delivery of the money?"

"Tomorrow afternoon."

"Where?"

"Aix."

"Where in Aix?"

"A café near the Place du General de Gaulle."

"What's the place called?"

"Le Provence—what else?"

"How's it supposed to go down?"

"Brossard is supposed to arrive first, at ten minutes past five. I'm supposed to join him at twenty past."

"Where will he be sitting?"

"At a table outside."

"And the money?"

"Brossard told me it would be in a metal attaché case."

"How inconspicuous."

"It was his choice, not mine."

"Is there a fallback if either one of you fails to show?"

"Le Cézanne, just up the street."

"How long will he wait there?"

"Ten minutes."

"And if you don't show?"

"The deal's off."

"Were there any other instructions?"

"No more phone calls," said Lacroix. "Paul's getting nervous about all the phone calls."

"I'm sure he is."

Gabriel looked up toward the flying bridge, but this time Keller was standing stock-still, a black figure against a black sky, a gun balanced in outstretched hands. The single shot, muted by a suppressor, opened a hole above Lacroix's left eye. Gabriel held the Frenchman's shoulders as he died. Then he spun around in a rage and leveled his own weapon at Keller.

"You'd better put that away before someone gets hurt," the Englishman said calmly.

"Why the hell did you do that?"

"He got on my bad side. Besides," Keller added as he slipped his gun into the waistband of his trousers, "we didn't need him anymore."

13

CÔTE D'AZUR, FRANCE

THEY SENT HIM TO THE bottom in the deep waters beyond the Golfe du Lion and then made for Marseilles. It was still dark when they drew into the Old Port; they slipped from *Moondance* a few minutes apart, climbed into their separate cars, and set out along the coast toward Toulon. Just before the town of Bandol, Gabriel pulled to the side of the road and loosened several engine cables. Then he telephoned the rental company and in the hysterical voice of Herr Klemp left a message saying where the "broken" car could be found. After wiping his fingerprints from the steering wheel and dashboard panel, he climbed into Keller's Renault and together they drove eastward into the rising sun to Nice. On the rue Verdi was an old apartment building, white as bone, where the Office kept one of its many French safe flats. Gabriel entered the building alone and remained inside long enough to retrieve the post, which included the copy of Madeline Hart's Party personnel file he had requested from Graham Seymour. He read it as Keller drove toward Aix along the A8 Autoroute.

"What does it say?" the Englishman asked after several minutes of silence.

"It says that Madeline Hart is perfect. But then we already knew that."

"I was perfect once, too. And look how I turned out."

"You were always a reprobate, Keller. You just didn't realize it until that night in Iraq."

"I lost eight of my comrades trying to protect your country from Saddam's Scuds," Keller said.

"And we are forever in your debt."

Mollified, Keller switched on the radio and tuned it to an English-language station based in Monaco that served the large British expatriate community living in the south of France.

"Homesick?" asked Gabriel.

"Occasionally, I like to hear the sound of my native language."

"You've never been back?"

"To England?"

Gabriel nodded.

"Never," answered Keller. "I refuse to work there, and I've never accepted a contract on a British subject."

"How noble of you."

"One has to operate by a certain code."

"So your parents have no idea you're alive?"

"They haven't a clue."

"Then you couldn't possibly be Jewish," admonished Gabriel. "No Jewish boy would ever allow his mother to think he was dead. He wouldn't dare."

Gabriel turned to the most recent entry in Madeline Hart's personnel file and read it silently as Keller drove. It was a copy of a letter, sent by Jeremy Fallon to the Party chairman, suggesting that Madeline be promoted to a junior post in a ministry and groomed for elected office. Then he looked at the snapshot of Madeline sitting at an outdoor café with the man they knew only as Paul.

Keller, watching him, asked, "What are you thinking?"

"I'm just wondering why a rising young star in Britain's governing party was sharing a bottle of champagne with a first-rate creep like our friend Paul."

"Because he knew she was having an affair with the British prime minister. And he was preparing to kidnap her."

"How could he have known?"

"I have a theory."

"Is it supported by fact?"

"A couple."

"Then it's only a theory."

"But at least it will help to pass the time."

Gabriel closed the file, as if to say he was listening. Keller switched off the radio.

"Men like Jonathan Lancaster always make the same mistake when they have an affair," he said. "They trust their bodyguards to keep their mouths shut. But they don't. They talk to each other, they talk to their wives, they talk to their girlfriends, and they talk to their old mates who've found work in London's private security industry. And before long the talk reaches the ears of someone like Paul."

"You think Paul is connected to the London security business?"

"He could be. Or he could know someone who is. However it happened," Keller added, "a piece of information like that is gold to someone like Paul. He probably put Madeline under watch in London and hacked into her mobile phone and e-mail accounts. That's how he found out she was coming to Corsica on holiday. And when she arrived, Paul was waiting."

"Why have lunch with her? Why take the risk of showing his face?"

"Because he needed to get her alone so he could get her cleanly."

"He seduced her?"

"He's a charming bastard."

"I don't buy it," said Gabriel after a moment of reflection.

"Why not?"

"Because at the time of her abduction, Madeline was romantically involved with the British prime minister. She wouldn't have been attracted to someone like Paul."

"Madeline was the prime minister's mistress," Keller countered, "which means there was very little romance in their relationship. She was probably a lonely girl."

Gabriel looked at the photo again—not at Madeline but at Paul. "Who the hell is he?"

"He's no amateur, that's for sure. Only a professional would know about the don. And only a professional would dare to knock on the don's door to ask for help."

"If he's such a professional, why did he have to rely on local talent to pull off the job?"

"You're asking why he doesn't have a crew of his own?"

"I suppose I am."

"Simple economics," Keller responded. "Maintaining a crew can be a complicated undertaking. And invariably there are personnel problems. When work is slow, the boys get unhappy. And when there's a big score, the boys want a big cut."

"So he uses freelancers on straight fee-for-service contracts to avoid having to share the profits."

"In today's competitive global business environment, everyone's doing it."

"Not the don."

"The don is different. We're a family, a clan. And you're right about one thing," Keller added. "Marcel Lacroix is lucky Paul didn't have him killed. If he'd dared to ask Don Orsati for more money after completing a job, he would have ended up on the bottom of the Mediterranean in a cement coffin."

"Which is where he is now."

"Absent the cement, of course."

Gabriel glared at Keller in disapproval but said nothing.

"You're the one who ripped his earring out."

"A torn earlobe is a temporary affliction. A bullet through the eye is forever."

"What were we supposed to do with him?"

"We could have run him over to Corsica and left him with the don."

"Trust me, Gabriel—he wouldn't have lasted long. Orsati doesn't like problems."

"And, as Stalin liked to say, death solves all problems."

"No man, no problem," said Keller, finishing the quotation.

"But what if the man was lying to us?"

"The man had no reason to lie."

"Why?"

"Because he knew he was never going to leave that boat alive." Keller lowered his voice and added, "He was just hoping we would give him a painless death instead of letting him drown."

"Is this another one of your theories?"

"Marseilles rules," replied Keller. "When things start out violently down here, they always end violently."

"And what if René Brossard isn't sitting at Le Provence at five ten with a metal attaché case at his feet? What then?"

"He'll be there."

Gabriel wished he could share Keller's confidence, but experience wouldn't allow it. He checked his wristwatch and calculated the time they had left to find her.

"If Brossard does happen to show," he said, "it might be better if we don't kill him before he can lead us to the house where they're hiding Madeline."

"And then?"

Death solves all problems, thought Gabriel. No man, no problem.

14

AIX-EN-PROVENCE, FRANCE

T HE ANCIENT CITY OF AIX-EN-PROVENCE, founded by Romans, conquered by Visigoths, and adorned by kings, had little in common with Marseilles, its gritty neighbor to the south. Marseilles had drugs, crime, and an Arab quarter where little French was spoken; Aix had museums, shopping, and one of the country's finest universities. The Aixois tended to look down their noses at Marseilles. They ventured there rarely, mainly to use the airport, then fled as quickly as possible, hopefully while still in possession of their valuables.

Aix's main thoroughfare was the Cours Mirabeau, a long, broad boulevard lined with cafés and shaded by two parallel rows of leafy plane trees. Just to the north was a tangle of narrow streets and tiny squares known as the Quartier Ancien. It was mainly a pedestrian quarter, with all but the largest streets closed to motor traffic. Gabriel performed a series of time-tested Office maneuvers to see whether he was being followed. Then, after determining he was alone, he made his way to a busy little square along the rue Espariat. In the center of the square was an ancient column topped by a Roman capital; and on the southeastern corner, partially obscured by a large tree, was Le Provence. There were a few tables on the square and more along the rue Espariat, where two old men sat staring into space, a bottle of pastis between them. It was a place for locals more than tourists, thought Gabriel. A place where a man like René Brossard would feel comfortable.

Entering, Gabriel went to the *tabac* counter and asked for a pack of Gauloises and a copy of *Nice-Matin*; and while waiting for his change, he surveyed the interior to make certain there was only one way in and out. Then he went outside to select a fixed observation post that would allow him to see the tables on both sides of the restaurant's exterior. As he was weighing his options, a pair of Japanese teenagers approached and in dreadful French asked if he would take their picture. Gabriel pretended not to understand. Then he turned and walked along the rue Espariat, past the blank stares of the two old Provençal men, to the Place du General de Gaulle.

The roar of the cars racing around the busy traffic circle was jarring after the pedestrian quiet of the Quartier Ancien. It was possible Brossard would leave Aix by another route, but Gabriel doubted it; a car could get no closer to Le Provence than the Place du General de Gaulle. It would happen quickly, he thought, and if they weren't prepared, they would lose him. He peered down the cours Mirabeau, at the leaves of the plane trees fluttering in the faint breeze, and calculated the number of operatives and vehicles it would take to do the job correctly. Twelve at least, with four vehicles to avoid detection during the pursuit to the isolated property where they were holding the girl. Shaking his head slowly, he walked over to a café at the edge of the traffic circle where Keller sat drinking coffee alone.

"Well?" asked the Englishman.

"We need a motorbike."

"Where's the money you took from Lacroix before I killed him?"

Frowning, Gabriel patted his midsection. Keller left a few euros on the table and rose to his feet.

There was a dealership not far away, on the boulevard de la République. After spending a few minutes scrutinizing the inventory, Gabriel selected a Peugeot Satelis 500 premium scooter, which Keller paid for in cash and registered under one of his false Corsican-based identities. While the clerk saw to the paperwork, Gabriel crossed the street to a men's clothing store where he purchased a leather jacket, black jeans, and a pair of leather boots. He changed in one of the shop's dressing rooms and put his old clothing in the storage compartment of the scooter. Then, after slipping on a black helmet, he climbed on board the bike and followed Keller down the boulevard to the Place du General de Gaulle.

By then, it was approaching five o'clock. Gabriel left the bike at the base of the rue Espariat and, with the helmet beneath his arm, made his way up the narrow street to the tiny square with a Roman column at the center. The two old men had yet to move from their table at Le Provence. Gabriel took a table at an Irish pub on the opposite side of the street and ordered a lager from the waitress; and for a moment he wondered why anyone would come to an Irish pub in the south of France. His thoughts were interrupted by the sight of a powerfully built man coming up the street through the shadows, a metal attaché case dangling from his right hand. The man entered the interior portion of Le Provence and emerged a moment later with a café crème and a shot of something stronger. His eyes swept slowly over the square as he sat down at an empty table, settling briefly on Gabriel before moving on. Gabriel looked at his watch. It was ten minutes past five exactly. He removed his mobile phone from his coat pocket and speed-dialed Keller.

"I told you he'd come," said the Englishman.

"How did he arrive?"

"Black Mercedes."

"What kind?"

"E-Class."

"Registration?"

"Guess."

"Same car that was waiting at the marina?"

"We'll know soon enough."

"Who was driving?"

"A woman, mid-twenties, maybe early thirties."

"French?"

"Could be. I'll ask her, if you'd like."

"Where is she now?"

"Driving in circles."

"Where are you?"

"Two cars behind her."

Gabriel severed the connection and slipped the phone back into his coat pocket. Then, from the other pocket, he removed one of the phones he had taken from Marcel Lacroix's boat. It would happen quickly, he thought again, and if they weren't prepared they would lose him. Twelve operatives, four vehicles—that's what he needed to do the job properly. Instead, he had only two vehicles, and the only other member of his team was a professional hit man who had once tried to kill him. He drank some of the lager, if only for the sake of his cover. Then he stared at the dead man's phone and watched the minutes tick slowly past.

15

AIX-EN-PROVENCE, FRANCE

T 5:18 TIME SEEMED TO stumble to a stop. The distant hum of the traffic faded; the figures in the tiny square froze, as though rendered in oil on canvas by the hand of Renoir. Gabriel, the restorer, was able to examine them at his leisure. A quartet of florid Germans examining the menu at the tapas bar. Two sandaled Scandinavian girls staring mystified at the last paper street map in all creation. A pretty woman sitting at the base of the Roman column with a boy of perhaps three on her knees. And a man seated at a café called Le Provence with no company other than a metal attaché case filled with one hundred thousand euros. One hundred thousand euros that had been supplied by a man without a country and with no name other than Paul. Gabriel looked at the woman and the child at the base of the column and in his thoughts saw a flash of fire and blood. Then he glanced again at the man sitting alone at Le Provence. It was now twenty minutes past five o'clock. At the instant Gabriel's watch ticked over to 5:21, the man rose to his feet, snatched up the attaché, and departed.

"Is there a fallback if either one of you fails to show?"

"Le Cézanne, just up the street."

"How long will he wait there?"

"Ten minutes."

"And if you don't show?"

"The deal's off."

But why would a professional criminal fail to appear for a lucrative payday of one hundred thousand euros? Because the criminal was at that very moment lying on the seafloor of the Mediterranean eight miles south-southeast of Marseilles with a bullet in his brain. René Brossard couldn't be allowed to know that, of course, which was why Gabriel had the dead man's phone at the ready. He watched Brossard moving swiftly along the shadowed street, attaché case in hand. Then he looked at the florid Germans, and the sandaled Scandinavians, and the mother and child who, somewhere in the darkest recesses of his memory, were still burning. It was 5:22. Eight minutes, he thought, and then the chase would be on. One mistake was all it would take. One mistake, and Madeline Hart would die. He drank more of the beer, but in his current state it tasted of wormwood. He stared at the woman and the child and watched helplessly as the flames consumed their flesh.

At 5:25 he rang Keller again.

"Where is she?"

"Still driving in circles."

"Maybe she's leading you on a wild goose chase. Maybe there's a second car."

"Are you always so negative?"

"Only when a young woman's life is at stake."

Keller said nothing.

"Where is she now?"

"If I had to guess, heading back in your direction."

Gabriel severed the connection and picked up the other phone. After speed-dialing Brossard's number, he placed his thumb tightly over the microphone and brought the phone to his ear. Two rings. Then the sound of Brossard's voice.

"Where the fuck are you?"

Gabriel pressed his thumb tighter against the microphone and said nothing.

"Marcel? Is that you? Where are you?"

Gabriel removed the phone from his ear and pressed the END button. Thirty seconds later he redialed. Once again he covered the microphone with his thumb and said nothing. Brossard picked up on the first ring.

"Marcel? Marcel? I thought I told you no more phones. You have three minutes. Then I'm gone."

This time it was Brossard who rang off first. Gabriel slipped the phone into his pocket and called Keller again.

"How did it go?" asked the Englishman.

"He thinks Lacroix is alive and well and in a spot with bad cell service."

"Very bad."

"Where is she now?"

"Getting close to the Place du General de Gaulle."

Gabriel killed the connection and checked the time. Three minutes, then Brossard would walk. He would be agitated, wary. It was possible he would notice a man following him on foot, especially if that man had been drinking lager in the Irish pub when Brossard had been at Le Provence. But if Brossard passed by the man on his way to the car, he might be less inclined to regard him with suspicion. It was one of Shamron's golden rules of physical surveillance. Sometimes, he preached, it was better to follow a man from in front rather than from behind.

Gabriel stared at his watch. Then, at the stroke of 5:28, he left his table at the pub and set out down the rue Espariat with his helmet beneath his arm. Le Cézanne was the last business on the right, at the point where the street emptied into the Place du General de Gaulle. Brossard was at a table outside. As Gabriel passed, he could feel the Frenchman's eyes boring into his back, but he forced himself not to turn and look. The motorbike was where he had left it, parked next to several others beneath a plane tree that was beginning to shed its leaves. Three had come to rest on the bike's saddle. Gabriel brushed them away. Then he climbed on board and pulled on the helmet.

In the rearview mirror he could see Brossard rising from his table and stepping into the narrow street. A few seconds later the Frenchman passed within a few inches of Gabriel's right shoulder. Close enough so that Gabriel could smell his cologne. Close enough that, if he were so inclined, he could have plucked the attaché case from his left hand. Earlier Brossard had carried the attaché in his right hand, but now that was not possible; he had a mobile phone in his right hand. And the phone was pressed hard against his ear.

Gabriel started the bike's engine as Brossard entered the esplanade at the edge of the Place du General de Gaulle, his head swiveling slowly from side to side like the turret of a tank looking for a target to engage and destroy. There were late-afternoon crowds milling about; Gabriel might have lost sight of him were it not for the attaché case, which shone like a newly minted coin in the gathering dusk. By the time Brossard reached the curb of the traffic circle, the mobile phone was back in his pocket and he was reaching for the front passenger door of a black Mercedes E-Class sedan that had pulled to the side. As he lowered himself into the seat, a Renault hatchback swept past and then turned into the boulevard de la République. The Mercedes did the same thing ten seconds later. Watching, Gabriel couldn't help but smile at their good fortune. Sometimes, he thought, it was better to follow a man from in front rather than from behind. He twisted the throttle of the motorbike and eased into the traffic, his eyes fixed on the taillights of the Mercedes. One mistake, he was thinking. That's all it would take. One mistake and the girl would die.

They followed the boulevard de la République to the route d'Avignon and then headed north. For a mile or so it was all storefronts and stoplights; but gradually the shops turned to apartment blocks and houses, and before long they were moving at speed along a split four-lane road. After a mile a gas station appeared on their right. Keller slowed and switched on his turn signal, and the Mercedes immediately overtook him. Then, with little warning, the road shrank to two lanes again. Gabriel settled into position about fifty meters behind the Mercedes, with Keller on his tail.

By then, the sun was gone and the autumn night was falling with the quickness of a curtain dropping onto a stage. The cypress pine lining the road turned from dark green to black; then the darkness devoured them. As the gloom settled over the countryside, Gabriel's world shrank: white headlights, red taillights, the whine of the bike's engine, the hum of Keller's Renault a few meters behind. His eyes were focused on the back of René Brossard's Mercedes, but in his mind he was gazing at a map of France. In this part of Provence the towns and villages were strung tightly together, like pearls on a necklace. But if they continued in this direction, they would cross into the Vaucluse. There, in the Lubéron, the villages would become more sparse and the terrain rugged. That would be the kind of place they would be keeping her, he thought. Somewhere isolated. Somewhere with only a single road in and out. That way they would know whether they were being watched. Or being followed.

They flashed through the edges of a nothing town called Lignane. Just beyond it, the Mercedes pulled into the deserted gravel parking lot of a business that sold ceramic garden pottery, leaving Gabriel and Keller no choice but to continue past. About two hundred meters farther along was a traffic circle. In one direction was Saint-Cannat; in the other, reached by a smaller road, was Rognes. With a hand signal, Gabriel sent Keller toward Saint-Cannat. Then, after switching off his headlamp, he leaned the bike toward Rognes and quickly sought shelter in the shadow of a cinderblock wall. A moment later the Mercedes came purring past, though now Brossard was behind the wheel and the woman, whom Gabriel could see clearly for the first time, was peering intently into the passenger-side mirror. He quickly dialed Keller and told him the news. Then he forced himself to count slowly to ten and eased the bike back onto the road.

On the road to Rognes, time receded. The pavement narrowed, the night darkened, the air turned colder as they rose steadily in elevation toward the base of the Alps. A three-quarter moon was ducking in and out of the clouds, illuminating the landscape one minute, plunging it into darkness the next. On both sides of the road, vineyards marched neatly into the blackening hills like soldiers heading off to war, but otherwise the land seemed empty of human habitation. Scarcely a light burned anywhere, and the road was deserted except for the black E-Class Mercedes. Gabriel hovered in its wake, with Keller trailing far behind where he was invisible to Brossard. Whenever possible, Gabriel navigated without aid of his headlamp. Buffeted by the cold wind, and robbed partially of the ability to see, he had the sensation of traveling at the speed of sound.

As they approached the outskirts of Rognes, a few cars and trucks finally appeared. In the center of the town, the Mercedes stopped a second time, outside a charcuterie and an adjoining boulangerie. Again Keller sped past, but Gabriel managed to conceal himself in the lee of an ancient church. There he watched as the woman climbed out of the car and entered the shops alone, emerging a few minutes later with several plastic sacks filled with food. It was enough to feed a house filled with people, thought Gabriel, with some left over for a hostage. The fact that they had stopped for supplies suggested that Brossard did not suspect he was being followed. It also suggested they were getting close to their destination.

The woman placed the items in the trunk, then, after a glance around the quiet street, lowered herself into the passenger seat. Brossard had the car moving again even before she closed the door. They sped through the streets of the *centre ville* and then turned onto the D543, a two-lane road that ran from Rognes to the reservoir at Saint-Christophe. Beyond the reservoir was the river Durance. Brossard crossed it at half past six and entered the Vaucluse.

They continued north through the picturesque villages of Cadenet and Lourmarin before finally scaling the southern slopes of the Massif du Lubéron. In the flatlands of the river valley, Gabriel had remained a kilometer or more behind Brossard; but in the winding roads of the mountains he had no choice but to close the gap and keep Brossard constantly in sight. Passing through the hamlet of Buoux, he felt a stab of fear that Brossard had finally become aware of his presence. But when the Mercedes continued apace for another ten kilometers without taking evasive action, his fears receded. He drove on through the night, past stone walls and granite outcroppings that glowed luminous white in the moonlight, his eyes fixed on the red taillights of the Mercedes and his thoughts on a woman he did not know.

Finally, Brossard turned through a gap in the trees lining the road and disappeared. Gabriel didn't dare follow him right away, so he continued along the road for another kilometer before doubling back. The road Brossard had taken was only partially paved and scarcely wide enough for two vehicles. It brought Gabriel to a tiny valley with a patchwork quilt of cultivated fields, separated by hedgerows and stands of trees. There were three villas in the valley, two at the western end and one standing alone in the east, behind a barrier of cypress pine. The Mercedes was nowhere to be seen; Brossard must have switched off his headlamps as a precaution. Gabriel calculated how long it had taken him to double back to the road, and how long it would take for Brossard to reach each of the villas. Then he stood astride the motionless bike, his eyes sweeping back and forth across the valley, thinking that, eventually, Brossard would have to stop somewhere. And when he did, his brake lights would give away his position. After ten more seconds, Gabriel stopped looking at the villas in the west, which were closer to his position, and focused his gaze on the distant villa in the east. And then he saw it, a burst of red light, like the flaring of a match. For an instant it seemed to float atop one of the cypress pines, like a warning light atop a spire. Then the light was extinguished, and the valley was plunged once more into darkness.

16

THE LUBÉRON, FRANCE

THE NEAREST VILLAGE HAD ONLY a dreary bed-and-breakfast, so they drove to Apt and checked into a small hotel on the perimeter of the ancient center. The dining room was empty of other patrons, and only a single elderly waiter was on duty. They ate at separate tables and then walked through the quiet, dark streets to the old basilica of Sainte-Anne. The domed nave smelled of candle smoke and incense and faintly of mildew. Gabriel studied the main altarpiece, his head tilted slightly to one side, and then sat next to Keller, before a stand of softly flickering votive candles. The Englishman's head was bowed and he was holding the bridge of his nose between his thumb and forefinger. When he spoke, it was in a repentant whisper.

"It turns out she was right after all."

"Who?"

"The *signadora*."

"Perhaps I'm mistaken," said Gabriel, lifting his eyes toward the dome, "but I don't recall the *signadora* mentioning anything about a villa in an agricultural valley in the Lubéron."

"But she did mention the sea and the mountains."

"And?"

"They brought her across the sea, and now they're hiding her in the mountains."

"Maybe," said Gabriel. "Or maybe they've already moved her to another location. Or maybe she's dead already."

"Jesus," whispered Keller. "Why are you always so goddamned negative?"

"Remember where you are, Christopher."

Keller rose, walked over to the votive candles, and lit one. He was about to return to the pew but stopped when he saw Gabriel staring at the donation box. He dug a few coins from his pocket and fingered them one by one through the slot. The sound seemed to echo in the dome long after he had retaken his seat.

"Spend much time in Catholic churches?" he asked.

"More than you might imagine."

Keller resumed his pose of penitential reflection. The red glass of the votive candles lent a pink cast to his face.

"Let us stipulate," he said after a moment, "that it is possible the girl is somewhere else. But let us also stipulate that all the evidence suggests that isn't the case. Otherwise, Brossard wouldn't be here. He'd be back in Marseilles, working on his next score."

"At the moment, he's probably trying to figure out why Marcel Lacroix didn't come to Aix to collect his money. And when he tells Paul what happened, Paul is going to get nervous."

"You don't spend much time with criminals, do you?"

"More than you might imagine," Gabriel said again.

"Brossard isn't going to say a word to Paul about what happened in Aix today. He'll tell him everything went down as planned. And then he'll keep the money for himself. Well, not all of it," Keller added. "I suppose he'll have to give some to the woman."

Gabriel nodded slowly in agreement, as though Keller had spoken words of great spiritual insight. Then he turned his head slightly to watch a woman walking up the center of the nave. She had dark hair combed straight back from a high forehead and wore a belted raincoat of synthetic material. Her footfalls, like the sound of Keller's coins, echoed in the quiet of the large church. Pausing before the main altar, she genuflected and made the sign of the cross, deliberately, forehead to heart, left shoulder to right. Then she sat on the opposite side of the nave and stared straight ahead.

"The only way we can determine whether she's there," Gabriel said after a moment, "is to watch the villa for an extended length of time. And there's no way we can do that without a proper fixed observation post."

Keller frowned in disapproval. "Spoken like a true indoor spy," he said.

"What's that supposed to mean?"

"It means that you and your ilk can't function in the field without safe flats and five-star hotels."

"Jews don't camp, Keller. The last time the Jews went camping, they spent forty years wandering in the desert."

"Moses would have found the Promised Land much more quickly if he'd had a couple of lads from the Regiment to guide him."

Gabriel looked at the woman in the raincoat; she was still staring straight ahead, her face expressionless. Then he looked at Keller and asked, "How would we do it?"

"Not we," answered Keller. "I'll do it alone, the way I used to in Northern Ireland. One man in a hide with a pair of binoculars and a bag for his waste. Old school."

"And what happens if a farmer spots you while he's working one of those fields?"

"A farmer could walk over the top of an SAS man in his hide and never see him." Keller watched the candles for a moment. "I once spent two weeks in an attic in Londonderry observing a suspected IRA terrorist who lived across the street. The Catholic family below me never knew I was in the house. And when it came time for me to leave, they never heard me go."

"What happened to the terrorist?"

"He had an accident. A pity, really. He was a true pillar of his community."

Gabriel heard footfalls and, turning, saw the woman exiting the church.

"How long can you stay in that valley?" he asked.

"With enough food and water, I could stay for a month. But forty-eight hours should be more than enough time to tell whether she's there or not."

"That's forty-eight hours we'll never get back again."

"But they'll be well spent."

"What do you need from me?"

"A ride would be nice. But once I'm in place, you can forget about me."

"Then you won't mind if I go to Paris for a few hours?"

"Why the hell do you need to go to Paris?"

"It's probably time I had a word with Graham Seymour."

Keller made no reply.

"Something bothering you, Christopher?"

"I'm just wondering why I have to sit in the mud for two days and you get to go to Paris."

"Would you prefer that I sit in the mud and you go to see Graham?"

"No," said Keller, patting Gabriel's shoulder. "You go to Paris. It's a good place for an indoor spy."

It had been a long time since they had slept, so they returned to the hotel ten minutes apart and repaired to their rooms. Gabriel drifted into unconsciousness within minutes and woke to find his room ablaze with a violent Provençal sunrise. By the time he made his way downstairs to the dining room, Keller was already there, freshly shaved and looking as though he had slept well. They nodded to one another like strangers and, separated by a pair of linened tables, ate their breakfasts in complete silence. Afterward, they returned to the ancient center of the town, this time to do a quick bit of shopping. Keller bought a heavy coat, a dark woolen sweater, a rucksack, and two waterproof tarpaulins. He also bought enough water, packaged processed food, and plastic ziplock bags to last him forty-eight hours. The shopping excursion complete, they ate a large lunch together, though Keller drank no wine with his. He changed into his new clothing as Gabriel drove through the mountains to the rim of the tiny valley with three villas and spoke not a word as he disappeared into a thicket of undergrowth, as swiftly as a deer alerted by a hunter's footfall. By then, it was sunset. Gabriel phoned Graham Seymour in London, spoke the name of a Paris landmark, and rang off again. That night, God in his infinite wisdom saw fit to send an autumn storm into the Lubéron. Gabriel lay awake in his hotel room, listening to the rain lashing against the window and thinking of Keller alone in the mud, in the valley with three villas. The next morning he ate breakfast in the dining room with only the papers and the white-haired waiter for company. Then he drove to Avignon and boarded a TGV train to Paris.

17

PARIS

WAS BEGINNING TO THINK I would never hear from you."

"It's only been five days, Graham."

"Five days can seem like an eternity when a prime minister is breathing down your neck."

They were walking along the Quai de Montebello, past the stalls of the *bouquinistes*. Gabriel wore denim and leather, Seymour a Chesterfield coat and handmade shoes that looked as though they had touched no surface other than the carpet running between his office and the director-general's. Despite the circumstances, he seemed to be enjoying himself. It had been a long time since he had walked down a street without bodyguards, in Paris or anywhere else.

"Are you in direct communication with him?" asked Gabriel.

"Lancaster?"

Gabriel nodded.

"Not anymore," said Seymour. "He's asked Jeremy Fallon to serve as a buffer."

"How do you communicate with him?"

"In person and with great care."

"Does anyone else know of your involvement?"

Seymour shook his head. "I do it all in my spare time," he said wearily, "when I'm not trying to keep watch on the twenty thousand jihadis who call our blessed isle home."

"How are you managing?"

"My director-general suspects I'm selling secrets to our enemies, and my wife is convinced I'm having an affair. Otherwise, I'm managing rather well."

Seymour paused at one of the trestle tables of the *bouquinistes* and made a show of inspecting the inventory. Standing at his back, Gabriel scanned the street for any evidence of surveillance—a pose that seemed too contrived, a face he had seen too many times before. The wind was making tiny whitecaps on the surface of the river. Turning, he found Seymour holding a faded copy of *The Count of Monte Cristo*.

"Well?" asked Seymour.

"It's a classic tale of love, deception, and betrayal," said Gabriel.

"I was asking whether we're being watched."

"It seems we've both managed to slip into Paris without attracting the attention of our mutual friends in the French security services."

Seymour returned the volume of Dumas to its place on the trestle table. Then, as they set off again, he delved into the breast pocket of his Chesterfield and removed an envelope.

"They left this taped to the bottom of a bench in Hampstead Heath last night," he said, handing the envelope to Gabriel. "Two days, or the girl dies."

"Still no demands?"

"No," said Seymour, "but they supplied a new proof-of-life photo."

"How did they tell you where to find it?"

"They placed a call to Simon Hewitt's mobile using an electronic voice generator. Hewitt retrieved the parcel during his morning jog, the first and only morning jog he's ever taken. Jeremy Fallon gave it to me this morning. Needless to say, the tension inside Number Ten is rather high at the moment."

"It's about to get worse."

"No progress?" asked Seymour.

"Actually," said Gabriel, "I think I've found her. The question is, what do we do now?"

They crossed the Petit Pont and walked in the esplanade outside Notre Dame while Gabriel quietly recounted what he had discovered thus far. That the man with whom Madeline Hart had lunched on the afternoon of her disappearance had called himself Paul. That Paul had hired a Marseilles-based smuggler named Marcel Lacroix to move Madeline from Corsica to the mainland. That Lacroix had negotiated an additional payment of one hundred thousand euros for his services, which was to be delivered by a man named René Brossard, in the French city of Aix. And that Brossard, upon the unsuccessful transfer of the money, had immediately driven into the mountains of the Lubéron, to an isolated agricultural valley with three villas.

"You think Madeline is being hidden in one of the villas?"

"René Brossard is a well-known Marseilles crime figure. Unless he's decided to go into the winemaking business, there's only one reason for him to be there."

Seymour shook his head. "The French police have been looking for her for more than a month," he said after a moment, "and yet you managed to find her in five days."

"I'm better than the French police."

"That's why I came to you."

Directly before them several young eastern Europeans were posing for a photograph with the cathedral in the background. Gabriel supposed they were Croatians or Slovaks but couldn't be certain; he had no ear for the Slavic tongues. He nudged Seymour to the left, and they walked past the tourist cafés lining the rue d'Arcole.

"You won't mind if I ask you a few questions," said Seymour.

"The less you know, the better, Graham."

"Humor me."

"If you insist."

"How did you learn about Paul?"

"I can't tell you that."

"Where's Marcel Lacroix?"

"Don't ask."

"Who's watching the villa?"

"An associate."

"From the Office?"

"Not exactly."

"Well," said Seymour, "that was informative."

Gabriel said nothing.

"How much do you know about Paul?"

"He speaks fluent French with an accent, changes his appearance to suit his needs, and apparently he likes movies."

"What are you talking about?"

Gabriel explained how Marcel Lacroix had seen Paul at the Cannes Film Festival, though he left out the part about the duct tape, the near drowning, and the bullet that Christopher Keller, a renegade SAS man whom the British government believed to be dead, had fired into Lacroix's brain.

"Paul sounds like a professional."

"He is," said Gabriel.

"He befriended Madeline before kidnapping her? Is that your theory?"

"Obviously, they were acquainted at the time of her disappearance," Gabriel said. "Whether they were friends, lovers, or something else is the topic of some debate. I suppose the only way we'll know for certain is to ask Madeline."

"How long have you had the house under surveillance?"

"Less than twenty-four hours."

"How long will it take you to establish whether she's there or not?"

"We may never know for certain, Graham."

"How long?" Seymour pressed.

"Another twenty-four hours."

"That would leave only one more day until the deadline expires."

"Which is why you have no choice but to take my information and give it to the French."

They rounded a corner into a quiet side street.

"And what should I say to the French when they ask how I got this information?" Seymour asked.

"Tell them a little bird told you. Make up a convincing cover story about a source or a communications intercept. Trust me, Graham, they won't press you on the source."

"And if they're able to rescue her? What then?" Seymour quickly answered his own question. "They will undoubtedly discover that she was having an affair with the prime minister. And then, because they are French, they will rub Lancaster's nose in it as publicly as possible."

"They might not."

"Lancaster would never take that chance."

"You asked me to find her," said Gabriel, "and I believe I've found her."

"And now I'm asking you to bring her out."

"If I go in there, people will die."

"The French will assume it was one gang of Marseilles criminals killing members of another gang. It happens all the time down there." Seymour paused, then added, "Especially when you're in town."

Gabriel ignored the remark. "And if I'm able to get her out? What am I supposed to do with her?"

"Bring her back to Britain and let us worry about the rest."

"You'll need a cover story."

"People disappear and reappear all the time."

"And if the video ever becomes public?"

"No missing girl, no scandal."

"She'll need a passport."

"I'm afraid I can't help you."

"Why not?"

"Because I can't generate a false passport with her picture on it without raising alarm bells. Besides," Seymour added, "you and your service are rather good at making false passports."

"We have to be."

They walked in silence for a moment along the quiet street. Gabriel had run out of objections and questions. He could only say no, something he was not prepared to do.

"She might not be in any condition to travel," Gabriel said at last. "In fact, it might be a while before she's ready for much of anything at all."

"What are you suggesting?"

"If she's actually in that villa," Gabriel began, "and if we can get her out, we'll have to take her to one of our French safe properties and clean her up. I'll bring in a team, a doctor, some nice girls to make her feel comfortable."

"And when she's ready to move?"

"We'll change her appearance, take her photograph, and stick it on an Israeli passport. And then we'll bring her across the Channel, at which point she will be your problem."

They had reached the end of the street. It had brought them back to the flank of Notre Dame. Seymour adjusted his scarf and pretended to admire the flying buttresses.

"You never told me where the villa is," he said indifferently.

"You'll know soon enough."

"And Marcel Lacroix?"

"He's dead," said Gabriel.

Seymour turned and extended his hand. "Is there anything I can do for you?"

"Walk to the Gare du Nord and get on the next train to London."

"It's more than a mile."

"The exercise will do you good. Don't take this the wrong way, Graham, but you look like hell."

As it turned out, Seymour couldn't recall the way to the Gare du Nord. He was an MI5 man, which meant he came to Paris only for conferences, holidays, or when he was trying to find the kidnapped mistress of his prime minister. Gabriel murmured the directions into Seymour's ear and then followed him to the station's entrance, where he vanished into a sea of beggars, drug dealers, and African taxi drivers.

Alone again, Gabriel rode the Métro to the Place de la Concorde and then made his way on foot to the Israeli Embassy at 3 rue Rabelais. After paying a courtesy call on the station chief, he contacted the operations desk at King Saul Boulevard to request a French safe house and a hostage reception committee. Five minutes later the desk phoned back to say a three-member team would be on the ground within twenty-four hours.

"What about the house?"

"We have a new property in Normandy, not far from the ferry terminal at Cherbourg."

"What's it like?"

"Four bedrooms, an eat-in kitchen, lovely views of the Channel, maid service optional."

Gabriel rang off and collected the keys to the house from the station chief's safe. It was approaching half past four, leaving him just enough time to make the five o'clock train to Avignon. He arrived in darkness and returned to his hotel in Apt. That night there was no rain, only a powerful wind that stalked the narrow streets of the town's ancient center. Gabriel lay awake in his bed, in solidarity with Keller. At breakfast the next morning, he drank more than his usual allotment of coffee.

"You didn't sleep well, Monsieur?" asked the elderly waiter.

"The mistral," replied Gabriel.

"Terrible," agreed the waiter.

The sign over the storefront read L'IMMOBILIERE DU LUBÉRON. Adopting the skeptical demeanor of Herr Johannes Klemp, Gabriel spent a moment scrutinizing the property photographs hanging in the window before entering. A woman of perhaps thirty-five greeted him. She wore a tan skirt and a white blouse that clung to her with an illusion of dampness. She didn't seem to find Herr Klemp's attempt at small talk appealing. Few women did.

He told her that he had fallen under the Lubéron's spell and that he planned to return for a longer stay. A hotel wouldn't do, he said. In order to experience the *real* Lubéron, he wanted to rent a villa. And not just any villa. It had to be something substantial, in an area where tourists rarely ventured. Herr Klemp was not a tourist; he was a traveler. "There's an important difference," he insisted, though, if there was one, it seemed entirely lost on the woman.

There was something in Herr Klemp's demeanor that told her this was going to be a lengthy ordeal. Unfortunately, she had seen many others like him before. He would want to see every property but, in the end, find none to his satisfaction. Still, it was the only job she could find in this place that so enchanted the likes of Herr Klemp, so she offered him a café crème from the automated machine and opened her brochures with as much enthusiasm as she could muster.

There was a lovely villa north of Apt, but he found it too pedestrian. And then there was a newly remodeled villa in Ménerbes, but its garden was much too small and its furnishings far too modern. And then there was the grand estate outside Lacoste, the one with its own clay tennis court and indoor lap pool, but this offended Herr Klemp's social democratic sense of fairness. And on it went, villa by villa, town by town, setting by setting, until all that remained was a property south of Apt, in a small agricultural valley planted with vineyards and lavender.

"It sounds perfect," said Herr Klemp hopefully.

"It's a bit isolated."

"Isolated is good."

By this point, the woman felt exactly the same way. In fact, if she'd had the power, she would have locked Herr Klemp in the most isolated property in France and thrown away the key. Instead, she opened the brochure and walked him through every room in the house. For some reason, he seemed particularly interested in the entrance hall. There was nothing unusual about it. A heavy timbered door with iron studs. A small decorative table. Two flights of limestone steps. One flight rose to the second level of the house, the other sank into the basement.

"Is there any other way down besides these stairs?"

"No."

"And no outside entrance to the basement?"

"No," the woman repeated. "If you have guests using the bedroom on the lower level, they'll have to use these stairs."

"Are there photos of the lower level?"

"I'm afraid there's not much to see. There's only a spare bedroom and a laundry room."

"Is that all?"

"There's also a storage room, but it's off-limits to renters. The owner keeps a padlock on that."

"Are there any outbuildings on the property?"

"There were a long time ago," she said, "but they were removed during the last renovation."

He smiled, closed the brochure, and pushed it across the desk toward the woman.

"I think we've finally found the place," he said.

"When are you interested in taking it?"

"Next spring. But if possible," he added, "I'd love to have a look at it now."

"I'm afraid it's occupied."

"Really? Until when?"

"The renters are scheduled to depart in three days' time."

"I'm afraid I'm leaving Provence before then."

"What a pity," said the woman.

Gabriel spent the rest of the afternoon pretending to tour the countryside of the Lubéron by motorbike, and at sunset he was parked in a secluded spot along the rim of the valley with three villas. Keller was due to emerge at six o'clock sharp, but at ten minutes past there was still no sign of him. Then Gabriel felt a presence at his back. Turning abruptly, he saw the Englishman standing in the darkness, as still as a statue.

"How long have you been there?" asked Gabriel.

"Ten minutes," replied Keller.

Gabriel started the engine. And then they were gone.

18

APT, FRANCE

ELLER TOLD THE CONCIERGE HE had been trekking through the mountains, thus the smudges of dirt on his cheeks, the soiled rucksack over his sturdy shoulder, and the smell of the outdoors that clung to his clothing. Upstairs in his room, he shaved with great care, soaked his weary body in a tub of scalding water, and smoked his first cigarette in two days. Then he repaired to the dining room, where he ate an inordinately large meal and drank the most expensive bottle of Bordeaux in the cellar, courtesy of Marcel Lacroix. Satiated, he walked through the quiet streets of the old town to the basilica. The nave was in shadow and deserted except for Gabriel, who was seated before the stand of votive candles. "But are you *sure?*" he asked when Keller joined him. Yes, said Keller, nodding slowly. He was sure.

"Did you ever see her?"

"No."

"Then how do you know she's there?"

"Because one knows a criminal operation when one sees one," said Keller assuredly. "They're either running a meth lab, assembling a dirty bomb, or babysitting a kidnapped English girl. I'm betting on the girl."

"How many people are in the house?"

"Brossard, the woman, and two other Marseilles boys. The boys stay inside during the day, but at night they come outside for a smoke and a bit of fresh air."

"Any visitors?"

Keller shook his head. "The woman left the villa once each day to do some shopping and wave to the neighbors, but there was no other activity."

"How long was she away?"

"One hour and twenty-eight minutes the first day, two hours and twelve minutes the second."

"I admire your precision."

"I didn't have much else to keep me occupied."

Gabriel asked how Brossard spent his days.

"He pretends to be on holiday," Keller replied. "But he also takes a walk around the property to have a look at things. He almost stepped on me a couple of times."

"What's the routine at night?"

"Someone is always awake. They watch television in the sitting room or hang out in the garden."

"How can you tell they're watching television?"

"I can see it flickering through the shutters. By the way," he added, "the shutters are never open. Never."

"Any other lights on at night?"

"Not inside," said Keller. "But the outside is lit up like a Christmas tree."

Gabriel frowned. Keller suppressed a yawn and asked about Paris.

"It was cold."

"Paris or the meeting?"

"Both," replied Gabriel. "Especially when I suggested letting the French handle the rescue."

"Why on earth would we do that?"

"That was Graham's reaction, too."

"What a shock."

"You seem to have your finger on the pulse of Downing Street."

Keller allowed the remark to pass without a response. Gabriel contemplated the flickering votive candles for a moment before telling Keller about the rest of his meeting with Graham Seymour: the Office safe house in Cherbourg, the Office reception committee, the quiet return to England on a forged Office passport. But it was all predicated on one thing. They had to get Madeline out of the villa quickly and quietly. No shootouts. No car chases.

"Shootouts are for cowboys," said Keller, "and car chases only happen in the movies."

"How do we get through the lights without being seen by the guards?"

"We don't."

"Explain."

Keller did.

"And if Brossard or one of the others comes downstairs?"

"It's possible they might get hurt."

"Permanently," added Gabriel. He looked at Keller seriously for a moment. "Do you know what's going to happen when the police find those bodies? They'll start asking questions in town. And before long they'll have a composite sketch of a former SAS man who was supposed to have died in Iraq. Hotel surveillance photographs, too."

"That's what the *macchia* is for."

"Meaning?"

"I'll go to ground in Corsica and wait it out."

"It might be a long time before you'll be able to ply your trade again," Gabriel said. "A very long time."

"It's a sacrifice I'm willing to make."

"For queen and country?"

"For the girl."

Gabriel regarded Keller in silence for a moment. "I take it you have a problem with men who harm innocent women?"

Keller nodded his head slowly.

"Anything you want to tell me?"

"You might find this hard to believe," said Keller, "but I'm really not in the mood to take a stroll down memory lane with you."

Gabriel smiled. "There's hope for you after all, Keller."

"A little," the Englishman replied.

Gabriel heard footfalls in the church and, turning, saw the woman in the belted raincoat coming slowly up the nave. Once again she paused before the main altar and made the sign of the cross with great care, forehead to heart, left shoulder to right.

"The deadline is tomorrow," said Gabriel. "Which means we have to go in tonight."

"The sooner the better."

"We need more people to do this the right way," Gabriel said gloomily.

"Yes, I know."

"A hundred things could go wrong."

"Yes, I know."

"She might not be able to walk."

"So we'll carry her," said Keller. "It won't be the first time I've carried someone off the battlefield."

Gabriel looked at the woman in the tan raincoat staring into space, then at the flickering light of the votive candles.

"Who do you suppose he is?" he asked after a moment.

"Who?"

"Paul."

"I don't know," said Keller, rising. "But if I ever see him, he's dead."

———

After leaving the church, Gabriel returned to the hotel and informed management he would be checking out. It was nothing serious, he assured them—a small crisis at home that only he, the peerless Herr Johannes Klemp of Munich, could disentangle. Management smiled regretfully but privately was pleased to see him go. The chambermaids had unanimously declared him the most annoying guest of the season, and Mafuz, the chief bellman, secretly wished him dead.

It was Mafuz, standing pillar-like at his post by the front door, who saw him gratefully into the night. He rode through the streets of the town for several minutes to make certain he was not being followed. Then, with his headlamp doused, he made his way to the narrow dirt-and-gravel track running along the rim of the valley with three villas. One of the villas, the one in the east, was illuminated as if for a special occasion. Keller was standing amid a coppice of pine, staring at the villa intently. Gabriel joined him and stared at it, too. After a few minutes a shadowed figure appeared in the garden and a lighter flared. Keller extended his arm and whispered, "Bang, bang, you're dead."

They remained in the pine trees until the man had returned to the villa. Then they sat in Keller's darkened Renault thrashing out the final details of their plan of attack—their positions, their sightlines, their firing lanes, their conduct inside the villa itself. After twenty minutes all that remained to be decided was who would take the shot that would set everything in motion. Gabriel insisted he be the one, but Keller objected. Then he reminded Gabriel that he had achieved the highest score ever recorded in the killing house at Hereford.

"It was an exercise," said Gabriel dismissively.

"A live-fire exercise," Keller countered.

"It was still an exercise."

"What's your point?"

"I once shot a Palestinian terrorist between the eyes from the back of a moving motorcycle."

"So what?"

"The terrorist was sitting in the middle of a crowded café on the boulevard Saint-Germain in Paris."

"Yes," said Keller, feigning boredom, "I think I remember reading something about that in one of my history books."

In the end it came down to a coin toss.

"Don't miss," said Gabriel, as he slipped the coin back into his pocket.

"I never miss."

By then, it was approaching ten o'clock, too early to move. Keller closed his eyes and slept while Gabriel sat staring at the lights of the easternmost villa. He imagined a small room on the lower level: a cot, handcuffs, a hood, a bucket for a toilet, insulation to muffle the screaming, a woman who was no longer herself. And for an instant he was walking through Russian snow, toward a dacha on the edge of a birch forest. He blinked away the image and absently fingered the hand of red coral hanging around his neck. When she is dead, he was thinking. Then you will know the truth.

Four hours later he squeezed Keller's shoulder. Keller woke instantly, climbed out, and removed the rucksack from the trunk of the car. Inside were two rolls of duct tape, a pair of heavy-duty twenty-four-inch bolt cutters, and two suppressors—one for Keller's HK45 compact, the other for Gabriel's Beretta. Gabriel screwed the suppressor into the end of the Beretta's barrel and swung the rucksack over his shoulder. Then he followed Keller down through the pine trees and over the rim of the valley. There was no moon or stars and not a breath of wind. Keller moved through the scrub and rock formations in complete silence, slowly, as if he were under water. Every few steps he would raise his right hand to freeze Gabriel in his tracks, but otherwise they did not communicate. They did not need to. Every step, every move, had been worked out in advance.

At the base of the hill, they parted. Keller went to the southern side of the villa and settled into a drainage ditch; Gabriel headed for the eastern side and concealed himself in a thicket of briar. His position was fifty feet beyond the line where the exterior lights of the villa died and the darkness reclaimed the night. Directly opposite was a row of French doors leading from the garden to the sitting room. Through the shutters he could see the flickering light of the television and, he assumed, the faint shadow of a man.

He looked at his watch. It was 2:37 a.m. Three hours of darkness left. After that, there could be no more trips to the garden for the man inside the villa. Surely he would step outside for one last breath of fresh air and one more glance at the sky, even if there was no moon or stars and not a breath of wind. Then, from the drainage ditch on the southern side of the villa, there would come a single shot. And then it would begin: a cot, handcuffs, a bucket for a toilet, a woman who was no longer herself.

He glanced at his watch again, saw that only two minutes had passed, and shivered in the cold. Perhaps Keller was right; perhaps he was an indoor spy after all. To help pass the time he removed himself mentally from the thicket of briar and placed himself before a canvas. It was the painting he had left behind in Jerusalem— Susanna bathing in her garden, watched over by the village elders. Once again he cast Madeline in the role of Susanna, though now the wounds he healed were caused not by time but by captivity.

He worked slowly but steadily, repairing the sores on her wrists, adding flesh to her atrophied shoulders and color to her hollow cheeks. And all the while he kept watch on the passing of the minutes, and on the villa, which appeared to him in the background of the painting. For two hours there was no movement. Then, as the first light appeared in the eastern sky, one of the French doors opened slowly and a man stepped into Madeline's garden. He stretched his arms, looked left, then right, then left again. At Madeline's request, Gabriel quickly completed the restoration. And when he saw a flash of light from the south, he rose from his knees, gun in hand, and started running.

19

THE LUBÉRON, FRANCE

B Y THE TIME GABRIEL BREACHED the outer limits of the light, he could see Keller charging hard and fast across the garden. The Englishman arrived at the open French door first and took up a position along the left side. Gabriel went to the right and looked briefly down at the man who, a few seconds earlier, had stepped into the garden for a breath of fresh air. There was no need to check for a pulse; the .45-caliber round fired by Keller's gun had entered the skull cleanly and exited in a mess. The man had never known what had hit him and probably had been dead before he fell. It was a decent way to depart this world, thought Gabriel. For a criminal. For a soldier. For anyone.

Gabriel looked at Keller. Their poses were identical: one shoulder against the exterior of the villa, two hands on the gun, the barrel pointed at the ground. After a few seconds Keller gave a terse nod. Then, raising the HK to eye level, he rotated silently inside. Gabriel followed and covered the right side of the room while Keller saw to the left. There was no movement and no sound other than the television, where Jimmy Stewart was pulling Kim Novak from the waters of San Francisco Bay. The room smelled of spoiled food, stale tobacco, and spilled wine. Empty cardboard containers littered every surface. A month in Provence, thought Gabriel, Marseilles underworld style.

Keller inched forward through the flickering light of the television, the HK extended, sweeping back and forth in a ninety-degree arc. Gabriel hovered a half step behind, his gun pointed in the opposite direction but moving in the same arc. They came to an archway separating the sitting room from the dining room. Gabriel pivoted inside, swiveled the gun in all directions, and then pivoted back to Keller's side. At the entrance to the kitchen, he quickly repeated the movement. Both rooms were unoccupied, but both were piled high with soiled plates and cutlery. The squalor of the place made the back of Gabriel's neck burn with anger. As a rule, captors who lived like pigs did not treat their hostages well.

At last they came to the entrance hall. It was the one place in the villa that still bore any resemblance to the photographs Gabriel had seen at the offices of L'Immobiliere du Lubéron. The heavy timbered door with iron studs. The small decorative table. The two flights of limestone steps, one rising to the second level of the house, the other sinking into the basement. Both were in total darkness.

Keller took up a post midway between the two as Gabriel drew a Maglite from his pocket. He left the light switched off and descended blindly into the gloom, slowly, one step, two steps, three steps, four. Halfway down, he heard a sound from above, footfalls, muffled and quick. Then came two dull thumps, the sound of an HK45 with a suppressor firing two shots in rapid succession.

Someone had come down the stairs.

Someone had bumped into the man who scored the highest total ever recorded in the killing house at Hereford.

Someone had died.

Gabriel switched on the Maglite and raced down the steps two at a time.

At the bottom was a foyer with a tile floor and doors on each of the three walls. The owner's storeroom was on the left. Caught by the beam of the Maglite, the padlock sparkled with a brightness that suggested it had not been there long. Gabriel swung the rucksack from his shoulders, removed the bolt cutters, and closed the jaws around the shackle. A few pounds of pressure were all it took to send the padlock clattering to the floor. Gabriel moved aside the latch and pushed open the door. The smell hit him instantly. Heavy and nauseatingly sweet. The smell of a human being in captivity. He played the beam of the Maglite around the interior. A cot. Handcuffs. A hood. A bucket for a toilet. Insulation to muffle the screaming.

But Madeline was gone.

Upstairs there were two more dull thuds from Keller's muted HK. Then two more.

The first body was in the entrance hall, at the base of the stairs leading to the second floor. It was one of the guards who hadn't shown his face outside the villa. Now, thanks to two hollow-nosed .45-caliber rounds, there was little left of it. The same was true for René Brossard, who was sprawled next to him, a gun still in his lifeless hand. The woman was on the second-floor landing. Keller hadn't wanted to shoot her, but he'd had no choice; she had pointed a gun at him and given every indication that she intended to fire. He had spared her face, though, shooting her twice in the upper torso. As a result, she was the only one of the three still alive. Gabriel knelt next to her and held her hand. It was already cold to his touch.

"Am I going to die?" she asked him.

"No," he said, squeezing her hand gently. "You're not going to die."

"Help me," she said. "Please help me."

"I will," answered Gabriel. "But you have to help me, too. You have to tell me where I can find the girl."

"She's not here."

"Where is she?"

The woman's mouth tried to form words but could not.

"Where is she?" Gabriel repeated.

"I swear I don't know." The woman shivered. Her eyes were losing focus. "Please," she whispered, "you have to help me."

"When was she here last?"

"Two days ago. No, three."

"Which was it?"

"I can't remember. Please, please, you have to—"

"Was it before or after you and Brossard went to Aix?"

"How do you know we went to Aix?"

"Answer me," said Gabriel, squeezing her hand again. "Was it before or after?"

"It was that night."

"Who took her?"

"Paul."

"Only Paul?"

"Yes."

"Where did he take her?"

"To the other safe house."

"Is that what he called it? A safe house?"

"Yes."

"Where is it?"

"I don't know."

"Tell me," repeated Gabriel.

"Paul never told us where it was. He called it operational security."

"Those were his exact words? Operational security?"

She nodded.

"How many safe houses are there?"

"I don't know."

"Two? Three?"

"Paul never told us that."

"How long was she here?"

"From the beginning," the woman said.

And then she died.

———

They laid the four bodies on the floor of the storage room and covered them in clean white linen. There was nothing to be done about the blood inside the house, but outside Gabriel quickly hosed down the paving stones of the garden to superficially erase the evidence of what had occurred there. He reckoned they had at least forty-eight hours; then the woman from L'Immobiliere du Lubéron would come calling to collect the keys from the departing clients and supervise the cleanup. After discovering the blood, she would immediately phone the gendarmes, who would in turn discover the four bodies in the owner's private storage room—a storage room that had been emptied of its contents and converted into a cell for a kidnap victim. Forty-eight hours, thought Gabriel. Perhaps a bit longer, but not much.

It was beginning to get light when they hiked out of the valley and returned to the spot where they had left the motorbike and Keller's old Renault. Gabriel paused for one last look; a single figure, a laborer, was moving through the vineyards but otherwise there was no activity in the valley below. They loaded the rucksacks into the trunk of Keller's car and drove separately to the town of Buoux, where they stopped for brioche and café crème in a café filled with ruddy-faced locals. The smell of freshly baked bread made Gabriel feel slightly ill. He rang Graham Seymour in London and in cryptic language reported that the mission had failed, that Madeline had been in the villa once but had been moved approximately seventy-two hours earlier. The trail had reached a dead end, he said before ringing off. All they could do now was wait for Paul to make his demands.

"But what if he decides it's too risky to make demands?" asked Keller. "What if he just kills her instead?"

"Why are you always so negative?"

"I suppose you're beginning to rub off on me."

They left the Lubéron by the same route they had taken the night they had followed René Brossard and the woman from Aix: down the slopes of the massif, across the river Durance, past the shore of the reservoir at Saint-Christophe, and, eventually, back to Marseilles. There was a ferry leaving for Corsica at noon. They each bought a ticket and then sat next to one another at separate tables at a café adjacent to the terminal. Gabriel drank tea, Keller beer. His mood was noticeably gloomy. It was not often he returned to Corsica having failed to fulfill his mission.

"It wasn't your fault," said Gabriel.

"I told you she was there," he answered. "She wasn't."

"But it *looked* like she was."

"Why?" Keller asked. "Why were the guards pulling night shifts when Madeline was already gone?"

Just then, Gabriel's mobile phone vibrated. He raised it to his ear slowly, listened in silence, then returned it to the tabletop.

"Graham?" asked Keller.

Gabriel nodded. "Someone left a phone taped to the underside of a bench in Hyde Park last night."

"Where's the phone now?"

"Downing Street."

"When is he supposed to call?"

"Five minutes."

Keller finished his beer and immediately ordered another. Five minutes passed, then five more. From outside came an announcement that the ferry for Corsica was beginning to board. It nearly drowned out the sound of Gabriel's phone buzzing against the tabletop. Again he raised it to his ear and listened in silence.

"Well?" asked Keller as Gabriel slipped the phone into his pocket.

"Paul made his demand."

"How much does he want?"

"Ten million euros."

"Is that all?"

"No," said Gabriel. "The prime minister would like a word."

Outside a line of cars was snaking into the belly of the ferry. Keller rose. Gabriel watched him go.

MARSEILLES–LONDON

THE NEXT FLIGHT TO HEATHROW was at five that evening. Gabriel purchased a change of clothing from a department store near the Old Port and then checked into a sad transit hotel adjacent to the train station to bathe and dress. He stuffed his old clothing into an overflowing rubbish bin behind a restaurant, left the motorbike in a spot where he was confident it would be stolen by nightfall, and took a taxi to the airport. The main terminal looked as though it had been abandoned to an advancing army. Gabriel checked the French Internet news sites to make certain the police hadn't found four bodies in a tranquil valley in the Lubéron; then he purchased a first-class ticket for London using the name Johannes Klemp. During the flight he refused all service and all attempts by his seatmate, a bald Swiss banker, to engage him in conversation, choosing instead to stare morosely out his window. There was not much to see that night; a thick layer of cloud blanketed the whole of northern Europe. Only when the plane was a few thousand feet from the ground again did the yellow sodium lamps of West London manage to prick the gloom. To Gabriel they looked like a sea of votive candles. He closed his eyes; and in his thoughts he saw a raincoated woman standing before the altar of a dark, ancient church, making the sign of the cross as though the very movement was unfamiliar to her.

Exiting the aircraft, Gabriel joined a line of travelers filing toward passport control. The customs officer, a bearded Sikh wearing a royal blue *dastar*, examined his passport with the skepticism it deserved, then, after stamping it violently, welcomed him to Great Britain. Gabriel returned the passport to his coat pocket and made his way to the arrivals hall, where an MI5 operative named Nigel Whitcombe stood alone amid the crowd clutching a wilted paper sign that read MR. BAKER. Whitcombe was Graham Seymour's acolyte and primary runner of off-the-record errands. He was in his mid-thirties but looked like an adolescent who had been stretched and molded into manhood. His cheeks were pink and hairless, and the fleeting smile he offered when shaking Gabriel's hand was as guiltless as a parson's. His benevolent appearance had proven to be a useful asset at MI5. It concealed a mind that was as cunning and devious as that of any terrorist or career criminal.

Owing to the secretive nature of Gabriel's visit, Whitcombe had come to Heathrow in his personal car, a Vauxhall Astra. He drove with the speed and ease of someone who spent his weekends racing rally cars. Indeed, it was not until they had reached West Cromwell Road that the speedometer dipped below eighty.

"It's a good thing we're close to a hospital," said Gabriel.

"Why?"

"Because if you don't slow down, we're going to need one."

Whitcombe eased off the throttle, but only slightly.

"Any chance we can stop at Harrods for tea?"

"I was told to bring you in straight away."

"I was joking, Nigel."

"Yes, I know."

"Do you know why I'm here?"

"No," Whitcombe answered, "but it must be something urgent. I haven't seen Graham like this since . . ."

His voice trailed off.

"Since when?" asked Gabriel.

"Since the day that al-Qaeda suicide bomber detonated himself in Covent Garden."

"Good times," said Gabriel darkly.

"That was one of our better ops, wouldn't you agree?"

"All except for the ending."

"Let's hope this one doesn't end that way, whatever it is."

"Let's," agreed Gabriel.

After successfully negotiating the traffic maelstrom at Hyde Park Corner, Whitcombe wound his way past Buckingham Palace to Birdcage Walk. As they were passing the Wellington Barracks, he pressed a button on his mobile phone, muttered something about delivering a package, and abruptly rang off. Two minutes later, in Old Queen Street, he pulled up behind a parked Jaguar limousine. Seated in the back, looking as though he had just dined poorly at his club, was Graham Seymour.

"I don't suppose you have anything approaching business attire?" he asked as Gabriel slid in next to him.

"I did," replied Gabriel, "but British Airways lost my luggage."

Seymour frowned. Then he glanced at his driver and said, "Number Ten."

Number 10 Downing Street, arguably the world's most famous address, had once been guarded by two ordinary London policemen, one who stood watch outside the rather drab black door, and another who sat in the entrance hall, in a comfortable leather chair. All that changed after the Provisional IRA attacked Downing Street with mortars in February 1991. Security barriers arose at the Whitehall entrance of the street, and heavily armed members of Scotland Yard's Diplomatic Protection Group took the place of the two ordinary London policemen. Downing Street, like the White House, was now a fortified encampment, visible only through the bars of a fence.

Originally, Number Ten was not one house but three: a town house, a cottage, and a sprawling sixteenth-century mansion called "the House at the Back" that served as a residence for members of the royal family. In 1732 King George II offered the property to Sir Robert Walpole, the first British prime minister in everything but title, who decided to join the three houses into one. The result was what William Pitt described as a "vast, awkward house," prone to sinking and cracking, where few British prime ministers chose to live. By the end of the eighteenth century, the house had fallen into such disrepair the Treasury recommended razing it; and after World War II, it grew so structurally unsound that limits were placed on the number of people who could be on the upper floors at any one time for fear the building would collapse beneath their weight. Finally, in the late 1950s, the government undertook a painstakingly exact reconstruction. Delayed by labor strikes and the discovery of medieval artifacts beneath the foundation, the project took three years to complete and cost three times more than projected. Harold Macmillan, the prime minister of the day, lived in the Admiralty House during the renovations.

Most visitors to Downing Street come through the security gate at Whitehall and enter Number Ten through the iconic black door. But on that evening Graham Seymour and Gabriel slipped onto the grounds through the gate along the Horse Guards Road and entered the residence through a French door overlooking the walled garden. Waiting in the foyer was a secretary from Lancaster's private office, a prim librarian of a woman who was holding a leather folio against her body as though it were a shield. She nodded to Seymour in greeting but avoided eye contact with Gabriel. Then, turning on her heel, she led them along a wide, elegant corridor to a closed door, against which she rapped her knuckles lightly. "Come," said the second-most-famous voice in Great Britain, and the prim woman led them inside.

21

10 DOWNING STREET

AFTER A LIFETIME OF SERVICE in the secret world, Gabriel had lost count of the number of times he had entered a room in crisis. The nature and setting didn't seem to matter; it was always the same. One man pacing the carpet, another staring numbly out a window, and still another trying desperately to appear calm and in control, even when there was no control to be had. In this case, the room was the White Drawing Room at Number Ten. The man pacing the carpet was Simon Hewitt, the man staring out the window was Jeremy Fallon, and the man trying to appear calm was Prime Minister Jonathan Lancaster. He was seated on one of two opposing couches before the fireplace. On the low rectangular table before him was a mobile phone—the phone that had been left in Hyde Park the previous evening. Lancaster was glaring at it as though the device, and not Madeline Hart, were somehow the source of his predicament.

Rising, he approached Gabriel and Seymour with the care of a man crossing the deck of a sailboat in rough seas. The television cameras had not done Lancaster justice. He was taller than Gabriel had imagined and, despite the strain of the moment, better looking. "I'm Jonathan Lancaster," he said somewhat absurdly as his large hand closed around Gabriel's. "It's about time we met. I only wish the circumstances could be different."

"So do I, Prime Minister."

Gabriel had intended the remark to be empathetic, but it was clear from Lancaster's narrowed eyes that he regarded it as a condemnation of his conduct. He released Gabriel's hand quickly, then gestured toward the two other figures in the room. "I assume you know who these gentlemen are," he said after regaining his composure. "The one wearing a hole in my carpet is Simon, my press spokesman. And that one over there is Jeremy Fallon. Jeremy's my brain, if you believe what you read in the newspapers."

Simon Hewitt stopped pacing long enough to nod vaguely in Gabriel's direction. Jacketless, with his shirtsleeves rolled to the elbow and his necktie loosened, he looked like a reporter on deadline who hadn't two facts to rub together. Jeremy Fallon, still at his post in the window, remained tightly buttoned and knotted. It had been written of Fallon that he saw himself as a prime minister until the instant he looked into a mirror. With his receding chin, lank hair, and sallow skin, he was best suited to the netherworld of politics.

Which left only the mobile phone. Without a word, Gabriel lifted it from the coffee table and checked the dialing directory. It showed the device had received a single call—the call that had been placed while Gabriel and Keller were at the ferry terminal in Marseilles.

"Who spoke to him?"

"I did," answered Fallon.

"What was his voice like?"

"It wasn't real."

"Computer generated?"

Fallon nodded.

"What time is he supposed to call back?"

"Midnight."

Gabriel switched off the phone, removed the battery and SIM card, and placed both on the coffee table.

"What's supposed to happen at midnight?"

It was Lancaster who responded.

"He wants an answer, yes or no. Yes means I agree to pay ten million euros in cash in exchange for Madeline and a promise the video will never be made public. If I say no, Madeline will die and everything will come out. Obviously," he added, exhaling heavily, "I have no choice but to agree to their demands."

"That would be the biggest mistake of your life, Prime Minister."

"The second biggest."

Lancaster lowered his long body onto the couch and covered his famous face with his hand. Gabriel thought of the people he had seen on the streets of London that evening going about their business, unaware of the fact their prime minister was at that moment paralyzed by scandal.

"What choice do I have?" Lancaster asked after a moment.

"You can still go to the police."

"It's too late for that."

"Then you have to negotiate."

"He said he wouldn't. He said he'd kill her if I didn't agree to pay the ten million."

"They always say that. But trust me, Prime Minister—if you agree, he'll get angry."

"At me?"

"At himself. He'll think he blew it by asking for only ten million.

He'll come back to you for more money. And if you agree to pay *that* number, he'll come back for even more. He'll bleed you dry, million by million, until there's nothing left."

"So what are you suggesting?"

"We wait for the phone to ring. And when it does, we tell him we'll pay one million, take it or leave it. And then we hang up the phone and wait for him to call back."

"What if he doesn't call back? What if he kills her?"

"He won't."

"How can you be so certain?"

"Because he's invested too much time, effort, and money. To him, this is business, nothing more. You have to act the same way. You have to approach this like any other tough negotiation. There are no shortcuts. You have to wear him down. You have to be patient. It's the only way we're going to get her back."

A heavy silence fell over the room. Jeremy Fallon had moved from his post in the window and was contemplating a painting, a London cityscape by Turner, as if noticing it for the first time. Graham Seymour seemed to have developed a passionate interest in the carpet.

"I appreciate your advice," Lancaster said after a moment, "but we've—" He stopped himself, then, deliberately, said, "*I've* decided to give them whatever they want. It is because of my reckless behavior that Madeline has been kidnapped. And I am obligated to do whatever is necessary to bring her home safely. It is the honorable thing to do, for her sake, and for the sake of this office."

The line sounded as though Jeremy Fallon had written it—and if the smug expression on Fallon's unfortunate face were any indicator, he had.

"Honorable, perhaps," said Gabriel, "but unwise."

"I disagree," said Lancaster. "And so does Jeremy."

"With all due respect," Gabriel said, turning to Fallon, "when was the last time you successfully negotiated the release of a hostage?"

"I think you'll agree," Fallon responded, "this isn't an ordinary kidnapping case. The target of the extortionists is the prime minister of the United Kingdom. And under no circumstances can I allow him to be incapacitated by a long, drawn-out negotiation."

Fallon had made this speech quietly and with the supreme confidence of someone who was used to whispering instructions into the ear of one of the world's most powerful men. It was an image that had been captured many times by the British news media. And it was why the cartoonists routinely depicted Fallon as a puppeteer, with Jonathan Lancaster dancing at the end of his string.

"Where do you intend to get the money?" asked Gabriel.

"Friends of the prime minister have agreed to lend it to him until he's in a position to repay them."

"It must be nice to have friends like that." Gabriel rose. "It looks as though you have everything under control. All you need now is someone to deliver the money. But make sure you find someone good. Otherwise, you're going to be back in this room in a few days, waiting for the phone to ring."

"Do you have any candidates?" asked Lancaster.

"Just one," said Gabriel, "but I'm afraid he's unavailable."

"Why?"

"Because he has a plane to catch."

"When's the next flight to Ben Gurion?"

"Eight a.m."

"Then I suppose there's no harm in staying a little longer, is there?"

Gabriel hesitated. "No, Prime Minister. I suppose there isn't."

By then, it was a few minutes past ten. Gabriel had no desire to spend the next two hours trapped with a politician whose career was about to go supernova, so he saw himself downstairs to the kitchen to raid the prime ministerial fridge. The night chef, a plump woman of fifty with the face of a cherub, made a plate of sandwiches and a pot of tea, then studied Gabriel attentively as he ate, as though she feared he were malnourished. She knew better than to ask about the nature of his visit. Few people came to Number Ten late at night dressed in clothing from a discount department store in Marseilles.

At eleven o'clock Graham Seymour came downstairs looking gray and very tired. He declined the chef's offer of food and then proceeded to devour the remnants of Gabriel's egg-and-dill sandwich. Afterward, they went outside to walk in the walled garden. It was silent except for the occasional crackle of a police radio and the wet rush of traffic along Horse Guards Road. Seymour extracted a packet of cigarettes from the pocket of his overcoat and lit one moodily.

"I never knew," said Gabriel.

"Helen made me quit years ago. I tried to get her to stop cooking, but she refused."

"She sounds like a good negotiator. Maybe we should let her deal with Paul."

"He wouldn't stand a chance." Seymour blew smoke at the starless sky and watched it drift beyond the walls. "It's possible you're wrong, you know. It's possible everything will go smoothly and Madeline will be home by tomorrow night."

"It's also possible that Britain will one day regain control of the American colonies," said Gabriel. "Possible, but unlikely."

"Ten million euros is a lot of money."

"Paying the money is the easy part," said Gabriel. "But getting the hostage back alive is another thing entirely. The person who delivers the money has to be an experienced professional. And he has to be prepared to walk away from the deal if he thinks the kidnappers are trying to deceive him." Gabriel paused, then added, "It's not a job for the faint of heart."

"Is there any chance you would consider doing it?"

"Under these circumstances," said Gabriel, "none whatsoever."

"I had to ask."

"Who put you up to it?"

"Who do you think?"

"Lancaster?"

"Actually, it was Jeremy Fallon. You made quite an impression on him."

"Not enough of an impression to make him listen to me."

"He's desperate."

"Which is exactly why he shouldn't go anywhere near that phone."

Seymour dropped his cigarette onto the wet grass and smothered it with his shoe, then led Gabriel back inside, to the White Drawing Room. Nothing had changed. One man pacing the carpet, another staring numbly out a window, and still another trying desperately to appear calm and in control, even when there was no control to be had. The phone was still lying in pieces on the coffee table. Gabriel inserted the battery and the SIM card and switched on the power. Then he sat on the couch opposite Jonathan Lancaster and waited for it to ring.

The call came through at midnight precisely. Fallon had set the volume to train whistle level and switched on the vibrate function, so the phone shimmied across the surface of the coffee table, as if moving to a private little earthquake. He reached for it at once, but Gabriel stayed his hand and held it for ten agonizing seconds before finally releasing it. Fallon seized and raised it swiftly to his ear. Then, with his eyes fixed on Lancaster, he said, "I agree to your terms." Gabriel admired Fallon's choice of words. The call had surely been recorded by GCHQ, Britain's eavesdropping service, and it would remain stored in its databases until the end of time.

For the next forty-five seconds, Fallon did not speak. Instead, with his gaze still fixed on Lancaster, he drew a fountain pen from his suit coat pocket and scribbled a few illegible lines on a notepad. Gabriel could hear the sound of the voice machine, thin, lifeless, and stressing all the wrong words, bleeding from the earpiece. "No," said Fallon finally, adopting the same laborious delivery, "that won't be necessary." Then, in response to another question, he said, "Yes, of course. You have our word." After that, there was another silence during which his eyes moved from Lancaster, to Gabriel, and then back to Lancaster. "That might not be possible," he said carefully. "I'll have to ask."

And then the line went dead. Fallon switched off the phone.

"Well?" asked Lancaster.

"He wants us to put the money into two rolling black suitcases. No tracking devices, no dye packs, no police. He'll call again tomorrow at noon to tell us what to do next."

"You didn't ask for proof of life," said Gabriel.

"He didn't give me a chance."

"Were there any additional demands?"

"Just one," said Fallon. "He wants you to deliver the money. No Gabriel, no girl."

22

LONDON

I T WAS A FEW MINUTES after one in the morning by the time Gabriel finally departed Downing Street. Graham Seymour offered to drive him, but he wanted to walk; it had been many months since he had been in London, and he thought the damp night air would do him good. He slipped out the back security gate along Horse Guards Road and headed westward through the empty parks to Knightsbridge. Then he made his way along Brompton Road to South Kensington. The street number of his destination was tucked away in the drawers of his prodigious memory: 59 Victoria Road, the last known British address of an SAS deserter and professional assassin named Christopher Keller.

It was a stout little house, with a wrought-iron gate and a fine flight of steps rising to a white front door. Flowers bloomed in the tiny forecourt, and in the window of the drawing room a single light burned. The curtain was parted a few inches; through the gap

Gabriel could see a man, Dr. Robert Keller, sitting upright in a wing chair—reading or sleeping, it was impossible to know. He was a bit younger than Shamron but, even so, not a man with long to live. For twenty-five years he had suffered under the belief that his son was dead, a pain that Gabriel knew only too well. It was a cruel thing that Keller had done to his parents, but it was not Gabriel's place to make it right. And so he stood alone in the empty street, hoping the old man could somehow feel his presence. And in his thoughts he told him that his son was a flawed man who had done evil things for money, but that he was also decent and honorable and brave and still very much alive.

After a moment the light was extinguished and Keller's father disappeared from view. Gabriel turned and made his way to Kensington Road. As he was nearing Queen's Gate, a motorcycle swept past him on the right. He had seen the bike a few minutes earlier as he was crossing Sloane Street, and a few minutes before that as he was leaving Downing Street. He had assumed then that the figure riding it was an MI5 watcher. But now, as he scrutinized the supple line of the back and the generous curve of the hips, he no longer believed that to be the case.

He continued eastward along the edge of Hyde Park, watching the taillight of the bike grow smaller, confident he would see it again soon. He did not have to wait long—two minutes, perhaps less. That was when he glimpsed it speeding directly toward him. This time, instead of passing him by, it swung a U-turn around a traffic pylon and stopped. Gabriel eased his leg over the seat and clasped his arms around the narrow waist. As the bike shot forward, he inhaled the familiar scent of vanilla and softly stroked the underside of a warm, rounded breast. He closed his eyes, at peace for the first time in seven days.

The flat was located in an ugly postwar building on Bayswater Road. It had been an Office safe flat once, but inside King Saul Boulevard— and MI5, too, for that matter—it was now known as Gabriel Allon's London pied-à-terre. Entering, he hung the key on the little hook just inside the kitchen door and opened the refrigerator. Inside was a carton of fresh milk, along with a crate of eggs, a lump of Parmesan cheese, mushrooms, herbs, and a bottle of Gabriel's favorite pinot grigio.

"The cupboard was bare when I arrived," said Chiara, "so I picked up a few things from that market around the corner. I was hoping we might have dinner together."

"When did you get in?"

"About an hour after you."

"How did you manage that?"

"I was in the neighborhood."

Gabriel looked at her seriously. "What neighborhood?"

"France," she answered without hesitation. "A farmhouse not far from Cherbourg, to be precise. Four bedrooms, an eat-in kitchen, lovely views of the Channel."

"You got yourself assigned to the reception team?"

"It wasn't like that."

"How was it exactly?"

"Ari did it for me."

"Whose idea was it?"

"His."

"Oh, really?"

"He thought I was perfect for the job, and I couldn't argue with him. After all, it's not as if I don't have some idea of what it's like to be kidnapped and held for ransom."

"Which is exactly why I wouldn't have let you anywhere near her."

"It was a long time ago, darling."

"Not that long."

"It seems like another lifetime. In fact, sometimes it seems like it never happened at all."

She closed the refrigerator door and kissed Gabriel softly. Her leather jacket still held the cold of the night ride across London, but her lips were warm.

"We waited all day for you to arrive," she said, kissing him again. "The operations desk finally sent us a message saying you'd boarded a British Airways flight from Marseilles to London."

"That's funny, but I don't remember mentioning my travel plans to the Operations Desk."

"They watch your credit cards, darling—you know that. They had a team from London Station waiting at Heathrow. They saw you leave with Nigel Whitcombe. And then they saw you entering Downing Street through the back door."

"I was slightly disappointed we didn't go through the front, but under the circumstances it was probably for the best."

"What happened in France?"

"Things didn't go according to plan."

"So what now?"

"Britain's prime minister is about to make someone a very rich man."

"How rich?"

"Ten million euros rich."

"So crime pays after all."

"It usually does. That's why there are so many criminals."

Chiara withdrew from Gabriel and removed her coat. She was

wearing a tight black sweater with a roll neck. She had arranged her hair to fit inside the helmet. Now, with her eyes fixed warily on Gabriel, she removed several clasps and pins, and it fell about her square shoulders in an auburn-and-chestnut cloud.

"So that's it?" she asked. "We can go home now?"

"Not exactly."

"What does that mean?"

"It means someone has to deliver the ransom money." He paused, then added, "And then someone has to bring her out."

Chiara narrowed her eyes. They seemed to have darkened in color, never a good sign.

"I'm sure the prime minister can find someone other than you," she said.

"I'm sure he can, too," said Gabriel, "but I'm afraid he doesn't have much of a choice in the matter."

"Why is that?"

"Because the kidnappers made one final demand tonight."

"You?"

Gabriel nodded. "No Gabriel, no girl."

Despite the lateness of the hour, Chiara wanted to cook. Gabriel sat at the tiny kitchen table, a glass of wine at his elbow, and recounted the journey he had taken after leaving her in Jerusalem. In any other marriage, the wife surely would have responded with incredulity and astonishment to such a story, but Chiara seemed preoccupied by the preparation of her vegetables and herbs. Only once did she look up from her work—when Gabriel told her about the empty holding cell in the house in the Lubéron, and the woman who had died in his arms. When he finished, she filled the center of her palm with salt, discarded a small portion into the sink, and poured the rest into a pot of boiling water.

"And after all that," she said, "you decided to take a midnight stroll to South Kensington."

"I considered doing a very foolish thing."

"More foolish than agreeing to deliver ten million euros in ransom to the kidnappers of the British prime minister's mistress?"

Gabriel said nothing.

"Who lives at Fifty-Nine Victoria Road?"

"Dr. and Mrs. Robert Keller."

Chiara was about to ask Gabriel why he had gone to see them, but then she understood.

"What on earth would you have told them?"

"That's the problem, isn't it?"

Chiara placed several mushrooms in the center of the cutting board and began slicing them precisely. "It's probably better they think he's dead," she said reflectively.

"And if it was your son? Wouldn't you want to know the truth?"

"If you're asking whether I would want to know that my son killed people for a living, the answer is no."

A silence fell between them.

"I'm sorry," Chiara said after a moment. "I didn't mean that to sound the way it did."

"I know."

Chiara placed the mushrooms in a sauté pan and seasoned them with salt and pepper. "Did she ever know?"

"My mother?"

Chiara nodded.

"No," said Gabriel. "She never knew."

"But she must have suspected something," Chiara said. "You were gone for three years."

"She knew I was involved in secret work and that it had something to do with Munich. But I never told her that I was the one who did the actual killing."

"She must have been curious."

"She wasn't."

"Why not?"

"Munich was a trauma for the entire country," Gabriel responded, "but it was especially hard on people like my mother—German Jews who had survived the camps. She could barely look at the newspapers or watch the funerals on television. She locked herself in her studio and painted."

"And when you came home after Wrath of God?"

"She could see the death in my eyes." He paused, then added, "She knew what it looked like."

"But you never talked about it?"

"Never," said Gabriel, shaking his head slowly. "She never told me what happened to her during the Holocaust, and I never told her what I had done while I was in Europe for three years."

"Do you think she would have approved?"

"It didn't matter to me what she thought."

"Of course it did, Gabriel. You're really not as fatalistic as all that. If you were, you wouldn't have gone to Keller's old house in the middle of the night to stare at his father through the window."

Gabriel said nothing. Chiara placed a bundle of fettuccine in the boiling water and stirred it once with a wooden spoon.

"What's he like?" she asked.

"Keller?"

She nodded.

"Extremely capable, utterly ruthless, and without a shred of conscience."

"He sounds like the perfect person to deliver ten million euros in ransom money to the kidnappers of Madeline Hart."

"Her Majesty's government is under the impression he's dead. Besides," Gabriel added, "the kidnappers specifically asked for me to deliver the money."

"Which is precisely the reason you have no business doing it."

Gabriel made no reply.

"How did they even know you were involved?"

"They must have spotted me in Marseilles or Aix."

"So why would they want a professional like you to deliver the money? Why not a flunky from Downing Street who they can manipulate?"

"I suppose they're entertaining thoughts of killing me. But that's going to be rather hard to do."

"Why?"

"Because I'll be in possession of ten million euros that they want very badly, which means *we* call the shots."

"We?"

"You don't think I'm going to do this alone, do you? I'm going to have someone watching my back."

"Who?"

"Someone extremely capable, utterly ruthless, and without a shred of conscience."

"I thought he was back in Corsica."

"He is," said Gabriel. "But he's about to get a wake-up call."

"What about me?"

"Go back to the house in Cherbourg. I'll bring Madeline there after paying the ransom. When she's ready to be moved, we'll bring her back to Britain. And then we'll go home."

Chiara was silent for a moment. "You make it sound so simple," she said at last.

"If they play by my rules, it will be."

Chiara placed a bowl of steaming fettuccine and mushrooms in the center of the table and sat down opposite Gabriel.

"No more questions?" he asked.

"Just one," she said. "What did the old woman in Corsica see when you dropped the oil into the water?"

By the time they finished the dishes, it was nearly four in the morning, which meant it was nearly five on Corsica. Even so, Keller sounded awake and alert when he took Gabriel's call. Using carefully coded language, Gabriel explained what had transpired at Downing Street and what was to happen later that day.

"Can you make the first flight to Orly?" he asked.

"No problem."

"Pick up a car at the airport and get up to the coast. I'll call you when I know something."

"No problem."

After severing the connection, Gabriel stretched out on the bed next to Chiara and tried to sleep, but it was no use. Each time he closed his eyes, he saw the face of the woman who had died in his arms in the Lubéron, in the valley with three villas. So he lay very still, listening to the sound of Chiara's breathing and the hiss of the traffic on Bayswater Road, as the gray light of a London dawn crept slowly into the room.

He woke Chiara with fresh coffee at nine o'clock and showered. When he emerged from the bathroom, Jonathan Lancaster was on the television discussing his costly new initiative to repair Britain's troubled families. Gabriel couldn't help but marvel at the prime minister's performance. His career was at that moment hanging by a gossamer thread, and yet he looked as commanding and unflappable as ever. Indeed, by the end of his remarks, even Gabriel was convinced that spending a few million more pounds in taxpayer money would solve the problems facing Britain's permanent underclass.

The next story had something to do with a Russian energy firm securing rights to drill for oil in the British territorial waters of the North Sea. Gabriel switched off the television, dressed, and extracted a 9mm Beretta pistol from the safe concealed beneath the floor of the closet. Then, after kissing Chiara one final time, he headed downstairs to the street. Waiting curbside behind the wheel of his Vauxhall Astra was Nigel Whitcombe. He made the drive to Number Ten in record time and deposited Gabriel at the back entrance along Horse Guards Road.

"Let's hope this one doesn't end like the last one," he said with false cheerfulness.

"Let's," agreed Gabriel, and he headed inside.

23

10 DOWNING STREET

JEREMY FALLON WAS WAITING IN the rear foyer of Number Ten. He offered Gabriel a warm, damp hand and then wordlessly led him to the White Drawing Room. This time, it was empty. Gabriel sat down without waiting for an invitation, but Fallon remained standing. He reached into his pocket and removed the keys to a rental car.

"It's a Passat saloon, as you requested. If you could return it in one piece, I would be eternally grateful. I'm not as well-to-do as the prime minister."

Fallon smiled weakly at his own joke. It was obvious why he didn't smile more often; he had teeth like a barracuda. He handed Gabriel the keys, along with a parking stub.

"It's in the car park at Victoria Station. The entrance is—"

"On Eccleston Street."

"Sorry," Fallon said sincerely. "Sometimes I forget who I'm dealing with."

"I don't," said Gabriel.

Fallon was silent.

"What color is the car?"

"Island Gray."

"What the hell is Island Gray?"

"The island mustn't be very nice, because the car is quite dark."

"And the money?"

"It's in the boot, two suitcases, just as they requested."

"How long has it been there?"

"Since early this morning. I dropped it off myself."

"Let's hope it's still there."

"The money or the car?"

"Both."

"Was that supposed to be a joke?"

"No," said Gabriel.

Frowning, Fallon sat down opposite Gabriel and contemplated his nails. There was little left of them.

"I owe you an apology for my behavior last night," he said after a moment. "I was only acting in what I believed to be the best interests of my prime minister."

"So was I," replied Gabriel.

Fallon seemed taken aback. Like most powerful men, he was no longer used to being spoken to honestly.

"Graham Seymour warned me that you could be blunt at times."

"Only when lives are at stake," Gabriel responded. "And the moment I climb behind the wheel of that car, my life will be in danger. Which means, as of this moment, I make all the decisions."

"I don't need to remind you that this affair has to be concluded as discreetly as possible."

"No, you don't. Because if it isn't, the prime minister isn't the only one who'll pay the price."

Fallon made no response other than to glance at his wristwatch. It was 11:40, twenty minutes before the phone was supposed to ring. He rose to his feet with the air of a man who had not slept well in many days.

"The prime minister is in the Cabinet Room, meeting with the foreign secretary. I'm supposed to join them for a few minutes. Then I'll bring him here for the call."

"What's the topic of the meeting?"

"British policy regarding the Israeli-Palestinian conflict."

"Don't forget who's delivering the money."

Fallon gave another dreadful smile and headed wearily toward the door.

"Did you know?" asked Gabriel.

Fallon turned slowly. "Know what?"

"That Lancaster and Madeline were having an affair."

Fallon hesitated before answering. "No," he said at last, "I didn't know. In fact, I never would have dreamed that he would do something to jeopardize all we'd worked for. And the irony of it all," he added, "is that I was the idiot who introduced them."

"Why did you?"

"Because Madeline was an integral part of our political operation. And because she was an extremely bright, capable woman whose future was limitless."

Gabriel was struck by Fallon's use of the past tense when talking about his missing colleague. Fallon noticed it, too.

"I didn't mean that the way it sounded," he said.

"What *did* you mean?"

"I'm not sure," he responded. They were three words he didn't often utter. "It's just that she isn't likely to be the same person after something like this, is she?"

"Humans are more resilient than you realize, especially women. With the right kind of help, she'll eventually be able to resume her normal life. But you are right about one thing," Gabriel added. "She'll never be the same person again."

Fallon reached for the door. "Is there anything else you need?" he asked over his shoulder.

"A few hours' sleep would be nice."

"How do you take it?"

"Milk, no sugar."

Fallon went out and closed the door softly behind him. Gabriel rose, walked over to the Turner cityscape, and stood before it with one hand resting on his chin and his head tilted slightly to one side. It was 11:43, seventeen minutes until the phone was supposed to ring.

Fallon returned just before noon, accompanied by Jonathan Lancaster. The change in the prime minister's appearance was remarkable. Gone was the Lancaster whom Gabriel had seen on television earlier that morning, the confident politician promising to repair the fabric of British society. In his place was a man whose life and career were in imminent danger of unraveling in the most spectacular political scandal in British history. It was obvious Lancaster could not endure much more before unraveling himself.

"Are you sure you want to be here for this?" Gabriel asked, shaking the prime minister's hand.

"Why wouldn't I?"

"Because you might not like everything you hear."

Lancaster sat down, making it clear he had no intention of going anywhere. Fallon withdrew the mobile phone from his coat pocket and placed it on the coffee table. Gabriel quickly removed the battery, exposing the serial number on the inside of the device, and used his personal BlackBerry to snap a photo of it.

"What are you doing?" asked Lancaster.

"In all likelihood, the kidnappers will tell me to leave this one in a place where it will never be found."

"So why are you photographing it?"

"Insurance," said Gabriel.

He slipped his BlackBerry back into his coat pocket and switched on the kidnappers' device. It was 11:57. There was nothing more to do now but wait. Gabriel excelled at waiting; by his own calculation, he had spent more than half of his life doing it. Waiting for a train or a plane. Waiting for a source. Waiting for the sun to rise after a night of killing. Waiting for the doctors to say whether his wife would live or die. He had hoped his placid demeanor would calm Lancaster, but it seemed to have the opposite effect. The prime minister was staring unblinking at the display screen of the phone. By 12:03 it had yet to ring.

"What the hell is going on?" he asked finally in frustration.

"They're trying to make you nervous."

"They're doing a damn good job of it."

"That's why I'm going to do the talking."

Another minute passed with no contact. Then, at 12:05, the phone rang and began dancing its way across the tabletop. Gabriel picked it up and looked at the caller ID while the phone vibrated in his grasp. As he had expected, they were using a different phone. He lifted the cover and very calmly asked, "How can I help you?"

There was a pause, during which Gabriel could hear the clatter of a computer keyboard. Then came the robotic voice.

"Who is this?" it asked.

"You know who this is," replied Gabriel. "Let's get going. My girl has been waiting a long time for this day. I want to get this over and done with as quickly as possible."

There was another pause, more typing. Then the voice asked, "Do you have the money?"

"I'm looking at it now," Gabriel responded. "Ten million euros, unmarked, nonsequential, no beacons, no dye packs, everything you asked for. I hope you have a nice dirty bank at your disposal because you're going to need it."

He cast a quick glance at Lancaster, who seemed to be chewing at something on the inside of his cheek. Fallon looked as though he had gone into respiratory arrest.

"Are you ready for the instructions?" the voice asked after another burst of typing.

"I've been ready for several minutes," answered Gabriel.

"Do you have something to write with?"

"Just go ahead," said Gabriel impatiently.

"Are you in London?"

"Yes."

"Do you have a car?"

"Yes, of course."

"Take the four-forty ferry from Dover to Calais. Forty minutes after departure, drop this phone into the Channel. When you get to Calais, go to the park on the rue Richelieu. Do you know it?"

"Yes, I know it."

"There's a rubbish bin on the northeast corner. The new phone will be taped to the bottom. After you get it, go back to your car. We'll call you and tell you where to go next."

"Anything else?"

"Come alone, no backup, no police. And don't miss the four-forty ferry. If you do, the girl dies."

"Are you finished?"

There was silence at the other end, no voice, no typing.

"I'll take that as a yes," said Gabriel. "Now listen carefully because I'm only going to say this once. This is your big day. You've worked very hard, and the end is almost in sight. But don't spoil it by doing something stupid. I'm only interested in bringing the girl home safely. This is business, nothing more. Let's do this like gentlemen."

"No police," said the voice after a few seconds' delay.

"No police," repeated Gabriel. "But let me say one more thing. If you try to harm either Madeline or me, my service is going to find out who you really are. And then they're going to hunt you down and kill you. Are we clear?"

This time there was no response.

"And one other thing," said Gabriel. "Don't ever keep me waiting five minutes for a call again. If you do, the deal's off."

With that, he severed the connection and looked at Jonathan Lancaster.

"I think that went well. Don't you, Prime Minister?"

It is rare to see a man stepping from the front door of 10 Downing Street dressed in blue jeans and a black leather jacket, but that is precisely what occurred at 12:17 p.m., on a rain-swept afternoon in early October. It was five weeks to the day after Madeline Hart's disappearance on the island of Corsica, eight days after her photograph and video were left at the home of press aide Simon Hewitt, and twelve hours after the prime minister of the United Kingdom of Great Britain and Northern Ireland agreed to pay ten million euros in ransom to secure her safe return. The policeman standing watch in the entrance hall knew none of this, of course. Nor did he realize that the unusually dressed man was the Israeli spy and assassin Gabriel Allon, or that beneath Gabriel's black leather jacket was a Beretta semiautomatic, fully loaded. As a result, he bade him a pleasant day and then watched as Gabriel made his way along Downing Street to the Whitehall security gate. As he passed through it, a camera snapped his photograph. It was 12:19.

Jeremy Fallon had left the Passat in the uncovered portion of the Victoria Station car park. Gabriel approached it the way he always approached cars that were not his own, slowly and with a feeling of dread. He circled it once, as if inspecting the paint for scratches, and then intentionally dropped the keys to the redbrick paving stones. Crouching, he quickly scanned the undercarriage. Seeing nothing out of the ordinary, he stood upright again and pressed the trunk release. The hatch rose slowly, revealing two nylon suitcases of discount manufacture. He tugged at the zipper of one, peered inside, and saw row upon row of tightly packed hundred-euro notes.

By London standards, the traffic at that hour was only mildly catastrophic. Gabriel crossed the Chelsea Bridge at one o'clock, and by half past he had put London's southern suburbs behind him and was speeding along the M25 motorway. At 2:00 p.m. he switched on Radio Four to listen to a news update. Little had changed since the morning; Jonathan Lancaster was still talking about curing the ills of Britain's poor, and a Russian oil company was still planning to drill for oil in the North Sea. There was no mention of Madeline Hart, or of a man in blue jeans and a leather jacket who was about to pay ten million euros to her kidnappers. The man listened to the latest weather bulletin and learned that conditions were expected to deteriorate rapidly throughout the afternoon, with heavy rain and dangerous winds along the Channel coast. Then he switched off the radio and absently fingered the Corsican talisman around his neck. When she is dead, he heard the old woman say. Then you will know the truth.

24

DOVER, ENGLAND

B
Y THE TIME GABRIEL TURNED onto the M20, the skies
were pouring with rain. He raced past Maidstone, Lenham
Heath, and Ashford, arriving in the port of Folkestone at
half past three. There he turned onto the A20 and continued east,
across a seemingly endless plain of the greenest grass he had ever
seen. Finally, he breasted a low hill, and the sea appeared, dark and
whitecapped. It promised to be an unpleasant crossing.

As the road descended into the Dover seafront, Gabriel glimpsed
a portion of the cliffs for the first time, chalky white against a background of gunmetal-gray cloud. The way to the ferry terminal was
clearly marked. Gabriel entered the ticket office and confirmed his
booking, all the while keeping his eyes fixed on the Passat. Then,
ticket in hand, he climbed behind the wheel again and joined the line
of cars waiting in the departure queue. *And don't miss the four-forty
ferry. If you do, the girl dies* . . . There was only one reason to make

such a demand, thought Gabriel. The kidnappers were now watching him.

It was against regulations for passengers to remain inside their cars during the crossing. Gabriel briefly considered bringing the suitcases with him but decided the act of lugging them up and down the passageways would leave him too vulnerable. So he locked the car tightly, checking the trunk and each of the four doors twice to make sure they were secure, and headed to the passenger lounge. As the ferry eased from the terminal, he went to the snack bar and ordered tea and a scone. Outside the skies gradually darkened, and by 5:15 the sea was no longer visible. Gabriel remained in his seat for another five minutes. Then he rose and made his way to an isolated corner of the windblown observation deck. None of the other passengers followed him. Therefore no one saw him drop a mobile phone over the railing.

Gabriel neither saw nor heard the device strike the surface of the sea. He stood at the rail for two more minutes before returning to his seat in the lounge. And there he remained, committing to memory each of the faces around him, until an announcement came over the public address system, first in English, then in French, alerting passengers it was time to return to their cars. Gabriel made certain he was the first to arrive on the vehicle deck. Opening the trunk of the Passat, he saw that the two suitcases were still in place and that both were still filled with money. Then he climbed behind the wheel and watched the other passengers filing toward their cars. In the next row a woman was unlocking the door of a small Peugeot. She had short blond hair, almost like a boy's, and a heart-shaped face. But Gabriel noticed something else. She was the only passenger on the ferry wearing gloves.

He stared straight ahead, both hands on the wheel.

She was the one. He was certain of it.

Calais was an ugly seaside town, part English, part German, scarcely French at all. The rue Richelieu was about a half mile from the ferry terminal in the *quartier* known as Calais-Nord, an octagonal artificial island ringed by canals and harbors. Gabriel parked outside a terrace of stucco houses and headed toward the park, watched by a trio of Afghan men in heavy coats and traditional *pakul* hats. The men were probably economic migrants waiting for a chance to hitch an illegal ride across the Channel to Britain. There had once been a large encampment in the sand dunes along the beach where, on a clear day, they could see the White Cliffs of Dover sparkling on the other side of the Channel. The good citizens of Calais, a stronghold of the Socialist Party, had referred to the camp as "the jungle" and had applauded the French police when they finally shut it down.

The trash receptacle stood to the right side of a footpath leading into the park. It was four feet in height and forest green in color. Next to it was a sign asking visitors not to harm the park's grass and flowers. It said nothing about searching for a hidden mobile phone beneath the rubbish bin, which is what Gabriel did after discarding his ferry ticket. He found it instantly; it was secured to the underside of the bin by packing tape. He tore it away and slipped it into his coat pocket before standing upright and heading back to the Passat. The phone was ringing as he started the engine. "Very good," said the computer-generated voice. "Now listen carefully."

It told him to go directly to the Hotel de la Mer, in the town of Grand-Fort-Philippe. A reservation had been made there under the name Annette Ricard. Gabriel was to check into the room using his own

credit card and explain that a Mademoiselle Ricard would be joining him later that evening. Gabriel had never heard of the hotel, or
even of the town where it was located. He found it using the Internet
browser on his personal mobile phone. Grand-Fort-Philippe was just
west of Dunkirk, scene of one of the greatest military humiliations in
British history. In the spring of 1940, more than three hundred thousand members of the British Expeditionary Force were evacuated
from Dunkirk's beaches as France was falling to Nazi Germany. In
their haste to leave, the British forces had no choice but to abandon
enough materiel to equip some ten divisions. It was possible the kidnappers hadn't realized any of this when they had chosen the hotel,
but Gabriel doubted it.

The Hotel de la Mer was not actually by the sea. Compact, tidy,
and covered with a fresh coat of white paint, it overlooked the tidal
river that split the town in two. Gabriel intentionally drove past the
entrance three times before finally easing into an angled parking
space along the quay. No one from the hotel came to help him; it was
not that kind of place. He waited for a lone car to pass before switching off the engine. Then, after burying the key deep in the front
pocket of his jeans, he climbed quickly out. The two suitcases were
surprisingly heavy. Indeed, had he not known the contents, he would
have assumed that Jeremy Fallon had filled them with lead weights.
Gulls circled slowly overhead, as if hoping he might collapse beneath
the weight of his burden.

The hotel had no proper lobby, only a cramped vestibule where a
bald, thin clerk sat somnambulantly behind a desk. Despite the fact
there were only eight rooms, it took a moment for him to locate the
reservation. Gabriel paid in cash, violating one of the kidnappers'
demands, and left a generous deposit for incidentals.

"Is there a second key for the room?" he asked.

"Of course."

"May I have it, please?"

"But what about Mademoiselle Ricard?"

"I'll let her in."

The clerk frowned disapprovingly as he slid the extra key across the desktop.

"There are no others?" asked Gabriel. "Just this one?"

"The maid has a master key, of course. And so do I."

"And you're sure there's no one in the room?" he asked.

"Positive," said the clerk. "I just finished preparing it myself."

For this thoughtful gesture, Gabriel placed a ten-euro note upon the desk. It was seized by a grimy hand and disappeared into the pocket of an ill-fitting blazer.

"Do you require assistance with your luggage?" he asked, as though assisting Gabriel was the last thing on his mind that evening.

"No, thank you," said Gabriel cheerfully. "I think I can manage."

He wheeled the suitcases across the linoleum floor, then did his best to make them appear weightless as he lifted them off the ground by their grips and started up the narrow staircase. His room was on the third floor, at the end of a dimly lit hall. Gabriel inserted the key into the lock with the care of a doctor wielding a medical probe. Entering, he found the room empty and a single light burning weakly on the bedside table. He rolled the bags just across the threshold. Then, after closing the door and drawing his Beretta, he quickly searched the closet and the bathroom. Finally, certain he was alone, he chained the door, barricaded it with every piece of furniture in the room, and wedged the two suitcases beneath the bed. As he stood upright again, the phone he had collected in Calais rang for the second time. "Very good," said the same computer-generated voice. "Now listen carefully."

This time, Gabriel issued several demands of his own. She had to come alone, with no backup, and no weapon. Gabriel reserved the right to search her—thoroughly and intrusively, he added, just so there were no misunderstandings. After that, she could take all the time she needed to verify that the notes were genuine and, when tallied, amounted to a sum of ten million euros. She could count the money, smell it, taste it, or make love to it—Gabriel didn't care, so long as she made no attempt to steal it. If she did that, said Gabriel, she would get hurt, badly, and the deal would be off. "And don't make any stupid threats about killing Madeline," he said. "Threats insult my intelligence."

"One hour," responded the voice, and the connection went dead.

Gabriel removed a straight-backed chair from his barricade and placed it in the room's arrow-slit of a window. And there he sat for the next sixty-seven minutes watching the street below. Forty minutes into his vigil, a man hurried past the hotel beneath an umbrella, pausing only long enough to pull at the latch of the Passat's front passenger-side door. After that, there were no more cars or pedestrians, only the gulls circling overhead, and a gang of street cats that feasted on the rubbish from the seafood restaurant next door. The waiting, he thought. Always the waiting.

When sixty minutes elapsed with no sign of her, Gabriel felt a stab of panic—a panic that worsened with each passing minute. Then, finally, a BMW wagon nosed into the empty space next to his. The door opened and a stylish boot emerged, followed in short order by a long, blue-jeaned leg. The leg belonged to a woman with coal-black hair that fell about her shoulders and shielded her face from Gabriel's view. He watched as she came across the street through the rain, watched the rhythm of her stride, the bend of her knees. It was a curious thing, the gait; it was like a fingerprint or a retina scan. A face could be easily changed, but even professional intelligence officers struggled to change the way they walked. Gabriel realized he had seen the walk before. She was the woman from the ferry.

He was certain of it.

25

GRAND-FORT-PHILIPPE, FRANCE

IT TOOK HER LESS THAN a minute to make her way from the street to the third floor of the hotel. Gabriel used the interval to remove the barricade of furniture from the entrance hall. Then he placed his ear against the door and listened to the tack-hammer clatter of her heels along the uncarpeted hall. It was a good door, solid and thick, enough to slow a bullet but not to stop one. The woman knocked lightly upon it, as though she suspected children were sleeping within.

"Are you alone?" asked Gabriel in French.

"Yes," she replied.

"Do you have a gun?"

"No."

"Do you know what will happen if I find a gun on you?"

"The deal is off."

Gabriel opened the door a few inches with the chain still in place. "Put your hand through," he said.

The woman hesitated for a moment and then obeyed. Her hand was long and pale. She wore a single ring, a band of woven silver, and there was a small tattoo of the sun on the webbing between her thumb and forefinger. Gabriel seized hold of the wrist and twisted it painfully. On the underside were the long-healed scars of a youthful suicide attempt.

"If you ever want to use this hand again," he said, "you'll do exactly as I tell you. Do you understand?"

"Yes," gasped the woman.

"Drop your handbag to the floor and push it to me with your foot."

Again, the woman obeyed. With his left hand still wrapped around her wrist, Gabriel reached down and emptied the contents of the handbag onto the floor. It was the usual detritus one would expect to find in the purse of a French female, with two notable exceptions: a jeweler's loupe and a handheld infrared lamp. Gabriel removed the chain from the door and, twisting the wrist to the point of breaking, drew the woman inside. With his foot, he closed the door. Then he pushed her face-first against the wall and, as promised, searched her thoroughly, confident in the belief he was going where many men had gone before.

"Are you enjoying yourself?" she asked.

"Yes," Gabriel said dully. "In fact, I haven't had this much fun since the last time I had a bullet removed."

"I hope it hurt."

He removed the dark wig and ran his hand through the woman's boyishly short blond hair.

"Finished?" she asked.

"Turn around."

She did, facing him for the first time. She was tall and thin, with the long limbs and small breasts of a Degas dancer. Her heart-shaped face was impish and innocent, and on her lips was the faintest trace of an ironic smile. The Office loved faces like hers. Gabriel wondered how many fortunes had been lost to it.

"How are we going to do this?" she asked.

"The usual way," answered Gabriel. "You're going to examine the money, and I'm going to hold a gun to your head. And if you do anything to make me nervous, I'm going to blow your brains out."

"Are you always this charming?"

"Only with girls I really like."

"Where's the money?"

"Under the bed."

"Are you going to get it for me?"

"Not a chance."

The woman exhaled heavily, knelt at the foot of the bed, and heaved the first bag into view. Opening it, she counted the number of stacks in each direction, first vertically, then horizontally. Then she pulled a stack from the center, like a climatologist drilling an ice core, and counted those, too.

"Finished?" asked Gabriel, mocking her.

"We're just getting started."

She selected six bundles of notes from six different parts of the bag at six different depths and counted the notes, setting one note aside from each bundle. She counted quickly, like someone who had worked in a bank or a casino. Or perhaps, thought Gabriel, she simply spent a lot of time counting stolen money.

"I need my things," she said.

"You don't really think I'm going to turn my back on you?"

She left the six hundred-euro notes on the bed and went to the entrance hall to collect her loupe and infrared lamp. Returning, she sat on the edge of the bed and used the loupe to examine each bill carefully, looking for any clue that it might be counterfeit—a poorly printed image, a missing number or character, a hologram or watermark that didn't look genuine. The examination of each bill took more than a minute. When she was finally finished, she set down the loupe and picked up the infrared lamp.

"I need to turn off the room lights."

"Turn that on first," said Gabriel, nodding toward the infrared lamp.

She did. Gabriel walked around the room switching off the lights until only the purplish glow of the infrared remained. She used it to examine each of the six bills. The security strips glowed lime green, proving the bills were genuine.

"Very good," she said.

"I can't tell you how happy I am you're pleased." Gabriel switched on the room lights. "Now I have a demand," he said. "Tell Paul to call me within the hour, or the deal's off."

"He's not going to like it."

"Tell him about the money," said Gabriel. "He'll get over it."

The woman returned the wig to her head, collected her things, and departed without another word. Gabriel watched her drive away from his outpost in the window. Then he remained there, staring into the wet street, and waited for the phone to ring. The call came through at 9:15 p.m., one hour to the minute. After enduring a computer-generated tirade, Gabriel calmly issued his demand. There was a silence, a burst of typing, and then the voice. Thin, lifeless, and stressing all the wrong words.

"I'm in charge," it said, "not you."

"I understand," Gabriel responded, calmer still. "But this is a business transaction, nothing more. Money for merchandise. And I would be remiss if I didn't do my due diligence before completing the sale."

Another pause, more typing, then the voice.

"This call has lasted too long. Hang up and wait for us to call back."

Gabriel did as he was told. A minute later a call came through from a different device. The voice issued a detailed set of instructions, which Gabriel copied onto a page of Hotel de la Mer stationery.

"When?" he asked.

"One hour," said the voice.

And then it was gone. Gabriel severed the connection and reread the instructions to make certain he had written them down correctly. There was only one problem.

The money.

During the next five minutes, Gabriel made three phone calls in rapid succession. The first two he placed from his room phone—one to the room next door, which went unanswered, and a second to the drowsy night clerk downstairs, who confirmed that the room was unoccupied. Gabriel reserved it for the night, promising payment in full within the hour. Then, from his personal mobile phone, he rang Christopher Keller.

"Where are you?" he asked.

"Boulogne," replied Keller.

"I need you to walk through the entrance of the Hotel de la Mer in Grand-Fort-Philippe in fifty-five minutes."

"Why would I do that?"

"Because I have an errand to run, and I need to make sure no one steals my luggage while I'm gone."

"Where's the luggage?"

"Under the bed in the room next door."

"Where are you going?"

"I have no idea."

Another hour, another wait. Gabriel used the time to put his room in order and to prepare perhaps the strongest cup of Nescafé ever brewed. He was going on his third night without sleep—the Lubéron, Downing Street, and now this. He was close; he could feel it. A few more hours, he thought, as he poured the bitter liquid down his throat. And then he would sleep for a month.

At ten minutes past ten, he headed downstairs to the lobby, where he told the night clerk that a Monsieur Duval would be arriving shortly. He paid the room charges in full and left behind an envelope, which was to be given to Monsieur Duval at check-in. Then he headed outside and climbed behind the wheel of the Passat. As he was driving away, he peered into the rearview mirror and saw Keller walking into the hotel, right on schedule.

This time they had given him not only a destination but a specific route as well. It took him across fields of windmills and eventually to the gasworks, refineries, and rail depots of west Dunkirk. Before him rose a mountain range of gravel, like a miniaturized version of the Alps. He sped past it in a cloud of dust and turned onto a narrow road running atop a long breakwater. On his right were the cargo cranes of Dunkirk harbor; on his left, the sea. He marked the starting point of the road with the TRIP setting on the odometer; then, exactly one and a half kilometers later, he pulled to the side and switched off the engine. The car shuddered in the heavy, wet wind. Gabriel climbed out and, turning up his coat collar, set out across the beach. The tide was out; the sand was as hard and flat as a parking lot. He stopped at the water's edge and hurled his Beretta into the sea. It was a fine place for a soldier's gun to end up, he thought as he started back toward the car. On the bottom of the sea, off the beaches of Dunkirk.

When he arrived back at the road, he looked in both directions, east, west, then east again. There were no other people about and no headlights approaching, only the lights of the cargo cranes and the distant glow of the gas fires burning atop the refineries. Gabriel opened the trunk and placed the key on the ground, just inside the left rear wheel. Then he climbed into the trunk, arranged his moderately sized frame in something like a fetal position, and pulled the hatch closed. A few seconds later the phone rang.

"Are you in?" asked the voice.

"I'm in."

"Five minutes," said the voice.

As it turned out, it was closer to ten minutes before Gabriel heard a car pull up behind him. He heard a door opening and closing, followed by the tack-hammer clatter of boots over asphalt. It was the woman, he thought as the car lurched forward. He was certain of it.

Once free of Dunkirk, she drove at speed for more than an hour, only twice coming to a complete stop. Then she turned onto a pitted track and continued to drive at speed, as if to punish Gabriel for the impertinence of asking for proof of life before surrendering ten million euros in ransom. At one point the Passat bottomed out with a heavy, scraping thud. To Gabriel it sounded as though they had just struck an iceberg.

The pitted track soon gave way to soft, deep gravel, and the gravel to the concrete floor of a garage. Gabriel knew this because, when the car came to a stop, the sound of the engine was vibrating back at him from the walls. After a moment it fell silent, and the woman climbed out, her heels clattering loudly over the floor. The trunk opened a few inches, and the long pale hand inserted a swath of cloth, which Gabriel immediately pulled over his head.

"Are you ready?" she asked.

"Yes."

"Do you know what's going to happen if that hood comes off?"

"The girl dies."

Gabriel heard the hatch of the trunk rise. Then two pairs of hands, obviously male, took hold of him, one by the shoulders, the other by the legs, and lifted him out. They placed him on his feet with surprising gentleness and made certain he was stable before binding his hands behind his back with a pair of flex-cuffs. Then they seized him by the elbows and frog-marched him across the gravel, slowing slightly to help him up two brick steps and through a doorway.

The flooring inside was wooden and uneven, like the floorboards of an old farmhouse. As they made a series of quick turns, Gabriel had the sensation of being guided by a figure of authority. They clambered down a flight of steep stairs, into a cool cellar that smelled of limestone and damp. The hands pushed him forward for several more feet, jerked him to a stop, and then eased him downward, onto the edge of a cot. Gabriel listened carefully to the footfalls of the captors as they withdrew, trying to determine their number. Then a heavy door slammed shut with the finality of a coffin lid. After that, there was no sound at all. Only the smell. Heavy and nauseatingly sweet. The smell of a human being in captivity.

Gabriel sat motionless and silent, convinced he had been left in the room alone. But after a few seconds, a hand removed the hood from his head. It belonged to a young woman, gaunt, pale as porcelain, yet still exquisitely beautiful.

"I'm Madeline Hart," she said. "Who are you?"

26

NORTHERN FRANCE

FOR NINE DAYS GABRIEL HAD struggled to paint her face clearly in his mind. She was a charcoal sketch, a name in an impressive file, a favor for an old friend. And now at long last she sat before him, the captive for whom he had tortured and killed, posed as if for her own portrait. She wore a dark blue tracksuit and canvas shoes with no laces. She was thinner than she had been in the videotape—thinner even than in the last proof-of-life photo—and her hair had grown at least an inch in length since her disappearance. It was combed straight back from her forehead and hung limply down the center of her back. There was a hard edge to her cheek-bones and dark patches like bruises beneath her blue-gray eyes. Her hands were folded neatly in her lap. Her wrists were all bone and sinew; her nails were gnawed to the quick. Even so, she managed to convey a sense of dignity and command. It was clear why Jeremy Fallon had declared her destined for a seat in Parliament—and why

Jonathan Lancaster had risked everything for her. Gabriel realized suddenly that he had, too.

"I'm here to bring you out, Madeline," he said, responding finally to her original question. "This is part of the endgame."

"You wanted to see whether I was still alive?"

He hesitated for a moment and then nodded.

"Well, I *am* alive," she said. "At least, I think I am. Sometimes I'm not so certain. I don't know the time, the day of the week, or the month. I don't even know where I am."

"I think you're in France," said Gabriel. "Somewhere in the north."

"You think?"

"I was brought here in the trunk of a car."

"I've spent a great deal of time in the trunk of a car," she said sympathetically. "And I think I remember a boat ride a few hours after they kidnapped me, but I can't be sure. They gave me a shot of something. After that, it was all a blur."

Gabriel assumed that their conversation was being monitored. Therefore, he did not tell Madeline that she had been brought from Corsica to the mainland aboard a thirty-six-foot motor yacht called *Moondance*, piloted by a smuggler named Marcel Lacroix, and accompanied by the man with whom she had lunched earlier that afternoon at Les Palmiers. Gabriel had many questions he wanted to ask her about the man he knew only as Paul. When did she meet him? What was the nature of their relationship? Instead, he asked if she could recall the circumstances of her kidnapping.

"It happened on the road between Piana and Calvi." She stopped herself. "Have you ever been?"

"To Corsica?"

"Yes."

"I've never set foot there."

"It's quite lovely, really," she said, sounding very English. "In any case, I was riding a little faster than I should have been, the way I always ride. A car pulled in front of me after a blind turn. I managed to squeeze the brakes, but I still hit the side of the car quite hard. It took an eternity for all the scrapes and bruises to heal." She rubbed the back of her hand. "How long has it been?" she asked. "How long have they been holding me?"

"Five weeks."

"Is that all? It seems longer."

"Have they treated you well?"

"Do I look as though I've been treated well?"

He didn't answer her.

"I've eaten nothing but bread and cheese and canned vegetables. Once they gave me a few scraps of chicken," she added, "but it made me sick, so they never gave it to me again. I asked for a radio but they refused. I asked for books to read or a newspaper so I could keep up with what's going on in the world, but they refused that, too."

"They didn't want you reading about yourself."

"What does the world know about me?"

"You're missing—that's all."

"And what about that dreadful video they forced me to make?"

"No one's seen it," he said. "No one but the prime minister and his closest aides."

"Jeremy?"

"Yes."

"Simon?"

Gabriel nodded.

"And what about you? You've seen it, too, I suppose."

Gabriel said nothing. Madeline was rubbing the back of her hand raw, as though she were trying to punish herself. Gabriel wanted to stop her but couldn't—not with his hands pinned behind his back.

"I had no choice but to make that video," she said at last.

"I know."

"They said they would kill me."

"I know."

"I tried to lie—you have to believe me. I tried to tell them there was nothing between Jonathan and me, but they knew everything. Times, dates, places—*everything*."

She stopped herself and looked at him quizzically.

"You're not English."

"Sorry," said Gabriel.

"Are you a policeman?"

"I'm a friend of the prime minister."

"So you're a spy, then?"

"Something like that."

She actually smiled briefly. It had been a beautiful smile once, but now there was something faintly mad about it. She would be well again eventually, thought Gabriel, but it was going to take time.

"Please stop, Madeline," he said.

"Stop what?"

"Your hands."

She looked down at them. She had drawn blood.

"Sorry." Her voice was full of submission. She bunched her hands into a tight knot and squeezed until her knuckles were white. "Why did they do this to me?"

"Money," answered Gabriel.

"They're blackmailing Jonathan?"

He nodded.

"How much?"

"It's not important."

"How *much*?" she insisted.

"Ten million."

"My God," she whispered. "And he agreed to pay it?"

"Without blinking."

"What happens now?"

"We find some way to make an exchange that satisfies the needs of both parties."

"How long?"

"We're close."

"How long?" she pressed.

"I'll do whatever it takes to get you out of here by morning."

"I'm afraid that doesn't mean anything to me."

"A few hours."

"And then?"

"We'll take you somewhere safe to clean you up and let you rest. And then you'll go home."

"To what?" she asked. "My life will be ruined, all because I made one silly mistake."

"No one will ever know about the ransom or the affair. It will be as if it never happened."

"Until the press finds out. And then they'll tear me limb from limb. That's what they do. That's *all* they do."

Gabriel was about to respond, but just then there was a knock at the door, two sharp blows with a hammer fist. Madeline gave a start that made Gabriel's stomach lurch sideways. She quickly covered his head with the black hood. He supposed she covered her own as well, but couldn't be sure; his hood was entirely opaque.

"You never told me your name," she said.

"It's not important."

"I loved him, you know. I loved him very much."

"I know."

"I can't take much more of this."

"I know."

"You have to get me out of here."

"I will."

"When?"

"Soon," he said.

They removed the flex-cuffs before placing him in the trunk and driving him down the pitted dirt track. The car bottomed out at the same pothole and after that ran smooth and fast over paved roads. It must have been raining very hard because the road spray beat ceaselessly against the wheel wells. The sound lulled Gabriel briefly to sleep. He dreamed that Madeline had scratched the back of her hand down to the bone.

"I can't take much more of this."

"I know."

"You have to get me out of here."

"I will."

Ten minutes after he awoke, the car finally came to a stop. The engine died, a door opened, boots clattered over pavement and receded into nothing. After that, there was only the rain and the distant crash-and-hiss of the surf. For a moment Gabriel feared they had left him to die a death that was akin to being buried alive. Then the phone rang in his coat pocket.

"We told you no backup," said the voice.

"You didn't really think I was going to leave ten million euros in a hotel room, did you?"

"From now on, do exactly as we say, or the girl dies."

"You have my word," said Gabriel.

There was silence, followed by a burst of typing.

"The spare key is taped to the lid directly above your head. Go back to your room and wait for our call."

"How long?"

The connection went dead. Gabriel reached up and tore loose the key. Then he pressed the trunk release and the rain fell benevolently upon his face.

27

GRAND-FORT-PHILIPPE, FRANCE

WHEN GABRIEL ENTERED HIS ROOM at the Hotel de la Mer, he found Keller propped up in bed, a cigarette burning between his fingers, his eyes fixed on the television. It was a replay of an English Premier League match, Fulham versus Arsenal. The sound was muted.

"Comfortable?" asked Gabriel.

"I saw you drive up." Keller aimed the remote at the screen and fired. "Well?"

"She's alive."

"How bad?"

"Bad."

"What do we do now?"

"We wait for the phone to ring."

Keller switched on the television and lit a fresh cigarette.

This time Gabriel's natural forbearance abandoned him. He tried to distract himself with the football match, but the sight of grown men in shorts chasing a ball around a pitch seemed offensive to him. Finally, he brewed another evil cup of the double-strength Nescafé and drank it at his outpost in the window. The current of the tidal creek had changed directions; it was flowing in instead of out. He looked at his wristwatch. The time had not changed since he had checked it last: 3:22 a.m. It was a provable fact, he told himself, that nothing good ever happened at 3:22 in the morning.

"They're not going to call," he said, more to himself than to Keller.

"Of course they're going to call."

"How can you be so sure?"

"Because they've come too far. And keep one other thing in mind," he added. "At this point, they want to get rid of Madeline as badly as you want her back."

"That's what I'm afraid of."

Keller looked at him seriously. "When's the last time you slept?"

"September."

"Any chance you'd allow me to deliver the money?"

"None whatsoever."

"I had to ask."

"I appreciate the gesture."

Keller frowned at the television. Evidently, someone had scored a goal because the men in shorts were jumping up and down like children on a playground. But not Gabriel; he was staring at the waters of the tidal creek and thinking about Madeline clawing the skin from the back of her hand. Consequently, when the phone finally rang at 3:48 a.m., it startled him like the scream of a terrified woman. The voice spoke to him, thin, lifeless, and stressing all the wrong words. After a few seconds he looked at Keller and nodded once.

It was time.

The night clerk was nowhere to be found. Gabriel placed both room keys in the pigeonhole behind the desk and wheeled the two suitcases into the wet street. The engine block of the Passat was still ticking from the last journey. He loaded the suitcases into the trunk and climbed behind the wheel. The phone started ringing as he was closing the door. He immediately switched the device to SPEAKER mode, just as he had been instructed.

"Go to the A16 and head toward Calais," said the voice. "And whatever you do, don't hang up. If the connection dies, the girl dies."

"What if I lose cell service?"

"Don't," said the voice.

It was a four-lane motorway with light towers down the center median and tabletop-flat farmland on either side. Gabriel kept to the posted speed limit of ninety kilometers per hour, despite the fact the road was nearly empty of any other traffic. He drove with one hand and held the phone with the other, watching the signal strength meter carefully. For the most part it remained at five bars, but for a few anxious seconds it fell to only three.

"Where are you?" the voice asked finally.

"Approaching the exit for the D219."

"Keep going."

He did. It was more of the same: farmland and lights, a bit of traf-fic, a power transmission line that stepped on the cell service. The next time the voice spoke, it was through a hailstorm of static.

"Where are you?"

"Coming up on the D940."

"Keep going."

The transmission lines fell away, the signal cleared.

"Where are you?"

"Approaching the A216 interchange."

"Keep going."

When the lights of Calais appeared, Gabriel stopped waiting for questions. Instead, he offered a running commentary of his where-abouts, if only to break the monotony of the call-and-response rhythm of the instructions. There was silence at the other end until Gabriel announced he was nearing the turnoff for the D243.

"Take it," said the voice, though it sounded more like a question than an order.

"Which direction?"

The answer came a few seconds later. They wanted him to head north, toward the sea.

The next town was Sangatte, a wind-whipped cluster of flint cottages that looked as though they had been plucked from the English countryside and plopped down in France. From there, they sent him farther west along the Channel coast, through the villages of Escalles, Wissant, and Tardinghen. There were periods lasting several minutes when there were no instructions. Gabriel could hear nothing at the other end of the call, but he had a sense he was near-ing the end. He decided it was time to force the issue.

"How much farther?" he asked.

"You're getting close."

"Where is she?"

"She's safe."

"This has gone on long enough," Gabriel snapped. "You've seen the money, you know I'm not being followed. Let's get this over with so she can come home."

There was silence on the line. Then the voice asked, "Where are you?"

"I'm passing through Audinghen."

"Can you see the traffic circle yet?"

"Wait," said Gabriel as he rounded a bend in the road. "Yes, I can see it now."

"Enter the circle, take the second exit, and go fifty meters."

"What then?"

"Stop."

"Is that where she is?"

"Just do as we say."

Gabriel obeyed the instructions. There was no shoulder along the road, leaving him no choice but to drive over a low concrete curb and park on the asphalt pedestrian walkway. Directly before him stood a commercial building of some sort, long and low, with chimneys at either end of the red tile roof. On his right a field of grain swirled in the wind and rain. And beyond the field was the sea.

"Where are you?" asked the voice.

"Fifty meters past the traffic circle."

"Very good. Now turn off the engine and listen carefully."

The instructions had obviously been preloaded into the computer, for they spewed forth in a disjointed but steady stream. Gabriel was to open the trunk of the car and throw the key into the field on his right. Madeline was approximately three kilometers down the road, in the rear storage compartment of a dark blue Citroën C4. The key to the Citroën was hidden in a magnetic box in the left-front wheel well. Gabriel was to keep the phone in his hand until he arrived at the car, with the connection left open so they could hear him. No police, no backup, no traps.

"It's not good enough," he said.

"You have fifteen minutes."

"Or what?"

"You're wasting time."

An image flashed in Gabriel's mind. Madeline in her cell, clawing herself bloody.

"I can't take much more of this."

"I know."

"You have to get me out of here."

"I will."

Gabriel climbed out of the car and hurled the key so hard that, for all he knew, it splashed into the Channel. Then he marked the time on the mobile phone and started running.

"Are we on?" asked the voice.

"We're on," said Gabriel.

"Hurry," said the voice. "Fifteen minutes, or the girl dies."

28

PAS-DE-CALAIS, FRANCE

THREE KILOMETERS WAS SLIGHTLY LESS than two miles, or seven and a half laps on a four-hundred-meter oval track. A world-class distance runner could be expected to complete the distance in under eight minutes; a fit athlete who jogged regularly, in about twelve. But for a middle-aged man who was wearing jeans and street shoes, and who had twice been shot in the chest, fifteen minutes was more than a fair test. And that was if the distance was truly three kilometers, he thought. If it was a few hundred meters longer, the time limit might be beyond his physical limits.

Mercifully, the road was flat. In fact, because Gabriel was moving toward the sea, it had a slight downhill pitch in places, though the wind blew hard and steady into his face. Fueled by a rush of adrenaline and anger, he set off at a maniacal sprint, but after a hundred meters or so he settled into what he assumed to be roughly a seven-minute-mile pace. He clutched the phone in his right hand but kept his left hand loose and relaxed. His breath was smooth at first, but it soon grew ragged and the back of his throat tasted like rust. It was Shamron's fault, he thought resentfully, as he pounded along the pavement with the rain stinging his face. Shamron and his damn cigarettes.

Beyond the commercial building there was nothing at all—no cottages or streetlamps, only black fields and hedgerows and the broken white line at the edge of the road that guided Gabriel through the dark. The gaps between the lengths of white line were equidistant to the lines themselves, two strides per line, two strides per gap. Gabriel used the lines to keep his motion rhythmic and even. Two strides per line, two strides per gap. Fifteen minutes to cover three kilometers.

"Or what?"

"You're wasting time."

After five minutes his calves felt like granite and he was sweating beneath the weight of his leather jacket. He tried to shed the coat while running but couldn't, so he paused long enough to remove it and hurl it into a farmer's field. When he started running again, he saw a faint dome of yellow light on the horizon. Then two lamps, the parking lamps of a vehicle, peaked over the crest of a small rise and headed toward him at high speed. The vehicle was a small paneled van, pale gray in color, well worn. As it shot past in a blur, Gabriel noticed that the driver and his passenger were both wearing balaclava masks. The bagmen, he thought, coming to collect their prize. He didn't bother turning to watch. Instead, he tried to ignore the burning in his calves and the sting of the rain on his face. Two strides per line, two strides per gap. Fifteen minutes to cover three kilometers.

When she is dead. Then you will know the truth . . .

Gabriel cleared the small rise and immediately saw a chain of lights glowing in the distance. They were the lights of Audresselles, he thought, the small coastal village just south of the lighthouse at Cap Gris Nez. He checked the time on the mobile phone. Eight minutes elapsed, seven remaining. His stride was beginning to falter, and the back of his neck felt numb. He lamented the fact he had not taken better care of his body, but mainly his thoughts were of Vienna. Of a car parked at the edge of a snowy square. Of an engine that wouldn't start right away because of a bomb drawing power from the battery. He looked at the phone. Nine minutes elapsed, six remaining. Two strides per line, two strides per gap.

He lifted the phone to his mouth. "Did you get the money?"

The voice responded a few seconds later.

"We got it. Thank you very much."

Thin, lifeless, stressing all the wrong words. Even so, Gabriel swore it was filled with mirth.

"You have to give me more time," he shouted.

"That's not possible."

"I can't make it."

"You have to try harder."

He looked at the clock. Ten minutes elapsed, five remaining. Three strides per line, three strides per gap.

"I'm coming for you, Leah," he shouted into the wind. "Don't turn the key again. Don't turn the key."

He sprinted past a sprawling manor house, new but built to look old, and immediately felt the pull of the sea. The road sank toward it, and the smell of it tasted of fish and salt on Gabriel's tongue. A sign materialized from the dark indicating there was beach access two hundred meters ahead. And then Gabriel saw the Citroën. It was waiting in a small sandy car park, its headlamps staring him straight in the face, seemingly watching him as he hurtled toward it like a madman. He glanced at the clock on the phone. Thirteen minutes elapsed, two remaining. He would make it with time to spare. Still, he forced himself to see the race to its end, pounding his feet on the asphalt, flailing his arms, until he thought his heart would burst. Starved of oxygen, his brain started to play tricks on him. He saw a Citroën parked by the beach one instant, but the next it was a dark blue Mercedes sedan in a snowy Vienna square. He swore he heard an engine struggling to start, and later he would remember shouting something incoherent before being blinded by the flash of an explosion. The blast wave hit him with the force of a speeding car and blew him off his feet. He lay on the cold asphalt for several minutes, gasping for breath, wondering whether it was real or only a dream.

PART TWO

THE
SPY

29

AUDRESSELLES, PAS-DE-CALAIS

THE HOUR WAS EARLY, THE location remote, and therefore the response was slow. Much later, a commission of inquiry would reprimand the chief of the local gendarmerie and issue a lofty set of recommendations that went largely ignored, for in the quaint little fishing village of Audresselles, recriminations were the last thing on anyone's mind. For many months afterward, its shocked residents would speak of that morning in the most somber of tones. One woman, an octogenarian whose family had lived in the village when it was ruled by an English king, would describe the incident on the beach as the worst thing she had seen since the Nazis hoisted a swastika over the Hôtel de Ville. No one took issue with her claim, though a few found it hyperbolic. Surely, they said, Audresselles had seen worse than this, though, when pressed, none could provide an example.

The commune of Audresselles is only two thousand acres in size, and the blast wave from the explosion rattled windows the length and breadth of it. Several startled residents immediately called the gendarmes, though twenty long minutes would elapse before the first mobile unit arrived at the little sand car park adjacent to the beach. There they discovered a Citroën C4 engulfed in a fire so hot no one could get within thirty meters of it. Another ten minutes would pass before the firefighters arrived. By the time they managed to smother the flames, the Citroën was little more than a blackened shell. For reasons that were never made clear, one of the firefighters took it upon himself to pry open the rear hatch. Instantly, he fell to his knees and was violently sick. The first gendarme to look inside fared no better. But the second, a veteran of some twenty years, managed to maintain his composure as he confirmed that the blackened contents of the car were indeed the remains of a human being. He then radioed the desk officer for the Pas-de-Calais region and reported that the exploding car on the beach at Audresselles was now a murder case—and a grisly one at that.

By daybreak more than a dozen detectives and forensic experts were working the crime scene, watched over by what seemed like half the town. Only one resident of Audresselles had anything useful to tell them: Léon Banville, owner of a recently built manor house on the edge of town. As it happened, Monsieur Banville had been awake at 5:09 a.m., when a man in street clothes had come running past his window shouting in a language he didn't recognize. Police immediately undertook a search of the road and found a leather jacket that looked as though it would fit a man of moderate height and build. Nothing else of interest was ever found—not the key that the running man had hurled into the field of grain, nor the Volkswagen car that it operated. The car vanished without a trace, along with the ten million euros hidden inside two suitcases in its trunk.

The intense heat of the fire did significant damage to the remains of the body in the back of the Citroën but did not destroy them completely. As a result, forensic examiners were able to determine that the victim had been a young woman, probably in her late twenties or early thirties, approximately five-foot-eight inches in height. The description was a rough match for Madeline Hart, the English girl who had gone missing on Corsica in late August. The French police quietly reestablished contact with their brethren across the Channel and within forty-eight hours had in their possession a DNA sample taken from Ms. Hart's London flat. An expedited comparison test showed that the sample matched DNA taken from the car. The French interior minister immediately sent word to the Home Office in London before making the findings public at a hastily called news conference in Paris. Madeline Hart was dead. But who had killed her? And why?

They held the funeral at St. Andrew's Church in Basildon, just down the road from the little council house where she had been raised. Prime Minister Jonathan Lancaster was not in attendance—his schedule would not permit it, or so said his press spokesman, Simon Hewitt. Nearly the entire staff of party headquarters was there, as was Jeremy Fallon. He wept openly at the graveside, which inspired one reporter to remark that perhaps he had a heart after all. Afterward, he spoke briefly to Madeline's mother and brother, who looked curiously out of place amid the well-dressed London crowd. "I'm so sorry," he was overheard telling them. "I'm so very sorry."

Once again, the Party's political team noticed a spike in Lancaster's approval ratings, though this time they had the decency not to invoke Madeline's name. With his popularity at an all-time high, the prime minister announced a sweeping program to make government more efficient and then jetted off on a high-profile trip to Moscow, where he promised a new era in Russian-British relations, especially in the arenas of counterterrorism, finance, and energy. A handful of conservative commentators gently criticized Lancaster for not meeting with the leaders of Russia's pro-democracy movement while in Moscow, but most of the British press applauded his restraint. With the domestic economy still on life support, they wrote, the last thing Britain needed was another cold war with the Russians.

Upon returning to London, Lancaster was questioned at every turn as to whether he intended to call an election. For ten days he toyed with the press while Simon Hewitt orchestrated a steady stream of leaks that made it clear an announcement was imminent. Therefore, when Lancaster finally rose in the Commons to declare his intention to seek a new mandate, it was an anticlimax. In fact, the most surprising news concerned the future of Jeremy Fallon, who planned to leave his powerful post at Downing Street to run for a safe seat in Parliament. There were numerous press reports, all unconfirmed, that if Lancaster were to win a second term as prime minister, Fallon would be appointed the next chancellor of the exchequer. Fallon denied the reports categorically, going so far as to claim that he and the prime minister had held no substantive discussions about his future. Not a single member of the Whitehall press corps believed him.

As October turned to November, and the campaign commenced in earnest, Madeline Hart again faded from the public consciousness. This proved to be a blessing for the French police, for it allowed them to conduct their investigation without the British press peering over their shoulders. Among the most promising developments was the discovery of four bodies at an isolated villa in the Lubéron. All four were known members of a violent Marseilles criminal gang. Three had been killed with professional-looking shots to the head; the fourth, a woman, had been hit twice in the upper torso. More important, however, was the discovery of a purpose-built holding cell in the lower level of the villa. It was clear to the police that Madeline had been held in the room after her abduction in Corsica, probably for a lengthy period of time. It was possible she was the victim of sexual enslavement, but it was unlikely, given the pedigrees of the four people who had been staying in the house with her. These people were not sexual predators; they were professional criminals interested only in money. All of which led the police to conclude that Madeline Hart had been held as part of a kidnap-for-ransom scheme—a scheme that, for some reason, was never reported to the authorities.

But why kidnap a girl from a working-class family who had been raised in a council house in Essex? And who had killed the four Marseilles criminals at the villa in the Lubéron? Those were just two of the questions the French police still could not answer a month after Madeline's terrible death on the beach at Audresselles. Nor did they have any clue about the identity of the man who had been spotted running past Monsieur Banville's house at 5:09 a.m., minutes before the car exploded. One veteran detective who had worked numerous kidnapping cases had a theory, though. "The poor devil was the bagman," he told his colleagues assuredly. "Somewhere along the line, he made a mistake, and the girl died for his sins." But where was he now? They assumed he was lying low somewhere, licking his wounds and trying to figure out what had gone wrong. And though the French police would never know it, they were entirely correct.

But there were many other things about the running man that the French police, even in their wildest dreams, would never imagine to be true. They would never know, for example, that he was Gabriel

Allon, the legendary Israeli spy and assassin who had been operating with impunity on French soil since he was a boy of twenty-two. Or that the man who had spirited him to safety after the bomb exploded was none other than Christopher Keller, the Corsican-based assassin about whom the French police had been hearing whispers for years. Or that the two men, once bitter rivals, had proceeded to a seaside villa near Cherbourg where a team of four Israeli operatives waited on standby. Keller had stayed at the villa only a few hours before returning quietly to Corsica, but Gabriel and Chiara remained there for a week while they waited for the many small cuts on Gabriel's face to heal. On the morning of Madeline Hart's funeral, they drove to Charles de Gaulle Airport and boarded an El Al flight to Tel Aviv. And by nightfall they were once again at the apartment in Narkiss Street.

In Gabriel's absence, Chiara had moved the painting and his supplies to the room that was supposed to be his studio. But the next morning, after she left for work at the museum, he promptly moved his things back to the sitting room. For three days he stood before the canvas almost without a break, from dawn each morning until late afternoon, when Chiara returned home. He tried to keep the memories of the nightmare in France at bay, but the subject matter of the painting, a beautiful young woman bathing in her garden, would not allow it. Madeline was in his thoughts constantly, especially on the fourth day, when he began work on the extensive losses to the hands of Susanna. Here he saw much evidence of Bassano's luminous brushwork. Gabriel imitated it so immaculately it was nearly impossible to discern the original from the retouching. Indeed, in Gabriel's humble opinion, he managed to outdo the master in places. He wished he could take credit for the high quality of his work, but he could not. It was Madeline who inspired him.

He forced himself to take a break for lunch early each afternoon, but inevitably he ate at the computer, where he scoured the Internet for news about the French investigation into Madeline's death. He knew the stories were far from complete, but it appeared the police were unaware of his involvement in the case. Nor could he find any evidence in the British press to suggest that Jonathan Lancaster might have been linked in any way to Madeline's disappearance and death. It seemed that Lancaster and Jeremy Fallon had pulled off the impossible—and now, according to the polls, they were headed toward a landslide victory. Needless to say, neither man tried to contact Gabriel. Even Graham Seymour waited three long weeks before calling. From the background noise, Gabriel guessed he was using a public phone in Paddington Station.

"Our mutual friend sends his regards," Seymour said carefully. "He was wondering whether there's anything you need."

"A new leather jacket," said Gabriel with more good humor than he was feeling.

"What size?"

"Medium," replied Gabriel, "with a hidden compartment for false passports and a weapon."

"Are you ever going to tell me how you managed to get away without being arrested?"

"Someday, Graham."

Seymour fell silent as the station announcer called a train for Oxford. "He's grateful," he said finally, speaking of Lancaster again. "He knows you did everything you could."

"It just wasn't enough to save her."

"Have you considered the possibility that they never intended to let her go?"

"I have," said Gabriel. "But for the life of me, I can't figure out why."

"Is there anything else you want me to tell him?"

"You might want to remind him that the kidnappers still have a copy of her video confession of the affair."

"No girl, no story."

If it had been Seymour's intention to lift Gabriel's spirits with the phone call, he failed miserably. In fact, in the days after, Gabriel's mood grew darker still. Dreams disturbed his sleep. Dreams of running toward a car that receded farther into the distance with each stride. Dreams of fire and blood. In his subconscious, Madeline and Leah became indistinguishable, two women, one whom he had loved, another whom he had sworn to protect, both consumed by fire. He was despondent with grief. More than anything, though, he was gripped by an overwhelming sense of failure. He had given Madeline his word he would get her out alive. Instead, she had died a nightmarish death, bound and gagged in a coffin of fire. He only hoped she had been sedated at the time, that she had been oblivious to the pain and terror.

But why had they killed her? Had Gabriel made a mistake during the drop that cost Madeline her life? Or had it always been their intention to kill her in front of Gabriel, so that he had no choice but to watch her burn? It was a question that Chiara posed one evening while they were walking along Ben Yehuda Street. Gabriel answered by telling her about the *signadora*'s vision, that she had seen an old enemy when peering into her magic potion of olive oil and water. Not an old enemy of Keller's, but of Gabriel's.

"I never knew you had any enemies inside the criminal underworld of Marseilles."

"I don't," replied Gabriel. "At least, none that I know about. But maybe they were acting at the behest of someone else when they kidnapped Madeline."

"Like who?"

222

"Someone who wanted to punish me for something I'd done in the past. Someone who wanted to humiliate me."

"Is there anything else the *signadora* said that you forgot to mention?"

"When she is dead," answered Gabriel. "Then you will know the truth."

It was a few minutes after nine o'clock by the time they returned to Narkiss Street, but Gabriel decided to spend some time at the easel. He slipped a copy of *La Bohème* into his paint-smudged portable CD player, lowered the volume to a whisper, and worked with a clarity of purpose that had eluded him since his return to Jerusalem. He did not hear when the opera reached its end, nor did he notice the sky beginning to lighten at his back. Finally, at dawn, he laid down his brush and stood motionless before the painting, his hand to his chin, his head tilted slightly to one side.

"Is it finished?" Chiara asked, watching him intently.

"No," replied Gabriel, still staring at the painting. "It's just getting started."

30

TIBERIAS, ISRAEL

THAT EVENING WAS SHABBAT. SHAMRON invited them to dinner at his home in Tiberias. It was not truly an invitation, for invitations can be politely declined. It was a commandment, chiseled into stone, inviolable. Gabriel spent the morning making arrangements to have the painting shipped to Julian Isherwood in London. Then he drove across Jerusalem to collect Chiara at the Israel Museum. As they sped down the Bab al-Wad, the staircase-like gorge linking Jerusalem to the Coastal Plain, Palestinian militants in the Gaza Strip unleashed a barrage of rockets that landed as far north as Ashdod. There were only minor injuries in the attack, but it snarled traffic across the narrow waist of the country as thousands of commuters were rushing home for the Sabbath. Only in Israel, thought Gabriel, as he waited an hour for the traffic to budge. It was good to be back home again.

After finally reaching the flatlands of the Coastal Plain, they headed north to the Galilee, then eastward through a string of Arab towns and villages to Tiberias. Shamron's honey-colored villa was a few miles outside the city, on a bluff overlooking the lake. To reach it required an ascent up a steeply sloped drive. As Gabriel and Chiara entered, it was Gilah who greeted them. Shamron was standing before the television, a phone pressed to his ear. His ugly metal spectacles were propped on his forehead, and he was pinching the bridge of his nose between his thumb and forefinger. If they ever erected a statue of him, thought Gabriel, it would be cast in that pose.

"Who is he talking to?" Gabriel asked of Gilah.

"Who do you think?"

"The prime minister?"

Gilah nodded. "Ari thinks we need to retaliate. The prime minister isn't so sure."

Gabriel handed Gilah a bottle of wine, a Bordeaux-style red from the Judean Hills, and kissed her cheek. It was as smooth as velvet and smelled of lilac.

"Tell him to get off the phone, Gabriel. He'll listen to you."

"I'd rather take a direct hit from one of those Palestinian rockets."

Gilah smiled and led them into the kitchen. Lining the counters were platters of delicious-looking food; she must have been cooking all day. Gabriel tried to snatch a piece of Gilah's famous eggplant with Moroccan spice, but she playfully patted the back of his hand.

"How many people are you planning to feed?" he asked.

"Yonatan and his family were supposed to come, but he can't get away because of the attack."

Yonatan was Shamron's eldest child. He was a general in the IDF, and there were rumors he was in the running to become the next chief of staff.

"We'll eat in a few minutes," Gilah said. "Go sit with him for a while. He missed you terribly while you were away."

"I was only gone for two weeks, Gilah."

"At this stage of his life, two weeks is a long time."

Gabriel opened the wine, poured two glasses, and carried them into the next room. Shamron was no longer on the phone, but he was still staring at the television.

"They just launched another barrage," he said. "The rockets should start landing in just a few seconds."

"Is there going to be a response?"

"Not now. But if this keeps up, we'll have no choice but to act. The question is, what will Egypt do, now that it's ruled by the Muslim Brotherhood? Will it stand idly by while we attack Hamas, which, after all, is a wing of the Muslim Brotherhood? Will the Camp David peace treaty hold?"

"What does Uzi say?"

"At the moment, the Office is unable to predict with certainty how the Egyptian leader will react if we go into Gaza. Which is why the prime minister, at least for the moment, is willing to do nothing while the rockets rain on his people."

Gabriel looked at the screen; rockets were beginning to fall. Then he switched off the television and led Shamron outside to the terrace. It was warmer here than in Jerusalem, and a soft wind from the Golan Heights was making patterns on the silvery surface of the lake. Shamron sat down in one of the wrought-iron chairs along the balustrade and immediately lit one of his foul-smelling cigarettes. Gabriel handed him a glass of wine and sat next to him.

"It's done nothing for my heart," Shamron said after drinking some of the wine, "but I've become fond of it in my dotage. I suppose it reminds me of all the things I never had time for when I was young—wine, children, holidays." He paused, then added, "Life."

"There's still time, Ari."

"Spare me the banalities," Shamron said. "Time is my enemy now, my son."

"So why are you wasting a minute of it involving yourself in politics?"

"There's a difference between politics and security."

"Security is merely an extension of politics, Ari."

"And if you were advising the prime minister on what to do about the missiles?"

"It's Uzi's job to advise him, not mine."

Shamron let the subject drop for the moment. "I've been following the news from London with great interest," he said. "It looks as though your friend Jonathan Lancaster is well on his way to victory."

"He is perhaps the luckiest politician on the planet."

"Luck is an important thing to have in life. I never had much of it. Neither did you, for that matter."

Gabriel said nothing.

"Needless to say," Shamron continued, "it is our fervent hope that current electoral trends continue and Lancaster prevails. If that is the case, we are confident he will be the most pro-Zionist British politician since Arthur Balfour."

"You're a ruthless bastard."

"Someone has to be." Shamron looked at Gabriel seriously for a moment. "I'm sorry I ever let you get mixed up in this business."

"You got exactly what you wanted," Gabriel said. "Lancaster might as well be on the Office payroll. He's the worst thing a leader can be. He's compromised."

"It was his doing, not ours."

"That's true," said Gabriel. "But it was Madeline Hart who paid the price."

"You have to do your best to forget her."

"I'm afraid I said something to the kidnappers that makes that impossible."

"You threatened to kill them if they harmed her?"

Gabriel nodded.

"Death threats are like vows of endless love whispered in the heat of passion—easily made, soon forgotten."

"Not when they're made by me."

Shamron crushed out his cigarette thoughtfully. "You surprise me, my son. But not Uzi. He predicted you would want to go after them, which is why he's already taken it off the table."

"So I'll do it without his support."

"That means you'll be out there in the field on your own, with no Office resources and no Office protection."

Gabriel was silent.

"And if I forbade you to go? Would you obey me?"

"Yes, Abba."

"Really?" asked Shamron, surprised.

Gabriel nodded in response.

"And if I permitted you to find these men and give them the justice they deserve? What would I get in return?"

"Must everything be a negotiation with you?"

"Yes."

"What do you want?"

"You know what I want." Shamron paused, then added, "And the prime minister wants it, too."

Shamron drank some of the wine and then lit another cigarette.

"These are consequential and turbulent times we are living through, and the challenges are only going to grow more serious. The decisions we make in the coming months and years will determine whether the enterprise succeeds or fails. How can you pass up the chance to shape history?"

"I already have shaped history, Ari. Many, many times."

"So put your gun on the shelf and use that brain of yours to defeat our enemies. Steal their secrets. Recruit their spies and generals as agents. Confuse and confound them. By way of deception, my son, thou shalt do war."

Gabriel lapsed into silence. The sky above the Golan was turning blue-black with the coming night, and the lake was now nearly invisible. Shamron loved the view because it allowed him to keep watch on his distant enemies. Gabriel loved it because he had beheld it while reciting his marriage vows to Chiara. Now he was about to take a vow of another sort, a vow that would make an old man very happy.

"I won't be a party to any sort of palace coup," Gabriel said at last. "Uzi and I have had our differences over the years, but we've become friends."

Shamron knew better than to speak. He had the interrogator's gift of silence.

"If the prime minister decides not to appoint Uzi to a second term," Gabriel continued, "I will consider an offer to become the next chief of the Office."

"I need better odds than that."

"They're the best you're going to get."

"Negotiating with kidnappers has sharpened your edge."

"Yes, it has."

"Where do you plan to start?"

"I haven't decided yet."

"What will you do for money?"

"I found a few thousand euros lying around a boat in Marseilles."

"Who did the boat belong to?"

"A smuggler named Marcel Lacroix."

"Where is he now?"

Gabriel told him.

"Poor devil."

"More to follow."

"Just make sure you're not one of them. I have plans for you."

"I said I would consider it, Ari. I haven't agreed to anything."

"I know," Shamron said. "But I also know that you would never mislead me to get something you wanted. You're not like me. You have a conscience."

"So do you, Ari. That's why you can't sleep at night."

"Something tells me I'll sleep well tonight."

"Don't get carried away," Gabriel said. "I still have to talk to Chiara about all this."

Shamron smiled.

"What's so funny?" asked Gabriel.

"Whose idea do you think it was?"

"You're a ruthless bastard."

"Someone has to be."

But where to begin his search for Madeline's killers? The most logical place was among the criminal organizations of Marseilles. He could locate associates of Marcel Lacroix and René Brossard, watch them, bribe them, interrogate them, hurt a few if necessary, until he learned the identity of the man who had called himself Paul. The man who had taken Madeline to lunch at Les Palmiers the day of her disappearance. The man who spoke French as though he had learned it from a tape. But there was one problem with that plan. If Gabriel went to Marseilles, he would surely cross paths with the French police. Besides, he thought, the man known as Paul was probably long gone by now. Therefore, he decided he would begin his search not with the perpetrators of the crime but with the two victims. Someone had known about the affair between Jonathan Lancaster and Madeline Hart. And someone had passed that information to the man known as Paul. Find that person, he reasoned, and he would find Paul.

For now, though, Gabriel needed to find someone else first. Someone who had followed Lancaster's rise to power. Someone who knew the dynamics of Lancaster's relationship with Jeremy Fallon. Someone who knew where the bodies were buried. He found that person the following morning while reading the coverage of the British election campaign. It would be complicated, dangerous even. But if it produced information that led Gabriel to Madeline's killers, it would be well worth the personal risk.

He spent the rest of the morning preparing a detailed dossier. Then he packed an overnight bag with two changes of clothing and two changes of identity. That evening he flew from Ben Gurion to Paris, and by noon the following day he was once again on the island of Corsica. He needed one more thing before he could begin his search. He needed an accomplice. Someone extremely capable, utterly ruthless, and without a shred of conscience.

He needed Christopher Keller.

31

CORSICA

T HE ISLAND HAD BEEN TRANSFORMED since Gabriel's last visit. The beaches were deserted, there were good tables to be had in the better restaurants, and the outdoor markets were free of the half-naked mainlanders who gawked admiringly but rarely reached into their wallets. Corsica was once again in the possession of the Corsicans. And for that, even the gloomiest of the island's residents were grateful.

There were many other things, however, that remained unchanged. The same intoxicating scent of the *macchia* greeted Gabriel as he turned inland from the coast; the same old woman pointed at him with her index and little fingers as he drove through the isolated hill town; and the same two guards nodded menacingly as he sped past the entrance of Don Anton Orsati's estate.

He followed the road until it turned to dirt, and then he followed it a little farther. And when he rounded the sharp left-hand bend near the three ancient olive trees, Don Casabianca's wretched palomino goat was there to block his path. Upon seeing Gabriel, its expression darkened, as though it recalled the circumstances of their last encounter and now planned to return the favor. Through the open car window, Gabriel politely asked the goat to give way. And when the beast lifted its chin defiantly, Gabriel climbed out of the car, leaned close to the goat's tattered old ear, and whispered a threat much like the one he had issued to the kidnappers of Madeline Hart. Instantly, the goat turned and beat a hasty retreat into the *macchia*. He was a coward, as most tyrants were.

Gabriel climbed back into the car and drove the rest of the way to Keller's villa. He parked in the drive, in the shade of a laricio pine tree, and called up a greeting to the terrace that went unanswered. The door was unlocked; Gabriel walked from one beautiful white room to the next but found each of them unoccupied. Then he went into the kitchen and opened the refrigerator. No milk, no meat, no eggs, nothing that might spoil. Only some beer, a container of Dijon mustard, and a bottle of rather good Sancerre. Gabriel opened the Sancerre and phoned Don Orsati.

Keller was away on business. Mainland Europe, a country other than France—that was as far as the don would go. If all went according to plan, Keller would be back on Corsica that evening, the following morning at the latest. The don told Gabriel to stay at Keller's villa and to make himself at home. He said he was sorry about what had happened "up in the north." Keller had obviously given him a full account.

"So what brings you back to Corsica?" asked the don.

"I paid someone a large sum of money, and they didn't deliver the merchandise as promised."

"A very large sum," the don agreed.

"What would you do if you were in my position?"

"I would have never agreed to help a man like Jonathan Lancaster in the first place."

"It's a complicated world, Don Orsati."

"Indeed," said the don philosophically. "As for your business problem, you have two choices. You can do your best to forget what happened to the English girl, or you can punish those responsible."

"What would you do?"

"Here on Corsica we have an old proverb: a Christian forgives, an idiot forgets."

"I'm not an idiot."

"Nor a Christian," said Orsati, "but I won't hold that against you."

The don asked Gabriel to stay on the line while he dealt with a minor crisis. It seemed a large shipment of oil to a restaurant in Zurich had gone missing. Gabriel could hear the don shouting at an underling in the Corsican dialect. Find the oil, he was saying, or heads will roll. At any other enterprise, the threat might have been dismissed as managerial bluster. But not at the Orsati Olive Oil Company.

"Where were we?" asked the don.

"You were saying something about Christians and idiots. And you were about to extract a steep price for the privilege of borrowing Keller."

"He *is* my most valuable employee."

"For obvious reasons."

The don was silent for a moment. Gabriel could hear him slurping coffee.

"It is important that this be about more than just blood," he said after a moment. "You have to recover the money as well."

"And if I'm able to?"

"A small payment of tribute to your Corsican godfather would be in order."

"How small?"

"One million should be sufficient."

"That's rather steep, Don Orsati."

"I was going to ask for five."

Gabriel thought about it for a moment and then accepted the terms. "But only if I can find the money," he stipulated. "Otherwise, I'm free to use Keller as I see fit, at no charge."

"Done," said Orsati. "But make sure you bring him home in one piece. Remember, money doesn't come from singing."

Gabriel settled in on the terrace with the Sancerre and the thick dossier on the inner workings of Downing Street under Jonathan Lancaster. But within an hour he was restless, so he called Don Orsati again and asked for permission to walk. The don gave his blessing and told Gabriel where he could find one of Keller's guns. A chunky HK 9mm, it was located in the drawer of a pretty French antique writing desk, directly beneath the Cézanne. "But be careful," the don cautioned. "Christopher sets his trigger pressure very light. He's a sensitive soul."

Gabriel slipped the weapon into the waistband of his jeans and set out along the narrow track, toward the three ancient olive trees. Thankfully, the goat had yet to return to its sentry post, which meant Gabriel was able to proceed into the village unmolested. It was the uncertain hour between late afternoon and evening. The houses were shuttered and the streets had been abandoned to cats and children. They watched Gabriel with great interest as he made his way to the main square. On three sides there were shops and cafés, and on the fourth was the church. Gabriel purchased a scarf for Chiara in one of the shops and then took a table at the least forbidding-looking of the cafés. He drank strong coffee to counter the effects of the Sancerre; then, as the sky darkened softly and the breeze turned chill, he drank rough Corsican red wine to counter the effects of the coffee. The doors of the church hung ajar. From inside came the murmur of prayer.

Gradually, the square began to fill with townspeople. Teenage boys sat astride their mopeds outside the ice cream parlor; a group of men started up a hard-fought game of *boules* in the center of the dusty esplanade. Shortly after six, about twenty people, old women mainly, came filing down the steps of the church. Among them was the *signadora*. Her gaze settled briefly on Gabriel, the unbeliever; then she disappeared through the doorway of her crooked little house. Soon after, two women came calling on her—an old widow dressed head to toe in black and a distraught-looking girl in her mid-twenties who, doubtless, was suffering the ill effects of the *occhju*.

A half hour later the two women reappeared, along with a boy, about ten years old, with long curly hair. The women made for the ice cream parlor, but the boy, after pausing a moment to watch the game of *boules*, came over to the café where Gabriel was sitting. In his hand was a slip of paper, pale blue and folded in quarters. He placed it on the table before Gabriel and then scurried off as though he feared he might catch something. Gabriel unfolded the slip of paper and in the fading light read the single line that had been written there:

I must see you at once.

Gabriel inserted the note into his coat pocket and sat there for several minutes debating what to do. Then he left a few coins on the table and headed across the square.

When he knocked on her door, a reedy voice invited him to enter. She was seated sleepily in a faded wing chair, her head lolling to one side, as though she were still suffering from the exertion of absorbing the evil that infected her previous visitors. Despite Gabriel's protests, she insisted on rising to greet him. This time there was no hostility in her expression, only concern. She touched Gabriel's cheek without speaking and stared directly into his eyes.

"Your eyes are so very green. You have your mother's eyes, yes?"

"Yes," said Gabriel.

"She suffered during the war, did she not?"

"Did Keller tell you that?"

"I've never spoken to Christopher about your mother."

"Yes," said Gabriel after a moment, "terrible things happened to my mother during the war."

"In Poland?"

"Yes, in Poland."

The *signadora* took one of Gabriel's hands in hers. "You're warm to the touch. Do you have fever?"

"No," said Gabriel.

She closed her eyes. "Your mother was a painter like you?"

"Yes."

"She was in the camps? The one that was named for the trees?"

"Yes, that's the one."

"I see a road, snow, a long line of women in gray clothing, a man with a gun."

Gabriel withdrew his hand quickly. The old woman's eyes opened with a start.

"I'm sorry. I didn't mean to upset you."

"Why did you want to see me?"

"I know why you came back here."

"And?"

"I want to help you."

"Why?"

"Because it is important that nothing happens to you in the days to come. The old man needs you. So does your wife."

"I'm not married," Gabriel lied.

"Her name is Clara, is it not?"

"No," said Gabriel, smiling. "Her name is Chiara."

"She is an Italian?"

"Yes."

"Then I will keep you in my prayers." She nodded toward her table where a plate of water and a vessel of olive oil stood next to a pair of burning candles. "Won't you sit down?"

"I'd rather not."

"You still don't believe?"

"I believe," he said.

"Then why won't you sit? Surely you're not afraid. Your mother named you Gabriel for a reason. You have the strength of God."

Gabriel felt as though a stone had been laid over his heart. He wanted to leave at once but curiosity made him stay. After helping the old woman into her chair, he sat opposite her and dipped his finger into the oil. Upon striking the surface of the water, the three drops shattered into a thousand before disappearing. The old woman nodded gravely, as if the test had confirmed her darkest fears. Then, for the second time, she took Gabriel's hand in hers.

"You're burning," she said. "Are you sure you're not unwell?"

"I was in the sun."

"At Christopher's house," she said knowingly. "You drank his wine. You have his gun on your hip."

"Go on."

"You're looking for a man, the man who killed the English girl."

"Do you know who he is?"

"No," she said. "But I know *where* he is. He's hiding in the east, in the city of heretics. You must never set foot there. If you do," she said firmly, "you will die."

She closed her eyes, and after a moment began to weep softly, a sign that the evil had flowed from Gabriel's body into hers. Then, with a nod, she instructed Gabriel to repeat the test of the oil and the water. This time the oil coalesced into a single drop. The old woman smiled in a way that Gabriel had never seen before.

"What do you see?" asked Gabriel.

"Are you sure you want to know?"

"Yes, of course."

"I see a child," she replied without hesitation.

"Whose child?"

She patted Gabriel's hand. "Go back to the villa," she said. "Your friend Christopher has returned to Corsica."

When Gabriel arrived at the villa, he found Keller standing before the open refrigerator. He wore a dark gray suit, wrinkled from travel, and a white dress shirt open at the neck. He withdrew the half-drunk bottle of Sancerre, gave it a demonstrative shake, and then dumped several inches of the wine into a glass.

"Rough day at the office, honey?" asked Gabriel.

"Brutal." He held up the bottle. "You?"

"I've had quite enough."

"I can see that."

"How was your trip?"

"The travel was hell," said Keller, "but everything else went smoothly."

"Who was he?"

Keller drank some of his wine without answering and asked Gabriel where he had been. When Gabriel told him that he had been to see the *signadora*, Keller smiled.

"We'll make a Corsican of you yet."

"It wasn't my idea," explained Gabriel.

"What did she want to tell you?"

"It was nothing," said Gabriel. "Just the usual hocus-pocus about the wind in the willows."

"Then why are you so pale?"

Gabriel made no response other than to place Keller's gun carefully on the countertop.

"From what I hear," Keller said, "you're going to need that."

"What do you hear?"

"I hear you're going on a hunting trip."

"Are you willing to help me?"

"Frankly," said Keller, raising his wineglass to the light, "I expected you a long time ago."

"I had a painting to finish."

"By whom?"

"Bassano."

"Studio of Bassano or Bassano Bassano?"

"A little of both."

"Nice," said Keller.

"How quickly can you be ready to move?"

"I have to check my calendar, but I suspect I'll be ready to go first thing in the morning. But you should know," he added, "that Marseilles is crawling with *flics* at the moment. And half of them are looking for us."

"Which is why we're not going anywhere near Marseilles, at least for now."

"So where are we going?"

Gabriel smiled. "We're going home."

32

CORSICA-LONDON

T HEY HAD DINNER IN THE village, then Gabriel settled into a guest suite on the lower level of the villa. The walls were white, the bedding was white, the armchair and otto-man were covered in sailcloth. The room's lack of color disturbed his sleep. That night, when he ran to Madeline in his dreams, he ran across an endless field of snow. And when she scratched at the back of her hand, the blood that flowed from the wound was the color of heavy cream.

In the morning they caught the first flight to Paris and then flew on to Heathrow. Keller cleared customs on a French passport, which Gabriel, who was waiting for him in the arrivals hall, thought was a most ignoble way for an Englishman to return to the land of his birth. They made their way outside and waited twenty minutes for a taxi. It crawled into central London through heavy traffic and rain.

"Now you know why I don't live here any longer," Keller said quietly in French as he stared out his rain-spattered window at the gray London suburbs.

"The moisture will do wonders for your skin," Gabriel replied in the same language. "You look like a piece of leather."

The taxi delivered them to Marble Arch. Gabriel and Keller walked a short distance along Bayswater Road, to the apartment house overlooking Hyde Park. The flat was precisely as he had left it the morning he had driven to France with the ransom money; in fact, Chiara's breakfast dishes were still in the sink. Gabriel dropped his bag in the main bedroom and took a gun from the floor safe. When he emerged, he found Keller standing in the window of the sitting room.

"Can you manage for a few hours on your own?" Gabriel asked.

"I'll be fine."

"Any plans?"

"I think I'll take a boat ride on the Serpentine and then pop over to Covent Garden for a bit of shopping."

"It might be better if you stayed here. You never know who you might bump into."

"I'm Regiment, luv."

Keller said nothing more; he didn't need to. He was SAS, which meant that, if he wanted, he could walk through a room of close friends and no one would know his name.

Gabriel headed down to the street and hailed a passing taxi. Twenty minutes later he was walking past the gated entrance of Downing Street, toward the Houses of Parliament. In his pocket was a single entry from his dossier, a lengthy article from London's *Daily Telegraph*. The headline read MADELINE HART—THE UNANSWERED QUESTIONS.

The article had been written by Samantha Cooke, the *Telegraph*'s chief Whitehall correspondent and one of Britain's most highly regarded journalists. She had been covering Jonathan Lancaster from the time he was a lowly backbencher and had chronicled his rise in a biography called *The Path to Power*. Despite the book's somewhat pretentious title, it had been well received, even by her competitors who were jealous of the advance paid by her London publisher. Samantha Cooke was the kind of reporter who knew much more than she could ever put into print, which is why Gabriel wanted to talk to her.

He rang the *Telegraph*'s switchboard and asked to be connected to her extension. The operator put him through without delay, and after a few seconds Samantha Cooke picked up. Gabriel suspected she was on a mobile phone because he could hear footsteps and the echo of baritone voices in a high-ceilinged room—perhaps the lobby of Parliament, which was just across the street from the café where Gabriel was sitting. He said he needed a few minutes of her time. He promised he would make it well worth her while. He never mentioned a name.

"Do you know how many calls I get like this every day?" she asked wearily.

"I can assure you, Ms. Cooke, you've never received a call like this before."

There was silence on the line. Clearly, she was intrigued.

"What's this about?"

"I'd rather not talk about it over the telephone."

"Oh, no, of course not."

"You're obviously skeptical."

"Obviously."

"Does your phone have an Internet connection?"

"Of course."

"A couple of years ago, a rather well-known Israeli intelligence officer was captured by Islamic terrorists and interrogated on camera. Their plan was to kill him, but it didn't work out that way. The video of the interrogation is still floating around on the Internet. Watch it and then call me."

He gave her a number and rang off. Two minutes later she called him back.

"I'd like to see you."

"Surely you can do better than that, Ms. Cooke."

"Please, Mr. Allon, would you consider granting me an audience?"

"Only if you apologize for treating me so rudely a moment ago."

"I offer my most profound and humble apology, and I hope you will find some way in your heart to forgive me."

"You're forgiven."

"Where are you?"

"Café Nero on Bridge Street."

"Unfortunately, I know it well."

"How soon can you be here?"

"Ten minutes."

"Don't be late," said Gabriel, and he severed the connection.

As it turned out, she *was* late—six minutes late, which explained why she came whirling through the door in a rush, a phone to her ear, her umbrella flapping in the wind that blew in with her. Most of the patrons in the café were tourists, but three gray-suited junior MPs were sipping lattes in the back. Samantha Cooke stopped to have a word with them before making her way to Gabriel's table. Her hair was ash blond and shoulder length. Her eyes were blue and probing. For several seconds they didn't move from Gabriel's face.

"My God," she said finally. "It really is you."

"What were you expecting?"

"Horns, I suppose."

"At least you're honest."

"It's one of my worst faults."

"Any others?"

"Curiosity," she said.

"Then you've come to the right place. Can I get you something to drink?"

"Actually," she said, looking around the room, "it might be better if we walked."

Gabriel rose and pulled on his coat.

They headed toward the Tower Bridge and then made a quick left onto the Victoria Embankment. The afternoon traffic moved slowly along the road, but the crowds that usually surged along the river walk had been chased away by the rain. Gabriel glanced over his shoulder to make certain they hadn't been followed from the café. Turning again, he noticed Samantha Cooke peering at him from beneath her umbrella as though he were on the endangered species list.

"You look much better than you did in that video," she said after a moment.

"It was all done with makeup."

She smiled in spite of herself. "Does it help?" she asked.

"To make jokes after something like that?"

She nodded.

"Yes," he said. "It helps."

"I met her once, you know."

"Who?"

"Nadia al-Bakari. It was when she was a nobody, a Saudi party girl, the spoiled daughter of Abdul Aziz al-Bakari, financier of Islamic terror." She looked at Gabriel's face for a reaction and seemed disappointed when there was none. "Is it true that you were the one who killed him?"

"Zizi al-Bakari was killed as the result of an operation initiated by the Americans and their allies in the global war on terror."

"But you were the one who actually pulled the trigger, weren't you? You killed him in Cannes, in front of Nadia. And then you recruited Nadia to take down Rashid al-Husseini's terror network. Brilliant," she said. "Truly brilliant."

"If I was so brilliant, Nadia would still be alive."

"But her death changed the world. It helped to bring democracy to the Arab world."

"And look how well that worked out," Gabriel said glumly.

They passed beneath the Hungerford Bridge as a train rumbled into Charing Cross. The rain eased. Samantha Cooke lowered her umbrella, wound it tightly, and inserted it into her handbag.

"I'm honored you came to me," she said, "but the Middle East isn't exactly my beat."

"This isn't about the Middle East. It's about Jonathan Lancaster."

She looked up sharply. "Why is a famous Israeli intelligence operative coming to a London reporter for information about the British prime minister?"

"It must be something important," Gabriel said evasively. "Otherwise, the famous Israeli operative would never dare to do such a thing."

"No, he wouldn't," she agreed. "But surely the famous operative has a great deal of information about Lancaster at his fingertips. Why would he ask a reporter for help?"

"Contrary to popular myth, we don't compile personal dossiers on our friends."

"Bullshit."

Gabriel hesitated for a moment. "This is a strictly personal matter, Ms. Cooke. My service isn't involved in any way."

"And if I agree to help you?"

"Obviously, I would give you something in return."

"A story?"

Gabriel nodded.

"But you can't tell me what it is," she said.

"Not yet."

"Whatever it is, it had better be something big."

"I'm Gabriel Allon. I only do big."

"Yes, you do." She stopped walking and gazed at the London Eye turning slowly on the opposite bank of the river. "All right, Mr. Allon, we have a deal. Perhaps you should tell me what this is all about."

Gabriel withdrew the *Telegraph* article from his coat pocket and held it up for her to see. Samantha Cooke smiled.

"Where would you like me to start?"

Gabriel returned the article to his coat pocket. Then he asked her to start with Jeremy Fallon.

33

LONDON

S HE WAS A GOOD REPORTER, and like all good reporters she provided her audience with the necessary background to put her story into proper context. Gabriel, a former resident of the United Kingdom, knew much of it already. He knew, for example, that Jeremy Fallon had been educated at University College London and had worked as an advertising copywriter before joining the political unit at Party headquarters. What Fallon discovered was that there was an antiquated campaign organization dedicated to selling a product that no one, least of all the British voting public, wanted to buy. His first priority was to change the way the Party did its polling. Fallon didn't care which party a particular voter supported; he wanted to know where the voter did his shopping, what programs the voter watched on television, and what hopes the voter had for his children. Most of all, Fallon wanted to know what the voter expected from his government. Quietly, working far from the public spotlight, Fallon set about retooling the Party's core policies to meet the needs of a modern British electorate. Then he went in search of the perfect pitchman to take his new product to market. He found one in Jonathan Lancaster. With Fallon's help, Lancaster successfully challenged for Party leader. Then, six months later, he was swept into Downing Street.

"Jeremy got the dream job as his reward," Samantha Cooke said. "Jonathan appointed him chief of staff and gave him more power than any other chief of staff in British history. Jeremy is Lancaster's gatekeeper and enforcer, a deputy prime minister in everything but name. Lancaster once told me it was the biggest mistake he'd ever made."

"On the record?"

"*Off*," she said pointedly. "Way, way, way off."

"If Lancaster knew it was a mistake, why did he do it?"

"Because without Jeremy, the Party would still be wandering in the proverbial political wilderness. And Jonathan Lancaster would still be a lowly opposition backbencher trying to make a name for himself once a week during PMQ. Besides," she added, "Jeremy is completely loyal to Lancaster. I'm quite confident he would kill for him and then volunteer to mop up the blood."

Gabriel wished he could tell her how right she was. Instead, he walked on in silence and waited for her to resume.

"But there was more to their relationship than just a bond of debt and loyalty. Lancaster *needed* Jeremy. He truly didn't believe he could govern the country without him at his side."

"So it's true, then?"

"What's that?"

"That Jeremy Fallon is Lancaster's brain."

"Actually, it's complete rubbish. But it didn't take long for that perception to take hold in the public. Even the Party's own internal polls showed a majority of Britons thought Jeremy was the one who was truly running the government." She paused thoughtfully. "That's why I was so surprised when Jeremy was at Lancaster's side the day he finally called the election."

"Surprised?"

"Not long ago there was a nasty rumor running round Whitehall that Lancaster was planning to push Jeremy out of Downing Street."

"Because he had become an electoral liability?"

Samantha Cooke nodded her head. "And because he was so unpopular within the Party that no one wanted to work for him."

"Why didn't you report it?"

"I didn't have the sourcing necessary to take it to print," she replied. "Some of us do have standards, you know."

"Do you think Jeremy Fallon heard the same rumors?"

"I can't imagine he didn't."

"Did he and Lancaster ever discuss it?"

"I was never able to confirm that, which is one of the reasons I didn't write about it. Thank God I didn't," she added. "I would have looked very foolish right about now."

They had reached Waterloo Bridge. Gabriel took her by the elbow and guided her toward the Strand.

"How well do you know him?" he asked.

"Jeremy?"

Gabriel nodded.

"I'm not sure anyone really knows Jeremy Fallon. I know him professionally, which means he tells me things he wants me to put in my newspaper. He's a manipulative bastard, which is why his performance at Madeline Hart's funeral was so peculiar. I never would have dreamed Jeremy was even capable of shedding a tear." She paused, then added, "I suppose it was true after all."

"What's that?"

"That Jeremy was in love with her."

Gabriel stopped and turned to face Samantha Cooke. "Are you saying that Jeremy Fallon and Madeline Hart were having an affair?"

"Madeline wasn't interested in Jeremy romantically," she replied, shaking her head. "But that didn't prevent her from using him to advance her career. She rose through the ranks rather too quickly, in my opinion. And I suspect it was all because of Jeremy."

A silence fell between them. They were standing on the pavement outside the Courtauld Gallery. Samantha Cooke was watching the traffic rushing along the Strand, but Gabriel was wondering why Jeremy Fallon had introduced a woman he loved to Jonathan Lancaster. Perhaps Fallon had wanted to create leverage over the man who was about to end his career in politics.

"Are you sure?" Gabriel asked after a moment.

"That Jeremy was smitten with Madeline?"

Gabriel nodded.

"As sure as one can be about something like that."

"Meaning?"

"I had it from multiple sources I trust. Jeremy used to make up the flimsiest excuses to contact her. Apparently, it was all rather pathetic."

"Why didn't you report it when she disappeared?"

"Because it didn't seem the right thing to do at the time," she replied. "And now that she's dead . . ."

Her voice trailed off. They entered the gallery, purchased two tickets, and climbed the staircase to the exhibition rooms. As usual, they were largely empty of visitors. In Room 7 they paused before the empty frame commemorating the theft of the Courtauld's signature piece, *Self-Portrait with a Bandaged Ear* by Vincent van Gogh.

"A pity," said Samantha Cooke.

"Yes," said Gabriel. He guided her to Gauguin's *Nevermore* and asked whether she had ever met Madeline Hart.

"Once," she replied, pointing toward the woman on the canvas, as though she were speaking about her rather than a woman who was dead. "I was doing a piece on the Party's efforts to connect with minority voters. Jeremy sent me to Madeline. I thought she was rather too pretty for her own good, but smart as a whip. Sometimes it seemed she was interviewing me rather than the other way around. I felt as though I was . . ." She lapsed into silence, as if searching for the right word. Then she said, "I felt as though I were being recruited— for what, I haven't a clue."

As the sound of her words died, Gabriel heard footsteps and, turning, saw a middle-aged couple enter the room. The man wore tinted eyeglasses and was bald except for a monkish tonsure. The woman was several years his junior and carried a museum guidebook open to the wrong page. They moved from painting to painting without speaking, stopping before each canvas for only a few seconds before moving mechanically to the next. Gabriel watched as the couple entered the adjoining exhibition room. Then he led Samantha Cooke downstairs, to the vast internal courtyard at the center of the building. In warm weather it was a popular gathering spot for Londoners who worked in the office blocks along the Strand. But now, in the chill rain, the metal café tables were empty and the dancing fountain splashed with the sadness of a toy in a nursery without children.

"You wrote well of Madeline after her disappearance," said Gabriel as they walked slowly around the perimeter of the courtyard.

"And I meant every word of it. She was remarkably composed and self-confident for someone of her upbringing." She paused and furrowed her brow thoughtfully. "I never understood the way her mother behaved during the days after she went missing. Most parents of missing persons talk to the press constantly. But not her. She was tight-lipped and insular throughout. And now it seems she's vanished from the face of the earth. Madeline's brother, too."

"What do you mean?"

"When I tried to contact her for that piece," she said, nodding toward the newspaper article in Gabriel's coat pocket, "there was no answer at their house. *Ever.* I finally drove out to bloody Essex and sat on the doorstep. A neighbor told me that Madeline's family hadn't been seen since shortly after the funeral."

Gabriel said nothing, but in his thoughts he was calculating the driving time between central London and Basildon, Essex, at the height of the evening rush.

"I've done a great deal of talking," Samantha Cooke was saying. "Now it's your turn. Why on earth is the great Gabriel Allon interested in a dead English girl?"

"I'm afraid I can't tell you yet."

"Will you ever?"

"That depends."

"You know," she said provocatively, "the very fact you're in London asking questions is quite a story."

"That's true," Gabriel admitted. "But you would never dare to report it or even mention our conversation to anyone."

"Why wouldn't I?"

"Because it would prevent me from giving you a much better story in the future."

Samantha Cooke smiled and looked at her wristwatch. "I'd love to spend about a week talking to you, but I really have to be going. I have a piece in tomorrow's paper."

"What are you writing about?"

"Volgatek Oil and Gas."

"The Russian energy company?"

"Very impressive, Mr. Allon."

"I try to keep up with the news. It helps in my line of work."

"I'm sure it does."

"What's the story?"

"The environmentalists and the global warming crowd are upset about the deal. They're predicting all the usual calamities—major oil spills, melting polar ice caps, oceanfront property in Chelsea, that sort of thing. They don't seem to care that the deal will generate billions of dollars in licensing fees and bring several thousand badly needed jobs to Scotland."

"So your piece will be balanced?" asked Gabriel.

"They always are," she shot back with a smile. "My sources tell me the deal was Jeremy's pet project, his last big initiative before leaving Downing Street to run for Parliament. I tried to talk to him about it, but he spoke two words that I'd never heard come out of his mouth before."

"What were they?"

"No comment."

With that, she gave him a business card, shook his hand, and disappeared through the arched passage that connected the courtyard to the Strand. Gabriel waited five minutes before following. As he turned into the street, he saw the man and woman from the gallery attempting to hail a taxi. He walked past them without a glance and continued to Trafalgar Square, where a thousand protesters were engaged in Two Minutes Hate directed against the State of Israel. Gabriel plunged into the throng and moved slowly through it, pausing now and again to see whether anyone was following. Finally, a heavenly cloudburst sent the demonstrators scurrying for cover. Gabriel fell in with a troupe of pro-Palestinian actors and artists who were heading off to the bars of Soho, but in Charing Cross Road he broke away and ducked into the Leicester Square Underground station. As he was riding the escalator downward into the warm earth, he called Keller.

"We need a car," he said in rapid French.

"Where are we going?"

"Basildon."

"Any particular reason?"

"I'll tell you on the way."

34

BASILDON, ESSEX

I T HAD BEEN CREATED AFTER World War II as part of a grand
scheme to reduce overcrowding in the bombed-out slums of London's East End. The result was what the central planners called
a New Town—a town without a history, without a soul, without a
purpose other than to warehouse the working classes. Its commercial
center, the Basildon town plaza, was a masterpiece of neo-Soviet ar-
chitecture. So, too, was the tower of council flats that loomed menacingly over one flank, like a giant slab of burnt toast.

A half mile farther to the east lay a tattered colony of apartment
blocks and terraced houses known as the Lichfields. The streets
all had agreeable names—Avon Way, Norwich Walk, Southwark
Path—but cracks split the pavements and weeds thrived in the
courts. A few of the houses had small front lawns, but the tiny unit
at the end of Blackwater Way had only a patch of broken concrete
where a worn-out car was usually parked. Its exterior was pebble-

dash on the ground floor and brown brick on the second. There were three small windows; all were curtained and dark. No light burned over the inhospitable little front door.

"Does anyone work?" asked Keller, as they drove slowly past the house for a second time.

"The mother works a few hours a week at the Boots pharmacy in the plaza," answered Gabriel. "The brother drinks for a living."

"And you're sure no one's in there?"

"Does it look occupied to you?"

"Maybe they like the dark."

"Or maybe they're vampires."

Gabriel eased the car into a common parking area around the corner and switched off the engine. Just beyond Keller's window was a sign warning that the entire area was under twenty-four-hour CCTV surveillance.

"I have a bad feeling about this."

"You just killed a man for money."

"Not on camera."

Gabriel said nothing.

"How long are you planning to stay in there?" asked Keller.

"As long as necessary."

"What happens if the police show up?"

"It might be a good idea if you let me know."

"And if they notice me sitting here?"

"Show them your French passport and tell them you're lost."

Without another word, Gabriel opened the car door and climbed out. As he started across the street, a dog began to bark somewhere in the estate. It must have been a very large dog, for each deep, sonorous volley echoed from the crumbling facades of the apartment blocks like cannon fire. For an instant Gabriel considered returning to the car—surely, he thought morosely, the beast had designs on his throat. Instead, he silently crossed the Harts' concrete garden and presented himself at their door.

There was no alcove or shelter from the steady rain. Gabriel tried the latch and, as expected, found it was locked. Then he withdrew a thin metal tool from his pocket and inserted it into the mechanism. A few seconds was all it took—indeed, a stranger might have assumed he was merely fumbling for his key in the dark. When he tried the latch a second time, it yielded without resistance. He eased the door open, stepped into the darkened void, and closed the door quickly. Outside the dog unleashed one last barrage of barks before finally falling silent. Gabriel returned the lock pick to his pocket, removed a small Maglite, and clicked the power switch.

He was standing in a cramped entrance hall. The linoleum floor was strewn with unread post, and on his right several cheap wool and oilskin coats hung from hooks. Gabriel emptied the coat pockets of litter—matchbooks, receipts, business cards—before following the beam of light into the sitting room. It was a claustro-phobic little space, about eight feet by ten, with three shabby arm-chairs arrayed around a television. In the center of the room was a low table with two overflowing ashtrays, and on one wall hung framed photographs of Madeline. Madeline as a young girl chasing a ball across a sunlit field. Madeline receiving her degrees from the University of Edinburgh. Madeline posing with Prime Minister Jonathan Lancaster at Downing Street. There was also a photo of the entire Hart family standing unhappily along a gray seashore. Gabriel stared at the broad, flat features of Madeline's parents and tried to imagine how they had been combined to produce a face as beautiful as hers. She was a mistake of nature, he thought. She was the child of a different God.

He left the sitting room and, after passing through a small dining room, entered the kitchen. Stacks of dirty dishes stood on the countertops, and in the basin was a pool of greasy water. The air was heavy with the stench of rot. Gabriel opened one of the foot-level cabinets and found a rubbish bin overflowing with spoiled food. There was more in the refrigerator. He wondered what could have possessed them to leave the house in such chaos.

Gabriel returned to the front entrance hall and climbed the narrow stairs to the second floor. There were three bedrooms—two tiny cells on the left side of the house and a larger room on the right, which he entered first. It belonged to Madeline's mother. The double bed had been left unmade, and a cold draft was pouring through an open window overlooking the dirt patch that was the rear garden. Gabriel opened the paper-thin closet door and shone the beam around the interior. The rod was hung with garments from end to end, and more clothing was stacked neatly on the shelf above it. Next he went to the dresser. All the drawers were filled to capacity except for the top left—the drawer, he thought, where a woman typically kept personal papers and keepsakes. Crouching, he shone a light beneath the bed but found nothing but clouds of dust. Then he went to the telephone. It stood on one of the matching bedside tables, next to an empty glass. He lifted the receiver to his ear but heard no dial tone. Then he pressed the playback button on the answering machine. There were no messages.

Gabriel crossed the hall and poked his head into one of the smaller bedrooms. It looked like the aftermath of a car bombing. Only the walls remained intact. They were plastered with the usual fare— football stars, supermodels, cars the occupant would never be able to afford. On the air hung a foul male odor that, thankfully, Gabriel had not encountered since leaving the army. He searched the room quickly but discovered nothing out of the ordinary—nothing except that it contained no object or slip of paper that bore the name of the creature who resided there.

The last room Gabriel entered was Madeline's room. It was not the Madeline who had been Jonathan Lancaster's lover, or the remnant of Madeline whom Gabriel had encountered in France, but the Madeline who had somehow survived a childhood spent in this sad little house. It seemed to Gabriel that she had accomplished it the same way she had survived a month in captivity, with neatness and order. Her bed was crisply made; her tiny schoolgirl's desk was ready for inspection. On it stood a row of classic English novels—Dickens, Austen, Forster, Lawrence. The volumes looked as though they had been read many times, and their pages were filled with underlined passages and notations written in a small, precise hand. Gabriel was about to slip one of the books, *A Room with a View*, into his coat pocket when his mobile phone vibrated softly. He picked up the call and brought the phone quickly to his ear.

"We've got company," said Keller.

"How many?"

"It looks like just one, but I can't be sure."

Gabriel parted the gauzy curtains of Madeline's window a fraction of an inch and saw a woman walking along Blackwater Way beneath the shelter of an umbrella. As she passed through a cone of yellow lamplight, he glimpsed her face briefly and realized at once that he had seen it somewhere before. The answer came to him as she veered into the concrete drive. It had been in an ancient church, in the mountains of the Lubéron. She was the woman who had crossed herself as though the movement were unfamiliar to her. And for some reason she was now inserting a key into Madeline Hart's front door.

Gabriel switched off the phone and drew the gun from the small of his back. He was tempted to steal down the stairs and confront the woman immediately, but decided it was better to wait. Eventually, he thought, the woman would tell him who she was and why she was here, preferably without realizing she had done so. That was always the best way to acquire a piece of intelligence—without the knowledge of the target. As Shamron always preached, it was better for a spy to be a pickpocket than a mugger.

And so Gabriel stood stock-still in Madeline Hart's childhood room, the barrel of the gun pressed reassuringly to his cheek, as the woman stepped into the entrance hall and quietly closed the door. She emitted a single syllable that was unfamiliar to Gabriel. Then came a series of swishes and rustles that suggested she was gathering up the post and placing it into a plastic bag. Next she moved into the sitting room, where she spent approximately two minutes. Then she entered the kitchen and again uttered the same single syllable. Gabriel suspected it was a vulgarity from a language other than English, Hebrew, French, Italian, or German. He suspected something else, too. The woman, whoever she was, was searching the house, just as Gabriel had before her arrival.

When her footfalls reached the base of the stairs, Gabriel was seized by a moment of indecision. If he was right about the woman's intentions—that she was looking for something—she would surely search Madeline's bedroom. He glanced around to see if there was a place to conceal himself but saw nothing suitable; the room was scarcely larger than the cell where Madeline had been held captive in France. As the woman's steps grew louder, Gabriel decided he had no choice but to leave. But where? The bathroom was just across the hall. As he entered it without a sound, he wondered what Shamron would be thinking if he could see the future chief of Israeli intelligence at this moment. He would approve, thought Gabriel. In fact, he was certain the great Ari Shamron had taken cover in places that were far more professionally degrading than the bathroom of a Basildon council house.

He left the door slightly ajar—a quarter inch, no more—and held the gun in his outstretched hands as the woman completed her journey up the stairs. She entered the largest bedroom first and, judging from the sound of opening drawers and slamming doors, searched it thoroughly. Five minutes later she emerged and walked past the bathroom without pausing, seemingly unaware a gun was at that instant pointed at her head. She was wearing the same tan raincoat she had worn in France, though her hair was arranged slightly differently. In her left hand was a green shopping bag from Marks & Spencer. It looked as though it contained more than just unread post.

When she entered Madeline's room, her search turned suddenly violent. It was a professional search, thought Gabriel, listening. *A crash search* . . . She tore clothing from the closet, ripped sheets from the bed, and emptied the contents of drawers onto the floor. Finally, there was a sharp crack, like the splintering of wood, followed by a heavy silence. It was broken a moment later by the sound of her voice. It was low and calm, the kind of voice one uses to deliver news to a superior over a device that transmitted a signal over the open airwaves. Gabriel couldn't understand what she was saying—he had no ear for Slavic tongues—but he was certain of one thing.

The woman was speaking Russian.

35

BASILDON, ESSEX

ER CAR, A BOXY OLD Volvo sedan, was parked across the street from the meanest of the Lichfields apartment blocks. She walked to it directly, the umbrella in her right hand, the green Marks & Spencer bag in her left. The umbrella was purely cosmetic, thought Gabriel, watching from Madeline's window, for the rain had ended. The bag looked heavy. After opening the car door, she swung the bag onto the front passenger seat, then climbed in, leaving the umbrella unfurled until she was safely inside. The engine hesitated before coughing to life. She waited until she had reached the perimeter of the estate before switching on the headlamps. She drove fast but smoothly, like a professional.

Gabriel took one last look at the destruction the woman had wrought in Madeline's room and then hurried down the stairs. By the time he stepped from the doorway, Keller had pulled the car around and was waiting outside in the street. Gabriel climbed in quickly and nodded for Keller to follow the woman.

"— be careful," he cautioned. "She's good."

"How good?"

"Moscow Center good."

"What are you talking about?"

"I could be wrong," said Gabriel, "but I believe the woman driving that car is KGB."

───────────

Technically, there was no KGB, of course. It had been disbanded not long after the collapse of the old Soviet empire. The Russian Federation now had two intelligence services: the FSB and the SVR. The FSB handled matters inside Russia's borders: counterintelligence, counterterrorism, the *mafiya*, the pro-democracy activists who were brave enough, or stupid enough, to challenge the men who now ruled Russia from behind the walls of the Kremlin. The SVR was Russia's foreign intelligence service. It ran its global network of spies from the same secluded campus in Yasenevo that had served as the headquarters of the KGB's First Chief Directorate. SVR officers still called the building Moscow Center—and, not surprisingly, even Russian citizens still referred to the SVR as the KGB. And for good reason. The Kremlin might have changed the name of Russia's intelligence service, but the SVR's mission remained the same—to penetrate and weaken the nations of the old Atlantic alliance, with the United States and Great Britain at the top of its list.

But why had an SVR field agent followed Gabriel and Keller to an ancient church in the mountains of the Lubéron? And why had the same SVR field agent just searched the family home of a dead

English girl named Madeline Hart? A girl who had been the lover of the British prime minister. A girl who had been kidnapped while on holiday on the island of Corsica and held for ransom. A girl who had burned to death in the trunk of a Citroën C4, on the beach at Audresselles.

"Let's not get ahead of ourselves," said Keller.

"I know what I heard," replied Gabriel.

"You heard a woman speaking Russian."

"No," countered Gabriel, "I heard a Moscow Center agent turning over a room."

They were headed west on the A127. The time was approaching eight o'clock. The eastbound lanes were still thick with the remnants of the London evening rush, but the westbound side was moving at speed. The woman was about two hundred yards ahead. Keller had no trouble keeping track of the old Volvo's distinctive taillights.

"Let's assume you're right," he said, staring straight ahead. "Let's assume that the KGB, or the SVR, or whatever the hell you want to call it, is somehow connected to the kidnapping of Madeline Hart."

"I would argue that, at this moment in time, that fact is beyond dispute."

"Point taken," said Keller. "But what's the link?"

"I'm still working on that. But if I had to guess, I'd say it was their operation from the beginning."

"Operation?" asked Keller incredulously. "You're saying the Russians kidnapped the mistress of the British prime minister?"

Gabriel made no reply. He didn't quite believe it yet, either.

"Would you allow me to remind you of a few salient facts?" Keller asked.

"Please do."

"Marcel Lacroix and René Brossard weren't Russian, and they didn't work for the SVR. They were both French organized crime figures with a long track record in Marseilles and the south of France."

"Maybe they didn't realize who they were working for."

"What about Paul?"

"We don't know anything about him except that he speaks French like he learned it from a tape—or so said the great Don Anton Orsati of Corsica."

"Peace be upon him."

Gabriel rapped his knuckle on the windshield and said, "She's too far ahead of you."

"I've got her."

"Close the gap some."

Keller accelerated for a few seconds, then eased off the throttle.

"You think Paul is Russian?" he asked.

"That would help explain why the French police were never able to attach a name to his face."

"But why would he hire French criminals to kidnap Madeline instead of doing the job himself?"

"Have you ever heard of a false flag operation?" asked Gabriel. "Intelligence services routinely conduct operations that would cause diplomatic or political damage if they were ever exposed. So they cloak those activities under a false flag. Sometimes they pose as operatives from another service. Or sometimes they pose as something else entirely."

"Like French criminals?"

"You'd be surprised."

"There's just one problem with your theory."

"Just one?"

"The SVR doesn't need money."

"I doubt very much that this was about money."

"You gave them two suitcases filled with ten million euros."

"Yes, I know."

"If this wasn't about money, what was the payment all about?"

"They flew the false flag until the end," said Gabriel.

Keller was silent for a moment. Finally, he asked, "But why did they kill Madeline?"

"I don't know."

"Where's her family?"

"I don't know."

"How did the Russians find out about Madeline and Lancaster?"

"I don't know that, either."

"There's someone who might."

"Who's that?"

"The woman driving that car," said Keller, pointing over the steering wheel toward the taillights of the Volvo.

"It's better to be a pickpocket than a mugger."

"What does that mean?"

"Close the gap," said Gabriel, rapping his knuckle against the glass. "She's too far ahead of you."

She passed beneath the M25 ring road, sped over a landscape of farms and fields, and then entered the suburbs of metropolitan London. After thirty minutes the suburbs gave way to the boroughs of the East End and, eventually, to the office towers of the City. From there, she headed across Holborn and Soho to Mayfair, where she pulled to the curb of a busy section of Duke Street, just south of Oxford Street. After engaging the emergency flashers, she climbed out of the Volvo and carried the Marks & Spencer bag toward a Mercedes sedan that was parked a few feet away. As she approached the car, the trunk lid rose automatically, though Gabriel could see no evidence the woman had been the one to open it. She placed the bag inside, closed the lid with a thump, and returned to the Volvo. Ten seconds later she eased carefully away from the curb and headed toward Oxford Street.

"What should I do?" asked Keller.

"Let her go."

"Why?"

"Because the person who opened the trunk of that Mercedes is watching to see if she's being tailed."

Keller scanned the street. So did Gabriel. There were restaurants on both sides, all of them catering to the tourist trade, and the pavements were crowded with pedestrians. Any one of them might have been carrying the key to the Mercedes.

"What now?" asked Keller.

"We wait."

"For what?"

"I'll know it when I see it."

"Pickpockets and muggers?"

"Something like that."

Keller was staring at the Mercedes, but Gabriel was looking around at the culinary nightmare that was upper Duke Street: Pizza Hut, Garfunkel's, something called Pure Waffle, whatever that meant. The class of the street was Bella Italia, a chain restaurant with locations scattered across the city, and it was there that Gabriel's gaze finally settled. A man and a woman several years apart in age were at that moment stepping from the doorway, presumably having finished their meal. The man wore a waxed hat against the light drizzle, and the woman was staring into her handbag as though she had misplaced something. Earlier that day, in the exhibition rooms of the Courtauld Gallery, she had been carrying a guidebook open to the wrong page, and the man had been wearing tinted eyeglasses. Now he wore no spectacles at all. After helping the woman into the front passenger seat of the Mercedes, he walked around to the driver's side and climbed behind the wheel. The engine, when started, seemed to make the street vibrate. Then the car shot away from the curb with a sharp chirp of its tires and barreled across Oxford Street at the instant the traffic signal turned to red.

"Well played," said Keller.

"Indeed," replied Gabriel.

"Should I try to follow him?"

Gabriel shook his head slowly. They were good, he thought. Moscow Center good.

The Grand Hotel Berkshire was not grand, nor was it in the enchanted English county of Berkshire. It stood at the end of a terrace of flaking Edwardian houses in West Cromwell Road, with a discount electronics store on one flank and a suspect Internet café on the other. Gabriel and Keller arrived at midnight. They had no reservation and no luggage; it was still inside the Bayswater safe flat, which Gabriel now assumed was under Russian surveillance. He paid for a two-night stay in cash and told the night clerk that he and his companion were expecting no guests and wanted no interruptions of any kind, including maid service. The night clerk found nothing unusual in Gabriel's instructions. The Grand Hotel Berkshire—or GHB, as management referred to it in shorthand—catered to those who took the road less traveled.

Their room was on the uppermost floor, the fourth, and had a sniper's view of the road. Gabriel insisted Keller sleep first. Then he sat in the window, with the gun in his lap and his feet resting on the sill, five questions running ceaselessly through his thoughts. Why would the Russian intelligence service be so reckless as to kidnap the mistress of the British prime minister? Why had there been a payment of ransom when surely money was not what the Russians wanted? Why had they killed Madeline? Where was her family? And how much did Jonathan Lancaster and Jeremy Fallon know? Satisfactory answers eluded him. He could make educated guesses, deductions, but nothing more. He needed to pick a few more pockets, he thought—and, if necessary, he would carry out a mugging or two as well. And then what? He thought of the old *signadora* and her prophecies about an old enemy and the city of heretics in the east.

You must never set foot there. If you do, you will die . . .

Just then, a newspaper delivery truck screeched to a halt outside the Tesco Express on the other side of the road. Gabriel looked at his wristwatch. It was nearly four o'clock, time to wake Keller and get a few hours' sleep himself. Instead, he picked up the volume of E. M. Forster he had taken from Madeline's room, opened it to a random page, and began to read:

> Some complicated game had been playing up and down the hillside all the afternoon. What it was and exactly how the players had sided, Lucy was slow to discover . . .

Gabriel closed the volume and watched the delivery truck move off along the wet, darkened street. And then he understood. But how to prove it? He needed the help of someone who knew the dark world of Russian business and politics. Someone who was just as ruthless as the men in the Kremlin.

He needed Viktor Orlov.

36

CHELSEA, LONDON

VIKTOR ORLOV HAD ALWAYS BEEN good with numbers. Born in Moscow during the darkest days of the Cold War, he had attended the prestigious Leningrad Institute of Precision Mechanics and Optics and had worked as a physicist in the Soviet nuclear weapons program. At the suggestion of his superiors, he joined the Communist Party—though many years later, in an interview with a British newspaper, he would claim he was never a true believer. "I joined the Party," he said without a trace of remorse, "because it was the only avenue of career advancement available to me. I suppose I could have been a dissident, but the gulag never seemed like a terribly appealing place to me."

When the Soviet Union finally breathed its last, Orlov did not shed a tear. In fact, he became wildly drunk on cheap Soviet vodka and ran through the streets of Moscow shouting, "The king is dead." The next morning, thoroughly hungover, he renounced his membership in the Communist Party, resigned from the Soviet nuclear program, and vowed to become rich. Within a few years, Orlov had earned a sizable fortune importing computers, appliances, and other Western goods for the nascent Russian market. Later, he used that fortune to acquire Russia's largest state-owned steel company along with Ruzoil, the Siberian oil giant, at bargain-basement prices. Before long, Viktor Orlov, a former government physicist who once had to share an apartment with two other Soviet families, was a billionaire many times over and the richest man in Russia. He was one of the original oligarchs, a modern-day robber baron who built his empire by looting the crown jewels of the Soviet state. Orlov was unapologetic about how he had become wealthy. "Had I been born an Englishman," he once told a British interviewer, "my money might have come to me cleanly. But I was born a Russian. And I earned a Russian fortune."

But in post-Soviet Russia, a land with no rule of law and rife with crime and corruption, Orlov's fortune made him a marked man. He survived at least three attempts on his life, and it was rumored that he had ordered several men killed in retaliation. But the greatest threat to Orlov would come from the man who succeeded Boris Yeltsin as president of Russia. He believed that Viktor Orlov and the other oligarchs had stolen the country's most valuable assets, and it was his intention to steal them back. After settling into the Kremlin, the new president summoned Orlov and demanded two things: his steel company and Ruzoil. "And keep your nose out of politics," he added ominously. "Otherwise, I'm going to cut it off."

Orlov agreed to relinquish his steel interests but not Ruzoil. The president was not amused. He immediately ordered prosecutors to open a fraud-and-bribery investigation, and within a week he had an arrest warrant in hand. Orlov wisely fled to London, where he became one of the Russian president's most vocal and effective critics. For several years, Ruzoil remained legally icebound, beyond the reach of both Orlov and the new masters of the Kremlin. Finally, Orlov was convinced to surrender it as part of a secret deal to secure the release of four people who had been taken hostage by a Russian arms dealer named Ivan Kharkov. In return, the British rewarded Orlov by making him a subject of the realm and granting him a brief and very private meeting with Her Majesty the Queen. The Office gave him a note of gratitude, which had been dictated by Chiara and handwritten by Gabriel. Ari Shamron delivered the note in person and burned it when Orlov had finished reading it.

"Will I ever get the opportunity to meet this remarkable man in person?" Orlov had asked.

"No," Shamron had replied.

Undeterred, Orlov had given Shamron his most private number, which Shamron had given to Gabriel. He called it later that morning, from a public phone near the Grand Hotel Berkshire, and was surprised when Orlov answered himself.

"I'm one of the people you saved by giving up Ruzoil," Gabriel said without mentioning his name. "The one who wrote you the note that the old man burned after you read it."

"He was one of the most disagreeable creatures I've ever met."

"Wait until you get to know him a little better."

Orlov emitted a small, dry laugh. "To what do I owe the honor?"

"I need your help."

"The last time you needed my help, it cost me an oil company worth at least sixteen billion dollars."

"This time it won't cost you a thing."

"I'm free at two this afternoon."

"Where?"

"Number Forty-Three," said Orlov.

And then the line went dead.

Number Forty-Three was the street address of Viktor Orlov's red-brick mansion on Cheyne Walk in Chelsea. Gabriel made his way there on foot, with Keller running countersurveillance a hundred yards behind. The house was tall and narrow and covered in wisteria. Like its neighbors, it was set back from the street, behind a wrought-iron fence. An armored Bentley limousine stood outside, a chauffeur at the wheel. Directly behind the Bentley was a black Range Rover, occupied by four members of Orlov's security detail. All were former members of Keller's old regiment: the elite Special Air Service.

The bodyguards watched Gabriel with obvious curiosity as he headed up the garden walk and presented himself at Orlov's front door. The doorbell, when pressed, produced a maid in a starched black-and-white uniform. After ascertaining Gabriel's identity, she conveyed him up a flight of wide, elegant stairs to Orlov's office. The room was an exact replica of the queen's private study in Buckingham Palace—all except for the giant plasma media wall that flickered with financial newscasts and market data from around the world. As Gabriel entered, Orlov was standing before it, as if in a trance. As usual, he wore a dark Italian suit and a lavish pink necktie bound in an enormous Windsor knot. His thinning gray hair was gelled and spiked. Reflected numbers glowed softly in the lenses of his fashionable eyeglasses. He was motionless except for the left eye, which was twitching nervously.

"How much did you make today, Viktor?"

"Actually," said Orlov, still staring at the video wall, "I think I lost ten or twenty million."

"I'm sorry to hear that."

"Tomorrow's another day."

Orlov turned and regarded Gabriel silently for a long moment before finally extending a manicured hand. His skin was cool to the touch and peculiarly soft. It was like shaking hands with an infant.

"Because I am a Russian," he said, "I'm not easily shocked. But I have to admit I am truly surprised to see you standing here in my office. I assumed we would never meet."

"I'm sorry, Viktor. I should have come a long time ago."

"I understand why you didn't." Orlov smiled sadly. "We have something in common, you and I. We were both targeted by the Kremlin. And we both managed to survive."

"Some of us have survived better than others," said Gabriel, glancing around the magnificent room.

"I've been lucky. And the British government has been very good to me," Orlov added pointedly, "which is why I want to do nothing that might upset the powers that be in Whitehall."

"Our interests are the same."

"I'm glad to hear that. So, Mr. Allon, why don't you tell me what this is all about?"

"Volgatek Oil and Gas."

Orlov smiled. "Well," he said, "I'm glad *someone* finally noticed."

37

CHEYNE WALK, CHELSEA

VIKTOR ORLOV HAD NEVER BEEN reluctant to talk about
money. In fact, he rarely talked about anything else. He
boasted that his suits cost ten thousand dollars each, that
his handmade dress shirts were the finest in the world, and that the
diamond-and-gold watch he wore on his wrist was among the most
expensive ever made. The current incarnation of the watch was actually his second. He had famously destroyed the first in Switzerland,
when he had struck it against a pine tree while skiing. "Silly me," he
told a British tabloid after the multimillion-dollar crash, "but I forgot
to take the damn thing off before leaving the chalet."

His wine of choice was Château Pétrus, the famous Pomerol that
he drank as though it were Evian. It was a bit early in the afternoon,
even for Orlov, so they had tea instead. Orlov drank his Russian
style, through a sugar cube that he held between his front teeth. His
arm was flung toward Gabriel along the back of an elegant brocade

couch, and he was twirling his costly spectacles by the stem, something he always did when he was speaking about Russia.

It was not the Russia of his childhood, or the Russia he had served as a nuclear scientist, but the Russia that had stumbled into existence after the collapse of the Soviet Union. It was lawless Russia—drunken, confused, lost Russia. Its traumatized people had been promised cradle-to-grave security. Now, suddenly, they had to fend for themselves. It was social Darwinism at its most vicious. The strong preyed on the weak, the weak went hungry, and the oligarchs reigned supreme. They became the new tsars of Russia, the new commissars. They blew through Moscow in bulletproof caravans surrounded by heavily armed security details. At night, the security details fought each other in the streets. "It was the Wild East," said Orlov reflectively. "It was madness."

"But you loved it," said Gabriel.

"What was not to love? We were gods, truly."

Early in his career as a capitalist, Orlov had run his burgeoning empire alone and with an iron fist. But after the acquisition of Ruzoil, he realized he needed a second-in-command. He found one in Gennady Lazarev, a brilliant theoretical mathematician he had worked within the Soviet nuclear weapons program. Lazarev knew nothing of capitalism, but like Orlov he was good with numbers. Lazarev learned the business from the ground up. Then Orlov placed him in charge of Ruzoil's day-to-day operations. It was, said Orlov, the biggest mistake he had ever made in business.

"Why?" asked Gabriel.

"Because Gennady Lazarev was KGB," Orlov answered. "He was KGB when he was working inside the nuclear weapons program, and he was KGB when I placed him in charge of Ruzoil."

"You never had any suspicions?"

Orlov shook his head. "He was very good—and very loyal to the sword and the shield, which is how the KGB thugs like to refer to themselves. Needless to say," Orlov added, "Lazarev betrayed me. He gave the Kremlin mountains of internal documents—documents that the state prosecutors then used to fabricate a case against me. And when I fled the country, Lazarev ran Ruzoil as though it were his own."

"He cut you out?"

"Completely."

"And when you agreed to give up Ruzoil in order to get us out of Russia?"

"Lazarev was already gone by then. He was running a new state-owned petroleum company. Apparently, the Russian president chose the name for this enterprise himself. He called it Volgatek Oil and Gas. There was a joke running round the Kremlin at the time that the president wanted to call the company KGB Oil and Gas but didn't think that would play well in the West."

Volgatek, Orlov resumed, was to have no role in domestic Russian oil production, which had already leveled off. Instead, its sole purpose was to expand Russia's oil and gas interests internationally, thus increasing the Kremlin's global power and influence. Backed by Kremlin money, Volgatek went on a shopping spree in Europe, purchasing a chain of oil refineries in Poland, Lithuania, and Hungary. Then, over the objections of the Americans, it signed a lucrative drilling agreement with the Islamic Republic of Iran. It also signed development deals with Cuba, Venezuela, and Syria.

"Do you see a pattern here?" asked Orlov.

"The deals Volgatek struck were all in the lands of the old Soviet empire or in countries hostile to the United States."

"Correct," said Orlov.

But Volgatek wasn't content to stop there, he added. It expanded its operations into Western Europe, signing distribution and refinery deals in Greece, Denmark, and the Netherlands. Then it set its sights on the North Sea, where it wanted to drill in two newly discovered fields off the Western Isles of Scotland. Volgatek's geologists estimated that production would eventually reach one hundred thousand barrels a day, with a large portion of profits flowing directly into the coffers of the Kremlin. The company applied to Britain's Department of Energy and Climate Change for a license. And then the secretary of state for energy asked Viktor Orlov to pop over to his office for a chat.

"And what do you think I told him?"

"That Volgatek was a wholly owned subsidiary of the Kremlin, run by a former member of the KGB."

"And what do you think the secretary of state for energy did with Volgatek's application to drill in territorial waters of Britain?"

"He dropped it into his shredder."

"Right before my eyes," added Orlov, smiling. "It was a most satisfying sound."

"Did the Kremlin know that you were the one who sabotaged the deal?"

"Not to my knowledge," replied Orlov. "But I'm sure Lazarev and the Russian president suspected I was somehow involved. They're always willing to believe the worst about me."

"What happened next?"

"Volgatek waited a year. Then it filed a second application for the drilling license. But this time, things were different. They had a friend inside Downing Street, a man who they'd spent a year cultivating."

"Who?"

"I'd rather not say."

"Fine," responded Gabriel. "Then I'll say it for you. Volgatek's man inside Downing Street was Jeremy Fallon, the most powerful chief of staff in British history."

Orlov smiled. "Perhaps we should have a bottle of Pétrus after all."

They had sailed into dangerous waters. Gabriel knew it, and Orlov surely knew it, too, for his left eye was beating a furious rhythm. When he was a child, the twitch had made him the target of merciless teasing and bullying. It had made him burn with hatred, and that hatred had driven him to succeed. Viktor Orlov wanted to beat everyone. And it was all because of the twitch in his left eye.

For now, the eye was staring into a goblet of dark-red Pomerol wine. Orlov had yet to drink from it. Nor had he answered the rather straightforward question that Gabriel had posed a moment earlier. Why Jeremy Fallon?

"Why *not* Fallon?" the Russian said at last. "Fallon was Lancaster's brain. Fallon was the puppet master. Fallon pulled a string, and Lancaster waved his hand. And better yet, he was vulnerable to an approach."

"How so?"

"He didn't have a pot to piss in. He was poor as a church mouse."

"Who suggested targeting him?"

"I'm told it came from the SVR *rezidentura* here in London."

Rezidentura was the word used by the SVR to describe its operations inside local embassies. The *rezident* was the station chief, the *rezidentura* the station itself. It was a holdover from the days of the KGB. Most things about the SVR were.

"How did they go about it?"

"Lazarev and Fallon started bumping into each other in all the wrong places: parties, restaurants, conferences, holidays. Rumor has it Fallon spent a long weekend at Lazarev's place in Gstaad and cruised the Greek islands on Lazarev's yacht. I'm told they got along famously, but that's not surprising. Gennady can be a charming bastard when he wants to be."

"But there was more than just a charm offensive, wasn't there, Viktor?"

"*Much* more."

"How much?"

"Five million euros in a numbered Swiss bank account, courtesy of the Kremlin. Very clean. Completely untraceable. The SVR handled all the arrangements."

"Says who?"

"Says I'd rather not say."

"Come on, Viktor."

"You obviously have your sources, Mr. Allon, and I have mine."

"At least tell me the direction your information comes from."

"It comes from the East," said Orlov, meaning it came from one of his many sources in Moscow.

"Go on," said Gabriel.

Orlov partook of the wine first. Then he explained how Volgatek filed a second application for a license to drill in the North Sea, this time with the backing of the second most powerful man in Whitehall. But the prime minister was still ambivalent at best, and the secretary of state for energy remained absolutely opposed. Fallon prevailed upon the secretary not to reject the application outright. It was technically alive, but just barely.

"And then," said Orlov, raising one arm toward the ceiling, "the secretary of state suddenly approves the license, Jonathan Lancaster jets off to Moscow for champagne toasts in the Kremlin, and the man who accepted five million euros in Russian money is about to become the next chancellor of the exchequer."

"I need to know your source for the five million."

"Asked and answered," replied the Russian curtly.

Gabriel changed the subject. "What's the state of relations between Volgatek and your business here in London?"

"As you might expect, we are in a state of war. It's rather like the Cold War—undeclared but vicious."

"How so?"

"Lazarev has outbid me on a number of acquisitions. It's easy for him," Orlov added resentfully. "He's not playing with his own money. He also takes great pleasure in hiring away my best people. He throws a pile of money at them—Kremlin money, of course— and they bolt for greener pastures."

"Are you on speaking terms?"

"I wouldn't go that far," Orlov said. "When we encounter one another in public, we nod politely and exchange frozen smiles. Our war is conducted entirely in the shadows. I must admit Gennady's gotten the better of me lately. And now he's going to be drilling for oil in the waters of a country I've come to love. It makes me sick to my stomach."

"Then maybe you should do something about it."

"Like what?"

"Help me blow up the deal."

Orlov stopped twirling his eyeglasses and stared directly at Gabriel for a moment without speaking. "What is your interest in this matter?" he asked finally.

"It's strictly personal."

"Why would someone like *you* care whether a Russian energy company gets access to North Sea oil?"

"It's complicated."

"Coming from you, I would expect nothing less."

Gabriel smiled in spite of himself. Then, quietly, he said, "I believe the Kremlin blackmailed Jonathan Lancaster into giving Volgatek those drilling rights."

"How?"

Gabriel was silent.

"I gave up a company worth sixteen billion dollars in order to get you and your wife out of Russia," Orlov said. "I believe that entitles me to an answer. How did they do it?"

"By kidnapping Lancaster's mistress from the island of Corsica."

Orlov didn't bat an eye. "Well," he said again. "I'm glad *someone* finally noticed."

They talked until the windows in Viktor Orlov's magnificent office turned to black, and then they talked a little longer. By the end of their conversation, Gabriel felt confident he understood how the game on the hillside had been played, but precisely how the players had sided themselves remained just beyond his grasp. He was certain of one thing, though; it was time to have a quiet word with Graham Seymour. He called him from a public phone in Sloane Square and confessed that he had once again entered the country without first signing the guestbook. Then he requested a meeting. Seymour recited a time and a place and rang off without another word. Gabriel replaced the receiver and started walking, with Christopher Keller running countersurveillance a hundred yards behind.

38

HAMPSTEAD HEATH, LONDON

THEY WALKED TO HYDE PARK CORNER, boarded a Picca-dilly Line train to Leicester Square, and then took the long slow ride on the Northern Line up to Hampstead. Keller entered a small café in the High Street and waited there while Gabriel made his way alone up South End Road. He entered the heath at the Pryors Field, skirted the banks of the Hampstead Ponds, and then climbed the gentle slope of Parliament Hill. In the distance, veiled by low cloud and mist, glowed the lights of the City of London. Graham Seymour was admiring the view from a wooden park bench. He was alone except for a pair of raincoated security men who stood with the stillness of chess pieces along the footpath at his back. They averted their eyes as Gabriel slipped wordlessly past them and sat down at Seymour's side. The MI5 man gave no sign he was aware of Gabriel's presence. Once again, he was smoking.

"You've really got to stop that," said Gabriel.

"And *you* really should have told me you were coming back into the country," replied Seymour. "I would have arranged a reception committee."

"I didn't want a reception committee, Graham."

"Obviously." Seymour was still contemplating the lights of central London. "How long have you been in town?"

"I came in yesterday afternoon."

"Why?"

"Unfinished business."

"Why?" asked Seymour again.

"Madeline," said Gabriel. "I'm here because of Madeline."

Seymour turned his head and looked at Gabriel for the first time. "Madeline is dead," he said slowly.

"Yes, Graham, I know that. I was there."

"I'm sorry," Seymour said after a moment. "I shouldn't have—"

"Forget about it, Graham."

The two men lapsed into an uneasy silence. It was the nature of this unfortunate case, thought Gabriel. They had both gotten into the intelligence business to protect their countries and their fellow citizens, not their politicians.

"You must have discovered something important," Seymour said finally. "Otherwise, you wouldn't have called me."

"You were always good, Graham."

"Not good enough to keep you from entering my country anytime you please."

Gabriel was silent.

"What have you got?"

"I believe I know who kidnapped Madeline Hart. More important," Gabriel added, "I believe I know *why* she was kidnapped."

"Who was it?"

"KGB Oil and Gas," answered Gabriel.

Seymour's head turned sharply. "What are you talking about?"

"It was the Volgatek deal, Graham. Madeline was kidnapped so the Russians could steal your oil."

There is no worse feeling for a professional spy than to be told something by an officer from another service that he should have already known himself. Graham Seymour suffered this indignity with as much grace as possible, with his chin up and his head held high. Then, after carefully weighing the consequences, he asked for an explanation. Gabriel began by telling him everything he had learned about Jeremy Fallon. That Fallon had been in love with Madeline Hart. That Fallon had worn out his welcome at Downing Street and was due to be pushed out before the next election. That Fallon had accepted a secret payment of five million euros from one Gennady Lazarev and had then used his power to push through the deal over the objections of the secretary of state for energy. Finally, he told Seymour about the Russian-speaking woman he had first seen in an ancient church in the Lubéron and then in an abandoned council house in Basildon.

"Who's the source for Jeremy Fallon and the five million?" asked Seymour.

"I'd like to claim a zone of exclusivity on that one, if you don't mind."

"I'm sure you would. But who's the source?"

Gabriel answered truthfully. Seymour shook his head slowly.

"Viktor Orlov is genetically incapable of telling the truth," he said. "He's always offering MI6 bits of so-called intelligence about Russia, and none of it ever pans out."

"Chiara and I wouldn't be alive if it wasn't for Viktor Orlov," Gabriel responded.

"That doesn't mean that everything he says is true."

"He knows more about the underside of the Russian oil industry than anyone else in the world."

Seymour did not challenge this assertion. "And you're sure about the man and the woman who drove off in the Mercedes?" he asked. "You're sure they were the same ones who followed you in the gallery?"

"Graham," said Gabriel wearily.

"We all make mistakes from time to time."

"Some of us more often than others."

Seymour tossed his cigarette into the darkness in anger. "Why am I hearing about this only now? Why didn't you call me last night while you had them under watch?"

"And what would you have done? Would you have alerted the chief of your Russian counterintelligence division? Would you have informed your director?" Gabriel was silent for a moment. "If I had come to you last night, it would have set in motion a chain of events that would have led to the destruction of Jonathan Lancaster and his government."

"So why are you coming to me now?"

Gabriel made no reply. Seymour started to light another cigarette, then stopped himself.

"Rather ironic, don't you think?"

"What's that?"

"I asked you to find Madeline Hart because I was trying to protect my prime minister from scandal. And now you're bringing me information that could destroy him."

"That wasn't my intention."

"You can't prove a word of it, you know. Not one word."

"I realize that."

Seymour exhaled heavily. "I am the deputy director of Her Majesty's Security Service," he said, more to himself than to Gabriel. "Deputy directors of MI5 do not bring down British governments. They protect them from enemies foreign and domestic."

"But what if the government is dirty?"

"What government isn't?" Seymour replied glibly.

Gabriel didn't answer. He was in no mood for a relativistic debate over ethics in politics.

"And if I prevailed upon you to walk away and forget about it?" asked Seymour. "What would you do?"

"I would abide by your wishes and go home to Jerusalem."

"And do what?"

"It seems Shamron has plans for me."

"Anything you want to tell me about?"

"Not yet."

Seymour was clearly intrigued but let it drop for now. "And what would you think of me?" he asked after a moment.

"What does it matter what I think?"

"It matters to me," said Seymour earnestly.

Gabriel made a show of thought. "I think you would spend the rest of your life wondering what the SVR was doing with all the money they were siphoning from the North Sea. And I think you would feel guilty that you'd done nothing to stop it."

Seymour made no reply.

"We have a saying in our service, Graham. We believe that a career without scandal is not a proper career at all."

"We're British," Seymour answered. "We don't have sayings, and we don't like scandals. In fact, we live in fear of making even the slightest misstep."

"That's why you have me."

Seymour looked at Gabriel seriously for a moment. "What exactly are you suggesting?"

"Let me go to war against Volgatek on your behalf. I'll find the proof that they stole your oil."

"And then what?"

"I'll steal it back."

Gabriel and Graham Seymour spent the next thirty minutes thrashing out the details of perhaps the most unorthodox operational accord ever reached between two sometimes-allied services. Later, it would come to be known as the Parliament Hill accord, though there were some inside British intelligence who referred to it as the Kite Hill accord, which was the other name for the knoll at the southern end of Hampstead Heath. Under the provisions of the agreement, Seymour granted Gabriel the license to operate on British soil as he saw fit, provided there was no violence and no threat to British national security. For his part, Gabriel pledged that any intelligence produced by the operation would be turned over to Seymour and that Seymour and Seymour alone would decide how to use it. The deal was sealed with a handshake. Then Seymour departed, trailed by his bodyguards.

Gabriel remained in the Heath for another ten minutes before walking back to Hampstead High Street to collect Keller. Together they rode the Underground to Kensington and then made their way on foot to the Israeli Embassy. The Office station was deserted except for a low-level clerk who leaped to attention when the legend came striding through the doorway unannounced. Gabriel deposited Keller in the anteroom, then made his way into the secure communications pod, which Office veterans such as himself referred to as the Holy of Holies. Shamron's home number in Tiberias was still loaded into the directory of emergency contacts. He answered after the first ring, as though he had been sitting by the phone.

Though the call was technically secure, the two men spoke in the terse patois of the Office, a language no translator or supercomputer could ever decipher. Gabriel quickly explained what he had discovered, what he planned to do next, and what he required to move forward. The resources for such an operation were not Shamron's to provide. Nor did he retain any official authority to approve it. Only Uzi Navot could launch such an endeavor—and only with the blessing of the prime minister himself.

And thus the groundwork was laid for a row that would go down in the annals as one of the worst in the storied history of the Office. It commenced at 10:18 p.m. Israel time, when Shamron rang Navot at home and told him that Gabriel intended to go to war against KGB Oil & Gas and that Shamron wanted the operation to proceed. Navot made it clear that such an undertaking was not in the cards. Not then. Not ever. Shamron hung up without another word and rang the prime minister before Navot had a chance to head him off.

"Why am I starting a war with the Russian president?" the prime minister asked. "It's only oil, for God's sake."

"It's not *only* about oil, not for Gabriel. Besides," Shamron added, "do you want him to be the next chief or not?"

"You know I want him, Ari."

"Then let him settle an old score with the Russians," Shamron said, "and he'll be yours."

"Who's going to tell Uzi?"

"I doubt he'll take my call."

And so it was that the Israeli prime minister, acting at the behest of Ari Shamron, called the chief of his foreign intelligence service and ordered him to approve an operation the chief wanted no part of. Witnesses would later attest to the fact that voices were raised, and there were rumors Navot threatened to resign. But they were only that, rumors, for Navot loved being the chief almost as much as Shamron had. In a sign of things to come, Navot refused to call Gabriel in London to personally bestow his blessing, leaving the task to a lowly desk officer instead. Gabriel received his formal operational charter shortly after midnight London time, in a phone call lasting less than ten seconds. After hanging up the phone, he and Keller left the embassy and set out through the quiet streets of London, toward the Grand Hotel Berkshire.

"What about me?" asked Keller. "Do I stay, or do I get on the next plane to Corsica?"

"It's up to you."

"I think I'll stay."

"You won't be disappointed."

"I don't speak Hebrew."

"That's good."

"Why?"

"Because we can make fun of you, and you'll never know it."

"How are you going to use me?"

"You speak French like a Frenchman, you have several clean passports, and you're rather good with a gun. I'm sure we'll think of something."

"May I offer a piece of advice?"

"Just one."

"You're going to need a Russian."

"Don't worry," said Gabriel. "I've got one."

39

GRAYSWOOD, SURREY

T HE RAMBLING TUDOR HOUSE STOOD a mile from the old Grayswood parish church, at the edge of the Knobby Copse. A rutted beech drive led to it; thick hedgerows shielded it from view. There was a tangled garden for thinking deep thoughts, eight private acres for wrestling with one's demons, and a stock pond that hadn't been fished in years. The bass that stalked its dark waters were now the size of sharks. Housekeeping, the Office division that acquired and maintained secure properties, referred to the pond as Loch Ness.

Gabriel and Keller arrived at the property shortly after noon the next day, in a four-wheel-drive Land Rover that had been supplied by Transport. In the back were two stainless steel crates filled with secure communications equipment taken from the embassy safe room, along with several bags of groceries from the Sainsbury's supermarket in Guildford. After loading the food into the pantry, they pulled the covers from the furniture, blew the cobwebs from the eaves, and searched the old house from end to end for listening devices. Then they went into the garden and stood on the banks of the stock pond. Dorsal fins carved slits in the black surface.

"They weren't joking," said Keller.

"No," said Gabriel.

"What do they eat?"

"They devoured one of my best officers the last time we were here."

"Is there any tackle?"

"In the mudroom."

Keller went inside and found a pair of rods leaning in the corner, next to a splintered old oar. While searching for a lure, he heard a dull thud, like the snapping of a tree limb. Stepping outside, he smelled the unmistakable odor of gunpowder on the air. Then he glimpsed Gabriel coming up the garden path, a silenced Beretta in one hand, a two-foot fish in the other.

"That hardly seems sporting," Keller said.

"I don't have time for sport," said Gabriel. "I have to figure out a way to get an agent inside a Russian oil company. And I have many mouths to feed."

―――――――

Late that afternoon, as the hedgerows melted into the gathering darkness and the air turned brittle with cold, there arrived at the isolated Tudor house at the edge of the Knobby Copse a caravan of three motorcars. The vehicles were of different make and model, as were the nine operatives who emerged from them, weary after a long day of clandestine travel. Within the corridors and conference rooms of King Saul Boulevard, the operatives were known as Barak, the Hebrew word for lightning, because of their ability to gather and strike quickly. The Americans, jealous of the unit's matchless list of operational accomplishments, referred to them as "God's team."

Chiara entered the house first, followed by Rimona Stern and Dina Sarid. Petite and dark-haired, Dina was the Office's top terrorism analyst, but she possessed a brilliant analytical mind that made her an asset in any kind of operation. Rimona, a Rubenesque woman with sandstone-colored hair, had started her career in military intelligence but was now part of the Office unit that focused exclusively on the Iranian nuclear program. She also happened to be Shamron's niece. Indeed, Gabriel's fondest memories of Rimona were of a fearless child on a kick scooter careening down the steep drive of her famous uncle's house in Tiberias.

Next came a pair of all-purpose field operatives named Oded and Mordecai, followed by Yaakov Rossman and Yossi Gavish. Yaakov, a hard figure with black hair and a pockmarked face, was an agent runner by trade who specialized in the recruitment and maintenance of Arab spies. Yossi was a senior officer from Research, the Office's analytical division. Born in London and educated at Oxford, he still spoke Hebrew with a pronounced British accent.

From the last car emerged two men—one of late middle age, the other in the prime of life. The elder of the two was none other than Eli Lavon: noted archaeologist, hunter of Nazi war criminals and looted Holocaust assets, and surveillance artist extraordinaire. As usual, Lavon was wearing many layers of mismatched clothing. He had thinning hair that defied styling of any sort and the vigilant brown eyes of a terrier. His suede loafers made no sound as he crossed the entrance hall and entered Gabriel's warm embrace. Eli Lavon did nearly everything silently. Shamron once said that the legendary Office watcher could disappear while shaking your hand.

"Are you sure you're up for this?" asked Gabriel.

"I wouldn't miss it for the world. Besides," Lavon added, "your leading man said he wouldn't go anywhere near the Russians unless I was watching his back."

Gabriel looked at the tall figure standing just behind Lavon's tiny shoulder. His name was Mikhail Abramov. Lanky and fair with a fine-boned face and eyes the color of glacial ice, he had immigrated to Israel from Russia as a teenager and joined the Sayeret Matkal, the IDF's elite special operations unit. Once described by Shamron as "Gabriel without a conscience," he had personally assassinated several of the top terror masterminds from Hamas and Palestinian Islamic Jihad. He now carried out similar missions on behalf of the Office, though his enormous talents were not limited strictly to the gun. It was Mikhail, working with a CIA officer named Sarah Bancroft, who had infiltrated the personal entourage of one Ivan Kharkov, thus initiating the long and bloody war between the Office and Ivan's private army. Had Viktor Orlov not surrendered Ruzoil to the Kremlin, Mikhail would have died in Russia, along with Gabriel and Chiara. Indeed, on Mikhail's porcelain cheekbone was a deep scar left by Ivan's sledgehammer fist.

"You don't have to do this," Gabriel said, touching the scar now. "We can find someone else."

"Like who?" asked Mikhail, glancing around the room.

"Yossi can do it."

"Yossi speaks four languages," Mikhail said, "but Russian doesn't happen to be one of them. They could be talking about slitting his throat, and he would think they were ordering chicken Kiev."

The members of Gabriel's fabled team had stayed in the house before, and so they settled into their old rooms with a minimum of bickering while Chiara headed into the kitchen to prepare an elaborate reunion meal. The main entrée was the enormous bass, which she roasted with white wine and herbs. Gabriel placed Keller to his right at dinner, a deliberate sign to the others that, for now at least, the Englishman was to be treated as a member of the family. At first the others were uneasy about his presence, but gradually they warmed to him. For the most part, they conducted the meal in English for his benefit. But when discussing their last operation, they reverted to Hebrew.

"What are they talking about?" Keller asked quietly of Gabriel.

"A new program on Israeli television."

"Are you telling me the truth?"

"No."

Their mood was more subdued than usual, for Ivan's shadow hung over them. They did not speak his name at dinner. Instead, they talked about the *matsav*, the situation. Yossi, deeply read in the classics and history, served as their guide. He saw a world spinning dangerously out of control. The promises of the great Arab Awakening had been exposed as lies, he said, and soon there would be a crescent of radical Islam stretching from North Africa to Central Asia. America was bankrupt, tired, and no longer able to lead. It was possible this turbulent new world disorder would produce a twenty-first-century axis led by China, Iran, and, of course, Russia. And standing alone, surrounded by a sea of enemies, would be Israel and the Office.

With that, they cleared away the dishes and repaired to the sitting room, where Gabriel finally explained why he had brought them all to England. They knew fragments of it already. Now, standing before them, a gas fire burning at his back, Gabriel swiftly completed the painting. He told them everything that had transpired, beginning with the desperate search for Madeline Hart in France and ending with the deal he had struck with Graham Seymour the previous evening in Hampstead Heath. There was one aspect of the affair, however, that he recounted out of sequence. It was his brief encounter with Madeline Hart, in the hours before her death. He had given Madeline his word he would bring her home safely. Having failed, he intended to keep that promise by undoing what was a Russian operation from beginning to end. To accomplish that, they were going to insert Mikhail into KGB Oil & Gas, he said. And then they were going to find proof that Madeline Hart had been murdered as part of a Russian plot to steal British oil from the North Sea.

"How?" asked Eli Lavon incredulously when Gabriel had finished speaking. "How in God's name are we going to get Mikhail inside a Kremlin-owned oil company run by Russian intelligence?"

"We'll find a way," said Gabriel. "We always do."

The real work began the next morning when the members of Gabriel's team began secretly burrowing into the state-owned Russian energy company known as Volgatek Oil & Gas. At the outset, the bulk of their material came from open sources such as business journals, press releases, and academic papers written by experts in the rough-and-tumble Russian oil industry. In addition, Gabriel requested help from Unit 1400, the Israeli electronic eavesdropping service. As expected, the Unit discovered that Volgatek's Moscow-based computer networks and communications were protected by high-quality Russian firewalls—the same firewalls, interestingly enough, used by the Kremlin, the Russian military, and the SVR. Late in the day, however, the Unit managed to hack into the computers of a Volgatek field office in Gdansk, where the company owned an important refinery that produced much of Poland's gasoline. The material was forwarded directly to the safe house in Surrey. Mikhail and Eli Lavon, the only members of the team who spoke Russian, handled the translation. Mikhail dismissed the intelligence as a dry hole, but Lavon was more optimistic. By getting their foot in the door of Gdansk, he said, they would learn much about how Volgatek operated beyond the boundaries of Mother Russia.

By instinct, they approached their target as if it were a terrorist organization. And the first order of business when confronted with a new terror group or cell, Dina reminded them needlessly, was to identify the structure and key personnel. It was tempting to focus on those who resided at the top of the food chain, she said, but the middle managers, foot soldiers, couriers, innkeepers, and drivers usually proved far more valuable in the end. They were the passed over, the forgotten, the neglected. They carried grudges, harbored resentments, and oftentimes spent more money than they earned. This made them far easier targets for recruitment than the men who flew on private planes, drank champagne by the bucketful, and had a stable of Russian prostitutes at their beck and call, no matter where they went in the world.

At the top of the organization chart was Gennady Lazarev, the former Russian nuclear scientist and KGB informant who had served as Viktor Orlov's deputy at Ruzoil. Lazarev's trusted deputy was Dmitry Bershov, and his chief of European operations was Alexei Voronin. Both were former officers of the KGB, though Voronin was by far the more presentable of the two. He spoke several European languages fluently, including English, which he had acquired while working in the KGB's London *reʒidentura* during the last days of the Cold War.

The rest of Volgatek's hierarchy proved harder to identify, which surely was no accident. Yaakov likened the company's profile to that of the Office. The name of the chief was public knowledge, but the names of his key deputies, and the tasks they carried out, were kept secret or concealed beneath layers of deception and misdirection. Fortunately, the e-mail traffic from the Gdansk field office allowed the team to identify several other key players inside the company, including its chief of security, Pavel Zhirov. His name appeared in no company documents, and all attempts to locate a photograph were fruitless. On the team's organizational chart, Zhirov was a man without a face.

As the days wore on, it became clear to the team that the enterprise Zhirov protected was about more than just oil. The company was part of a larger Kremlin stratagem to turn Russia into a global energy superpower, a Eurasian Saudi Arabia, and to resurrect the Russian Empire from the ruins of the Soviet Union. Eastern and Western Europe were already overly dependent on Russian natural gas. Volgatek's mission was to extend Russian dominance over Europe's energy market through its purchases of oil refineries. And now, thanks to Jeremy Fallon, it had a foothold in the North Sea that would eventually send billions in oil profits gushing into the Kremlin. Yes, Volgatek Oil & Gas was about Russian avarice, the team agreed. But it was first and foremost about Russian revanchism.

But how to plant an agent inside such an organization? It was Eli Lavon who found a possible solution, which he explained to Gabriel while they were walking in the tangled garden. After purchasing the refinery in Gdansk, he said, Volgatek had made a local Polish hire to serve as the refinery's nominal director. In practice, the Pole had absolutely nothing to do with the day-to-day operations of the refinery. He was window dressing, a bouquet of flowers designed to smooth over hurt Polish feelings over the Russian bear gobbling up a vital economic asset. Furthermore, Lavon explained, Poland wasn't the only place Volgatek hired local helpers. They did it in Hungary, Lithuania, and Cuba as well. None of those managers fared any better than the one from Gdansk. To a man, they were all marginalized, ignored, and cut out of the loop.

"They're walking coffee cups," said Lavon.

"Which means they have no access to the kind of closely held information we're looking for," Gabriel pointed out.

"That's true," replied Lavon. "But if the local hire also happened to be Russian by birth or ancestry, Volgatek central command might look more kindly upon him, especially if he happened to be the sharpest knife in the drawer. If that were the case, they might be tempted to give him actual responsibilities. Who knows? They might even let him into the inner sanctum in Moscow."

"It's brilliant, Eli."

"Yes, it is," Lavon conceded. "But it has one serious problem."

"What's that?"

"How do we get Volgatek to take notice of him in the first place?"

"That's easy."

"Really?"

"Yes," said Gabriel, smiling. "Really."

Gabriel did not take part in the family meal that night. Instead, he drove to Cheyne Walk in Chelsea, where he dined alone with Viktor Orlov. His nascent plan met no resistance from the Russian; in fact, Orlov offered several key suggestions that made it better. At the conclusion of the meal, Gabriel handed Orlov the boilerplate document given to all non-Office individuals who participate in Office operations. It barred Orlov from ever disclosing his role in the affair and left him no legal recourse if he or his businesses were harmed in any way. Orlov refused to sign it. Gabriel had expected nothing less.

After leaving Orlov's mansion, Gabriel drove up to Hampstead and then made his way on foot to Parliament Hill. Graham Seymour was waiting on the bench, flanked by his two bodyguards. They moved out of earshot as Gabriel spoke about the operation he was about to undertake and what he required in the way of unofficial British assistance. Listening, Seymour couldn't help but smile. It was unorthodox, but then most Office operations were, especially when conceived by Gabriel and his team.

"You know," Seymour said, "it might actually work."

"It *is* going to work, Graham. The question is," he added, "do you want me to go forward with it?"

Seymour was silent for a moment. Then he rose to his feet and turned his back on the lights of London. "Bring me proof the Russians were behind Madeline's kidnapping and murder," he said calmly, "and I'll make sure those bastards in the Kremlin never see a drop of our oil."

"Let me do it for you, Graham. That way, you won't—"

"This is something only I can do," Seymour said. "Besides, a very wise man once told me a career without scandal is not a proper career at all."

"Type my name into a Google box, and then tell me whether you think I'm so wise."

Seymour smiled. "You're not having second thoughts, are you?"

"None," replied Gabriel.

"Good lad," said Seymour. "But do keep one thing in mind."

"What's that?"

"It might be easy for you to get Mikhail *into* Volgatek, but getting him out again might be quite another thing entirely."

With that, Seymour returned to the company of his bodyguards and melted into the darkness. Gabriel remained on the bench for another five minutes. Then he walked to his car and headed back to the house at the edge of the Knobby Copse.

40

GRAYSWOOD, SURREY

THE EDUCATION OF MIKHAIL ABRAMOV, future employee of the state-owned Russian energy company known as Volgatek Oil & Gas, commenced at nine o'clock the following morning. His first tutor was none other than Viktor Orlov. Despite Gabriel's objections, Orlov insisted on traveling to Surrey in his Mercedes Maybach limousine, trailed by a Land Rover filled with bodyguards. The small motorcade caused something of a commotion in Grayswood, and for much of the day a rumor floated about the village that the occupant of the car had been the prime minister himself. But Jonathan Lancaster was nowhere near Surrey; he was campaigning that morning in Sheffield. The latest polls gave him a commanding lead over the opposition candidate. Britain's most famous political analyst was now predicting a landslide of historic proportions.

Orlov returned to the safe house the following morning, and

the morning after that as well. His lectures were a reflection of his unique personality: brilliant, arrogant, opinionated, condescending. He spoke mainly in English to Mikhail, with occasional forays into Russian that only Eli Lavon could understand. And sometimes he mixed the two languages together into a bizarre tongue the team referred to as "Rusglish." He was indefatigable, irritating, and impossible not to love. He was a force to be reckoned with. He was Orlov on a mission.

He began his tutorial with a history lesson: life under Soviet Communism, the fall of an empire, the lawless era of the oligarchs. Much to everyone's surprise, Orlov admitted that he and the other robber barons of Russia had sown the seeds of their own destruction by growing far too rich, far too quickly. In doing so, he added, they had helped to bring about the circumstances that had led to a return of authoritarianism. The current president of Russia was a man with no ideology or belief system other than the exercise of naked power. "He is a fascist in everything but name," Orlov said. "And I created him."

The next phase of Mikhail's hasty education began on the fourth day, when he undertook what Eli Lavon described as the shortest MBA program in history. His professor was from Tel Aviv, but he had attended the Wharton School of Business and had worked briefly for ExxonMobil before returning to Israel. For seven long days and nights, he lectured Mikhail on the basics of business administration: accounting, statistics, marketing, corporate finance, risk management. Mikhail proved to be a quick study—hardly surprising, for his parents had both been prominent Soviet academics. At the conclusion of the course, the professor predicted that Mikhail had a bright future, though he had no idea what that future might hold. Then he happily signed Gabriel's nondisclosure pledge and boarded a flight home to Israel.

While Mikhail labored over his studies, the rest of the team worked diligently on the identity that would cloak him once he entered the field. They built him as a novelist might construct a character upon the page: ancestry and education, loves and losses, triumphs and disappointments. For several days his name eluded them, for it had to suit a man who had one foot in the West and another still rooted firmly in the East. It was Gabriel who finally chose the name Nicholas Avedon, an English perversion of Nicolai Avdonin. With Graham Seymour's blessing, they forged him a well-traveled British passport and wrote a long and detailed curriculum vitae to match. Then, when Mikhail had completed his coursework, they took him on a tour of a life that had never been lived. There was the house in a leafy London suburb that he had never entered, and the college at Oxford where he had never cracked a book, and the offices of an unheralded drilling services firm in Aberdeen where he had never earned a paycheck. They even flew him to America so that he could recall what it was like to walk the streets of Cambridge on a chilly autumn afternoon, though he had never been to Cambridge, in autumn or any other time of the year.

Which left only the matter of Mikhail's appearance. It had to be altered dramatically. Otherwise, Volgatek's friends in the SVR would remember Mikhail from operations past. Plastic surgery was not an option; the healing time was too long, and Mikhail refused to allow anyone to touch his face with a knife. It was Chiara who conceived of a potential solution, which she demonstrated to Gabriel on one of the computers. On the screen was the photograph she had taken of Mikhail for his false British passport. She pressed a single button, and the photo reappeared, with one distinct change.

"I barely recognize him myself," Gabriel said.

"But will he go for it?"

"I'll make it clear that he has no choice."

That evening, in the presence of the entire team, Mikhail shaved his head bald. Yaakov, Oded, and Mordecai shaved theirs in solidarity, but Gabriel refused. His commitment to unit cohesion, he said, went only so far. The following morning, the women took Mikhail into London for a shopping excursion that raised more than a few eyebrows in the accounting department of King Saul Boulevard. Upon their return to Grayswood, they found Viktor Orlov waiting to give Mikhail a final examination, which he passed with flying colors. To celebrate, Viktor opened several bottles of his beloved Château Pétrus. As he was raising a glass in his student's honor, there came from the garden the dull thump of a suppressed Beretta.

"What was that?" asked Orlov.

"I think we're having fish for dinner," said Mikhail.

"Someone should have told me," Orlov replied. "I would have brought a nice Sancerre instead."

Not long after Viktor Orlov received his British passport, he purchased a controlling interest in a failing newspaper, the venerable *Financial Journal* of London, as a means of raising his profile among the city's smart set. A few members of the staff, including the renowned investigative reporter Zoe Reed, had resigned in protest, but most stayed on, in part because they had nowhere else to go. Under the terms of the ownership agreement, Orlov had agreed to play no role whatsoever in shaping the newspaper's editorial content. It was a pledge he had somehow managed to keep, despite his desire to use the paper as a cudgel with which to beat his enemies in the Kremlin.

That didn't mean, however, that Orlov was averse to calling his editors with the occasional news tip, especially when it concerned his own business. And so it was that, three days later, a small item appeared deep in the paper regarding a new addition to the staff at Viktor Orlov Investments, LLC. Orlov confirmed the hiring in a press release later that morning, saying that a thirty-five-year-old executive named Nicholas Avedon would be taking control of VOI's energy portfolio, along with its oil futures trading desk. Within minutes, the Internet was swirling with rumors that Orlov had chosen a successor and was preparing a gradual withdrawal from the company's day-to-day operations. By that evening, the rumors were so intense that Orlov felt compelled to make a rare appearance on CNBC to deny them. His performance was hardly convincing. Indeed, one prominent commentator said it raised many more questions than it answered.

No one in London's financial circles would ever know that the rumors of Orlov's imminent retirement were started by a team of men and women working from an isolated house in Surrey. Nor would they know that the same rumors were injected into the bloodstream of Moscow's business community, or that they reached the highest level of the state-owned energy company known as Volgatek Oil & Gas. Gabriel and his team were aware of this, because they read about it in a caustic e-mail sent by Alexei Voronin, Volgatek's chief of European operations, to the head of the Gdansk field office. Eli Lavon presented a printout of the e-mail to Gabriel over dinner and translated the text, even the parts that were unfit for polite company. Gabriel responded by opening a leftover bottle of the Château Pétrus and pouring a glass for each member of the team. All in all, it was an auspicious beginning. Mikhail was now Viktor Orlov's heir apparent. And KGB Oil & Gas was watching.

41

MAYFAIR, LONDON

T HE OFFICES OF Viktor Orlov Investments, LLC, occupied four floors of a luxury Mayfair office block, not far from the American Embassy. When Nicholas Avedon arrived there early the next morning, the entire senior staff of the firm was waiting in the main conference room to greet him. Orlov made a few brief remarks, followed by a round of hasty introductions, all of which were unnecessary because Mikhail had memorized the names and faces of Orlov's team during his preparation at the safe house in Surrey.

If they had expected him to ease into the job slowly, they were sadly mistaken. Because within an hour of settling into his new corner office overlooking Hanover Square, he had begun a top-to-bottom review of VOI's lucrative investments in the energy field. Never mind that he had conducted the same review already within the walls of the safe house, or that his insightful findings had already been written for him by Victor Orlov. The review sent a signal to the rest of the staff that Nicholas Avedon was not a man to be taken lightly. He had been brought to VOI to do a job. And heaven help the fool who tried to stand in his way.

His days quickly acquired a strict routine. He would arrive at his desk early, having read the morning business journals and checked the Asian markets, and then spend an hour or two with his spread-sheets and charts before joining the morning senior staff meeting, which was always held in Orlov's spacious office. He tended to keep his own counsel during large gatherings, but when he did choose to speak, his remarks set new standards for brevity. Most days he lunched alone. Then he would labor at his desk until seven or eight, when he would return to the spacious flat Gabriel had rented for him in Maida Vale. Housekeeping had taken a smaller flat in the building across the street as well. Whenever Mikhail was at home, a member of the team watched over him. And when he was at work, a high-resolution video camera with a secure transmitter kept a vigil for them.

As it turned out, Volgatek was watching him, too. Gabriel and the team knew this because Unit 1400 had finally managed to break into Volgatek's computer network, and they were now reading the e-mail of top company executives almost in real time. The name Nicholas Avedon featured prominently in several—including one sent by Gennady Lazarev to Pavel Zhirov, Volgatek's faceless security chief, requesting a background check. Nicholas Avedon was now a flash-ing light on Volgatek's radar screen. It was time, said Gabriel, to make him burn a little brighter.

The next morning, Nicholas Avedon presented the findings of his review to Viktor Orlov and the entire team at VOI. Orlov declared them brilliant, which was hardly a surprise, since he had conceived and written them himself. Over the next few days, he undertook a series of bold market moves, all of which had been long in the planning, that radically altered VOI's position in the global energy sector. During a whirlwind round of print and broadcast interviews, Orlov called it "energy for the twenty-second century and beyond"—and whenever possible, he gave credit to the plan's nominal architect: Nicholas Avedon. The moneymen from the City liked what they saw of Orlov's young protégé. And so, it seemed, did KGB Oil & Gas.

They had demonstrated competence on the part of Nicholas Avedon. Now it was time to reveal the level to which Viktor Orlov had grown dependent upon him. Stock analysts and middle managers, said Gabriel, were a dime a dozen. Gennady Lazarev would make a play for Nicholas Avedon for one reason and one reason only—in order to screw his former mentor and business partner.

And so began what the team described as the Viktor and Nicholas Follies. For the next two weeks, they were inseparable. They lunched together, dined together, and wherever Viktor went in public, Nicholas was at his side. On several occasions he was seen leaving Orlov's Cheyne Walk mansion late in the evening, and he spent a weekend relaxing at Orlov's sprawling Berkshire estate, a perquisite bestowed upon no other employee of the firm. As their relationship grew closer, tensions began to rise inside VOI's Mayfair headquarters. Orlov's other division chiefs didn't like the fact that Nicholas Avedon began sitting in on what were usually one-on-one meetings with the boss—or that Avedon was often seen whispering advice into Viktor's cocked ear. A few of the other staff declared open war on him, but most trimmed their sails accordingly. Avedon was besieged with invitations for after-work drinks and working dinners. He turned them all down. Viktor, he said, required his full attention.

Next they took the Follies on a tour of the Continent. There was the business forum in Paris, where they were dazzling. And the gathering of Swiss bankers in Geneva, where they couldn't put a foot wrong. And the rather tense meeting in Madrid with the CEO of an Orlov-owned pipeline company, who was given six months to show a profit or he would find himself looking for another job, along with the rest of Spain.

Finally, they flew to Budapest for a meeting of business and government leaders from the so-called emerging markets of Eastern Europe. Gazprom, the Russian gas giant, sent a representative to assure those present that they had nothing to fear from their overdependence on Russian energy, that the Kremlin would never dream of turning off the spigot as a means of imposing its will on the lost lands of its former empire. That evening, at a cocktail reception held on the banks of the Danube, the man from Gazprom introduced himself to Nicholas Avedon and found, much to his surprise, that he spoke fluent Russian. Clearly, the Gazprom executive was impressed by what he heard, because a few minutes after the encounter an e-mail arrived in Gennady Lazarev's in-box. Gabriel and the team read it even before Lazarev managed to open it. It seemed that Nicholas Avedon was now in play. "Hire him," said the man from Gazprom. "If you don't, we will."

But how to bring the two sides together so that the relationship could be consummated? Never one to wait by the phone, Gabriel wanted to force the issue by placing Mikhail and Lazarev in close proximity, in a place where they might have a moment or two for a private chat. He saw his chance when Unit 1400 intercepted an e-mail that had been sent to Lazarev by his secretary. The topic was Lazarev's itinerary for the upcoming Global Energy Forum, the biennial gathering of something called the International Association of Petroleum Producers. Reading it, Gabriel smiled. The Follies were going to Copenhagen. And the Office was going with them.

42

COPENHAGEN, DENMARK

FIVE ANXIOUS DAYS LATER, the lords of oil began flowing into Copenhagen from the four corners of the earth: Saudis and Emiratis, Azeris and Kazakhs, Brazilians and Venezuelans, Americans and Canadians. The global warming activists were predictably appalled by the gathering, with one group issuing the hysterical claim that the carbon emitted by the conference itself would eventually cause the oceans to swallow a village in Bangladesh. The delegates seemed not to notice. They arrived in Copenhagen aboard private jets and roared through its quaint streets in armored limousines powered by internal combustion engines. Perhaps one day the oil would run out and the planet would grow too hot to sustain human life. But for now at least, the extractors of fossil fuels still reigned supreme.

The competition for resources in Copenhagen was intense. Dinner reservations were impossible to come by, and the Hotel d'Angleterre, a white luxury liner of a building overlooking the sprawling King's New Square, was filled to capacity. Viktor Orlov and Mikhail arrived at its graceful entrance in a blinding snowstorm and were escorted by management to a pair of neighboring suites on an upper floor. Mikhail's contained a platter of Danish treats and a bottle of Dom Pérignon, which was chilling in an ice bucket. The last time he had stayed in a hotel on Office business, he had used the complimentary champagne to inflict an injury on his knee for the sake of his cover. Surely, he thought, his cover for this operation demanded that he partake of a glass or two. As he was removing the cork he heard a discreet knock at the door—curious, because he had hung the DO NOT DISTURB sign on the latch before generously tipping the bellman. He opened the door slowly and peered over the security bar at the man of medium height and build standing in the corridor. He wore a mid-length woolen coat with a German-style collar and a Tyrolean felt hat. His hair was lush and silver; his eyes brown and bespectacled. A soft-sided leather briefcase, scuffed and weathered, dangled from his right hand.

"How can I help you?" asked Mikhail.

"By opening the door," replied Gabriel softly.

Mikhail disengaged the security bar, stepped to one side so Gabriel could enter, and then closed the door again quickly. Turning, he saw Gabriel moving slowly about the hotel room with his BlackBerry extended in his right hand. After a moment he nodded at Mikhail to indicate that the room was free of listening devices. Mikhail walked over to the champagne bucket and poured himself a glass of the Dom Pérignon.

"You?" he asked, waving the bottle in Gabriel's direction.

"It gives me a headache."

"Me, too."

Mikhail lowered his lanky frame onto the couch and propped his feet upon the coffee table, a busy executive weary from a long day of travel and meetings. Gabriel looked around at the lavishly appointed suite and shook his head.

"I'm glad Viktor is footing the bill for this place," he said. "Uzi's already on my back over expenses."

"Tell Uzi that I need to be maintained in the style to which I've become accustomed."

"It's good to know all this success hasn't gone to your head."

Mikhail drank some of the champagne but said nothing.

"You need to shave."

"I shaved this morning," Mikhail said, rubbing his chin.

"Not there," replied Gabriel.

Mikhail ran a palm over his glistening pate. "You know," he said, "I'm actually getting used to it. In fact, I'm thinking about adopting it as my look when this operation is over."

"You look like an alien, Mikhail."

"Better an alien than a character from *The Sound of Music*." Mikhail snatched a small shrimp sandwich from the platter and devoured it whole.

"Since when do you eat shellfish?"

"Since I became an Englishman of Russian descent who works for an investment company owned by an oligarch named Viktor Orlov."

"With a bit of luck," said Gabriel, "it's only a stepping stone to bigger and better things."

"Inshallah," said Mikhail, raising his champagne glass in a mock toast. "Have my future employers arrived yet?"

Gabriel delved into his battered briefcase and withdrew a manila file folder. Inside were three freshly printed color photographs, which he arrayed on the coffee table before Mikhail in the order they had been snapped. They depicted three men descending the airstair of a small private jet and climbing into the back of a waiting limousine. They had been taken from a considerable distance, by a camera fitted with a long lens. Snowfall blurred the image.

"Who got the pictures?" asked Mikhail.

"Yossi."

"How did he get onto the tarmac?"

"He has a press pass for the forum," replied Gabriel. "So does Rimona."

"Who are they working for?"

"An industry newsletter called the *Energy Times*."

"Doesn't ring a bell."

"It's new."

Smiling, Mikhail picked up the first photo, the one showing the three figures moving in single file down the airstair. Leading the way, looking nothing at all like the bookish mathematician he had once been, was Gennady Lazarev. A step behind was Dmitry Bershov, Volgatek's deputy CEO, and behind Bershov was a short, compact man whose face was obscured by the brim of a fedora.

"Who is he?" asked Mikhail.

"We haven't been able to figure that out."

Mikhail picked up the second photograph, then the third. In neither was the man's face visible.

"He's rather good, isn't he?" asked Mikhail.

"You noticed that, too."

"Hard to miss, actually. He knew where the cameras were, and he made certain no one got a good shot of him." Mikhail dropped the photos onto the coffee table. "Why do you suppose he did that?"

"The same reason you and I do it."

"He works for the Office?"

"He's a professional, Mikhail. The real thing. Maybe he's retired SVR and does it out of habit. But it looks to me as though he's still on active duty."

"Where is he now?"

"The Hotel Imperial, along with the rest of them. Gennady is rather disappointed with his accommodations."

"How do you know that?"

"Because Mordecai and Oded paid a visit to his room an hour before the Volgatek plane landed, and they left a little something under the night table."

"How did you know which room was Lazarev's?"

"The Unit hacked into the Imperial's reservation system."

"And the door?"

"Mordecai has a new magic card key. The door practically opened itself." Gabriel returned the photographs to the file folder and the folder to the briefcase. "You should know that Gennady has been talking about more than just the quality of his room," he said after a moment. "He's obviously looking forward to meeting you."

"Any idea when he might make his move?"

"No," said Gabriel, shaking his head. "But you should expect it to be subtle."

"Do I know him?"

"You know his name," said Gabriel, "but not his face."

"And if he makes a pass at me?"

"I've always found it best to play hard to get."

"And look where it's gotten you." Mikhail poured another inch of champagne into his glass but said nothing more.

"Is there something you wish to say to me, Mikhail?"

"I suppose congratulations are in order."

"For what?"

"Come on, Gabriel. Don't make me say it out loud."

"Say what?"

"People talk, Gabriel, especially spies. And the talk around King Saul Boulevard is that you're going to be the next chief."

"I haven't agreed to anything."

"That's not what I hear," Mikhail said. "I hear it's a done deal."

"It's not."

"Whatever you say, boss."

Gabriel exhaled heavily. "How much does Uzi know?"

"Uzi knew from the minute he took the job that he was everyone's second choice."

"It's not something I sought."

"I know. And I suspect Uzi knows it, too," Mikhail added. "But that's not going to make it any easier when the prime minister tells him he won't be serving a second term as chief."

Mikhail raised his glass to the light and watched the bubbles rising to the surface of his champagne.

"What are you thinking about?" asked Gabriel.

"The time we were in Zurich, at that little café near the Paradeplatz. It was when we were trying to get Chiara back from Ivan. Do you remember that place, Gabriel? Do you remember what you said to me that afternoon?"

"I believe I might have told you to marry Sarah Bancroft and leave the Office."

"You have a good memory."

"What's your point?"

"I was just wondering whether you still thought I should leave the Office."

Gabriel hesitated before answering. "I wouldn't do that if I were you," he said at last.

"Why not?"

"Because if I become the next chief, you have a bright future, Mikhail. Very bright."

Mikhail rubbed his scalp. "I need to shave," he said.

"Yes, you do."

"Are you sure you won't have some of this champagne?"

"It gives me a headache."

"Me, too," said Mikhail as he poured another glass.

Before leaving the hotel suite, Gabriel installed a piece of Office software on Mikhail's mobile phone that turned it into a full-time transmitter and automatically forwarded all his calls, e-mails, and text messages to the team's computers. Then he headed down to the lobby and spent a few minutes searching for familiar faces amid the crowd of well-lubricated oilmen. Outside the afternoon blizzard had ended, but a few thick flakes were falling lazily through the lamplight. Gabriel headed westward across the city, along a winding pedestrian shopping street known as the Strøget, until he came to the Rådhuspladsen. The bells in the clock tower were tolling six o'clock. He was tempted to pay a visit to the Hotel Imperial, which was located not far from the square, on the fringes of the Tivoli Gardens. Instead, he walked to a despondent-looking apartment building on a street with a name only a Dane could pronounce. As he entered the small flat on the second floor, he found Keller and Eli Lavon hunched over a notebook computer. From its speakers came the sound of three men conversing quietly in Russian.

"Have you been able to figure out who he is?" asked Gabriel.

Lavon shook his head. "It's funny," he said, "but these Volgatek boys aren't big on names."

"You don't say."

Lavon was about to reply but was stopped by the sound of one of the voices. He was speaking in a low murmur, as though he were standing over an open grave.

"That's our boy," Lavon said. "He always talks like that. Like he assumes someone is listening."

"Someone *is* listening."

Lavon smiled. "I sent a sample of his voice to King Saul Boulevard and told them to run it through the computers."

"And?"

"No match."

"Forward the sample to Adrian Carter at Langley."

"And if Carter asks for an explanation?"

"Lie to him."

Just then, the three Russian oil executives collapsed in uproarious laughter. As Lavon leaned forward to listen, Gabriel moved slowly to the window and peered into the street. It was empty except for a young woman walking along the snowy pavement. She had Madeline's alabaster skin and Madeline's cheekbones. Indeed, the resemblance was so startling that for an instant Gabriel felt compelled to run after her. The Russians were still laughing. Surely, thought Gabriel, they were laughing at him. He drew a deep breath to slow the clamorous beating of his heart and watched Madeline's wraith pass beneath his feet. Then the darkness reclaimed her and she was gone.

43

COPENHAGEN, DENMARK

THEY HELD THE FORUM IN the Bella Center, a hideous glass-and-steel convention hall that looked like a giant greenhouse dropped from outer space. A pack of reporters stood shivering outside the entrance, behind a cordon of yellow tape. Most of the arriving executives had the good sense to ignore their shouted taunts, but not Orlov. He paused to answer a question about the sudden spike in global oil prices, from which he profited wildly, and soon found himself holding forth on subjects ranging from the British election to the Kremlin's crackdown on Russia's pro-democracy movement. Gabriel and the team heard every word of it, for Mikhail was standing at Orlov's side in plain sight of the cameras, his mobile phone in his hand. In fact, it was Mikhail who finally put an end to Orlov's impromptu news conference by taking hold of his coat sleeve and tugging him toward the center's open door. Later, a British reporter would remark that it was the first time she had ever seen anyone—"And I mean *anyone!*"—dare to lay so much as a finger on Viktor Orlov.

Once inside, Orlov was a whirlwind. He attended every panel discussion the morning had to offer, visited every booth on the exhibition floor, and accepted every hand that was extended his way, even those that were attached to men who loathed him. "This is Nicholas Avedon," he would say to anyone within earshot. "Nicholas is my right hand and my left. Nicholas is my north star."

Lunch was a vertical affair—Orlov-speak for a buffet meal with no assigned seating—and there was no alcohol or pork in deference to the many delegates from the Muslim world. Orlov and Mikhail sailed through it without a bite and then settled in for the afternoon's first panel, a somber discussion of the lessons learned from BP's disaster in the Gulf of Mexico. Gennady Lazarev was in attendance as well, seated two rows behind Orlov's right shoulder. "Like an assassin," Orlov murmured to Mikhail. "He's circling for the kill. It's only a matter of time before he draws his gun."

The remark was clearly audible in the little flat on the street with an unpronounceable name, and the sentiments expressed were shared by Gabriel and the rest of his team. In fact, thanks to the camera hanging around Yossi's neck, they had the photographs to prove it. During the morning session of the forum, Lazarev had kept a safe distance. But now, as the afternoon wore on, he was moving ever closer to his target. "He's like a jetliner in a holding pattern," said Eli Lavon. "He's just waiting for the tower to give him clearance to land."

"I'm not sure the weather conditions on the ground will allow it," replied Gabriel.

"When do you expect a window to open?"

"Here," said Gabriel, tapping his forefinger on the final entry of the first-day schedule. "This is when we'll set him down."

Which meant that Gabriel and the team were forced to endure two more hours of what Christopher Keller described as "oil babble." There was a deeply boring speech by an Indian government minister about the future energy needs of the world's second most populous nation. Then it was a chiding lecture by France's new president about taxation, profit, and social responsibility. And finally there was a re-markably honest panel discussion about the environmental dangers posed by the extraction technique known as hydraulic fracturing. Not surprisingly, Gennady Lazarev was not in attendance. As a rule, Russian oil companies regarded the environment as something to be exploited, not protected.

With that, the delegates filed onto the escalators and headed to the center's upper gallery for a cocktail reception. Gennady Lazarev had arrived early and was talking to a couple of tieless Iranian oil executives in the far corner of the room. Orlov and Mikhail each snagged a glass of champagne from a passing tray and settled among a group of festive Brazilians. Orlov had turned his back to Lazarev, but Mikhail had a clear view of him. Therefore, it was Mikhail who saw the Russian separate himself from the Iranians and begin a slow journey across the room.

"Now might be a good time for you to take a walk, Viktor."

"Where?"

"Finland."

A skilled cocktail party actor, Orlov drew his mobile phone from his suit pocket and raised it to his ear. Then, frowning as though he could not hear, he moved swiftly away in search of a quiet place to talk. In Orlov's absence, Mikhail turned his back to the room and fell into a serious discussion with one of the Brazilians about investment opportunities in Latin America. But two minutes into the conversa-tion, he became aware of the fact that a man was standing behind him. He knew this because the smell of the man's rich cologne had overwhelmed all other scents within its zone of influence. He knew it, too, because he could see it in the wandering eye of the Brazilian. Turning, he found himself staring directly into the face that had adorned the wall of the Grayswood safe house. Training and experience allowed him to react with nothing more than a blank stare.

"Forgive me for interrupting," the face said in Russian-accented English, "but I wanted to introduce myself before Viktor returns. My name is Gennady Lazarev. I'm from Volgatek Oil and Gas."

"I'm Nicholas," said Mikhail, accepting the outstretched hand. "Nicholas Avedon."

"I know who you are," said Lazarev, smiling. "In fact, I know everything there is to know about you."

The conversation that came next was one minute and twenty-seven seconds in length. The quality of the recording was remarkably clear except for the background hum of the cocktail reception and a dull pile-driver thumping that the team later identified as the sound of Mikhail's heart. Gabriel's own heart beat a matching rhythm as he listened to the recording five times from beginning to end. Now, as he clicked the PLAY icon and listened to the recording for a sixth time, he seemed to have no pulse at all.

"I know who you are. In fact, I know everything there is to know about you."

"Really? Why is that?"

"Because we've been watching some of the moves you've been making with Viktor's portfolio, and we're very impressed."

"Who's we?"

"*Volgatek, of course. Who did you think I was talking about?*"

"*The business environment in Russia is rather different than it is in the West. Pronouns can be tricky things.*"

"*You're very diplomatic.*"

"*I have to be. I work for Viktor Orlov.*"

"*Sometimes it looks as though Viktor is working for you.*"

"*Looks can be deceiving, Mr. Lazarev.*"

"*So the rumors on the street aren't true?*"

"*What rumors are those?*"

"*That you've taken control of Viktor's day-to-day operations? That Viktor is nothing more than a name and a flashy necktie?*"

"*Viktor is still the master strategist. I'm just the one who pushes the buttons and pulls the levers.*"

"*You're very loyal, Nicholas.*"

"*As the day is long.*"

"*I like that in a man. I'm loyal, too.*"

"*Just not to Viktor.*"

"*You and Viktor have obviously talked about me.*"

"*Only once.*"

"*I can't imagine he had anything decent to say about me.*"

"*He said you were very smart.*"

"*Did he mean it as a compliment?*"

"*No.*"

"*Viktor and I had our differences—I won't deny that. But that's all in the past. I've always respected his opinion, especially when it comes to people. He was always a good talent spotter. That's why I wanted to meet you. I have an idea I'd like to discuss.*"

"*I'll tell Viktor you'd like to have a word.*"

"*This isn't a Viktor Orlov idea. It's a Nicholas Avedon idea.*"

"*I'm an employee of Viktor Orlov Investments, Mr. Lazarev.*

There is no Nicholas Avedon, at least not where Viktor's money is concerned."

"This has nothing to do with Viktor's money. It's about your future. I'd like a few minutes of your time before you leave Copenhagen."

"I'm afraid my calendar is a nightmare."

"Take my card, Nicholas. My private cell number is on the back. I promise to make it well worth your while. Don't disappoint me. I don't like to be disappointed."

Gabriel clicked the STOP icon and looked at Eli Lavon.

"Sounds to me as if you've got him," Lavon said

"Maybe," replied Gabriel. "Or maybe Gennady's got us."

"It can't hurt to meet with him."

"It might hurt," Gabriel said. "In fact, it might hurt a lot."

Gabriel slid the toggle bar of the audio player back to the beginning of the conversation and clicked PLAY again.

"I know who you are. In fact, I know everything there is to know about you."

He pressed STOP.

"Figure of speech," said Lavon. "Nothing more."

"You're sure about that, Eli? You're one hundred percent sure?"

"I am sure the sun will rise tomorrow morning and that it will set tomorrow night. And I am reasonably confident Mikhail will survive a drink with Gennady Lazarev."

"Unless Gennady serves him a glass of polonium punch."

Gabriel reached for the computer mouse, but Lavon stilled his hand. "We came to Copenhagen to make the meeting," Lavon said. "Now make the meeting."

Gabriel picked up his phone and dialed Mikhail's mobile. The bleating of his ringtone came back at him from the speakers of the computer, as did the sound of Mikhail's voice when he answered.

"Do it tomorrow night," said Gabriel. "Control the venue to the best of your ability. No surprises."

Gabriel hung up without another word and listened while Mikhail dialed Gennady Lazarev's number. Lazarev answered immediately.

"I'm so glad you called."

"What can I do for you, Mr. Lazarev?"

"You can have dinner with me tomorrow night."

"I have something with Viktor."

"Make up an excuse."

"Where?"

"I'll find some place out of the way."

"Not *too* out of the way, Mr. Lazarev. I can't be out of pocket for more than an hour or so."

"How's seven?"

"Seven is fine."

"I'll send a car for you."

"I'm at the Hotel d'Angleterre."

"Yes, I know," said Lazarev before severing the connection. Gabriel switched the audio source of the computer from Mikhail's phone to the transmitter in Gennady Lazarev's room at the Imperial. The three Russians were laughing uncontrollably. Surely, thought Gabriel, they were laughing at him.

44

COPENHAGEN, DENMARK

THE SECOND DAY OF THE forum was a tired rerun of the first. Mikhail remained loyally at Viktor Orlov's side throughout, smiling with the overbright air of a man who was about to commit adultery. At the cocktail reception, he once again clung to the festive embrace of the Brazilians, who seemed crestfallen when he turned down their invitation to join them for a romp through some of Copenhagen's livelier nightclubs. Taking his leave, he extracted Viktor from the clutches of the Kazakh oil minister and herded him into the back of their hired limousine. He waited until they were a few blocks from the D'Angleterre before saying that he hadn't the strength for dinner. He did so in a voice that was loud enough to be picked up by any Russian transmitters present.

"What's her name?" asked Orlov, who already knew of Mikhail's plans for that evening.

"It isn't that, Viktor."

"What is it then?"

"I have a catastrophic headache."

"I hope it's nothing serious."

"I'm sure it's only a brain tumor."

Upstairs in his room, Mikhail made a few phone calls to London for the sake of his cover and sent a naughty e-mail to his secretary to let the cybersleuths of Moscow Center know that he was human after all. Then he showered and laid out his clothes for the evening, which proved to be more of a challenge than he first imagined. How does one dress, he thought, when one is betraying his ersatz employer by meeting with executives of an oil company owned and operated by Russian intelligence? He settled on a plain suit, Soviet gray in color, and a white dress shirt with French cuffs. He decided against a necktie for fear it would make him appear overeager. Besides, if it was their intention to kill him, he didn't want to wear an article of clothing that could be used as a murder weapon.

At Gabriel's instruction, he left every light in the room burning and hung the DO NOT DISTURB sign on the latch before making his way to the elevators. The lobby was a sea of delegates. As he headed toward the door, he saw Yossi, newly minted reporter for the nonexistent *Energy Times*, interviewing one of the tieless Iranians. Outside a gritty snow was blowing like a sandstorm across the expanse of King's New Square. A black Mercedes S-Class sedan waited curbside. Standing next to the open rear door was an eight-foot Russian. If his name wasn't Igor, it should have been.

"Where are we going?" Mikhail asked as the car shot forward with a lurch.

"Dinner," grunted Igor the driver.

"Well," said Mikhail quietly, "I'm glad we cleared that up."

The Russian driver did not hear Mikhail's remark, but Gabriel did. He was behind the wheel of an Audi sedan, parked on a side street around the corner from the hotel's entrance. Keller was beside him, a tablet computer on his knees. On the screen was a map of Copenhagen, with Mikhail's position depicted as a blinking blue light. At that instant, the light was moving rapidly away from King's New Square, headed toward a section of Copenhagen not known for its restaurants. Gabriel turned the key with no sense of urgency. Then he looked at the blue light and followed carefully after it.

It soon became apparent that Mikhail and Gennady Lazarev would not be dining in Copenhagen that evening. Because within minutes of leaving the hotel, the big black Mercedes was headed out of town at speeds that suggested Igor was accustomed to driving in snowy weather. Gabriel had no need to match the car's reckless pace. The blue light on Keller's computer screen told him everything he needed to know.

After clearing Copenhagen's southern districts, the light moved onto the E20 motorway and headed southward, into the region of Denmark known as Zealand. And when the highway turned inland toward the ancient market town of Ringsted, the light detached itself and floated toward the coastline. Gabriel and Keller did the same and soon found themselves on a narrow two-lane road, with the black waters of Køge Bay on their left and fields of snow on their right. They followed the road for several miles until they came upon a settlement of summer cottages huddled along a rocky, windswept beach, and it was there the blinking light finally stopped moving.

Gabriel eased to the side of the road and increased the volume on his earpiece. He heard a car door opening, footfalls over snowy paving stones, and the pile-driver beating of Mikhail's restive heart.

———

The cottage was among the finest of the lot. It had a small U-shaped drive, an open-sided carport with a red tile roof, and a terraced front garden framed by manicured hedges and stout little brick walls. Twelve steps rose to a veranda with a white balustrade; two potted trees stood like sentries on either side of the paned-glass door. As Mikhail approached, the door swung open and Gennady Lazarev stepped onto the veranda to greet him. He was wearing a roll-neck pullover and a thick Nordic-style cardigan. "Nicholas!" he called, as though to a deaf relation. "Come inside before you catch your death of cold. I'm sorry to drag you all the way down here, but I've never felt comfortable doing serious business in restaurants and hotels."

He offered Mikhail his hand and pulled him across the threshold, as though he were dragging a drowning man from the sea. Then, after closing the door too quickly, he relieved Mikhail of his coat and spent a moment carefully regarding his captured prize. Despite his power and riches, Lazarev still looked like a government scientist. With his round spectacles and furrowed brow, he had the air of a man who was forever struggling to solve a mathematical equation.

"Did you have any trouble getting away from Viktor?" he asked.

"None," replied Mikhail. "In fact, I think he was happy to be rid of me for a few hours."

"It seems you two get along quite well."

"We do."

"But you came in any case," Lazarev pointed out.

"I felt that I had to."

"Why?"

"Because when a man like Gennady Lazarev asks for a meeting, it's usually a good idea to take the meeting."

Mikhail's words were obviously pleasing to Lazarev. Clearly, the Russian was not immune to flattery.

"And you didn't tell him where you were going?" he asked.

"Of course not."

"Very good." Lazarev clamped his delicate hand on Mikhail's shoulder. "Come and have a drink. Meet the others."

Lazarev escorted Mikhail into a great room with windows looking onto the sea. Two men waited there in the sort of uncomfortable silence that usually follows a quarrel. One was pouring a drink at the trolley; the other was warming himself in front of the fire. The one at the trolley had the shadow of a heavy beard and dark thinning hair combed close to his scalp. Mikhail couldn't see much of the man at the fire because his back was turned to the room.

"This is Dmitry Bershov," Lazarev said, indicating the man at the trolley. "I'm sure you've heard the name. Dmitry is my number two."

"Yes, of course," said Mikhail, accepting the outstretched hand. "It's a pleasure to meet you."

"Likewise," intoned Bershov.

"And that man over there," said Lazarev, pointing toward the figure at the fire, "is Pavel Zhirov. Pavel handles corporate security and any other dirty deed that needs to be done. Isn't that right, Pavel?"

The man at the fire rotated slowly around, until he was staring directly into Mikhail's face. He wore a black woolen sweater and charcoal-gray trousers. His gray-blond hair was cut short; his face was angular and dominated by a small, rather cruel-looking mouth. Mikhail realized instantly he had seen the face before. It was in a photograph of a luncheon that had occurred on the island of Corsica, a few hours before Madeline Hart's disappearance. Now the face came toward him out of the firelight, with the small mouth formed into something like a smile.

"Have we ever met?" Zhirov asked, grasping Mikhail's hand.

"No, I don't think so."

"You look familiar to me."

"I get that a lot."

The smile faded, the eyes narrowed. "Did you bring a phone?" Zhirov asked.

"I shower with my phone."

"Would you mind switching it off, please?"

"Is that really necessary?"

"It is," he said. "And take out the battery as well. One can never be too careful these days."

Thirty seconds later the blue light on the tablet computer was extinguished. Gabriel removed his earpiece and frowned.

"What just happened?" asked Keller.

"Mikhail went behind the moon."

"What does that mean?"

Gabriel explained. Then he drew his mobile phone from his coat pocket and rang Eli Lavon in the safe flat. They spoke for a few seconds in terse operational Hebrew.

"What's going on?" Keller asked after Gabriel severed the connection.

"A couple of SVR hoods from the Copenhagen *rezidentura* are searching Mikhail's room at the d'Angleterre."

"Is that a good thing?"

"That's a very good thing."

"You sure about that?"

"No."

Gabriel returned the phone to his pocket and stared out the window at the windblown waves lapping against the frozen beach. The waiting, he thought. Always the waiting.

45

ZEALAND, DENMARK

A TABLE HAD BEEN LAID WITH a sumptuous all-Russian buffet. The origin of the food was unclear, for there was no evidence of anyone else in the house besides the three executives. Mikhail wondered how they had secured the property on such short notice. They hadn't, he decided. Surely it was an existing Volgatek safe house. Or maybe it was an SVR safe house. Or maybe it didn't matter. Maybe it was a distinction without a difference.

For now, the food remained only a decoration. A drink had been placed in Mikhail's hand—vodka, of course—and he had been deposited in a chair of honor with a fine view of the black sea. Dmitry Bershov, the company athlete, was pacing the edges of the room with the determined slowness of a man about to enter the ring. Pavel Zhirov, keeper of Volgatek's secrets, kidnapper of Madeline Hart, was staring at the ceiling as though calculating how much rope to use for Mikhail's hanging. Eventually, Zhirov's hard gaze settled on Gennady Lazarev, who had claimed the spot by the fire. Lazarev was staring into the flames and pondering a question that Mikhail had posed a moment earlier: "Why am I here?"

"Why *are* you here?" the Russian replied finally.

"I'm here because you asked me to come."

"Do you always accept meetings with the enemies of the man who signs your paycheck?" Lazarev turned slowly to listen to Mikhail's response.

"Is that what this is about?" Mikhail asked after a moment. "Are you recruiting me to spy on Viktor?"

"You seem familiar with the language of espionage, Nicholas."

"I read books."

"What kind of books?"

Mikhail set down his drink deliberately. "This is beginning to sound too much like an interrogation," he said calmly. "If you don't mind, I think I'd like to go back to my hotel now."

"That would be a mistake on your part," Lazarev said.

"Why?"

"Because you haven't heard my offer yet."

Smiling, Lazarev collected Mikhail's untouched drink and carried it over to the trolley for refreshing. Mikhail looked at Pavel Zhirov and returned his lifeless stare. Inwardly, though, he was exchanging Zhirov's dark woolen clothing for the bright summer costume he had worn to lunch at Les Palmiers restaurant in Calvi. When the drink reappeared, Mikhail wiped the image from his thoughts like chalk from a blackboard and looked only at Lazarev. His brow was furrowed, as though he were struggling over an equation with no possible solution.

"Do you mind if we conduct the rest of this conversation in Russian?" he asked at last.

"I'm afraid my Russian is only good enough for restaurants and taxicabs."

"I have it on the highest authority that your Russian is rather good. Fluent, actually."

"Who told you that?"

"A friend from Gazprom," Lazarev answered truthfully. "He spoke to you briefly in Prague when you were there with Viktor."

"Word gets around fast."

"I'm afraid there are no secrets in Moscow, Nicholas."

"So I hear."

"Did you study Russian at school?"

"No."

"That means you must have learned it at home."

"I must have."

"Your parents are Russian?"

"And my grandparents, too," replied Mikhail.

"How did they end up in England?"

"The usual way."

"What does that mean?"

"They left Russia after the fall of the tsar and settled in Paris. And then they came to London."

"Your ancestors were bourgeoisie?"

"They weren't Bolsheviks, if that's what you're asking."

"I suppose I am."

Mikhail appeared to weigh his next words carefully. "My great-grandfather was a moderately successful businessman who didn't want to live under communism."

"What was his name?"

"The family name was Avdonin, which he eventually changed to Avedon."

"So your real name is Nikita Avdonin," Lazarev pointed out.

"Nicolai," Mikhail corrected him.

"May I call you Nicolai?"

"If you wish," answered Mikhail.

When Lazarev spoke next, it was in Russian. "Have you ever been to Moscow?" he asked.

"No," replied Mikhail in the same language.

"Why not?"

"I've never had a reason to."

"You're not curious to see where you come from?"

"England is my home," Mikhail said. "Russia is the land my family fled."

"Were you an opponent of the Soviet Union?"

"I was too young to be an opponent."

"And our current government?"

"What about it?"

"Do you share Viktor Orlov's opinion that our president is an authoritarian kleptocrat?"

"This might surprise you, Mr. Lazarev, but Viktor and I don't talk about politics."

"That does surprise me."

Mikhail said nothing more. Lazarev let it drop. His gaze moved from Bershov to Zhirov before settling once again on Mikhail. When he spoke next, it was in English again.

"I assume you've read about the licensing deal we reached with the British government that will allow us to conduct drilling operations in the North Sea."

"Two newly discovered fields off the Western Isles," Mikhail said as though reading from a prospectus. "Projected output at maturity of one hundred thousand barrels a day."

"Very impressive."

"It's my business, Mr. Lazarev."

"Actually, it's *my* business." Lazarev paused, then added, "But I'd like *you* to run it for me."

"The Western Isles project?"

Lazarev nodded.

"I'm sorry, Mr. Lazarev," Mikhail said deferentially, "but I'm not a project manager."

"You did similar work in the North Sea for KBS Oil Services."

"Which is why I don't want to do it again. Besides, I'm already under contract with Viktor." Mikhail rose to his feet. "You'll forgive me if I don't stay for dinner, Mr. Lazarev, but I really should be getting back."

"But you haven't heard the rest of my offer yet."

"If it's anything like the first part," Mikhail said tersely, "I'm not interested."

Lazarev seemed not to hear. "As you know, Nicolai, Volgatek is expanding its operations in Europe and elsewhere. If we are to succeed in this venture, we need talented people like you. People who understand the West *and* Russia."

"Was that supposed to be an offer?"

Lazarev took a step forward and placed his hands proprietarily on Mikhail's shoulders. "The Western Isles are only the beginning," he said, as though there was no one else in the room. "I want you to help me build an oil company with truly global reach. I'm going to make you rich, Nicolai Avdonin. Rich beyond your wildest dreams."

"I'm doing quite nicely already."

"If I know Viktor, he's giving you a bit of loose change from his pockets." Lazarev smiled and squeezed Mikhail's shoulders. "Come to Volgatek, Nicolai. Come home."

The southern end of Køge Bay is not the sort of place where two men can sit for long in a parked car without being noticed, so Gabriel and

Keller drove to the nearest town and took a table in a small, warm restaurant that served an unappetizing mix of Italian and Chinese food. Keller ate enough for the both of them, but Gabriel had only black tea. In his earpiece there was silence, and in his thoughts there were images of Mikhail being marched to his death through a snow-covered forest of birch trees. Twice Gabriel started to rise to his feet out of fear and frustration, and twice Keller told him to sit down and wait it out. "You've done your job," Keller said calmly, a false operational smile affixed to his suntanned face. "Let it play out."

Finally, one hour and thirty-three minutes after Mikhail entered the house by the sea, Gabriel heard a sharp electronic crackle in his ear, followed by the roaring of the wind—the same wind that rattled the panes of the frosted window a few inches from his face. Then, much to his relief, he heard the sound of Mikhail's voice, thin with cold.

"I'll think about it, Gennady. Truly, I will."

"Don't think too long, Nicolai, because my offer has a deadline."

"How long do I have?"

"I'd like an answer in a week. Otherwise, I'm going to have to go in another direction."

"And if I say yes?"

"We'll bring you to Moscow for a few days so you can meet the rest of the team. If we both like what we see, we'll take the next step. If not, you'll stay with Viktor and pretend this never happened."

"Why Moscow?"

"Are you afraid to come to Moscow, Nicolai?"

"Of course not."

"You shouldn't be. Pavel will take very good care of you."

The words were the last spoken by either man. After that, a door slammed, a car engine turned over, and the blue light began to move across the screen of the tablet computer. As it approached the coordinates of the café, Gabriel turned his head and saw the big black Mercedes blow past in a cloud of swirling snow. Mikhail had survived reentry. All they had to do now was pluck him from the sea and bring him home.

———

The return trip to Copenhagen lasted forty-five minutes and was so uneventful it bordered on tedium. Gabriel allowed Keller to handle the driving so he could focus all his considerable powers of concentration on the audio feed streaming live into his ear. There was no sound other than the velvety rumble of a Mercedes engine and a monotonous tapping. At first, Gabriel assumed there was something loose beneath the car. Then he realized it was Mikhail drumming his fingers on the armrest, something he always did when he was on edge.

When he emerged from the car at the Hotel d'Angleterre, however, Mikhail looked like a man without a care in the world. Entering the lobby, he found the Brazilians drinking in the bar and decided to join them for a much-deserved nightcap. Afterward, he headed up to his room, which bore no trace of the highly professional search that had taken place in his absence. Even his laptop computer, which had been subjected to a digital ransacking, was precisely as he had left it. He used it to dash off a priority flash alert to the team, a printout of which Eli Lavon was holding in his hand as Gabriel and Keller returned to the safe flat on the street with an unpronounceable name.

"You did it, Gabriel," Lavon was saying. "You've got him."

"Who?" asked Gabriel.

"Paul," replied Lavon, smiling. "Pavel Zhirov of Volgatek Oil and Gas is *Paul*."

The quarrel that came next was among the worst in the team's long history together, yet it was conducted so quietly that Keller scarcely knew it was taking place at all. Uncharacteristically, they split roughly in two, with Yaakov assuming control of the rebel faction. His case was simple and passionately argued. They had undertaken the operation for one reason: to find proof that the Russians had carried out the kidnapping of Madeline Hart as part of a conspiracy to gain access to British oil. Now that proof was sitting in his room at the Imperial Hotel in the form of Pavel Zhirov, Volgatek's chief of security and a Moscow Center thug if ever there was one. They had no choice but to move against him immediately, Yaakov argued. Otherwise, Zhirov would slip beyond their reach forever.

Unfortunately for Yaakov, the leader of the opposing faction was none other than his future chief, Gabriel Allon, who calmly explained all the reasons why Pavel Zhirov would be leaving Copenhagen in the morning as scheduled. They had no time to plan or rehearse the operation properly, he said. Nor would they be presented with an opportunity to get Zhirov cleanly that matched any existing Office criteria. Crash operations were always risky, said Gabriel. And a crash operation without a plan was a recipe for a disaster the Office could not afford at this time. Pavel Zhirov would be allowed to walk. And, if necessary, the Office would carry his bags for him.

And so it was that, at ten the following morning, Pavel Zhirov, aka Paul, strode from the doorway of the Imperial Hotel, accompanied by Gennady Lazarev and Dmitry Bershov. Together they rode to the Copenhagen airport in a chauffeured limousine and boarded a private plane bound for Moscow. Yossi snapped one final departure photo for a newsletter that did not exist and then boarded a flight for London. By that evening he and the other members of the team were once again gathered around Gabriel in the Grayswood safe house. Nicolai Avdonin was going to the city of heretics for a job interview, he said. And the team was going with him.

46

GRAYSWOOD, SURREY

T HE SUMMONS ARRIVED VIA THE secure link late the following afternoon. Gabriel considered ignoring it, but the
message made it clear that a failure to appear would result
in the immediate revocation of his operational charter. And so, at
six that evening, he reluctantly drove to central London and slipped
into the Israeli Embassy through the back door. The station chief,
a battle-scarred careerist named Natan, waited tensely in the foyer.
He escorted Gabriel downstairs to the Holy of Holies and then
quickly fled, as though he feared being injured by flying debris.
The room was unoccupied, but resting upon the table was a tray
of tea sandwiches and Viennese butter cookies. There was also a
bottle of mineral water, which Gabriel locked in a cabinet. He did
so out of habit. Office doctrine dictated that the site of a potentially
hostile encounter be cleared of any object that could be used as a
weapon.

For twenty minutes no one else entered the room. Then, finally, there appeared a man with the thick physique of a wrestler. He wore a dark suit that seemed a size too small and a fashionable high-collared dress shirt that left the impression his head was bolted onto his shoulders. His hair had once been strawberry blond in color; now it was silver gray and cropped short to conceal the fact it was falling out at an alarming rate. He stared at Gabriel for a moment through a pair of narrow spectacles, as though he were debating whether to shoot him now or at dawn. Then he walked over to the tray of food and shook his head slowly.

"Do you think my enemies know?"

"What's that, Uzi?"

"That I am incapable of resisting food. Especially these," Navot added, snatching one of the butter cookies from the tray. "I suppose it's genetic. My grandfather loved nothing better than a butter cookie and a good cup of Viennese coffee."

"Better to have a problem with sweets than gambling or women."

"That's easy for you to say," Navot replied resentfully. "You're like Shamron. You don't have any weaknesses. You're incorruptible." He paused, then added, "You're perfect."

Gabriel could see where this was headed. He remained silent while Navot stared at the butter cookie in his hand as though it were the source of all his problems.

"I suppose you do have *one* weakness," Navot said at last. "You've always allowed personal feelings to enter into your decision making. You'll have to rid yourself of that when you become chief."

"This isn't personal, Uzi."

Navot gave an artificial smile. "So you're not going to deny that Shamron has talked to you about becoming the next chief?"

"No," replied Gabriel, "I'm not going to deny it."

Navot was still smiling, though barely. "You have one other weakness, Gabriel. You're honest. Far too honest for a spy."

Navot finally sat down and placed his heavy forearms upon the tabletop. The surface seemed to settle beneath the weight. Watching him, Gabriel recalled an unpleasant afternoon, many years earlier, when he had been paired with Navot for a session of silent-killing training. Gabriel lost count of how many times he died that day.

"How long do I have?" Navot asked.

"Come on, Uzi. Let's not do this."

"Why not?"

"Because it's not going to do either one of us any good."

"You must be feeling guilty then."

"Not at all."

"How long have you been planning to take my job?"

"You know me better than that, Uzi."

"I thought I did."

Navot pushed the tray of food away and looked around the room. "Would it kill them to leave me a bottle of water?"

"I locked it in the cabinet."

"Why?"

"Because I didn't want you to hit me with it."

Navot placed his hand on Gabriel's elbow and squeezed. Instantly, Gabriel felt his hand go numb.

"Get it for me," Navot said. "It's the least you can do."

Gabriel rose and retrieved the bottle. When he sat down again, Navot's anger seemed to have subsided, but only slightly. He unscrewed the aluminum cap using only his thumb and forefinger and slowly poured several inches of the effervescent water into a clear plastic cup. He offered none to Gabriel.

"What did I do to deserve this?" he asked, more of himself than of Gabriel. "I've been a good chief, a damn good chief. I've managed the affairs of the Office with dignity and kept my country out of any major foreign entanglements. Have I been able to shut down the Iranian nuclear program? No, I haven't. But I didn't get us into a catastrophic war, either. That's the first job of the chief, to make certain the prime minister doesn't go off half-cocked and drag the country into a needless conflict. You'll learn that once you settle into my chair."

When Gabriel offered no reply, Navot drank some of the water, deliberately, as though it were the last on earth. He was right about one thing; he *had* been a good chief. Unfortunately, the successes that had occurred under his watch had all been Gabriel's.

"There's something else you'll learn quickly," Navot resumed. "It's very difficult to run an intelligence service with a man like Shamron looking over your shoulder."

"It's his service. He built it from the ground up and turned it into what it is today."

"The old man is just that—an old man. The world has changed in the century since Shamron was chief."

"You don't really mean that, Uzi."

"Forgive me, Gabriel, but I'm not feeling terribly charitable toward Shamron at the moment. Or you, for that matter."

Navot lapsed into a sulky silence. Natan, the station chief, peered through the soundproof glass walls, saw two men glaring at one another over a table, and returned to his bunker.

"How long do I have?" Navot asked.

"Uzi . . ."

"Am I going to be allowed to finish my term?"

"Of course."

"Don't say it like it's the most obvious thing in the world, Gabriel.

Because from where I sit, nothing seems terribly obvious at the moment."

"You've been a fine chief, Uzi. The best since Shamron."

"And what is my reward? I'll be put out to pasture before my time. Because heaven knows we can't have a chief and a former chief inside King Saul Boulevard at the same time."

"Why not?"

"Because there's no precedent for it."

"There's no precedent for any of this."

"Sorry, Gabriel, but I'd rather not end my career as a sympathy case."

"Don't cut off your nose to spite your face, Uzi."

"You sound like my mother."

"How is she?"

"Good days and bad."

"Anything I can do?"

"Go see her the next time you're in town. She always loved you, Gabriel. Everyone loves you."

Navot treated himself to another butter cookie. Then another.

"By my calculation," he said, brushing the crumbs from his thick fingers, "I have fourteen months remaining in my term, which means I'm the one who gets to decide whether to send several of our best people to the most dangerous city in the world."

"You gave me the authority to run the operation."

"I had a gun to my head at the time."

"It's still there."

"I realize that, which is why I would never dream of pulling the plug on your little gambit. Instead, I'm going to ask you to take a deep breath and come to your senses."

Greeted by silence, Navot leaned forward across the table and stared directly into Gabriel's eyes. Absent from his face was any trace of anger.

"Do you remember what it was like the last time we went to Moscow, Gabriel, or have you managed to repress it?"

"I remember it all, Uzi."

"So do I," Navot replied distantly. "It was the worst day of my life."

"Mine, too."

Navot narrowed his eyes, as if truly perplexed. "So why in God's name do you want to go back there?"

When Gabriel offered no answer, Navot removed his spectacles thoughtfully and massaged the spot on the bridge of his nose where the pads carved into his skin. The eyeglasses, like everything else he was wearing, had been chosen by his demanding wife, Bella. She had worked for the Office briefly as an analyst on the Syria desk and loved the status that came with being the wife of the chief. Gabriel had always suspected her influence extended far beyond her husband's wardrobe.

"It's over," Navot said finally. "You beat him. You won."

"Beat who?"

"Ivan," replied Navot.

"This has nothing to do with Ivan."

"Of course it does. And if you can't see that, maybe you're not fit to run this operation after all."

"So pull my charter."

"I'd love to. But if I do, it will start a war I can't possibly win." Navot slipped on his glasses and smiled briefly. "That's the other thing you'll have to learn when you become chief, Gabriel. You have to choose your battles carefully."

"I already have."

"Since I'm still the chief for fourteen more months, why don't you do me the courtesy of giving me the broad strokes of your plan."

"I'm going to pull Pavel Zhirov aside for a chat. He's going to tell me why he kidnapped and murdered an innocent young woman for the sake of Volgatek's bottom line. He's also going to explain how Volgatek is nothing more than a front for the KGB. And then I'm going to burn them to a crisp, Uzi. I'm going to prove to the civilized world once and for all that the current crowd sitting in the Kremlin isn't much better than the one that came before them."

"I'll let you in on a little secret, Gabriel. The civilized world already knows, and it couldn't care less. In fact, it's so broke and frightened about the future that it's about to allow the mullahs to realize their nuclear dreams."

Gabriel said nothing. Navot exhaled heavily in capitulation.

"A confession? Is that what you're saying?"

"On camera," added Gabriel. "Just like the one he forced Madeline to make before he killed her."

"And what if he doesn't talk?"

"Everyone talks, Uzi."

"What are you going to do about Keller?"

"He's coming with me."

"He's a professional assassin who once tried to kill you."

"We've let bygones be bygones. Besides," Gabriel added, "I'm going to need a bit of extra muscle."

"What else do you need?"

"Passports, visas, travel, accommodations—the usual, Uzi. And I also need Moscow Station to put Pavel Zhirov under immediate full-time surveillance."

"Is that all?"

"No," said Gabriel. "I need you, too."

Navot was silent.

"I didn't ask for this, Uzi."

"I know," Navot replied. "But that still doesn't make it any easier."

It was nearly midnight by the time Gabriel returned to the Grays-wood safe house. Entering the room he shared with Chiara, he found her seated upright in bed, with a cup of herbal tea on the bedside table and a stack of glossy magazines on her lap. Her hair was arranged into a careless bun with many stray tendrils, and she was wearing the stylish new glasses she required for reading. Chiara was self-conscious about the glasses, but Gabriel took secret pleasure in the slight weakening of her vision. It gave him hope that perhaps one day she might look less like his daughter and more like his wife.

"How did it go?" she asked without looking up.

"With rest and proper rehabilitation, there's a chance I might regain partial use of my left hand."

"That bad?"

"He's angry. And I don't blame him."

Gabriel removed his coat and tossed it over the back of a chair. Chiara rolled her eyes in disapproval. Then she licked the tip of her finger and turned the page of the magazine.

"He'll get over it," she said.

"It's not the sort of thing that one gets over, Chiara. And it would have never happened if you and Shamron hadn't conspired behind my back."

"It wasn't like that, darling."

"How was it exactly?"

"Shamron came to see me when you were in France looking for

Madeline. He said he wanted to put the screws to you one last time about becoming chief, and he wanted my blessing."

"It was nice of him to ask."

"Don't be angry, Gabriel. It's what he wants." She paused, then added, "And it's what I want, too."

"You?" asked Gabriel, surprised. "Do you realize what it's going to be like after I take my oath?"

"We're sharing a room in a safe house with eight other people, including a man who once tried to kill you. I think I can handle your being chief."

Gabriel walked over to the bed and leafed through the stack of magazines lying next to Chiara. One was devoted to women who were pregnant. He held it up for her to see and asked, "Is there something you want to tell me?"

She snatched the magazine from his grasp without responding. Gabriel scrutinized her for a moment with his head tilted to one side and his hand resting against his chin.

"Don't look at me like that," she said.

"Like what?"

"Like I'm a painting."

"I can't help it."

She smiled. Then she asked, "What are you thinking?"

"I'm thinking that I wish we were alone instead of in a safe house surrounded by eight other people."

"Including a man who once tried to kill you," she added. "But what are you *really* thinking?"

"I'm wondering why you haven't asked me not to go to Moscow."

"So am I."

"Why haven't you?"

"Because they locked her in a car and burned her to death."

"No other reason?"

"None," she replied. "And if you're wondering whether I want to go to Moscow with the rest of the team, the answer is no. I don't think I'd be able to handle being back there. I might make a mistake."

Without a word, Gabriel crawled into bed and laid his head upon Chiara's womb.

"Aren't you going to take off your clothes?" she asked.

"I'm too tired to take off my clothes."

"Do you mind if I read a little longer?"

"You can do anything you want."

Gabriel closed his eyes. The sound of Chiara gently turning the pages of her magazine nudged him toward sleep.

"Are you still awake?" she asked suddenly.

"No," he murmured.

"Did she know this was going to end in Moscow, Gabriel?"

"Who?"

"The old woman in Corsica. Did she know?"

"Yes," said Gabriel. "I suppose she did."

"Did she warn you not to go?"

"No," said Gabriel as the knife of guilt twisted in his chest. "She told me I would be safe there."

"Did she see anything else?"

"A child," said Gabriel. "She saw a child."

"Whose child?" asked Chiara, but Gabriel didn't hear her. He was running toward a woman, across an endless field of snow. The woman was burning. The snow was stained with blood.

47

GRAYSWOOD, SURREY

U ZI NAVOT, DIRECTOR OF ISRAEL'S secret intelligence service, arrived at the Grayswood safe house at twenty minutes past seven the next morning, as a gray December dawn was breaking over the bare trees of the Knobby Copse. The first person he encountered was Christopher Keller, who was chasing down a Ping-Pong ball that Yaakov had just flicked past him for a winner. The score in the match was eight to five, with Yaakov leading and Keller closing hard.

"Who are you?" Keller asked of the unsmiling, bespectacled figure standing in the entrance hall.

"None of your business," replied Navot.

"Strange name. Hebrew, is it?"

Navot frowned. "You must be Keller."

"I must be."

"Where's Gabriel?"

"He and Chiara went to Guildford."

"Why?"

"Because we ate all the fish in the stock pond."

"Who's in charge?"

"The inmates."

Navot smiled. "Not anymore."

With Navot's unorthodox arrival, the team went on war footing. It was an undeclared war, as all its conflicts were, and it would be fought in a hostile land, against an enemy of superior size and capability. The Office was regarded as one of the most capable intelligence services in the world, yet it was no match for the brotherhood of the sword and the shield. The intelligence services of the Russian Federation were heirs to a proud and murderous tradition. For more than seventy years, the KGB had ruthlessly protected Soviet communism from enemies both real and perceived and had acted as the Party's vanguard abroad, recruiting and planting thousands of spies around the world. Its power had been almost without limit, allowing it to operate as a virtual state within a state. Now, with the collapse of the Soviet Union, it *was* the state. And Volgatek was its oil company.

It was this connection—the connection between Volgatek and the SVR—that Gabriel emphasized time and time again as the team began its work. The oil company and Russia's intelligence service were one and the same, he said, which meant that Mikhail would be in enemy hands the minute his plane left the ground in London. His cover identity had been sound enough to fool Gennady Lazarev, but it would not survive long in the interrogation rooms of Lubyanka. And neither would Mikhail, for that matter. Lubyanka was the place where agents and operations went to die, warned Gabriel. Lubyanka was the end of the line.

For the most part, though, Gabriel's thoughts remained focused on Pavel Zhirov, Volgatek's chief of security and the mastermind behind the operation to gain access to Britain's North Sea oil. Within twenty-four hours of Navot's arrival at the safe house, the Office station in Moscow had determined that Zhirov resided in a fortified apartment building in Sparrow Hills, the exclusive highlands on the banks of the Moscow River. His typical daily schedule was illustrative of the bifurcated nature of his work—mornings at Volgatek's flashy headquarters on Tverskaya Street, afternoons at Moscow Center, the SVR's wooded compound in Yasenevo. The Moscow surveillance team managed to snap several photographs of Zhirov climbing in and out of his chauffeured Mercedes limousine, though none showed his face clearly. Gabriel couldn't help but admire the Russian's professionalism. He had already proven himself to be a worthy opponent with the false flag kidnapping of Madeline Hart. Plucking him from the streets of Moscow, said Gabriel, would require an operation of matching skill.

"With two important differences," Eli Lavon pointed out. "Moscow isn't Corsica. And Pavel Zhirov won't be riding a motorbike on an isolated road, wearing only a sundress."

"Then I suppose we'll have to figure out a way to get Mikhail into Zhirov's car," replied Gabriel. "With a loaded gun in his back pocket, of course."

"How do you intend to do that?"

"Like this."

Gabriel sat down at one of the computers and with a few quick keystrokes retrieved the recording of Gennady Lazarev's final words to Mikhail in Denmark.

"We'll bring you to Moscow for a few days so you can meet the rest of the team. If we both like what we see, we'll take the next step. If not, you'll stay with Viktor and pretend this never happened."

"Why Moscow?"

"Are you afraid to come to Moscow, Nicolai?"

"Of course not."

"You shouldn't be. Pavel will take very good care of you."

Gabriel clicked the STOP icon and looked at Lavon. "I could be wrong," he said, "but I suspect Nicholas Avedon's Russian homecoming isn't going to be without problems."

"What kind of problems?"

"The kind only Pavel can solve."

"And when Mikhail is in the car?"

"He's going to give Pavel a simple choice."

"A choice between coming quietly or having his brains splattered over the inside of his nice Mercedes?"

"Something like that."

"What about Shamron's golden rule?"

"Which one?"

"The one about waving guns around in public."

"There's a little-known exception when it comes to sticking a gun in the ribs of a hood like Pavel."

Lavon made a show of thought. "We'll have to take the driver, too," he said finally. "Otherwise, every FSB officer and militiaman in Russia will be looking for us."

"Yes, Eli, I realize that."

"Where do you intend to conduct the interrogation?"

"Here," said Gabriel, tapping the keyboard again.

"Lovely," said Lavon, looking at the screen. "Who does it belong to?"

"A Russian businessman who couldn't stand living in Russia any-more."

"Where does he live now?"

"Just down the road from Shamron."

With a click of the mouse, Gabriel removed the image from the screen.

"That leaves just one last thing," Lavon said.

"Getting Mikhail out of Russia."

Lavon nodded. "He'll have to leave as someone other than Nicho-las Avedon."

"Preferably with as few Russian hurdles to clear as possible," added Gabriel.

"So how do we do it?"

"The same way Shamron got Eichmann out of Argentina."

"El Al?"

Gabriel nodded.

"Naughty boy," said Lavon.

"Yes," replied Gabriel, smiling. "And I'm just getting started."

Navot approved Gabriel's plan immediately, which left the team five days until Mikhail was to give Gennady Lazarev an answer as to whether he was coming to Moscow. Five days to see to a thousand details large and small—or, as Lavon put it, five days to determine whether Mikhail's visit to Russia would turn out better than his last. Passports, visas, identities, travel arrangements, lodgings: every-thing had to be procured on a crash basis. And then there were the bolt-holes, the backup plans, and the backup plans for the backup plans. Their task was made even more difficult by the fact that Gabriel could not tell them where or when the snatch of Zhirov would take place. They were going to have to improvise in a city that, throughout its long and bloody history, had never been particularly kind to freethinkers.

Gabriel drove his team hard during those long days and nights; and when his back was turned, Navot drove them even harder. There was no visible tension between the two men, no evidence that one was in ascendance and the other was headed toward the exits. Indeed, several members of the team wondered if they might be witnessing the formation of a partnership that could survive long after Gabriel assumed his rightful place as chief of the Office. Yaakov, the most fatalistic of the lot, scoffed at the notion. "It would be like the new wife deciding to let the first wife keep her old room. It will never happen." But Eli Lavon wasn't so sure. If there was anyone who was confident enough to allow his predecessor to stay on in some capacity, it was Gabriel Allon. After all, Lavon said, if Gabriel could make peace with Christopher Keller, he could reach an accommodation with Navot.

All talk of Gabriel's future plans ended whenever Chiara entered the room. At first, she tried to work alongside the others, but the endless talk of Russia quickly darkened her mood. She was alive only because the members of the team had once risked their lives to save her. Now, as they struggled against the deadline, she assumed the role of their caretaker. Despite the tension inside the house, she made certain the atmosphere remained familial. Each evening they sat down to a lavish meal and, at Chiara's insistence, spoke of anything except the operation—books they had read, films they had seen, the future of their troubled country. Then, after an hour or so, Gabriel and Navot would rise restlessly to their feet, and the work would start up again. Chiara happily saw to the dishes each night. Alone at the basin, she sang softly to herself to drown out the sound of the conversation in the next room. Later, she would confess to Gabriel that the mere sound of a Russian word produced a hollow aching in her abdomen.

The man at the center of the operation remained happily oblivious to the team's efforts, or so it seemed to anyone who encountered Nicholas Avedon after his return to London. His demeanor was of a man who no longer cared to conceal the fact he was going places others could only dream about. Orlov doted on his protégé as though he were the son he'd never had, and with each passing day seemed to grow more dependent upon him. The pronoun *we* entered Orlov's vocabulary for the first time when talking about his business, a change in tone that did not go unnoticed in the City. He informed the staff that he would be spending much of January at an undisclosed location in the Caribbean. "I need a nice long break," he said. "And now that I have Nicholas, I can finally take one."

With Orlov seemingly in retreat, word spread through financial circles that Nicholas Avedon was now the man to see at VOI. Most suitors had to wait a week or more for a chance to sit at his feet. But when he received a call from a Jonathan Albright of something called Markham Capital Advisers, he agreed to a meeting without delay. It took place in his office overlooking Hanover Square, though the topic had nothing to do with business or investing. At the conclusion of the meeting, he placed a call to a number in Moscow that lasted three minutes and was satisfactory in outcome. Then he walked Mr. Albright to the elevators with the contented air of a man who could do no wrong. "I'll run it past Viktor," he said loudly enough for everyone in close proximity to hear. "But it sounds to me as if all systems are go."

That night, a car appeared outside Mikhail's apartment house in Maida Vale. Later, Graham Seymour would identify the man who emerged from it as a courier from the SVR's generously staffed London *rezidentura*. The man took possession of Mikhail's false passport and carried it back to the Russian Embassy in Kensington Gardens. One hour later, when he returned it, the passport had been stamped with a hastily issued Russian visa. Tucked inside was a boarding pass for a British Airways flight to Moscow, leaving Heathrow at ten the following morning.

Mikhail slipped the ticket and passport into his briefcase. Then he rang Orlov at Cheyne Walk to say he needed a few days off. "Sorry, Viktor," he said, "but I'm burnt to a crisp. And, please, no phone calls or e-mails. I'm going off the grid."

"For how long?"

"Wednesday. Thursday at the latest."

"Take the week."

"You sure about that?"

"I promise not to make a mess of things while you're gone."

"Thanks, Viktor. You're a dream."

Mikhail tried to sleep that night, but it was no good; he had never been able to sleep the night before an operation. And so shortly after four the next morning, he rose from his bed and clothed himself in the armor of Nicholas Avedon, aka Nicolai Avdonin. A car appeared outside his door at six; it ferried him to Heathrow where he passed effortlessly through security, with Christopher Keller and Dina Sarid watching his back. As he entered the departure gate, he saw a heavily altered version of Gabriel reading a copy of the *Economist* with what appeared to be inordinate interest. Mikhail walked past him without a glance and boarded the aircraft, but Gabriel waited until the doors were about to close before finally stumbling into the first-class cabin in a rush. After takeoff, British controllers routed the plane directly over the town of Basildon, and at half past ten precisely it passed into international airspace. Mikhail drummed his fingers nervously on the center console. He was now in the hands of his enemy. And so was the future chief of Israeli intelligence.

48

MOSCOW

T HE PROTESTERS TRICKLED INTO Red Square in small clusters so that the Moscow City Militia and leather-jacketed thugs of the FSB wouldn't notice—artists, writers, journalists, punk rockers, even a few old babushkas who dreamed of spending their last years on earth in a truly free country. By noon, the crowd numbered several hundred, too large to conceal its true motives. Someone unfurled a banner. Someone else produced a bullhorn and accused the Russian president of having stolen the last election, which had the advantage of being entirely true. Then he made a joke about all the other things the president had stolen from the Russian people, which the leader of the leather-jacketed FSB thugs didn't find funny at all. With scarcely more than a nod, he unleashed the militiamen, who responded by smashing everything in sight, including several of the more important heads. The man with the bullhorn got the worst of it. When last seen, he was being hurled bloody and semiconscious into the back of a police van. Later, the Kremlin announced he would be charged with attempting to instigate a riot, an offense that carried a ten-year sentence in the neo-gulag. The subservient Russian press referred to the protesters as "hooligans," the same label the Soviet regime applied to its opponents, and not a single commentator dared to criticize the heavy-handed tactics. They were to be forgiven for their silence. Journalists who annoyed the Kremlin these days had a funny way of ending up dead.

At Moscow's Sheremetyevo Airport, the news from Red Square flashed briefly across the television screens as Mikhail stepped from the Jetway, followed thirty seconds later by Gabriel. As they approached passport control, Gabriel noticed a man in a tailored suit standing next to a malnourished border policeman in a threadbare uniform. The suited man had a photograph in his hand, which he consulted twice as Mikhail drew near. Then he walked over to Mikhail and said something to him in Russian that Gabriel couldn't understand. Mikhail smiled and shook the man's hand before following him through an unmarked doorway. Alone, Gabriel proceeded to passport control, where an unsmiling woman scrutinized his face for an uncomfortably long moment before vehemently stamping his passport and waving him on. Welcome to Russia, he thought, as he entered the crowded arrivals hall. It was good to be back again.

Stepping outside, Gabriel immediately inhaled a blast of tobacco smoke and diesel fumes that made his head swim. The evening skies were hard and clear; the air was serrated with cold. Glancing to his left, Gabriel saw Mikhail and his Volgatek escort settling into the warmth of a waiting Mercedes sedan. Then he joined the long queue for a taxi. The cold of the concrete ate its way through the thin soles of his Western loafers; and by the time he finally crawled into the back of a rattletrap Lada, his jaw was so frozen he was nearly incapable of speech. Asked for a destination, he replied that he wished to be taken to the Hotel Metropol, though it sounded as if he'd requested a manhole.

After leaving the airport, the driver headed to the Leningradsky Prospekt and started the long, slow slog into the center of Moscow. It was a few minutes past seven, the tail end of the city's murderous evening rush. Even so, their pace was glacial. The driver tried to engage Gabriel in conversation, but his English was as impenetrable as the traffic. Gabriel made thoughtful noises every now and again; mainly, he stared out the window at the crumbling Soviet-era buildings lining the dirty old *prospekt*. For a brief period they had been merely hideous. Now they were ruins. On every street corner, and upon every rooftop, billboards assaulted the eye with promises of luxury and copulation. It was the Communist nightmare with a new coat of capitalism, thought Gabriel. And it was crushingly depressing.

Eventually, they crossed the Garden Ring, and the *prospekt* gave way to Tverskaya Street, Moscow's version of Madison Avenue. It bore them down a long gentle hill, past Volgatek's glittering new headquarters, to the redbrick walls of the Kremlin, where it emptied into the eight lanes of Okhotnyy Ryad Street. Turning left, they sped past the Russian Duma, the old House of Unions, and the Bolshoi Theatre. Gabriel saw none of them. He had eyes only for the floodlit yellow fortress perched atop the heights of Lubyanka Square.

"KGB," said the driver, pointing over the top of the wheel.

"There is no KGB," Gabriel replied distantly. "The KGB is a thing of the past."

The driver muttered something about the naïveté of foreigners and guided the taxi toward the entrance of the Metropol. The lobby had been faithfully restored to its original decor, but the middle-aged woman at the check-in counter hadn't fared nearly as well. She greeted Gabriel with a frozen smile, made polite inquiries about the nature of his travel, and then handed him a long registration form, a copy of which would be forwarded to the relevant authorities. Gabriel completed it swiftly as Jonathan Albright of Markham Capital Advisers and was rewarded with a key to his room. A bellman offered to assist with his bag and seemed relieved when Gabriel said he could manage on his own. Nevertheless, he gave the bellman a tip for his troubles. Its size suggested he was unfamiliar with the value of Russian currency.

His room was on the fourth floor, overlooking the ten lanes of Teatralny Prospekt. Gabriel assumed it was bugged and therefore made no effort to search it. Instead, he placed two phone calls to clients who were not really his clients and then hacked his way through the stack of e-mail that had piled up in his in-box during the flight from London. One of them was from a lawyer in New York and concerned the tax implications of a certain investment of dubious legality. Its true sender was Eli Lavon, who was staying in a room down the hall, and its true content was revealed when Gabriel keyed in the proper password. It seemed that Gennady Lazarev had taken his prospective new employee to the O2 Lounge at the Ritz for drinks and a nosh. Also in attendance were Dmitry Bershov, Pavel Zhirov, and four pieces of Russian eye candy. Surveillance photos to follow, courtesy of Yaakov and Dina, who were in a booth on the opposite side of the room.

Gabriel rekeyed the password, and the message returned to its original text. Then he slipped on a pair of headphones and patched into a secure feed of the audio from Mikhail's mobile phone. He heard clinking glass, laughter, and the twitter of the Russian eye candy, which sounded inane, even in a language he could not comprehend. Then he heard the familiar voice of Gennady Lazarev murmuring a confidence into Mikhail's ear. "Make sure you get some rest to-night," he was saying. "We have big plans for you tomorrow."

They remained in the lounge until eleven, when Mikhail repaired to his luxury suite at the Ritz with no company other than a raging headache. Despite Lazarev's admonition, he did not sleep that night, for his thoughts were a swirl of operations past, strung together like a television newsreel of the century's most catastrophic events. He craved activity, movement of any kind, but the surveillance cameras that were surely hidden within the room wouldn't allow it. And so he lay tangled in the damp sheets of his bed with the stillness of a corpse until 7:00 a.m., when his wakeup call lifted him gratefully to his feet.

His coffee arrived a minute later, and he drank it while watching the morning business news from London. Afterward, he headed down to the health club, where he put in an impressive workout witnessed by a watcher from one of the Russian intelligence services. Returning to his room, he subjected himself to an ice-water shower to beat some life into his weary bones. Then he dressed in his finest gray chalk-stripe suit—the one Dina had chosen for him at Anthony Sinclair of Savile Row. He saw her in the breakfast room fifteen minutes later, staring into the eyes of Christopher Keller as if they held the secret to eternal happiness. A few tables away, Yossi was in the process of sending back his scrambled eggs. "I asked for them runny," he was saying, "but these should have been served in a glass." The remark bounced off the waiter like a pebble thrown at a freight train. "You want your eggs in a glass?" he asked.

At nine o'clock sharp, having read the morning papers and tidied up a few loose ends in London via e-mail, Mikhail made his way to the Ritz's ultramodern lobby. Waiting there was the same Volgatek factotum who had plucked him from the passport control line at Sheremetyevo the previous evening. He was smiling with all the pleasantness of a broken window.

"I trust you slept well, Mr. Avedon?"

"Never better," lied Mikhail cordially.

"Our office is very close. I hope you don't mind walking."

"Will we survive?"

"The chances are good, but there are no guarantees in Moscow this time of year."

With that, the factotum turned and led Mikhail into Tverskaya Street. As he climbed the slope of the hill, leaning hard into the battering-ram wind, he realized that the anonymous lump of wool and fur walking two steps behind him was Eli Lavon. The lump escorted him silently to Volgatek's front door, as if to remind Mikhail that he was not alone after all. Then it floated into the glare of the Moscow morning sun and was gone.

If there were any misunderstandings about Volgatek's true mission, they were put to rest by the vast metal sculpture that stood in the lobby of its Tverskaya Street headquarters. It depicted the earth, with an outsize Russia in the dominant position, pumping life-giving energy to the four corners of the planet. Standing beneath it, a tiny smiling Atlas in a handmade Italian suit, was Gennady Lazarev. "Welcome to your new home," he called out as his hand closed around Mikhail's. "Or should I call it your *real* home?"

"One step at a time, Gennady."

Lazarev squeezed Mikhail's hand a little harder, as if to say he would not be denied, and then led him into a waiting executive elevator that shot them to the building's uppermost floor. In the foyer was a sign that read WELCOME NICOLAI! Lazarev paused to admire it, as though he had put a great deal of effort into the wording, before conveying Mikhail into the large office that would be his to use whenever he was in town. It had a view of the Kremlin and came with a dangerously pretty secretary called Nina.

"What do you think?" asked Lazarev earnestly.

"Nice," said Mikhail.

"Come," said Lazarev, taking Mikhail by the elbow. "Everyone is anxious to meet you."

It turned out that Lazarev was not exaggerating when he said "everyone." Indeed, during the next two and a half hours, it seemed that Mikhail shook the hand of every employee in the company, and perhaps a few others for good measure. There were a dozen vice presidents of varying shapes, sizes, and responsibilities, and a cadaverous figure called Mentov who did something with risk analysis that Mikhail couldn't even pretend to comprehend. Next he was introduced to Volgatek's scientific team—the geologists who were searching for new sources of oil and gas around the world, the engineers who were devising inventive new ways of extracting it. Then he headed down to the lower floors to meet the little people—the young account executives who dreamed of being in his shoes one day, the walking dead who were clinging to their desks and their red Volgatek coffee cups. He couldn't help but wonder what happened to an employee who was terminated by a company owned and operated by the successor of the KGB. Perhaps he received a gold watch and a pension, but Mikhail doubted it.

Finally, they returned to the top floor and entered Lazarev's large atrium-like office, where he spoke at length about his vision for Volgatek's future and the role he wanted Mikhail to play in it. His starting position at the firm would be chief of Volgatek UK, the subsidiary that would be formed to run the Western Isles project. Once the oil was flowing, Mikhail would assume greater responsibilities, primarily in Western Europe and North America.

"Would that be enough to keep you interested?" asked Lazarev.

"It might be."

"What would it take to convince you to leave Viktor and come to me?"

"Money, Gennady. Lots of money."

"I can assure you, Nicolai, money isn't an issue."

"Then you have my full attention."

Lazarev opened a leather folio and removed a single sheet of paper. "Your compensation package will include apartments in Aberdeen, London, and Moscow," he began. "You will fly private, of course, and you will have use of a Volgatek villa that we keep in the south of France. In addition to your base salary, you will receive bonuses and incentives that will bring your total compensation to something like this."

Lazarev placed the sheet of paper in front of Mikhail and pointed to the figure near the bottom of the page. Mikhail looked at it for a moment, scratched his hairless head, and frowned.

"Well?" asked Lazarev.

"Not even close."

Lazarev smiled. "I thought that would be your answer," he said, delving into the folio again, "so I took the liberty of preparing a second offer." He placed it in front of Mikhail and asked, "Any better?"

"Warmer," said Mikhail, returning Lazarev's smile. "Definitely warmer."

49

RED SQUARE, MOSCOW

B Y FOUR THAT AFTERNOON, they had the broad outlines of an agreement. Lazarev drew up a one-page deal memo, booked a private room at Café Pushkin for the celebration, and sent Mikhail back to the Ritz for a few hours of rest. He made the short walk with no escort other than Gabriel, who was shadowing him along the opposite pavement, his coat collar around his ears, a flat cap pulled low over his brow. He watched Mikhail turn into the hotel's grand entrance and then continued along Tverskaya Street to Revolution Square. There he paused briefly to watch a Lenin imper- sonator exhorting a group of bewildered Japanese tourists to seize the means of production from their bourgeoisie overlords. Then he slipped beneath the archway of Resurrection Gate and entered Red Square.

Darkness had fallen and the wind had decided to give the city a reprieve to go about its evening business in peace. Head down, shoulders hunched, Gabriel looked like just another jaded Muscovite as he hurried along the northern wall of the Kremlin, past the blank stares of the frozen guards standing watch outside the Lenin Mausoleum. Directly ahead, awash in white light, rose the swirling candy-cane domes of St. Basil's Cathedral. Gabriel glanced at the clock in the Savior Tower and then made his way to the spot along the Kremlin wall where Stalin, the murderer of millions, slumbered peacefully in a place of honor. Eli Lavon joined him a moment later.

"What do you think?" asked Gabriel in German.

"I think they should have buried him in an unmarked grave in a field," Lavon responded. "But that's just one man's opinion."

"Are we clean?"

"As clean as we can be in a place like Moscow."

Gabriel turned without a word and led Lavon across the square to the entrance of GUM. Before the fall of the Soviet Union, it had been the only department store in the country where Russians could reliably find a winter coat or a pair of shoes. Now it was a Western-style shopping mall stuffed with all the useless trinkets capitalism had to offer. The soaring glass roof reverberated with the chatter of the evening shoppers. Lavon stared at his BlackBerry as he walked at Gabriel's side. These days, it was a very Russian thing to do.

"Gennady Lazarev's secretary just sent an e-mail to his senior staff about tonight's dinner at Café Pushkin," Lavon said. "Pavel Zhirov was on the invitation list."

"I never heard his voice when Mikhail was inside Volgatek today."

"That's because he wasn't there," Lavon replied, still gazing at his BlackBerry. "After leaving his apartment in Sparrow Hills, he went straight to Yasenevo."

"Why today of all days? Why wasn't he at Volgatek to meet the new boy?"

"Maybe he had other business to attend to."

"Like what?"

"Maybe there was someone else who needed to be kidnapped."

"That's what worries me."

Gabriel paused in the window of a jewelry store and gazed at a display of glittering Swiss watches. Next door was a Soviet-style cafeteria where plump women in white aprons joylessly spooned cheap Russian food onto gray Brezhnev-era plates. Even now, more than twenty years after the fall of communism, there were still Russians who clung to the nostalgia of their totalitarian past.

"You're not getting cold feet, are you?" Lavon asked.

"It's December in Moscow, Eli. It's impossible not to."

"What do you want to do about it?"

"I'd like the hotel to give Nicholas Avedon his special amenity a little earlier than planned."

"Amenities like that are frowned upon at Café Pushkin."

"Anyone who's anyone carries a gun at Pushkin, Eli."

"It's risky."

"Not as risky as the alternative."

"Why don't we skip dinner and go straight to dessert?"

"I'd love to," said Gabriel, "but the rush-hour traffic won't allow it. We have to wait until after ten o'clock. Otherwise, we'll never be able to get him out of town. We'll be dead in the water."

"A poor choice of words."

"Send the message, Eli."

Lavon typed a few characters into his BlackBerry and led Gabriel outside, into Il'inka Street. The wind was getting up again, and the temperature had plummeted. Tears flowed freely from Gabriel's eyes as they walked past the Easter-egg facades of the heavy imperial buildings. In his earpiece he could hear Nicholas Avedon humming softly to himself as he ran a bath in his room at the Ritz.

"I want full coverage on him the entire time," Gabriel said. "We take him to dinner, we sit with him at dinner, and then we take him back to his hotel. That's when the fun begins."

"Only if Pavel agrees to ride to Mikhail's rescue."

"He's the chief of Volgatek security. If Volgatek's newest executive believes his life is in danger, Pavel will come running. And then we'll make him very sorry that he did."

"I'd feel better if we could take him to another country."

"Which one, Eli? Ukraine? Belarus? Or how about Kazakhstan?"

"Actually, I was thinking about Mongolia."

"Bad food."

"Terrible food," agreed Lavon, "but at least it isn't Russia."

At the end of the street, they turned to the left and climbed the hill toward Lubyanka Square.

"Do you think it's ever been done before?" asked Lavon.

"What's that?"

"Kidnapping a KGB officer *inside* Russia."

"There is no KGB, Eli. The KGB is a thing of the past."

"No, it isn't. It's called the FSB now. And it occupies that big ugly building directly ahead of us. And they're going to be rather upset when they find out one of their brethren is missing."

"If we get him cleanly, they won't have time to do anything about it."

"If we get him cleanly," Lavon agreed.

Gabriel was silent.

"Do me a favor tonight, Gabriel. If you don't have the shot, don't take it." He paused, then added, "I'd hate to miss out on the opportunity of working for you when you become the chief."

They had arrived at the top of the hill. Lavon slowed to a stop and gazed at the enormous yellow fortress on the opposite side of Lubyanka Square. "Why do you suppose they kept it?" he asked seriously. "Why didn't they tear it down and put up a monument to its victims?"

"For the same reason they didn't remove Stalin's bones from the Kremlin wall," answered Gabriel.

Lavon was silent for a moment. "I hate this place," he said finally. "And at the same time, I love it dearly. Am I crazy?"

"Certifiable," said Gabriel. "But that's just one man's opinion."

"I'd feel better if we could take him to another country."

"So would I, Eli. But we can't."

"How far *is* it to Mongolia?"

"Too far to drive," said Gabriel. "And the food is terrible."

Five minutes later, as Gabriel entered the Metropol's overheated lobby, Yossi Gavish stepped from his fourth-floor room at the Ritz-Carlton Hotel dressed in a banker's gray suit and a silver necktie. In his left hand was a gold name tag that read ALEXANDER—a student of history, Yossi had chosen it himself—and in his right was a glossy blue gift bag bearing the hotel's logo. The bag was heavier than Yossi made it appear, for it contained a Makarov 9mm pistol, one of several weapons that Moscow Station had acquired from illicit local sources before the team's arrival. For three days the weapon had been concealed between the mattress and box spring in Yossi's room. He was understandably relieved to finally be rid of it.

Yossi waited until he was certain the corridor was unoccupied before quickly affixing the name tag to his lapel. Then he made his way to the doorway of Room 421. From the opposite side he could hear a man singing "Penny Lane" quite well. He knocked twice, firm but polite, the knock of a concierge. Then, upon receiving no answer, he knocked again, louder. This time a man in a white toweling robe answered. He was tall, impossibly fit, and pink from his bath.

"I'm busy," he snapped.

"I'm so sorry to interrupt, Mr. Avedon," replied Yossi in a neutral cosmopolitan accent, "but management would like to offer you a small gift of our appreciation."

"Tell management thanks but no thanks."

"Management would be disappointed."

"It's not more bloody caviar, is it?"

"I'm afraid management didn't say."

The pink man in the white robe snatched the gift bag and slammed the door on Yossi's false hotelier's smile. With that, Yossi turned on his heel and, after plucking the name tag from his lapel, headed back to his own room. There he quickly removed his suit and changed into a pair of jeans and a heavy woolen sweater. His suitcase stood at the foot of the bed; if everything went according to plan, a courier from Moscow Station would collect it in a few hours and destroy the contents. Yossi stuffed the suit into a side pocket and pulled the zipper closed. Then he wiped down every object he had touched in the room and left it for what he hoped would be the last time.

Downstairs in the lobby, he saw Dina leafing skeptically through an English-language Moscow newspaper. He walked past her as though they were unacquainted and stepped outside. A Range Rover waited at the curb, its tailpipe sending a plume of vaporous exhaust into the bitterly cold night. Seated behind the wheel was Christopher Keller. He pulled into the evening rush-hour traffic on Tverskaya Street even before Yossi had closed the door. Directly before them rose the Kremlin's Corner Arsenal Tower, its red star glowing like a warning light. Keller whistled tunelessly as he drove.

"Do you know the way?" asked Yossi.

"Left on Okhotnyy Ryad Street, left on Bol'shaya Dmitrovka Street, and then another left on the Boulevard Ring."

"Spend much time in Moscow, do you?"

"Never had the pleasure."

"Can you at least pretend to be nervous?"

"Why should I be nervous?"

"Because we're about to kidnap a KGB officer in the middle of Moscow."

Keller smiled as he made the first left turn. "Easy peasy lemon squeezy."

It took Keller and Yossi the better part of twenty minutes to make the short drive to their holding point on the Boulevard Ring. Upon arrival, Yossi fired off a secure message to Gabriel at the Metropol, and Gabriel in turn bounced it to King Saul Boulevard, where it flashed across the status screen in the Op Center. Seated in his usual chair was Uzi Navot. He was staring at a live video image of the Ritz-Carlton's lobby, courtesy of the miniature transmitter concealed in Dina's handbag. The time was 7:36 in Moscow, 6:36 in Tel Aviv. At 6:38 the phone at Navot's elbow rang. He brought the receiver swiftly to his ear, grunted something that sounded like his own name, and heard the voice of Orit, his executive secretary. Inside King Saul Boulevard, she was known as "the Iron Dome" because of her unrivaled ability to shoot down requests for a moment with the chief.

"No way," responded Navot. "Not a chance."

"He's made it clear he's not going to leave."

Navot sighed heavily. "All right," he said. "Send him down, if you have to."

Navot hung up the phone and stared at the image of the hotel lobby. Two minutes later he heard the sound of the Op Center door opening and closing behind him. Then, from the corner of his eye, he saw a liver-spotted hand place two packs of Turkish cigarettes on the tabletop, along with a battered old Zippo. The lighter flared. A cloud of smoke blurred the image on the screen.

"I thought I pulled all your passes," Navot said quietly, still staring straight ahead.

"You did," replied Shamron.

"How did you get in the building?"

"I tunneled in."

Shamron twirled the old lighter in his fingertips. Two turns to the right, two turns to the left.

"You have a lot of nerve showing your face around here," Navot said.

"This isn't the time or the place, Uzi."

"I know it isn't," Navot said. "But you still have a lot of nerve."

Two turns to the right, two turns to the left . . .

"Would it be possible to turn up the volume on the audio feed from Mikhail's phone?" Shamron asked. "My hearing isn't what it once was."

"Your hearing isn't the only thing."

Navot caught the eye of one of the technicians and gestured for him to increase the volume.

"What's that song he's singing?" Shamron asked.

"What difference does it make?"

"Answer the question, Uzi."

"It's 'Penny Lane.'"

"The Beatles?"

"Yes, the Beatles."

"Why do you suppose he chose that song?"

"Maybe he likes it."

"Maybe," said Shamron.

Navot glanced at the clock. It was 7:42 in Moscow, 6:42 in Tel Aviv. Shamron crushed out his cigarette and immediately lit another.

Two turns to the right, two turns to the left . . .

Mikhail was still singing to himself as he departed his hotel room, dressed for dinner. The gift bag was in his right hand as he entered the elevator, though it was absent when he came out of the lobby men's room three minutes after that. The team in the Ops Center saw him for the first time at 7:51 as he passed within range of Dina's camera and started toward the hotel entrance. Waiting there, his arm raised as though he were signaling a rescue aircraft, was Gennady Lazarev. The hand seized Mikhail by the shoulder and drew him into the back of a waiting Maybach limousine. "I hope you managed to get a little rest," Lazarev said as the car eased gracefully away from the curb, "because tonight you're going to get a taste of the real Russia."

50

CAFÉ PUSHKIN, MOSCOW

I N THE AFTERMATH, WHEN THEY were tidying up their files and writing their after-action reports, there would be a heated debate over the true meaning of Gennady Lazarev's words. One camp saw them as a harmless expression of goodwill; the other as a clear warning that Gabriel, a chief in waiting, would have been wise to heed. As usual, it was Shamron who settled the dispute. Lazarev's words were without consequence, he declared, for Mikhail's fate had been sealed the instant he climbed into the car.

The setting for what transpired next, Moscow's renowned Café Pushkin, could not have appeared any more inviting, especially on a December evening, with the air brittle and snow dancing on a Siberian wind. It was located at the corner of Tverskaya Street and the Boulevard Ring, in a stately old eighteenth-century house that looked as though it had been imported from Renaissance Italy. Beyond its pretty French doors ran three lanes of traffic; and beyond the traffic was a small square where Napoleon's soldiers had once pitched their tents and burned the lime trees for warmth. Muscovites hurried home along the gravel footpaths, and a few brave mothers sat on the benches in the lamplight, watching their overbundled children playing on the snow-whitened lawns. Mordecai and Rimona sat silently among them, Mordecai watching the entrance of Café Pushkin, Rimona the children. Keller and Yossi had found a parking space fifty yards short of the restaurant. Yaakov and Oded, also in a Land Rover, were fifty yards beyond it.

The dinner had been called for eight, but owing to the heavier than normal traffic in Moscow that evening, Lazarev and Mikhail did not arrive until twelve minutes past. Mordecai made a note of the time, as did the teams in the Land Rovers. So did Gabriel, who quickly flashed a message to the Op Center at King Saul Boulevard. The message was unnecessary, of course, because Navot and Shamron were closely monitoring the live audio feed from Mikhail's phone. Therefore, they heard his heavy footfalls over the unpolished floorboards in Pushkin's entrance. And the rattle of the old elevator that bore him to the second floor. And the round of throaty Russian applause that greeted him as he entered the private room that had been set aside for his coronation.

A place had been reserved for Mikhail at the head of the table, with Lazarev to his right and Pavel Zhirov, Volgatek's chief of security, to his left. Zhirov alone seemed to take no joy in the acquisition of Viktor Orlov's protégé. Throughout the evening, he wore the blank expression of an experienced gambler who was losing badly at roulette. His gaze, narrow and dark, never strayed long from Mikhail's face. He seemed to be calculating his losses and deciding whether he had the stomach for another turn of the wheel.

If Zhirov's brooding presence made Mikhail uneasy, he gave no sign of it. Indeed, all those who listened in on Mikhail's performance that evening would describe it as one of the finest they had ever heard. He was the Nicholas Avedon whom they had all fallen in love with from afar. The witty Nicholas. The edgy Nicholas. The smarter than everyone else in the room Nicholas—save for Gennady Lazarev, who was perhaps smarter than anyone else in the world. As the evening wore on, he spoke less English and more Russian, until he stopped speaking English altogether. He was one of them now. He was Nicolai Avdonin. A Volgatek man. A man of Russia's future. A man of Russia's past.

The transformation was made complete shortly after ten o'clock when he did a spot-on imitation of Viktor Orlov, along with the twitching left eye, which brought down the house. Only Pavel Zhirov seemed not to find it amusing. Nor did he join in the ovation that followed Gennady Lazarev's benedictory remarks. Afterward, the party spilled onto the pavement, where a line of Volgatek limousines waited at the curb. Lazarev offhandedly asked Mikhail to stop by the office on his way out of town in the morning to tie up a few loose ends on the deal memo. Then he guided him toward the open rear door of a waiting Mercedes. "If you wouldn't mind," he said through his mathematician's smile, "I'm going to have Pavel run you back to the hotel. He has a few questions he'd like to ask you on the way."

Mikhail heard himself say "No problem, Gennady." Then, without an instant's hesitation, he slid into the waiting car. Pavel Zhirov, the night's only loser, sat opposite, staring inconsolably out his window. He said nothing as the car pulled into the street. Mikhail tapped his finger against the armrest. Then he forced himself to stop.

"Gennady said you had a few questions for me."

"Actually," replied Zhirov in his underpowered voice, "I only have one."

"What is it?"

Zhirov turned and looked at Mikhail for the first time. "Who the fuck are you?"

"Sounds like Pavel just moved the goalposts," Navot said.

Shamron frowned; he considered the use of sports metaphors to be inappropriate for a business as vital as espionage. He looked up at one of the video panels and saw lights moving quickly across a map of central Moscow. The light depicting Mikhail's position flashed red. Four blue lights moved along with it, two in front, two behind.

"Looks like we've got him boxed in," said Shamron.

"Quite nicely, actually. The question is, does Pavel have backup of his own, or is he flying solo?"

"I'm not sure it matters much at this point."

"Any suggestions?"

"Kick the ball," said Shamron, lighting a fresh cigarette. "Quickly."

They shot past Tverskaya Street in a blur and continued on along the Boulevard Ring.

"My hotel is that way," said Mikhail, jerking his thumb over his shoulder.

"You seem to know Moscow well," replied Zhirov. Clearly, it was not meant as a compliment.

"Habit of mine," said Mikhail.

"What's that?"

"Getting to know my way around foreign cities. Hate having to ask for directions. Don't like doing the tourist thing."

"You like to blend in?"

"Listen, Pavel, I don't like the sound of where this is—"

"Or maybe you've been to Moscow before," Zhirov suggested.

"Never."

"Not recently?"

"No."

"Not as a child?"

"Never means never, Pavel. Now if you don't mind, I'd like to go back to my hotel."

Zhirov was looking out his window again. Or was he peering into the driver's sideview mirror? Mikhail couldn't be sure.

"You still haven't answered my question," Zhirov said finally.

"I haven't answered it because it doesn't deserve one," Mikhail shot back.

"Who are you?"

"I'm Nicholas Avedon," Mikhail said calmly. "I'm an employee of Viktor Orlov Investments in London. And thanks to this little display of yours, I'm going to remain one."

Zhirov was obviously unconvinced. "Who are you?" he asked again.

"I'm Nicholas. I grew up in England. I went to Cambridge and Harvard. I worked in the oil biz in Aberdeen for a time. And then I came to Viktor."

"Why?"

"Why did I grow up in England? Why did I go to Harvard?"

"Why did you go to work for a known enemy of the Kremlin like Viktor Orlov?"

"Because he was looking for someone to take over his oil portfolio. And at this moment, I'm sorry I betrayed him."

"Did you know about his politics when you went to work for him?"

"I don't care about his politics. In fact, I don't care about anyone's politics."

"You're a freethinker?"

"No, Pavel, I'm a businessman."

"You are a spy."

"A spy? Are you off your meds, Pavel?"

"Who are you working for?"

"Take me back to my hotel."

"The British?"

"My hotel, Pavel."

"The Americans?"

"You were the ones who approached *me*, remember, Pavel? It happened in Copenhagen, at the oil forum. We met at the house in the middle of nowhere. I'm sure you were there."

"Who are you working for?" Zhirov asked again, a teacher to a dull pupil.

"Stop the car. Let me out."

"Who?"

"Stop the fucking car."

It did stop, but not because of Zhirov; they had reached Petrovka Street. It was a large intersection, with streets leading away in several different directions. The light had just turned red. Directly in front of them was a Land Rover with two men in front. Mikhail shot a glance over his shoulder and saw a second Rover behind them. Then he felt his mobile phone give three short bursts of vibration.

"What was that?" asked Zhirov.

"Just my mobile."

"Turn it off and remove the battery."

"You can never be too careful, right, Pavel?"

"Turn it off," Zhirov snapped.

Mikhail reached into his overcoat, drew the Makarov, and screwed the barrel hard into Zhirov's ribs. The Russian's eyes widened, but he said nothing. He looked at Mikhail for a few seconds, then his gaze moved toward Yaakov, who was climbing out of the Land Rover in front of them. Keller had already climbed out of the second Land Rover and was approaching the Mercedes from behind.

"Tell the driver to put the car in park," Mikhail said quietly. "Otherwise, I'm going to put a bullet in your heart. Tell him, Pavel, or you're going to die right now."

When Zhirov made no response, Mikhail thumbed back the hammer of the weapon. Keller was now standing at Zhirov's window.

"Tell him, Pavel."

The traffic light turned green. Somewhere a car horn sounded. Then another.

"Tell him!" Mikhail barked in Russian.

Zhirov glanced into the rearview mirror, met the driver's gaze, and nodded once. The driver slipped the car into park and placed his hands atop the wheel.

"Tell him to get out of the car and do exactly as he's told."

Another glance into the mirror, another nod of the head. The driver responded by opening the door and climbing slowly out. Yaakov waited there to take possession of him. After murmuring a few words into the driver's ear, he led him to the Land Rover, shoved him into the backseat, and slid in after him. By then, Keller had taken the driver's place behind the wheel of the Mercedes. When the Land Rover moved off, he slipped the car into gear and followed after it. Mikhail still had the Makarov to Zhirov's ribs.

"Who are you?" Zhirov asked.

"I'm Nicholas Avedon," Mikhail answered.

"Who are you?" Zhirov repeated.

"I'm your worst nightmare," said Mikhail. "And if you don't shut your mouth, I'm going to kill you."

In the Op Center at King Saul Boulevard, the lights of the team were moving vertically up the video map of Moscow—all but one, which was motionless on Teatralny Prospekt, just down the hill from Lubyanka Square. There were no celebrations, no congratulations on a job well done. The setting wouldn't allow it. Moscow had a way of fighting back.

"Thirty seconds from start to finish," Navot said, his eyes fixed on the screen. "Not bad."

"Thirty-three," said Shamron. "But who's counting?"

"You were."

Shamron gave a faint smile; he *had* been counting. In fact, he had been counting his entire life. The number of family members lost to the fires of the Holocaust. The number of countrymen lost to the bullets and the bombs. The number of times he had cheated death.

"How far is it to the safe house?"

"One hundred and forty-seven miles from the Outer Ring."

"What's the weather forecast?"

"Horrendous," replied Navot, "but they can handle it."

Shamron said nothing more. Navot stared at the lights moving across Moscow.

"Thirty seconds," he repeated. "Not bad."

"Thirty-three," said Shamron. "And let's hope no one else was watching."

Though Shamron did not know it, those were the same thoughts running through the head of the man standing in the window of his fourth-floor room at the Hotel Metropol. He was gazing down the curve of Teatralny Prospekt, toward the yellow fortress looming over Lubyanka Square. He wondered whether he would be able to detect some sort of reaction—lights coming on in the upper floors, cars careening out of the garage—but decided it was unlikely. Lubyanka had always been good at hiding her emotions, just as Russia had always been good at hiding her dead.

He turned away from the window, switched off his computer, and stuffed it into the side pocket of his overnight bag. Then he rode the elevator down to the lobby, accompanied by a pair of prostitutes, seventeen going on forty-five. Outside a Volvo SUV idled at the curb, watched over by a miserable-looking valet. He gave the valet a large tip, climbed behind the wheel, and drove away. Twenty minutes later, having rounded the walls of the Kremlin, he joined the river of steel and light flowing north out of Moscow. In the Op Center at King Saul Boulevard, however, he was but a single red light, an angel of vengeance alone in the city of heretics.

51

TVER OBLAST, RUSSIA

I T WAS ONCE THE DACHA of a powerful man—a member of the Central Committee, maybe even the Politburo. No one could say for certain, for in the chaotic days after the collapse all had been lost. State-owned factories had remained shuttered because no one could find the keys; government computers had slept because no one could remember the codes. Russia had stumbled into the brave new millennium without a map or a memory. There were some who said it had no memory still, though now its amnesia was deliberate.

For several years, the forgotten dacha sat empty and derelict, until a newly well-to-do Moscow developer named Bloch acquired it for a song and rebuilt it from the ground up. Eventually, like many of Russia's early rich, Bloch ran afoul of the new crowd in the Kremlin and decided to leave the country while he still could. He settled in Israel, in part because he thought he might be a little bit Jewish, but mainly because no other country would have him. Over time, he sold off his Russian assets, but not the dacha in Tver Oblast. He gave that to Ari Shamron and told him to use it in good health.

It stood by a lake with no name and was reached by a road that appeared on no map. It was not truly a road, more like a groove that had been beaten into the birch forest long before anyone had ever heard of a place called Russia. The dacha's original gate remained, as did the old Soviet NO TRESPASSING sign that Bloch, a child of the Stalinist era, had been too terrified to remove. It flashed briefly through Gabriel's headlamps as he came bumping up the snowbound drive. Then the dacha appeared, heavy and timbered, with a peaked roof and broad porches all around. Parked outside were several vehicles, including an S-Class Mercedes owned by Volgatek Oil & Gas. As Gabriel climbed out of the Volvo SUV, a cigarette flared in the darkness.

"Welcome to Shangri-La," said Christopher Keller. He was wearing a heavy down parka and holding a Makarov pistol.

"How's the perimeter?" asked Gabriel.

"Cold as hell, but clean."

"How long can you stay out here?"

Keller smiled. "I'm Regiment, luv."

Gabriel slipped past Keller and entered the dacha. The rest of the team were scattered in various states of repose across the rustic furnishings in the great room. Mikhail was still dressed for dinner at Café Pushkin. He was soaking his right hand in a bowl of ice water.

"What happened?" Gabriel asked.

"I bumped it."

"Against what?"

"Another man's face."

Gabriel asked to see the hand. It was badly swollen, and three of the knuckles had no skin.

"How many times did you bump it?" asked Gabriel.

"Once or twice. Or maybe it was more like ten or twelve."

"How's the face?"

"See for yourself."

"Where is he?"

Mikhail pointed toward the floor.

Among the dacha's many luxury features was a nuclear fallout shelter. It had once contained a year's worth of food, water, and supplies. Now it contained two men. Both were heavily trussed in duct tape: hands, feet, knees, mouths, eyes. Even so, it was obvious that the face of the elder man had suffered significant damage as a result of repeated collisions against Mikhail's dangerous right hand. He was propped against one wall, with his legs stretched before him across the floor. Upon hearing the opening of the door, his head began to swivel from side to side, a radar dish in search of an invading aircraft. Gabriel crouched before him and tore away the duct tape covering the eyes, taking part of one brow with it, which left him with an expression of permanent surprise. There was a deep gash on one cheek and dried blood around the nostrils of his now-crooked nose. Gabriel smiled and removed the duct tape from the mouth.

"Hello, Pavel," he said. "Or should I call you Paul?"

Zhirov said nothing. Gabriel scrutinized the broken nose.

"That must hurt," he said. "But these things happen in a place like Russia."

"I look forward to returning the favor, Allon."

"So you *do* recognize me."

"Of course," Zhirov said a little too confidently. "We've been watching you since the moment you set foot in Russia."

"Who's *we?*" asked Gabriel. "Volgatek? The SVR? The FSB?

Or shall we just put aside the niceties and call you the KGB, which is exactly what you are."

"You're dead, Allon—you and all your people. You'll never leave Russia alive."

Gabriel's smile was still firmly in place. "I've always found it best not to make hollow threats, Pavel."

"I couldn't agree more."

"Then perhaps you should drop the pretense that you knew I was in Moscow, or that you knew Nicholas Avedon was my creation. You would have never made a move against him tonight without FSB backup if you'd known he was my agent."

"Who says I didn't have backup?"

"I do."

"You're wrong, Allon. But then you have a long history of being wrong. The FSB is just waiting to make sure they've identified all the members of your team. You've got a few hours at most. Then *you'll* be the one sitting in a cell with a broken nose."

"Then I suppose we should get started."

"On what?"

"Your confession," said Gabriel. "You're going to tell the world how you kidnapped an English girl named Madeline Hart so Volgatek Oil and Gas could gain access to the North Sea."

Zhirov feigned surprise. "The English girl? Is that what this is about?"

Gabriel shook his head slowly, as if disappointed by Zhirov's response. "Come on, Pavel," he said. "Surely you can do better than that. You plucked her from the coast road near Calvi a few hours after having lunch with her at Les Palmiers. A Marseilles lowlife named Marcel Lacroix took you to the mainland, where you handed her over to another Marseilles lowlife named René Brossard for safe-keeping. Then, after collecting ten million euros in ransom from the

British prime minister, you left her in the back of a car on the beach at Audresselles and lit a match."

"Not bad, Allon."

"Actually, it wasn't all that difficult. You left plenty of clues to follow. But that was your intention. You wanted Madeline's kidnapping and murder to appear to be the work of French criminals. But you made one mistake, Pavel. You should have listened when I warned you not to harm her. I told you exactly what would happen if you did. I told you that I would find you. I also told you that I would kill you."

"So why haven't you? Why put your people at risk by kidnapping me and bringing me here?"

"We didn't kidnap you, Pavel. We captured you. And we brought you here because, in spite of your current circumstances, this is your lucky day. I'm going to give you something that doesn't come along often in our business. I'm going to give you a second chance."

"What do I have to do for this second chance?"

"Answer a few questions, tie up a few loose ends."

"That's all?"

Gabriel nodded.

"And then?"

"You'll be free to go."

"Go where?" asked Zhirov seriously.

"Back to Volgatek. Back to the SVR. Back to the rock you crawled out from under."

Zhirov managed a condescending smile. "And what do you think will happen to me when I return to Yasenevo after answering your questions and tying up your loose ends?"

"I suppose you'll be given *vysshaya mera*," Gabriel said. "The highest measure of punishment."

Zhirov gave a nod of admiration. "You know a great deal about my service," he said.

"Not by choice," replied Gabriel. "And to be perfectly honest with you, Pavel, I couldn't care less what your service does to you."

"You should," said Zhirov through the same condescending grin. "You see, Allon, what you are offering me is a choice between death and death."

"I'm offering you a chance to see one more Russian sunrise, Pavel. And don't worry," Gabriel added. "I'll make sure you have plenty of time in a nice quiet place to think up a good story to tell your masters at the SVR. Something tells me you'll be all right in the end."

"And if I refuse?"

"Then I'm going to personally put a bullet in the back of your neck for killing Madeline."

"I need some time to think."

Gabriel reapplied the duct tape to Zhirov's eyes and mouth.

"You have five minutes."

As it turned out, ten minutes would elapse before Mikhail, Yaakov, and Oded carried Zhirov from the fallout shelter to the dining room, where they secured him tightly to a heavy chair. Gabriel was seated opposite; behind him stood Yossi, his eyes fixed on the display screen of a tripod-mounted video camera. After making a small adjustment to the angle of the shot, Yossi nodded to Mikhail, who ripped the tape from Zhirov's eyes and mouth. The Russian blinked rapidly several times. Then his eyes swept slowly around the room, recording every face, every detail, before finally settling on the photograph in Gabriel's hands. It showed Zhirov, looking very different than he did now, having lunch with Madeline Hart at Les Palmiers in Calvi.

"How did you meet her?" asked Gabriel.

"Meet who?" replied Zhirov.

Gabriel laid the photograph upon the table and told Yossi to shut off the camera.

They cut him away from the chair, tied a length of rope to his wrists, and carried him outside, to the shore of the lake. A dock stretched fifty feet into the darkness; and at the end was a patch of water that had yet to freeze. Zhirov entered it gracelessly, as a heavily bound man is prone to do when hurled by three angry men.

"Do you know the survival time for water like that?" asked Keller.

"He'll start to lose feeling and dexterity in two minutes. And there's a good chance he'll be unconscious in about fifteen."

"If he doesn't drown first."

"There's always that," said Gabriel.

Keller watched the thrashing figure in silence for a moment. "How will you know when he's had enough?" he asked finally.

"When he starts to sink."

"Remind me never to get on your bad side."

"These things happen in a place like Russia."

52

TVER OBLAST, RUSSIA

TWO MINUTES IN THE LAKE was all it took. After that, there were no more protestations of innocence, no more threats that the FSB would soon be riding to his rescue. Resigned to his fate, he became a model prisoner. He made only one request, that they do something about his appearance. Like most spies, he had spent his career avoiding cameras, and he didn't want to make his star turn looking like the loser of a prizefight.

There is a truism about the intelligence trade: contrary to popular belief, most spies like to talk, especially when confronted with a situation that renders their career unsalvageable. At that point, they spill their secrets in a torrent, if only to prove to themselves that they had been more than simply a cog in the covert machine, that they had been important, even if they were not.

Therefore, it came as no surprise to Gabriel that Pavel Zhirov, after recovering from his plunge into the lake, was suddenly in a talkative mood. Dressed in dry clothing, warmed by sweetened tea and a bit of brandy, he began his account not with Madeline Hart but with himself. He had been a child of the *nomenklatura*, the Communist elite of the Soviet Union. His father had been a senior official at the Soviet Foreign Ministry under Andrei Gromyko, which meant that Zhirov had attended special schools reserved for the children of the elite and had been allowed to shop in special Party stores that contained luxury goods most Soviet citizens could only dream of. And then there was the almost unheard-of luxury of foreign travel. Zhirov had spent much of his childhood outside the Soviet Union—mainly in the Soviet vassal states of Eastern Europe, which was his father's area of expertise, though he did spend six months in New York once when his father was working at the United Nations. He hated New York because, as a loyal child of the Party, he had been bred and educated to hate it. "We didn't see the wealth and greed of the United States as something to be emulated," he said. "We saw it as something we could use against the Americans to destroy them."

Despite the fact he was an indifferent and oftentimes disruptive student, Zhirov won admission to the prestigious Moscow Institute of Foreign Languages. Upon graduation, it was assumed he would go to work at the Foreign Ministry. Instead, a recruiter from the Committee for State Security, better known as the KGB, came calling at the Zhirovs' apartment in Moscow. The recruiter said the KGB had been watching Pavel since he was a child and believed he possessed all the attributes of a perfect spy.

"I was incredibly flattered," Zhirov admitted. "It was 1975. Ford and Brezhnev were making nice in Helsinki, but behind the facade of détente the contest between East and West, capitalism and socialism, was still raging. And I was going to be a part of it."

But first, he added quickly, he had to attend another institute: the Red Banner Institute, the KGB's Moscow training center. There he learned the basics of KGB tradecraft. Mainly, though, he learned how to recruit spies, which, for the KGB, was an excruciatingly slow, tightly controlled process lasting a year or more. His training complete, he was assigned to the Fifth Department of the First Chief Directorate and posted to Brussels. Several other Western European postings followed, until it became clear to Zhirov's superiors at Moscow Center that he had a flair for the darker side of the trade. He was transferred to Department S, the unit that oversaw Soviet agents living "illegally" abroad. Later, he worked for Department V, the KGB division that handled *mokriye dela*.

"Wet affairs," said Gabriel.

Zhirov nodded. "I wasn't a trigger man like you, Allon. I was an organizer and planner."

"Did you ever run any false flag operations when you were at Department V?"

"We ran them all the time," Zhirov admitted. "In fact, false flags were standard operating procedure. We almost never moved against a target unless we could create a plausible cover story that someone else was behind it."

"How long were you at Department V?"

"Until the end."

By that, he meant the end of the Soviet Union, which crumbled in December 1991. Almost overnight, the once-mighty superpower became fifteen separate countries, with Russia, the heart of the old union, the first among equals. The KGB was broken into two separate services. Before long, Moscow Center, once a cathedral of intelligence, fell on hard times. Cracks appeared in the exterior of the building, and the lobby was filled with uncollected trash. Unshaven officers in wrinkled clothing wandered the halls in an alcoholic daze.

"There wasn't even toilet paper in the men's room," Zhirov said, disgust creeping into his voice. "The entire place was a pigsty. And no one was in charge."

That changed, he said, when Boris Yeltsin finally exited the stage and the *siloviki*, men from the security services, took control of the Kremlin. Almost immediately, they ordered the SVR to increase operations against the United States and Great Britain, both nominal allies of the new Russian Federation. Zhirov was named the SVR's new chief *rezident* in Washington, one of the most important posts in the service. But on the day he was supposed to depart Russia, he received a summons to the Kremlin. It seemed the president, an old colleague from the KGB, wanted a word.

"I assumed he wanted to give me some parting instructions about how to handle my job in Washington," Zhirov said. "But as it turned out, he had other plans for me."

"Volgatek," said Gabriel.

Zhirov nodded. "Volgatek."

To understand what happened next, Zhirov said, it was first necessary to understand the importance of oil to Russia. He reminded his audience that, for decades, the Soviet Union was the world's second-largest oil producer, trailing only Saudi Arabia and the emirates of the American-dominated Persian Gulf. The oil shocks of the 1970s and '80s had been a boon to the wobbly Soviet economy—they were like a respirator, said Zhirov, that prolonged the life of the patient long after the brain had ceased functioning. The new Russian president understood what Boris Yeltsin had not, that oil could turn Russia into a superpower again. So he showed the oligarchs like Viktor Orlov the door and brought the entire Russian energy sector under effective Kremlin control. And then he started an oil company of his own.

"KGB Oil and Gas," said Gabriel.

"More or less," agreed Zhirov, nodding slowly. "But our company was to be different. We were tasked with acquiring drilling rights and downstream assets *outside* Russia. And we were KGB from top to bottom. In fact, a substantial percentage of our profits now flow directly into the accounts at Yasenevo."

"Where does the rest of it go?"

"Use your imagination."

"Into the pockets of the Russian president?"

"He didn't get to be Europe's richest man by wisely investing his KGB pension. Our president is worth about forty billion dollars, and much of his wealth comes from Volgatek."

"Whose idea was it to drill in the North Sea?"

"It was his," replied Zhirov. "He took it very personally. He said he wanted Volgatek to stick a straw into British territorial waters and suck on it until there was nothing left. For the record," he added, "I was against it from the beginning."

"Why?"

"Part of my job as chief of security and operations was to survey the playing field before we made a move on an asset or a drilling contract. My assessment of the situation in Britain wasn't promising. I predicted that the political tensions between London and Moscow would lead to a rejection of our application to drill off the Western Isles. And, regrettably, I was proven correct."

"I take it the president was disappointed."

"He was angrier than I'd ever seen him," Zhirov said. "Mainly because he suspected Viktor Orlov had played a role in it. He called me into his Kremlin office and told me to use any and all means necessary to get that contract."

"So you set your sights on Jeremy Fallon."

Zhirov hesitated before responding. "You obviously have very good sources in London," he said after a moment.

"Five million euros in a Swiss bank account," said Gabriel.

"That's what you gave Jeremy Fallon to get the contract for you."

"He drove a hard bargain. Needless to say," Zhirov added, "we were extremely disappointed when he failed to deliver. He said there was nothing he could do. Lancaster and the energy secretary were dead set against the deal. We had to do something to change the dynamic—shape the battlefield, if you will."

"So you kidnapped the prime minister's mistress."

Zhirov made no reply.

"Say it," said Gabriel, "or we're going to take another moonlight swim."

"Yes," Zhirov said, looking directly into the camera, "I kidnapped the prime minister's mistress."

"How did you know Lancaster was having an affair with her?"

"The London *rezidentura* had been hearing rumors for some time about a young woman from Party headquarters coming to Downing Street late at night. I asked them to press a little harder on the issue. It didn't take them long to figure out who she was."

"Did Fallon know that you were planning to kidnap her?"

Zhirov shook his head. "I waited until after delivering Madeline's confession before telling Fallon that we were behind it. I told him to use the opportunity to get the deal done. Otherwise, I was going to burn him, too."

"By leaking the fact that he took a five-million-euro bribe from a Kremlin-owned Russian oil company."

Zhirov nodded.

"When were you in contact with him?"

"I traveled to London while you and your little friend from Corsica were tearing up France looking for her. Lancaster was so incapacitated by stress he told Fallon to do whatever he wanted. Fallon pushed through the deal despite the objections of the energy secretary. Then I initiated the endgame."

"The ransom demand," said Gabriel. "Ten million euros, or the girl dies. And Fallon knew all along that it was nothing more than a charade designed to cover up Volgatek's role in Madeline's disappearance."

"And his role, too," Zhirov added.

"How much did Lancaster know?"

"Nothing," Zhirov responded. "He still believes he paid ten million euros to save his mistress and his political career."

"Why did you insist that I be the one to deliver the money?"

"We wanted to have a little fun at your expense."

"By killing Madeline in front of me?"

Zhirov was silent.

"Say it for the cameras, Pavel. Admit that you killed Madeline."

"I killed Madeline Hart," he recited.

"How?"

"By placing her in the back of a Citroën with a gasoline bomb."

"Why?" asked Gabriel. "Why did you kill her?"

"She had to die," Zhirov said. "There was no way she could be allowed to return to England."

"Why didn't you kill me, too?"

"Trust me, Allon, nothing would have made us happier. But we thought you were more useful alive than dead. After all, who better to authenticate that Madeline had been killed as part of a garden-variety kidnap-for-ransom scheme than the great Gabriel Allon?"

"Where's the ten million euros?"

"I gave it to the Russian president as a gift."

"I'd like it back."

"Good luck with that."

Gabriel placed the photograph of the luncheon at Les Palmiers on the table again.

"What's going on here?" he asked.

"I suppose you could call it the final stages of a romantic recruitment."

Gabriel gave a skeptical frown. "Why would a beautiful young girl like Madeline be interested in a creep like you?"

"I'm good at my job, Allon. Just like you. Besides," Zhirov added, "she was a lonely girl. She was easy."

"Watch yourself, Pavel." Gabriel made a show of scrutinizing the photograph more carefully. "It's funny," he said after a moment, "but the two of you look very comfortable together."

"It was our third meeting."

"Meeting?"

"Date," Zhirov said, correcting himself.

"It doesn't look to me as though you're having a good time," said Gabriel, still staring at the photo. "In fact, if I didn't know better, I'd say you were quarreling."

"We weren't," Zhirov said quickly.

"You sure about that?"

"I'm sure."

Gabriel wordlessly set aside the photograph.

"Any more questions?" asked Zhirov.

"Just one," said Gabriel. "How did you know Madeline was having an affair with Jonathan Lancaster?"

"I've already answered that question."

"I know," said Gabriel. "But this time, I want you to tell me the truth."

He offered up the same explanation—the one about rumors reaching the ears of the SVR *rezident* in London—but Gabriel was having none of it. He gave Zhirov one more chance; then, when told the same lie, he marched the Russian out to the end of the dock and pressed the barrel of a Makarov against the nape of his neck. And there, at the edge of the frozen lake with no name, the truth came spilling out. A part of Gabriel had suspected it all along. Even so, he could scarcely believe the story Zhirov told. But it had to be true, he thought. In fact, it was the only possible explanation for all that had happened.

Back inside the dacha, Zhirov recited the story again, this time for the video camera, before being returned, bound and gagged, to the fallout shelter. The operation was now almost complete. They had obtained proof that Volgatek had bribed and blackmailed its way into the lucrative North Sea oil market. All they had to do now was make their way to the airport and board their separate flights home. Or, suggested Gabriel, they could postpone their departure to conduct one last piece of business. It was not a decision he could make alone so, uncharacteristically, he put it to a vote. There were no dissenters.

53

ST. PETERSBURG, RUSSIA

G ABRIEL DECIDED IT WAS SAFER to take the train. There was a station in the town of Okulovka; he could catch the first local of the morning and be in St. Petersburg by early afternoon. Privately, he was relieved when Eli Lavon insisted on coming with him. He needed Lavon's eyes. And he needed his Russian, too.

It was only forty miles to Okulovka, but the dreadful roads and weather stretched the trip to nearly two hours. They left the Volvo SUV in a small windblown car park and hurried into the station, a newly built redbrick structure that looked oddly like a factory. The train was already boarding by the time Lavon managed to secure a pair of first-class tickets from one of the surly glass-enclosed agents. They shared a compartment with two Russian girls who chattered without pause and a thin elegantly dressed businessman who never once looked up from his phone. Lavon passed the time by reading the morning papers from Moscow, which contained no mention of a missing oil executive. Gabriel stared out the frosted window at the endless fields of snow until the swaying of the carriage lulled him into something like sleep.

He woke with a start as the train rattled into St. Petersburg's Moskovsky Station. Upstairs the great vaulted hall was in turmoil; it seemed the afternoon bullet train to Moscow had been delayed by a Chechen bomb threat. Trailed by Lavon, Gabriel picked his way through the sobbing children and quarreling couples and headed into Vosstaniya Square. The Hero City Obelisk rose skyward from the center of the swirling traffic circle, its golden star tarnished by the falling snow. Streetlamps burned up and down the length of Nevsky Prospekt. It was only two in the afternoon, but whatever daylight there had been was long gone.

Gabriel set out along the *prospekt* with Lavon floating watchfully in his wake. He was no longer in Russia, he thought. He was in a tsarist dreamland, imported from the West and built by terrorized peasants. Florence called to him from the facades of the Baroque palaces, and, crossing the Moyka River, he dreamed of Venice. He wondered how many bodies lay beneath the ice. Thousands, he thought. Tens of thousands. No other city in the world concealed the horrors of its past more beautifully than St. Petersburg.

Near the end of the *prospekt* was its only eyesore—the old Aeroflot building, a hideous flint-gray monstrosity inspired by the Doge's Palace in Venice, with a dash of Florentine Medici thrown in for good measure. Gabriel turned into Bolshaya Morskaya Street and followed it through the Triumphal Arch, into Palace Square. As he neared the Alexander Column, Lavon drew alongside him to say that he was not being followed. Gabriel glanced at his wristwatch, which seemed frozen to his arm. It was twenty minutes past two. *It happens the same time every day*, Zhirov had said. *They all go a little crazy when they come home after a long time in the cold.*

Adjacent to Palace Square was a small park, green in summer, now bone-white with snow. Lavon waited there on an icy bench while Gabriel walked alone to the Palace Embankment. The Neva had been stilled by ice. He glanced at his watch one final time. Then he stood alone at the barrier, as motionless as the mighty river, and waited for a girl he did not know.

He saw her at five minutes to three, coming across the Palace Bridge. She wore a heavy coat and boots that rose nearly to her knees. A wool hat covered her pale hair. A scarf concealed the lower half of her face. Even so, Gabriel knew instantly it was her. The eyes betrayed her—the eyes and the contour of her cheekbones. It was as if Vermeer's girl with a pearl earring had been freed from her canvas prison and was now walking along a riverbank in St. Petersburg.

She passed him as if he were invisible and made her way toward the Hermitage. Gabriel waited to see whether she was under surveillance before following, and by the time he entered the museum she was already gone. It didn't matter; he knew where she was going. *Same painting every time*, Zhirov had said. *No one can figure out why.*

He purchased an admission ticket and walked along the endless corridors and loggias to Room 67, the Monet Room. And there she sat alone, staring at *The Pond at Montgeron*. When Gabriel sat down next to her, she glanced at him only briefly before resuming her study of the painting. His disguise was better than hers. He meant nothing to her. He supposed he never had.

When another minute passed and he had yet to move, she turned and looked at him a second time. That was when she noticed the copy of *A Room with a View* balanced upon his knee. "I believe this belongs to you," he said. Then he placed the book carefully into her trembling hand.

54

LUBYANKA SQUARE, MOSCOW

O N THE FOURTH FLOOR OF FSB Headquarters is a suite of rooms occupied by the organization's smallest and most secretive unit. Known as the Department of Coordination, it handles only cases of extreme political sensitivity, usually at the behest of the Russian president himself. At that moment its longtime chief, Colonel Leonid Milchenko, was seated at his large Finnish-made desk, a telephone to his ear, his eyes on Lubyanka Square. Vadim Strelkin, his number two, was standing anxiously in the door. He could tell by the way Milchenko slammed down the phone it was going to be a long night.

"Who was it?" Strelkin asked.

Milchenko delivered his response to the window.

"Shit," replied Strelkin.

"Not shit, Vadim. Oil."

"What did he want?"

"He'd like a word in private."

"Where?"

"His office."

"When?"

"Five minutes ago."

"What do you think it is?"

"It could be anything," Milchenko said. "But if Volgatek is involved, it can't be good."

"I'll get the car then."

"Good idea, Vadim."

It took longer to haul the car from the bowels of Lubyanka than it did to make the short drive over to Volgatek headquarters on Tverskaya Street. Dmitry Bershov, the firm's second-ranking officer, was waiting tensely in the lobby as Milchenko and Strelkin entered—another bad sign. He said nothing as he led the two FSB men into an executive elevator and pressed a button that shot them directly into an office on the building's top floor. The office was the biggest Milchenko had ever seen in Moscow. In fact, it took a few seconds for him to spot Gennady Lazarev seated at one end of a long executive couch. Milchenko chose to remain on his feet while the Volgatek CEO explained that Pavel Zhirov, his chief of security, had not been seen or heard from since eleven the previous evening. Milchenko knew the name; he and Zhirov had been contemporaries at the KGB. He dropped a leather-bound notebook on Lazarev's glass coffee table and sat down.

"What was going on at eleven last night?"

"We were having a party at Café Pushkin to celebrate an important new hire at the firm. By the way," Lazarev added, "the new hire is missing, too. So is the driver."

"You might have mentioned that at the outset."

"I was getting to it."

"What's the new hire's name?"

Lazarev answered the question.

"Russian?" asked Milchenko.

"Not really."

"What does that mean?"

"It means he's of Russian ancestry but carries a British passport."

"So he is, in fact, British."

"He is."

"Anything else I should know about him?"

"He's currently employed by Viktor Orlov in London."

Milchenko exchanged a long look with Strelkin before staring wordlessly at his notebook. He had yet to write anything in it, which was probably wise. A missing former KGB officer and a missing associate of the Kremlin's most vocal opponent. Milchenko was beginning to think he should have called in sick that morning.

"I take it they left Café Pushkin together," he said finally.

Lazarev nodded.

"Why?"

"Pavel wanted to ask him a few questions."

"Why am I not surprised?"

Lazarev said nothing.

"What kind of questions?" Milchenko asked.

"Pavel had suspicions about him."

"Meaning?"

"He thought he might be connected to a foreign intelligence service."

"Any service in particular?"

"For obvious reasons," Lazarev said carefully, "his suspicions centered on the British."

"So he was planning to give him a good going-over."

"He was going to ask him a few questions," Lazarev said deliberately.

"And if he didn't like the answers?"

"*Then* he was going to give him a good going-over."

"I'm glad we cleared that up."

The phone at Lazarev's elbow emitted a soothing purr. He lifted the receiver to his ear, listened in silence, then said, "Right away," before replacing the receiver.

"What is it?" asked Milchenko.

"The president would like a word."

"You shouldn't keep him waiting."

"Actually," said Lazarev, "you're the one he wants to see."

55

ST. PETERSBURG, RUSSIA

A T THAT SAME MOMENT, the man responsible for Colonel Milchenko's summons to the Kremlin was walking along Admiralty Prospekt in St. Petersburg. He could no longer feel the cold, only the place on his arm where her hand had alighted briefly before they parted. His heart was banging against his breastbone. Surely they had been watching her. Surely he was about to be arrested. To calm his fears, he told himself lies. He was not in Russia, he thought. He was in Venice and Rome and Florence and Paris, all at the same time. He was safe. And so was she.

St. Isaac's Cathedral, the colossal marble church that the Soviets had turned into a museum of atheism, appeared before him. He entered it from the square and made his way up the narrow winding staircase, to the cupola surrounding the single golden dome. As expected, the platform was abandoned. The fairy-tale city stirred beneath his feet, traffic moving sluggishly along the big *prospekts*.

On one a woman walked alone, a hat covering her pale hair, a scarf concealing the lower half of her face. A few moments later he heard her footfalls in the stairwell. And then she was standing before him. There were no lights in the cupola. She was barely visible in the darkness.

"How did you find me?"

The sound of her voice was almost unreal. It was the English accent. Then Gabriel realized it was the only accent she had.

"It's not important how I found you," he replied.

"How?" she asked again, but this time Gabriel said nothing. He took a step closer to her so she could see his face clearly.

"Do you remember me now, Madeline? I'm the one who risked everything to try to save your life. It never occurred to me at the time that you were in on it from the beginning. You fooled me, Madeline. You fooled us all."

"I was never *in* on it," she shot back. "I was just doing what I was ordered to do."

"I know," he said after a moment. "I wouldn't be here otherwise."

"Who are you?"

"Actually," said Gabriel, "I was about to ask you the same thing."

"I'm Madeline," she said. "Madeline Hart of Basildon, England. I followed all the rules. Did well at school and university. Got a job at Party headquarters. My future was limitless. I was going to be an MP one day. Maybe even a minister." She paused, then added, "At least, that's what they said about me."

"What's your real name?"

"I don't know my real name," she answered. "I barely speak Russian. I'm *not* Russian. I'm Madeline. I'm an English girl."

She dug the copy of *A Room with a View* from her coat pocket and held it up. "Where did you find this?"

"In your room."

"What were you doing in my room?"

"I was trying to find out why your mother left Basildon without telling anyone."

"She's not my mother."

"I know that now. Actually," he added, "I think I knew when I saw a photograph of you standing next to her and your father. They look like—"

"Peasants," she said spitefully. "I hated them."

"Where are your mother and brother now?"

"In an old KGB training center in the middle of nowhere. I was supposed to go there, too, but I refused. I told them I wanted to live in St. Petersburg, or I would defect to the West."

"You're lucky they didn't kill you."

"They threatened to." She looked at him for a moment. "How much do you really know about me?"

"I know that your father was an important general in the First Chief Directorate of the KGB, maybe even the big boss himself. Your mother was one of his typists. She overdosed on sleeping pills and vodka not long after you were born, or so the story goes. After that, you were placed in something like an orphanage."

"A KGB orphanage," she interjected. "I was raised by wolves, truly."

"At a certain point," Gabriel resumed, "they stopped speaking Russian to you in the orphanage. In fact, they said nothing at all in your presence. You were raised in complete silence until you were about three years old. Then they started speaking English to you."

"KGB English," she said. "For a while I had the inflection of a newsreader on Radio Moscow."

"When did you meet your new parents for the first time?"

"When I was about five. We lived together in a KGB camp for a year or so to get to know one another. Then we settled in Poland.

And when the great Polish migration to London began, we went with it. My KGB parents already spoke perfect English. They established new identities for themselves and engaged in low-level espionage. Mainly, they looked after me. We never spoke Russian inside the house. Only English. After a while, I forgot I actually was Russian. I read books to learn how to be a proper English girl—Austen, Dickens, Lawrence, Forster."

"*A Room with a View.*"

"That's all I ever wanted," she said. "A room with a view."

"Why the council house in Basildon?"

"It was the nineties," she replied. "Russia was broke. The SVR was a shambles. There was no budget to support a family of illegals in London, so we settled in Basildon and went on the dole. The British welfare state nurtured a spy within its midst."

"What happened to your father?"

"He contracted the illegal disease."

"He went stir-crazy?"

She nodded. "He told Moscow Center he wanted out. Otherwise, he was going to go to MI5. The Center brought him back to Russia. God only knows what they did to him."

"*Vysshaya mera.*"

"What does that mean?"

"It doesn't matter."

Nothing mattered now other than this girl, he thought. He peered into the darkened square and saw Eli Lavon stamping his feet against the cold. Madeline saw him, too.

"Who is he?"

"A friend."

"A watcher?"

"The best."

"He'd better be."

She turned away and set out slowly along the parapet.

"When did they activate you?" Gabriel asked of her long, elegant back.

"When I was at university," she replied. "They told me they wanted me to prepare for a career in government. I studied political science and social work, and the next thing I knew I had a job at Party headquarters. Moscow Center was thrilled. Then Jeremy Fallon took me under his wing, and Moscow Center was over the moon."

"Did you sleep with him?"

She turned and smiled for the first time. "Have you ever seen Jeremy Fallon?"

"I have."

"Then I'm sure you won't doubt me when I say that, no, I did not sleep with Jeremy Fallon. He wanted to sleep with me, though, and I gave him just enough hope that he gave me everything I wanted."

"Like what?"

"A few minutes alone with the prime minister."

"Whose idea was it?"

"It was Moscow Center's," she replied. "I never did anything without their approval."

"They thought Lancaster might be vulnerable to an approach?"

"They're *all* vulnerable," she answered. "Unfortunately for Jonathan, he gave in to temptation. He was totally compromised the moment he made love to me for the first time."

"Congratulations," said Gabriel. "You must have been very proud of yourself."

She turned sharply and looked at him for a moment without speaking. "I'm not proud of what I did," she said finally. "I became very fond of Jonathan. I never wanted any harm to come to him."

"Then perhaps you should have told him the truth."

"I thought about it."

"What happened?"

"I went on holiday to Corsica," she said, smiling sadly. "And then I died."

But there was more to it than that, of course, beginning with the message she received from Moscow Center directing her to meet with a fellow SVR officer at Les Palmiers restaurant in Calvi. The officer informed her that her mission in England was over, that she would be returning to Russia, that they had to make it appear like a kidnapping in order to fool British intelligence.

"You quarreled," said Gabriel.

"Quietly but vehemently," she said. "I told him I wanted to stay in England and live out the rest of my life as Madeline Hart. He said that wasn't possible. He told me that if I didn't do exactly as he said, the kidnapping would be real."

"So you left your villa on your motorbike and had an accident."

"I'm lucky they didn't kill me. I still have the scars from the collision."

"How much time did you actually spend in the hands of the French criminals?"

"Too much," she answered. "But most of the time I was with an SVR team."

"What about the night I came to see you?"

"Everyone in that house was SVR," she said. "Including the girl they sent to count the money."

"You gave quite a performance that night, Madeline."

"It wasn't all a performance." She paused. "I did want you to get me."

"I tried," said Gabriel. "But the cards were stacked against me."

"It must have been terrible."

"Especially for the girl they stuffed in the trunk of that car."

She said nothing.

"Who was she?" Gabriel asked.

"Some girl they plucked off the streets of Moscow. They spread her DNA around my apartment in London, and then . . ." Her voice trailed off.

"They lit a match."

Her expression darkened. She turned away and looked out over the dark, frozen city.

"It's not so bad here, you know. They gave me a lovely flat. It has a view. I can spend the rest of my life here and pretend that I'm in Rome or Venice or Paris."

"Or Florence," said Gabriel.

"Yes, Florence," she agreed. "Just like Lucy and Charlotte."

"Is that what you want?"

She turned to face him again. "What choice do I have?"

"You can come with me."

"It can't be done," she said, shaking her head slowly. "You'll get yourself killed. Me, too."

"If I can find you in St. Petersburg, Madeline, I can get you out."

"How *did* you find me?" she asked again.

"I still can't tell you that."

"Who are you?"

"I can't tell you that, either."

"Where will you take me?"

"Home," he said, "with one stop along the way."

She lived in a grand old building on the other side of the Neva with a view of the Winter Palace. Eli Lavon saw her clandestinely to her door while Gabriel checked into the Astoria Hotel. Upstairs in his room, he composed a priority update for King Saul Boulevard, a copy of which was handed to a bleary-eyed Uzi Navot at 5:47 p.m. Tel Aviv time. Navot read it in silence, then looked at Shamron.

"What is it, Uzi?"

"He wants to change the departure city from Moscow to St. Petersburg."

"Why?"

"You wouldn't believe me if I told you."

Navot handed the update to Shamron, who read it through a haze of smoke. By the time Shamron had finished, Navot was handed a second update.

"He's about to feed us some video."

"Of what?"

Before Navot could answer, Paul Zhirov's swollen face appeared on one of the monitors.

"Looks like he took a nasty fall," Shamron said.

"Several," said Navot.

"What's he saying?"

Navot instructed the techs to increase the volume.

"We were tasked with acquiring drilling rights and downstream assets outside Russia. And we were KGB from top to bottom. In fact, a substantial percentage of our profits now flow directly into the accounts at Yasenevo."

"Where does the rest of it go?"

"Use your imagination."

"Into the pockets of the Russian president?"

"He didn't get to be Europe's richest man by wisely investing his KGB pension . . ."

Shamron smiled. "Now that's what I call an ace in the hole," he said.

"Plus a pair of kings."

"What time does the next El Al flight leave for St. Petersburg?"

Navot tapped a few keys on the computer in front of him. "Flight six two five departs Ben Gurion at one ten a.m. and lands in St. Petersburg at eight in the morning. The crew spends the day resting at a downtown hotel. Then they bring the plane back to Tel Aviv that night."

"Call the head of El Al," Shamron said. "Tell him we need to borrow that airplane."

Navot reached for the phone. Shamron watched the video monitor.

"Say it for the cameras, Pavel. Admit that you killed Madeline."

"I killed Madeline Hart."

"How?"

"By placing her in the back of a Citroën with a gasoline bomb."

"Why? Why did you kill her?"

"She had to die. There was no way she could be allowed to return to England . . ."

56

LUBYANKA SQUARE, MOSCOW

I T WAS AT TIMES LIKE THESE, thought Colonel Leonid Milchenko, that Russia's immense size was more of a curse than a blessing. He was standing before a map in his Lubyanka Square office, Vadim Strelkin at his side. They had just returned from the Kremlin where the federal president, the tsar himself, had ordered them to spare no effort to find the three missing men. The tsar had not been disposed to explain why it was so important, only that it concerned the vital interests of the federation and its relations with the United Kingdom. It was Strelkin, during the drive back to Lubyanka, who reminded Milchenko that Volgatek had just secured lucrative rights to drill for oil in the North Sea.

"You think Volgatek pulled a fast one to get that license?" Milchenko asked now, his eyes still on the map.

"I wouldn't want to prejudge the situation without knowing all the facts," Strelkin replied cautiously.

"We work for the FSB, Vadim. We never worry about the facts."

"You know what they call Volgatek, don't you, boss."

"KGB Oil and Gas."

Strelkin said nothing.

"So let's assume Volgatek didn't play it straight when they secured that license," Milchenko said.

"They rarely do. At least that's what one hears on the street."

"Let's assume they bribed someone."

"Or worse."

"And let's assume British intelligence responded by trying to insert an agent into the company."

"Let's," Strelkin said, nodding.

"Let us also assume the British were listening when Zhirov pulled their man into his car and started pounding him with questions."

"They probably were."

"And that the British assumed their man was in danger."

"He was."

"And that the British responded by pulling their man out."

"With extreme prejudice."

"And that they took Zhirov and his driver with him."

"They probably had no choice."

Milchenko lapsed into a thoughtful silence. "So where's Zhirov now?" he asked finally.

"He'll turn up eventually."

"Dead or alive?"

"The British don't like *mokriye dela*."

"Wherever did you hear a thing like that?" Milchenko took a step closer to the map. "If you were the British," he said, "what would you be trying to do right now?"

"I'd be trying to get my man out of the country as quickly as possible."

"How would you do it?"

"I suppose I could drive him to one of the western border crossings, but the quickest way out is Sheremetyevo."

"He'll be carrying a different passport."

"And wearing a new face," added Strelkin.

"Get over to the Ritz," Milchenko said. "Get some pictures of him from hotel security. And then get those pictures into the hands of every passport control officer and militiaman at Sheremetyevo."

Strelkin started toward the door.

"One more thing, Vadim."

Strelkin stopped.

"Do the same thing in St. Petersburg," Milchenko said. "Just to be on the safe side."

The man in question was at that moment resting comfortably in an isolated dacha in Tver Oblast, along with the other members of the Israeli team. Shortly after 5:00 a.m., having passed yet another sleepless night, they departed the dacha in twos and threes and made their way to the train station in Okulovka—all but Christopher Keller, who remained at the dacha alone to keep watch on Pavel Zhirov and the driver.

The train from Okulovka was late in departing, which was not true of El Al Flight 625. It left Ben Gurion Airport promptly at 1:10 a.m. and landed in St. Petersburg two minutes ahead of schedule, at 8:03 a.m. Its twelve-member flight and cabin crew remained with the aircraft until it had been emptied of its passengers. Then, after clearing customs, they climbed into an unmarked El Al ground services van for the twenty-minute drive to the Astoria Hotel, where they had rooms for the day. One of the flight attendants was a tall woman with dark hair and eyes the color of caramel. After leaving her small rolling bag at the foot of her bed, she walked to a room at the end of the corridor and, ignoring the DO NOT DISTURB sign hanging from the latch, knocked softly. Receiving no answer, she knocked again. This time the door opened a few inches, just wide enough for her to pass, and she slipped inside.

"What are you doing here?" asked Gabriel.

Chiara lifted her eyes to the ceiling, as if to remind her husband, the future chief of Israeli intelligence, that they were in a Russian hotel room and that the Russian hotel room was probably bugged. He indicated to her that the room was clean. Then he repeated the question. His hands were on his hips and his green eyes were narrowed. He was angrier than Chiara had seen him in a very long time.

"Silly me," she said, "but I actually allowed myself to think that you would be happy to see me."

"How did you manage this?"

"We needed girls for the flight crew. I volunteered."

"And Uzi couldn't find anyone other than my wife?"

"Actually, Uzi was against it."

"So how did you get on the team?"

"I went behind Uzi's back to Shamron," she said. "I told him that I wanted in on the operation, and that if he didn't give me what I wanted, I wouldn't give him what *he* wanted."

"Me?"

She smiled.

"Clever girl."

"I learned from the best."

"I thought you said you didn't want to come to Russia. I thought you said you wouldn't be able to hold up under the pressure."

"I changed my mind."

"Why?"

"Because I wanted to share this with you." Chiara walked over to the window and peered into the darkness of St. Isaac's Square. "Does it ever get light here?"

"This is light."

Chiara drew the blind over the window and turned around. In her blue skirt and crisp white blouse, she looked irresistible. Gabriel was no longer angry that she had come to Russia against his wishes. In fact, he was pleased to have her company. It would make the waiting of the next few hours much more bearable.

"What's she like?" Chiara asked.

"Madeline?"

"Is that what we call her?"

"It's the only name she knows," said Gabriel. "She was . . ."

"What?"

"Raised by wolves," he said.

"Maybe she's a wolf, too."

"She isn't."

"You're sure about that?"

"I'm sure, Chiara."

"Because she fooled you once before."

Gabriel was silent.

"I'm sorry, Gabriel, but you must have considered the possibility that she's still loyal to her service."

"I must have," said Gabriel, unable to keep a trace of irritation out of his voice. "But if she's clean when she leaves her apartment this afternoon, I'm bringing her in. And then I'm bringing her home."

"Where's home?"

"England."

"She's going to cause quite a stir."

"Quite," agreed Gabriel.

"What are you going to do with her?"

"I'm going to use her to repay a small debt," replied Gabriel. "And then I'm going to place her in the capable hands of Graham Seymour."

"Poor Graham." Chiara sat on the edge of the bed and removed her pumps.

"How was the flight?" asked Gabriel.

"I managed not to injure any of the passengers during the food service."

"Well done."

"There was a baby in first class that cried all the way from Ankara to Minsk. A few of the passengers were quite upset about it. The mother was mortified." Chiara paused, then added, "And all I could think was that she was the luckiest woman in the world."

"Maybe you shouldn't have come," Gabriel said after a moment.

"I *had* to come," Chiara replied. "I'm going to enjoy this very much."

She wriggled out of her skirt, laid it neatly on the bed, and began unbuttoning her blouse.

"What are you doing?" asked Gabriel.

"What does it look like?"

"It looks like a very pretty flight attendant is taking her clothes off in my hotel room."

"I have to get some rest. And so do you," she added as she removed her blouse. "Don't take this the wrong way, Gabriel, but you look terrible. Sleep for an hour or two. You'll feel better."

"I couldn't possibly sleep now."

"What are you going to do? Stand in that window all day and worry yourself to death?"

"That was my plan."

"There'll be plenty of time for that when you become chief. Come to bed," she said. "I promise not to hurt you."

Gabriel relented, slipped out of his shoes and jeans, and crawled into bed next to her. Her body felt feverish. Her lips, when kissed, tasted of honey. She ran her fingertip along the line of his nose.

"Chiara . . ."

"What is it, darling?" she asked, kissing him again.

"I'm on duty."

"You're always on duty. And you're going to remain on duty for the rest of your life."

She kissed him again. His lips. His neck. His chest.

"I suppose she was right all along," she said.

"Who?" murmured Gabriel.

"The old woman from Corsica. She said you would know the truth when Madeline was dead. In a way, she died that morning in France. And now you know the truth."

"The old woman was wrong about one thing, though. She warned me not to go to the city of heretics. She said I would die there."

Chiara stopped kissing him and looked directly into his eyes. "I thought you told me that she said you would be safe."

"I did."

"So you lied to me."

"I'm sorry, Chiara. I shouldn't have."

She kissed him again. "I knew you were lying all along," she said.

"Really?"

"I always know when you're lying, Gabriel."

"But I'm a professional."

"Not when it comes to me." She pulled his shirt over his head and sat astride his hips. "It's still a possibility, you know."

"What's that?"

"That you could die in the city of heretics."

"She was referring to Moscow. I think I'm safe now."

"Actually," she said, running her hands over his stomach, "you're in grave danger."

"I'm sensing that."

She took him into the tender warmth of her body. He was no longer in Russia, he thought. He was in the room in Venice where he made love to her for the first time, in a bed of white linen. He was safe. And so was she.

"Maybe she won't come," Chiara said afterward, as Gabriel was drifting toward sleep.

"She'll come," he said. "And then we'll take her home."

"I want to go home, too."

"Soon," he said.

"Is it ever going to get light out?"

"No, Chiara. Not today."

57

ST. PETERSBURG, RUSSIA

THEY HAD DONE IT A dozen times before, on a dozen secret battlefields, and so a few minutes over a street map in Gabriel's room at the Astoria was all it took to put their plan in place—the route, the static posts, the fallbacks, the parachutes. Gabriel referred to it as Moscow Center's last chance. They were going to troll her through the streets of St. Petersburg one final time to make sure she was clean. And then they were going to reel her in and make her disappear. Again.

And so it was that, shortly after two on that lightless afternoon in St. Petersburg, six officers of Israel's secret intelligence service slipped from the Astoria Hotel and made their way past the dreamlike churches and palaces to their holding points. Eli Lavon had the farthest to travel, for it was Lavon who was waiting outside Madeline's apartment house when she emerged at 2:52 p.m.—the precise time that Gabriel had told her to appear if it was her intention to defect. She crossed the Palace Bridge on foot, strode through the Embankment entrance of the Hermitage Museum, and then went directly to the Monet Room, where she was seated on her usual bench at seven minutes past three. Lavon joined her two minutes later. "So far so good," he said quietly in English. "Now listen carefully and do exactly as I say."

They ran her across the Palace Square, beneath the Triumphal Arch, and up the Nevsky Prospekt. She had a coffee and a slice of Russian cake at the Literary Café, strolled the Roman colonnade of the Cathedral of Our Lady of Kazan, and did a bit of shopping at Zara. At each point along the route, she passed a member of the team. And each member reported that there was no sign of the opposition.

Leaving Zara, she headed to the Moyka River and made her way along the Venetian walkways to the sprawl of St. Isaac's Square, where Dina waited, a mobile phone pressed to her right ear. Had she been holding the phone to her left ear, it would have been a signal to Madeline to keep walking. The right meant it was safe for her to enter the lobby of the Hotel Astoria, which she did at 3:48 p.m. Eli Lavon joined her in the elevator and rode with her to the third floor. Madeline stared at the snow on her boots. Lavon stared at the ornate ceiling. When the doors rattled open, he held out his hand formally and said, "After you." Madeline slipped past him without a word and headed toward the room at the end of the hall. The door opened as she approached. Gabriel drew her inside.

"Who are you?" she asked.

"I can't tell you that."

"Where am I going?"

"You'll know soon enough."

The update flashed across the status screens in the Op Center at King Saul Boulevard two minutes later. Uzi Navot stared at it for a moment, almost in disbelief. Then he looked at Shamron.

"They've actually done it, Ari. They've got her."

"That's good," replied Shamron joylessly. "Now let's see if they can keep her."

He lit another cigarette.

Two turns to the right, two turns to the left . . .

They blackened her hair and her eyebrows and added the color of the Mediterranean to her Baltic cheeks. Mordecai took her photograph and inserted it into the passport she would use to exit the country. For now, she was Ilana Shavit. She had been born in October 1985 and lived in the Tel Aviv suburb of Rishon LeZion, which happened to be one of the first Jewish settlements in Palestine. Before joining El Al, she had served in the IDF. She was married but childless. Her brother had been killed in the most recent Lebanon war. Her sister had been murdered by a Hamas suicide bomber during the Second Intifada. This was not an invented life, Gabriel told her. This was an Israeli life. And for a few hours it would be Madeline's.

If there was a chink in her armor, it was her inability to speak more than a few hastily learned words of Hebrew. This weakness was alleviated to some degree by the fact that her English contained no trace of a Russian accent, and by the fact that cockpit and cabin crews cleared passport control in a group. It was likely to be a pro forma affair, little more than a glance at the photograph and a wave of the hand. Gabriel was confident that Madeline would resist the natural impulse to respond to a question spoken in Russian. She had been doing it her entire life. She had to tell one more lie, give one last performance. And then she would be free of them forever.

And so, a few minutes after 5:00 p.m., the girls removed the last of Madeline's Russian clothing, dressed her in her crisp El Al uniform, and coiffed her newly black hair. Then they presented her to Gabriel, who studied her for a long moment as though she were a painting upon an easel.

"What is your name?" he asked tersely.

"Ilana Shavit."

"When were you born?"

"October 12, 1985."

"Where do you live?"

"Rishon LeZion."

"What does that mean in Hebrew?"

"First to Zion."

"What was your brother's name?"

"Moshe."

"Where was he killed?"

"Lebanon."

"What was your sister's name?"

"Dalia."

"Where was she killed?"

"The Dolphinarium discotheque."

"How many others were killed that day?"

"Twenty."

"What is your name?"

"Ilana Shavit."

"Where do you live?"

"Rishon LeZion."

"What street in Rishon LeZion?"

"Sokolow."

Gabriel had no more questions. He placed one hand to his chin and tilted his head to one side.

"Well?" she asked.

"Five minutes," he said. "Then we leave."

Eli Lavon was drinking coffee in the paneled gloom of the lobby. Gabriel sat down next to him.

"I've got a funny feeling," said Lavon.

"How funny?"

"Two outside the door, two in the bar, and one hanging around the concierge desk."

"Could be anything," said Gabriel.

"Could be," Lavon agreed uncertainly.

"They might be watching a guest of the hotel."

"That's what I'm afraid of."

"*Another* guest, Eli."

Lavon said nothing.

"Are you sure she was clean when we brought her in?"

"As a whistle."

"Then she's clean now," said Gabriel.

"So why is the lobby filled with FSB officers?"

"Could be anything."

"Could be," Lavon repeated.

Gabriel looked out the window at the El Al van idling outside the hotel's entrance.

"What are we going to do?" asked Lavon.

"We're going to leave as planned."

"Are you going to tell her?"

"Not a chance."

Lavon sipped his coffee. "Good call," he said.

It would be three long minutes before the first members of the El Al cabin crew emerged from the elevators into the lobby. Two trim young women, they were both in fact employed by Israel's national carrier, which was not true of the four women and two men who followed, all of whom were veteran Office field agents. Next came the captain and the flight engineer, followed a moment later by a heavily disguised version of Mikhail, who was posing as the first officer. The FSB man at the concierge desk had turned his head and was staring unabashedly at the backside of one of the ersatz flight attendants. Watching the scene from across the lobby, Gabriel permitted himself a brief smile. If the FSB man had time to check out the Israeli talent, chances were good he wasn't looking for a missing Russian illegal.

Finally, at 5:10 p.m., Chiara and Madeline appeared, trailing their smart El Al rolling suitcases behind them. Chiara was recounting a story about a recent flight in rapid Hebrew, and Madeline was laughing as though it was the most amusing thing she had heard in a long time. The other members of the crew absorbed them into their midst. Then, together, they headed outside and climbed into the waiting van. The doors closed. And then they were gone.

"What do you think?" asked Gabriel.

"I think she's very good," replied Eli Lavon.

"Are we clean?"

"As a whistle."

Gabriel rose without another word, collected his overnight bag, and headed outside, into the eternal night.

A taxi was waiting outside the hotel; it bore him down one last *prospekt*. Past a hulking statue of Lenin leading his people into seventy years of stagnation and murder. Past the monuments to a war no one could remember. Past mile after mile of ruined apartment houses. And, finally, to the international terminal at Pulkovo Airport. He checked in for the flight to Tel Aviv, slipped effortlessly through passport control as Jonathan Albright of Markham Capital Services, and then made his way to El Al's heavily fortified departure gate. The Russians claimed the barriers were for the safety of the Israel-bound passengers. Even so, Gabriel had the uncomfortable feeling he was entering Europe's last ghetto.

He settled into an empty seat in the corner of the lounge, near a large family of haredim. No one was speaking Russian, only Hebrew. Were it not for his disguise, they surely would have recognized him. But now he sat among them as a stranger, their secret servant, their invisible guardian angel. Soon he would be the chief of their vaunted intelligence service. Or would he? Surely, he thought, this would be a fine way to end a career. He had obtained proof that an oil company owned and operated by Russian intelligence had destabilized the government of the United Kingdom in order to gain access to North Sea oil—all at the behest of the Russian president himself. There would be no more resets after this, he thought. No more happy talk about Russia as a friend of the West. He would prove once and for all that the former members of the KGB who now ran Russia were ruthless, authoritarian, and not to be trusted—that they were to be marginalized and contained, just like in the old days of the Cold War.

But it would be meaningless, he thought, if he lost the girl. He glanced at his wristwatch, then looked up in time to see Yossi and

Rimona entering the departure lounge. Next came Mordecai and Oded. Then Yaakov and Dina. Then, lastly, Eli Lavon, looking as though he had wandered into the airport by mistake. He roamed the lounge for a moment, inspecting each empty chair with the diligence of a man who lived in fear of germs, before settling opposite Gabriel. They stared past one another without speaking, two sentinels on a night watch without end. There was nothing to do now but wait. The waiting, thought Gabriel. Always the waiting. Waiting for a source. Waiting for the sun to rise after a night of killing. And waiting for his wife to carry a dead girl back to the land of the living.

He looked at his watch again, then at Lavon.

"Where are they?" he asked.

Lavon delivered his response to his open newspaper. "They've already cleared passport control," he said. "The customs boys are just having a peek inside their luggage."

"Why?"

"How should I know?"

"Tell me there's no problem with the luggage."

"The luggage is fine."

"So why are they searching it?"

"Maybe they're bored. Or maybe they just like touching ladies' underwear. They're Russians, for God's sake."

"How long, Eli?"

"Two minutes. Maybe less."

Lavon's two minutes passed with no sign of them. Then a third. And then an interminable fourth. Gabriel stared at his watch, and at the filthy carpet, and at the child next to him—anything but the entrance of the departure lounge. And then, finally, he glimpsed them from the corner of his eye, a flash of blue and white, like the waving of a banner. Mikhail was walking at the side of the captain, and Madeline was next to Chiara. She was smiling nervously and seemed to be holding Chiara's arm for support. Or was it the other way around? Gabriel couldn't be sure. He watched them turn in unison toward the gate and disappear down the Jetway. Then he looked at Lavon.

"I told you everything would be fine," he said.

"You were never worried?"

"Terrified beyond description."

"Why didn't you tell me?"

Lavon didn't answer. He just sat there reading his newspaper until the flight was called. Then he rose to his feet and followed Gabriel onto the plane. One last check for opposition surveillance, just to be certain.

They had given her a seat in the third row next to the window. She was peering out at the dark oily apron of Pulkovo, her last glimpse of a Russia she never knew. In her blue-and-white uniform, she looked curiously like an English schoolgirl. She glanced at Gabriel as he slid into the seat next to her but quickly turned away. Gabriel fired off one last message to King Saul Boulevard on his secure BlackBerry. Then he watched his wife preparing the cabin for takeoff. As the aircraft thundered down the runway, Madeline's eyes glistened; and as the wheels rose from Russian soil, a tear broke onto her cheek. She reached out for Gabriel's hand and held it tightly.

"I don't know how to thank you," she said in her prim English accent.

"Then don't," he answered.

"How long is the flight?"

"Five hours."

"Will it be warm in Israel?"

"Only in the south."

"Will you take me there?"

"I'll take you anywhere you want to go."

Chiara appeared and handed them each a glass of champagne. Gabriel raised his glass toward Madeline in a silent toast and then placed it on the center console without drinking any.

"You don't like champagne?" she asked.

"It gives me a terrible headache."

"Me, too."

She drank some of the champagne and stared out her window at the darkness below.

"How did you find me down there?" she asked.

"It's not important."

"Are you ever going to tell me who you are?"

"You'll know soon enough."

PART THREE

THE SCANDAL

58

LONDON-JERUSALEM

THE NEXT MORNING BRITAIN WENT to the polls. Jonathan Lancaster cast his ballot early, accompanied by his wife, Diana, and their three photogenic children, before returning to Downing Street to await the verdict of the voters. The day held little suspense; a final election-eve survey predicted Lancaster's Party would almost certainly increase the size of its parliamentary majority by several seats. By midafternoon Whitehall was swirling with rumors of an electoral massacre, and by early evening the champagne was flowing at the Party's Millbank headquarters. Even so, Lancaster appeared curiously somber when he strode onto the stage at the Royal Festival Hall to deliver his victory speech. Among the political reporters who took note of his serious demeanor was Samantha Cooke of the *Daily Telegraph*. The prime minister, she wrote, looked like a man who knew his second term would not go as well as his first. But then, she added, second terms rarely did.

Lancaster's troubles began later that week when he undertook the traditional reshuffling of his Cabinet and personal staff. As widely predicted, Jeremy Fallon, now member of Parliament from Bristol, was appointed chancellor of the exchequer, which meant that Lancaster's brain and puppet master would be his Downing Street neighbor as well. The man whom the press had once characterized as a deputy prime minister in name only now appeared to all of Whitehall like a prime minister in waiting. Fallon quickly gathered up the remaining members of his old Downing Street staff—at least, those who could still stand to work for him—and used his influence inside Party headquarters to fill key political positions with loyalists. The stage was now set, wrote Samantha Cooke, for a power struggle of Shakespearean proportions. Soon, she said, Fallon would be knocking on the door of Number Ten and asking for the keys. Jeremy Fallon had created Lancaster. And surely, she predicted, Fallon would try to destroy Lancaster as well.

At no point during the post-election political maneuverings did Madeline Hart's name appear in the press, not even when the Party chairman decided the time had come to fill her vacant post. A headquarters underling saw to the morbid chore of removing the last of her things from her old cubicle. There wasn't much left—a few dusty files, her calendar, her pens and paper clips, the dog-eared copy of *Pride and Prejudice* she used to read whenever she had a spare moment or two. The underling delivered the items to the Party chairman, who in turn prevailed upon his secretary to quietly dispose of them with as much dignity as possible. And thus the final traces of an unfinished life were expunged from Party headquarters. Madeline Hart was finally gone. Or so they thought.

At first it seemed she had traded one form of captivity for another. This time the apartment that served as her prison cell overlooked not the river Neva in St. Petersburg but the Mediterranean Sea in Netanya. The building's management had been told she was convalescing after a long illness. It wasn't far from the truth.

For a week she did not set foot beyond the flat's walls. Her days lacked any discernible routine. She slept late, she watched the sea, she reread her favorite novels, all under the watchful gaze of an Office security team. A doctor came once each day to check on her. On the seventh day, when asked whether she had any ailments, she answered that she was suffering from terminal boredom.

"Better to die from boredom than from a Russian poison," the doctor quipped.

"I'm not so sure about that," she replied in her English drawl.

The doctor promised to appeal the conditions of her confinement to higher authority; and on the eighth day of her stay, higher authority allowed her to take a brief walk on the cold, windswept stretch of sand that lay beneath her terrace. The day after that she was allowed to walk a little farther. And on the tenth day she trekked nearly to Tel Aviv before her minders placed her gently in the back of an Office car and ran her back to the flat. Entering, she found an exact copy of *The Pond at Montgeron* hanging on the wall in the sitting room—exact except for the signature of the artist who had painted it. He rang her a few minutes later and introduced himself properly for the first time.

"*The* Gabriel Allon?" she asked.

"I'm afraid so," he answered.

"And who was the woman who helped me onto the plane?"

"You'll know soon enough."

Gabriel and Chiara arrived in Netanya at noon the following day, after Madeline had returned from her morning walk along the beach. They took her to Caesarea for lunch and a stroll through the Roman and Crusader ruins; then they headed farther up the coast, nearly to Lebanon, to wander the sea caves at Rosh HaNikra. From there, they moved eastward along the tense border, past the IDF listening posts and the small towns that had been depopulated by the last war with Hezbollah, until they arrived in Kiryat Shmona. Gabriel had booked two rooms at the guesthouse of an old kibbutz. Madeline's had a fine view of the Upper Galilee. An Office security guard spent the night outside her door, and another sat outside the room's garden terrace.

The next morning, after taking breakfast in the kibbutz's communal dining hall, they drove into the Golan Heights. The IDF was expecting them; a young colonel took them to a spot along the Syrian border where it was possible to hear the regime's forces shelling rebel positions. Afterward, they paid a brief visit to the Nimrod Fortress, the ancient Crusader bastion overlooking the flatlands of the Galilee, before making their way to the ancient Jewish city of Safed. They ate lunch in the artists' quarter, at the home of a woman named Tziona Levin. Though Gabriel referred to Tziona as his *doda*, his aunt, she was actually the closest thing he had to a sibling. She didn't seem at all surprised when he appeared on her doorstep accompanied by a beautiful young woman whom the entire world believed to be dead. She knew that Gabriel had a habit of returning to Israel with lost objects.

"How's your work?" she asked over coffee in her sunlit garden.

"Never better," replied Gabriel, with a glance at Madeline.

"I was talking about your art, Gabriel."

"I just finished restoring a lovely Bassano."

"You should be focused on your own work," she said reproach-fully.

"I am," he responded vaguely, and Tziona let it drop. When they had finished their coffee, she took them into her studio to see her newest paintings. Then, at Gabriel's request, she unlocked her storage room. Inside were hundreds of paintings and sketches by Gabriel's mother, including several works depicting a tall man wearing the uniform of the SS.

"I thought I told you to burn these," Gabriel said.

"You did," Tziona admitted, "but I couldn't bring myself to do it."

"Who is he?" asked Madeline, staring at the paintings.

"His name was Erich Radek," Gabriel answered. "He ran a secret Nazi program called Aktion 1005. Its goal was to conceal all evidence that the Holocaust had taken place."

"Why did your mother paint him?"

"He nearly killed her on the death march from Auschwitz in January 1945."

Madeline raised one eyebrow quizzically. "Wasn't Radek the one who was captured in Vienna a few years ago and brought to Israel for trial?"

"For the record," replied Gabriel, "Erich Radek *volunteered* to come to Israel."

"Yes," said Madeline dubiously. "And I was kidnapped by French criminals from Marseilles."

The next day they drove to Eilat. The Office had rented a large private villa not far from the Jordanian border. Madeline passed her days lying next to the swimming pool, reading and rereading a stack of classic English novels. Gabriel realized that she was preparing herself to return to the country that wasn't truly hers. She was no one, he thought. She was not quite a real person. And, not for the first time, he wondered whether she might be better off living in Israel than in the United Kingdom. It was a question he put to her on the final night of their stay in the south. They were seated atop an outcropping of rock in the Negev, watching the sun sinking into the badlands of the Sinai.

"It's tempting," she said.

"But?"

"It's not my home," she answered. "It would be like Russia. I'd be a stranger here."

"It's going to be hard, Madeline. Much harder than you think. The British will put you through the wringer until they're certain of your loyalties. And then they'll lock you away somewhere the Russians will never find you. You'll never be able to go back to your old life. Never," he repeated. "It's going to be miserable."

"I know," she said distantly.

Actually, she didn't know, thought Gabriel, but perhaps it was better that way. The sun hung just above the horizon. The desert air was suddenly cold enough to make her shiver.

"Should we be getting back?" he asked.

"Not yet," she answered.

He removed his jacket and draped it over her shoulders. "I'm going to tell you something I probably shouldn't," he said. "I'm going to be the chief of Israeli intelligence soon."

"Congratulations."

"Condolences are probably in order," replied Gabriel. "But it means I have the power to look after you. I'll give you a nice place to live. A family. It's a dysfunctional family," he added hastily, "but it's the only family I have. We'll give you a country. A home. That's what we do in Israel. We give people a home."

"I already have a home."

She said nothing more. The sun slipped below the horizon. Then she was lost to the darkness.

"Stay," said Gabriel. "Stay here with us."

"I can't stay," she said. "I'm Madeline. I'm an English girl."

The next night was the gala opening of the Pillars of Solomon exhibit at the Israel Museum in Jerusalem. The president and prime minister were in attendance, as were the members of the Cabinet, most of the Knesset, and numerous important writers, artists, and entertainers. Chiara was among those who spoke at the ceremony, which was held in the newly built exhibition hall. She made no mention of the fact that her husband, the legendary Israeli intelligence officer Gabriel Allon, had discovered the pillars, or that the beautiful dark-haired woman at his side was actually a dead English girl named Madeline Hart. They remained at the cocktail reception for only a few minutes before driving across Jerusalem to a quiet restaurant located on the old campus of the Bezalel Academy of Arts and Design. Afterward, while they were walking in Ben Yehuda Street, Gabriel again asked Madeline if she wanted to remain in Israel, but her answer was the same. She spent her final night in Israel in the spare bedroom of Gabriel's Narkiss Street apartment, the room meant for a child. Early the next morning they drove to Ben Gurion Airport in darkness and boarded a flight for London.

59

LONDON

F OR SEVERAL DAYS GABRIEL DEBATED whether to warn Graham Seymour that he was about to be the recipient of a rather unusual Russian defector. In the end, he decided against it. His reasons were personal rather than operational. He simply didn't want to spoil the surprise.

As a result, the reception team waiting at Heathrow Airport late that same morning was Office rather than MI5. It took clandestine possession of Gabriel and Madeline in the arrivals hall and ferried them to a hastily procured service flat in Pimlico. Then Gabriel rang Seymour at his office and told him that, once again, he had entered the United Kingdom without signing the guestbook.

"What a surprise," said Seymour dryly.

"More to come, Graham."

"Where are you?"

Gabriel gave him the address.

Seymour had a meeting with a visiting delegation of Australian spies that couldn't be put off, so an hour would elapse before his car appeared in the street outside the building. Entering the flat, he found Gabriel alone in the sitting room. On the coffee table was an open notebook computer, which Gabriel used to play a video of Pavel Zhirov confessing the many sins of the Kremlin-owned energy firm known as Volgatek Oil & Gas. By the time the video ended, Seymour appeared stricken. Which proved one of Ari Shamron's favorite maxims, thought Gabriel. In the intelligence business, as in life, sometimes it was better not to know.

"He's the one who had lunch with Madeline in Corsica?" Seymour asked finally, still staring at the computer screen.

Gabriel nodded his head slowly. "You told me to find him," he said, "and I found him."

"What happened to his face?"

"He said something to Mikhail he shouldn't have."

"Where is he now?"

"Gone," said Gabriel.

"There are degrees of gone, you know."

The blank expression on Gabriel's face made it clear that Pavel Zhirov was gone permanently.

"Do the Russians know?" Seymour asked.

"Not yet."

"How long before they find out?"

"Spring, I'd say."

"Who killed him?"

"Another story for another time."

Gabriel ejected the DVD disk from the computer and offered it to

Seymour. Accepting it, he exhaled slowly, as though he were trying to keep his blood pressure in check.

"I've been in this game a long time," he said at last, "and that video is the single most explosive thing I've ever seen."

"You haven't seen everything yet, Graham."

"I don't know if you noticed," Seymour said as though he hadn't heard Gabriel's warning, "but we had an election in this country recently. Jonathan Lancaster just won by one of the biggest landslides in British history. And Jeremy Fallon is now the chancellor of the exchequer."

"Not for long," said Gabriel.

Seymour made no reply.

"You're not thinking about letting him get away with it, are you, Graham?"

"No," he said. "But it's going to be a bloodbath."

"You always knew it would be."

"But I was hoping the blood wouldn't spatter on me, too." He lapsed into a heavy silence.

"Is there something you need to get off your chest, Graham?"

"The prime minister has offered me a promotion," he said after a hesitation.

"What kind of promotion?"

"The kind I couldn't turn down."

"Director general?"

Seymour nodded. "But not of MI5," he added quickly. "You're looking at the future chief of Her Majesty's Secret Service. You and I are going to be running the world together—covertly, of course."

"Unless you bring down the Lancaster government."

"Correct," replied Seymour. "If I do that, there's a good chance I'll be swept out to sea with the rest of them. And *you* will lose a close ally in the process." He lowered his voice and added, "I would think a man in your position would want to hang on to a friend like me. You don't have many these days."

"But you can't possibly allow a KGB-owned energy company to drill for oil in your territorial waters."

"That would be a dereliction of duty," Seymour agreed genially.

"Nor can you allow a paid agent of the Kremlin to continue serving as the chancellor. Otherwise," Gabriel added, "he might be your next prime minister."

"I shudder at the very thought."

"Then you have to destroy him, Graham." Gabriel paused. "Or you have to avert your eyes while I do it for you."

Seymour was silent for a moment. "How would you go about it?"

"By repaying a favor."

"What about Lancaster?"

"He was guilty of an affair. There's a good chance the British people will forgive him, especially when they learn that Jeremy Fallon has five million euros sitting in a Swiss bank account." Gabriel paused, then added, "And there is one other mitigating circumstance I haven't told you about yet."

"What is it?"

Gabriel smiled and rose to his feet.

He entered the bedroom and returned a moment later with a beautiful young woman at his side. She had coal-black hair and her once-pale skin was deeply tanned by the sun of the Red Sea. Seymour rose chivalrously and, smiling, extended his hand. As it hovered there unaccepted, his face took on a puzzled expression. And then he understood. He looked at Gabriel and whispered, "Dear God."

She told Graham Seymour the story from the beginning—the same story she had told Gabriel on that frozen afternoon in St. Petersburg, in the cupola of St. Isaac's Cathedral. Then, calmly, primly, she declared that she wished to defect to the United Kingdom and, if possible, to one day resume her old life.

As deputy director of MI5, Graham Seymour did not possess the authority to grant defector status to a Russian spy; the only person who could do that was Madeline's former lover, Jonathan Lancaster. Which explained why, at two fifteen that afternoon, Seymour presented himself at Number Ten unannounced and demanded a word with the prime minister in private. Coincidentally, the encounter took place in the Study Room. There, beneath the same glowering portrait of Baroness Thatcher, Seymour told the prime minister everything he had learned. That the Russian president had ordered Volgatek to use any means possible to gain access to the oil of the North Sea. That Jeremy Fallon, Lancaster's closest aide and confidant, had betrayed him for five million pieces of Russian silver. And that Madeline Hart, his former lover, was a Russian-born spy who was still very much alive and requesting asylum in Britain. To his credit, Lancaster, though visibly shaken, did not hesitate before giving his answer. Fallon had to go, Madeline had to stay, and let the chips fall where they may. He made only one request, that he be given the chance to break the news to his wife.

"I wouldn't wait too long if I were you, Prime Minister."

Lancaster reached slowly for the telephone. Seymour rose to his feet and slipped silently from the room.

Which left only the name of the reporter who would be granted the most sensational exclusive in British political history. Seymour suggested Tony Richmond at the *Times* or perhaps Sue Gibbons from the *Independent*, but Gabriel overruled him. He had made a promise, he said, and he planned to keep it. He rang her mobile, got her voice mail, and left a brief message. She rang him back right away. Four o'clock at Café Nero, he said. And this time don't be late.

Much to Graham Seymour's chagrin, Gabriel and Madeline insisted on taking one last walk together. They headed up Millbank through a gusty wind—past the Victoria Tower Gardens, Westminster Abbey, and the Houses of Parliament—and at ten minutes to four entered the café. Gabriel ordered black coffee; Madeline had milky Earl Grey tea and a digestive biscuit. She removed a compact from her handbag and checked her face in the mirror.

"How do I look?" she asked.

"Very Israeli."

"Is that supposed to be a compliment?"

"Put it away," said Gabriel.

She did as Gabriel instructed. Then she looked out the window at the crowds moving along the pavements of Bridge Street. As though she had never seen them before, thought Gabriel. As though she would never see them again. He glanced around the interior of the café. No one recognized her. Why should they? She was dead and buried—buried in a churchyard in Basildon. A town without a soul for a girl without a name or a past.

"You don't have to do this," he said after a moment.

"Of course I do."

"I have enough without you. I have the video of Zhirov."

"The Kremlin can deny Zhirov," she answered. "But it can't deny me."

She was still staring out the window.

"Take a good look," Gabriel said, "because if you do this, it's going to be a long time before they let you come back to London."

"Where do you suppose they'll put me?"

"A safe house in the middle of nowhere. Maybe a military base until the storm passes."

"It doesn't sound very appealing, does it?"

"You can always come back to Israel with me."

She made no reply. Gabriel leaned forward across the table and took hold of her hand. It was trembling slightly.

"I keep a cottage in Cornwall," he said quietly. "The town isn't much, but it's by the sea. You can stay there if you like."

"Does it have a view?" she asked.

"A lovely view," he answered.

"I might like that."

She smiled bravely. Across the road Big Ben tolled four o'clock.

"She's late," Gabriel said incredulously. "I can't believe she's late."

"She's always late," Madeline said.

"You made quite an impression on her, by the way."

"She wasn't the only one."

Madeline laughed in spite of herself and drank some of her tea. Gabriel frowned at his wristwatch. Then he looked up in time to see Samantha Cooke rushing through the door. A moment later she was standing at their table, slightly out of breath. She looked at Gabriel for a moment before turning her gaze toward the beautiful dark-haired girl seated across from him. And then she understood.

"Dear God," she whispered.

"Can we get you something to drink?" Madeline asked in her English accent.

"Actually," stammered Samantha Cooke, "it might be better if we walked."

60

LONDON

THIRTEEN HOURS LATER A JUNIOR functionary from Downing Street delivered a bundle of newspapers to a redbrick house in the Hampstead section of London. The house belonged to Simon Hewitt, press spokesman for Prime Minister Jonathan Lancaster, and the thud the papers made upon hitting his doorstep woke him from an unusually sound sleep. He had been dreaming of an incident from his childhood when a schoolyard bully had blackened his eye. It was a slight improvement over the previous night, when he dreamed he was being torn to pieces by wolves, or the night before that, when a cloud of bees had stung him bloody. It was all part of a recurring theme. Despite Lancaster's triumph at the polls, Hewitt was gripped by a sense of impending doom quite unlike any he had experienced since coming to Downing Street. He was convinced that the quiet in the press was illusory. Surely, he thought, the earth's crust was about to move.

All of which explained why Hewitt was slow to rise from his bed and open his front door that cold London morning. The act of retrieving the bundle of newspapers from his doorstep sent his back into spasm, a reminder of the toll the job had taken on his health. He carried the parcel into the kitchen, where the coffeemaker was emitting the wheezy death rattle that signaled it was nearing the end of its cycle. After pouring a large cup and whitening it with heavy cream, he removed the newspapers from their plastic cover. As usual, Hewitt's old paper, the *Times*, was on top. He scanned it quickly, found nothing objectionable, then moved on to the *Guardian*. Next it was the *Independent*. Then, finally, the *Daily Telegraph*.

"Shit," he said softly. "Shit, shit, shit."

At first the press was at a loss over exactly what to call it. They tried the Madeline Hart Affair, but that seemed too narrow. So did the Fallon Fiasco, which was en vogue for a few hours, or the Kremlin Connection, which enjoyed a brief run on ITV. By late morning the BBC had settled on the Downing Street Affair, which was bland but broad enough to cover all manner of sins. The rest of the press quickly fell into line, and a scandal was born.

For most of that day, the man at the center of it, Prime Minister Jonathan Lancaster, remained curiously silent. Finally, at six that evening, the black door of Number Ten swung open, and Lancaster emerged alone to face the country. His tone was remorseful, but he remained dry-eyed and steady. He acknowledged that he had carried on a brief and unwise affair with a young woman from Party headquarters. He also admitted that he had retained the services of a foreign intelligence operative to find the young woman after her disappearance, that he had improperly withheld information from the

British authorities, and that he had paid ten million euros in ransom and extortion money. At no point, he insisted, did he ever suspect that the young woman was actually a Russian-born sleeper spy. Nor did he suspect that her disappearance was part of a well-orchestrated conspiracy by a Kremlin-owned energy company to obtain drilling rights in the North Sea. He had approved the Volgatek license, he said, at the suggestion of his longtime aide and chief of staff, Jeremy Fallon. And that deal, he added pointedly, was now dead.

Fallon wisely issued his first statement in written form, for even on his best days he looked like a man who was guilty of something. He acknowledged having helped the prime minister deal with the consequences of his "reckless personal conduct" but denied categorically that he had accepted a payment of money from anyone connected to Volgatek Oil & Gas. The commentators took note of the statement's sharp tone. It was clear, they said, that Jeremy Fallon believed that Lancaster might not survive and that the premiership might be his for the taking. This was shaping up to be a fight for survival, they said. Perhaps even a fight to the death.

The next statement came not in London but in Moscow, where the Russian president called the allegations against the Kremlin and its oil company a malicious Western lie. In a clear sign the affair would have geopolitical repercussions, he accused British intelligence of involvement in the disappearance of Pavel Zhirov, the man upon whose word the allegations were based. Then, without offering any evidence, he suggested that Viktor Orlov, the Russian oil oligarch now residing in the United Kingdom, was somehow linked to the affair. Orlov issued a taunting denial from his Mayfair headquarters in which he called the Russian president a congenital liar and kleptocrat who had finally shown his true stripes. Then he promptly handed himself over to an MI5 security detail for protection and disappeared from view.

But who was the mysterious operative from a foreign intelligence service whom Lancaster had retained to find Madeline Hart after her disappearance in Corsica? Citing issues of national security, Lancaster refused to identify him. Nor did Jeremy Fallon shed any light on the matter. Initially, speculation centered on the Americans, with whom Lancaster was known to be close. That changed, however, when the *Times* reported that the noted Israeli intelligence operative Gabriel Allon had been seen entering Downing Street on two separate occasions during the period in question. The *Daily Mail* then reported that a senior MP had spotted the same Gabriel Allon having coffee with a young woman at Café Nero, one day before the scandal broke. The *Mail* story was dismissed as tabloid silliness—surely the great Gabriel Allon would not be so foolish as to sit openly in a busy London coffeehouse—but the *Times* account proved tougher to deflate. In a break with tradition, the Office released a terse statement denying both reports, which the British press saw as ironclad confirmation of Allon's involvement.

With that, the scandal fell into a predictable cycle of leaks, counterleaks, and naked political warfare. The opposition leader declared his revulsion and demanded Lancaster's resignation. But when a head count in the Commons revealed that Lancaster would narrowly survive a vote of no confidence, the opposition leader didn't bother to schedule one. Even Jeremy Fallon seemed to have weathered the storm. After all, there was no proof he had accepted any payment from Volgatek, only the word of a Russian oil executive who seemed to have disappeared from the face of the earth.

And there it all might have ended, with the Lancaster-Fallon marriage badly damaged but still intact, were it not for the edition of the *Daily Telegraph* that landed with a thud on Simon Hewitt's doorstep on the second Tuesday of January. On the front page, next to an article by Samantha Cooke, was a photograph of Jeremy Fallon entering a small private bank in Zurich. A few hours later Lancaster again appeared alone outside the famous black door of 10 Downing Street, this time to announce the firing of his chancellor of the exchequer. A few minutes later Scotland Yard announced that Fallon was now the target of a bribery-and-fraud investigation. Once again, Fallon declared his innocence. Not a single member of the Whitehall press corps believed him.

He left Downing Street for the last time at sunset and returned to his empty bachelor's apartment in Notting Hill, which was surrounded, it seemed, by every reporter and cameraman in London. The inquest would never determine how or when he eluded them, though a CCTV camera captured a clear image of his stricken face at 2:23 the next morning as he walked along a deserted stretch of Park Lane, one end of a rope already tied around his neck. Using a nautical knot taught to him by his father, he tied the other end of the rope to a lamppost at the center of the Westminster Bridge. No one happened to see Fallon hurl himself over the edge, and so he hung there through the long night, until the sun finally shone upon his slowly swaying body. Thus lending proof to an ancient and wise Corsican proverb: He who lives an immoral life dies an immoral death.

61

CORSICA

B UT WHO HAD BEEN THE source of the damning photograph that drove Jeremy Fallon from office and over the railing of Westminster Bridge? It was a question that would dominate British political circles for months to come; but on the enchanted island where the scandal had its genesis, only a few north-looking sophisticates gave much thought to it. Occasionally, a couple would have their photograph taken at Les Palmiers, posed as Madeline Hart and Pavel Zhirov on the afternoon of their fateful lunch, but for the most part the island did its best to forget the small role it had played in the death of a senior British statesman. As the winter took hold, the Corsicans instinctively returned to the old ways. They burned the *macchia* for warmth. They waggled their fingers at strangers to ward off the evil eye. And in an isolated valley near the southwestern coast, they turned to Don Anton Orsati for help when they could turn to no one else.

On a blustery afternoon in the middle of February, while seated at the oaken desk in his large office, he received an unusual telephone call. The man at the other end was not looking to have someone eliminated—hardly surprising, thought the don, for the man was more than capable of seeing to his own killing. Instead, he was looking for a villa where he might spend a few weeks alone with his wife. It had to be in a place where no one would recognize him and where he had no need of bodyguards. The don had just the place. But there was one problem. There was only one road in and out—and the road passed the three ancient olive trees where Don Casabianca's wretched palomino goat made his encampment.

"Is there any way it can have a tragic accident before we arrive?" asked the man on the telephone.

"Sorry," replied Don Orsati. "But here on Corsica some things never change."

They arrived on the island three days later, having flown from Tel Aviv to Paris and then from Paris to Ajaccio. Don Orsati had left a car at the airport, a shiny gray Peugeot sedan that Gabriel drove with Corsican abandon southward down the coast, then inland through the valleys thick with *macchia*. When they arrived at the three ancient olive trees, the goat rose menacingly from its resting place and blocked their path. But it quickly gave ground after Chiara spoke a few soothing words into its tattered ear.

"What did you say to it?" asked Gabriel when they were driving again.

"I told him you were sorry for being mean to him."

"But I'm not sorry. He was definitely the aggressor."

"He's a goat, darling."

"He's a terrorist."

"How can you possibly run the Office if you can't get along with a goat?"

"Good question," he said glumly.

The villa was a mile or so beyond the goat's redoubt. It was small and simply furnished, with pale limestone floors and a granite terrace. Laricio pine shaded the terrace in the morning, but in the afternoon the sun beat brightly upon the stones. The days were cold and pleasant; at night the wind whistled in the pines. They drank Corsican red wine by the fire and watched the swaying of the trees. The fire burned blue-green from the *macchia* wood and smelled of rosemary and thyme. Soon, Gabriel and Chiara smelled of it, too.

They had no plan other than to do little of anything at all. They slept late. They drank their morning coffee in the village square. They ate fish for lunch by the sea. In the afternoon, if it was warm, they would sun themselves on the granite terrace; and if it was cold they would retreat to their simple bedroom and make love until they slept with exhaustion. Shamron left numerous plaintive messages that Gabriel happily ignored. In a year his every waking moment would be consumed by the job of protecting Israel from those who wished to destroy it. For now, though, there was only Chiara, and the cold sun and the sea, and the intoxicating smell of the pine and the *macchia*.

For the first few days, they avoided the newspapers, the Internet, and the television. But gradually Gabriel reconnected with a world of problems that would soon be his. The head of the IAEA, the UN's nuclear watchdog agency, predicted Iran would be a nuclear power within a year. The next day there was a report the regime in Syria had transferred chemical weapons to Hezbollah. And the day after that the Muslim Brother who now ran Egypt was caught on tape talking about a new war with Israel. Indeed, the only good news Gabriel could find occurred in London, where Jonathan Lancaster, having survived the Downing Street Affair, appointed Graham Seymour to be the next chief of MI6. Gabriel called him that evening to offer his congratulations. Mainly, though, he was curious about Madeline.

"She's doing better than I expected," said Seymour.

"Where is she?"

"It seems a friend offered her a cottage by the sea."

"Really?"

"It's a bit unorthodox," Seymour conceded, "but we decided it was as good a place as any."

"Just don't turn your back on her, Graham. The SVR has a very long reach."

It was because of that long reach that Gabriel and Chiara kept a deliberately low profile on the island. They rarely left the villa after dark, and several times each night Gabriel stepped onto the terrace to listen for movement in the valley. A week into their stay, he heard the familiar rattle of a Renault hatchback, then, a moment later, saw lights burning for the first time in Keller's villa. He waited until the following afternoon before dropping by unannounced. Keller was wearing a pair of loose-fitting white trousers and a white pullover. He opened a bottle of Sancerre, and they drank it outside in the sun. Sancerre in the afternoon, Corsican red in the evening—Gabriel thought he could get used to this. But there was no turning back now. His people needed him. He had an appointment with history.

"The Cézanne could use a bit of work," Gabriel said offhandedly. "Why don't you let me clean it up for you while I'm in town?"

"I like the Cézanne exactly the way it is. Besides," Keller added, "you came here to rest."

"You don't need any?"

"What's that?"

"Rest," answered Gabriel.

Keller said nothing.

"Where have you been, Christopher?"

"I had a business trip."

"Olive oil or blood?"

When Keller raised an eyebrow to indicate it was the latter, Gabriel shook his head reproachfully.

"Money doesn't come from singing," said Keller quietly.

"There are other ways of making money, you know."

"Not when your name is Christopher Keller and you're supposed to be dead."

Gabriel drank some of his wine. "I didn't include you on the team because I needed your help," he said after a moment. "I wanted to show you that there's more to life than killing people for money."

"You wanted to restore me? Is that what you're saying?"

"It's a natural instinct of mine."

"Some things are beyond repair." Keller paused, then added, "Beyond redemption."

"How many men have you killed?"

"I don't know," Keller shot back. "How many have *you* killed?"

"Mine are different. I'm a soldier. A secret soldier, but a soldier nevertheless." He looked at Keller seriously for a moment. "And you can be one, too."

"Are you offering me a job?"

"You'd have to become an Israeli citizen and learn to speak Hebrew to work for the Office."

"I've always felt a little Jewish."

"Yes," said Gabriel, "you mentioned that before."

Keller smiled, and a silence fell between them. The afternoon wind was starting to get up.

"There is one other possibility, Christopher."

"What's that?"

"Did you happen to notice who was just named the new director-general of MI6?"

Keller made no reply.

"I'll go on the record for you with Graham. He can give you a new identity. A new life."

Keller raised his wineglass to the valley. "I have a life. A very nice life, in fact."

"You're a hired gun. You're a criminal."

"I'm an honorary bandit. There's a difference."

"Whatever you say." Gabriel added a half inch of wine to his glass.

"Is this why you came to Corsica? To talk me into going home again?"

"I suppose it is."

"If I let you restore the Cézanne, will you promise to leave me alone?"

"No," answered Gabriel.

"Then maybe we should enjoy the silence."

62

CORSICA

THREE DAYS LATER THE DON invited Gabriel to drop by his office for a chat. It was not truly an invitation, for invitations can be politely declined. It was a Shamronian commandment, chiseled into stone, inviolable.

"How about lunch?" asked Gabriel, knowing that Orsati was likely to be in a good mood then.

"Fine," answered the don. Then he added ominously, "But perhaps it would be better if you came alone."

Gabriel left the villa shortly after noon. The goat allowed him to pass without a confrontation, for it recognized him as an associate of the beautiful Italian woman. The guards outside Don Orsati's estate allowed him to pass, too, for the don had left word that the Israelite was expected. He found the don in his large office, hunched over his ledger books.

"How's business?" asked Gabriel.

"Never better," replied Orsati. "I have more orders than I can possibly fill."

Whether the don was speaking of blood or oil, he did not say. Instead, he led Gabriel to a dining room where a table had been laid with a Corsican feast. With its whitewashed walls and simple furnishings, the room reminded Gabriel of the pope's private dining room in the Apostolic Palace. There was even a heavy wooden crucifix on the wall behind the chair reserved for the don.

"Does it bother you?" asked Orsati.

"Not at all," replied Gabriel.

"Christopher tells me you know your way around Catholic churches."

"What else did he tell you?"

Orsati frowned but said nothing more as he filled Gabriel's plate with food and his glass with wine.

"The villa is to your liking?" he asked finally.

"It's perfect, Don Orsati."

"And your wife is happy here?"

"Very."

"How long do you plan to stay?"

"As long as you'll have me."

The don was curiously silent.

"Have I worn out my welcome already, Don Orsati?"

"You can stay here on the island as long as you like." The don paused, then added, "So long as you don't involve yourself in matters that affect my business."

"You're obviously referring to Keller."

"Obviously."

"I meant no disrespect, Don Orsati. I was just—"

"Meddling in affairs that don't concern you."

The don's mobile phone buzzed softly. He ignored it.

"Did I not help you when you first came to the island looking for the English girl?"

"You did," said Gabriel.

"And did I not give you Keller free of charge to help you find her?"

"I couldn't have done it without him."

"And did I not overlook the fact that I was never offered any of the ransom money you surely recovered?"

"The money is in the bank account of the Russian president."

"So you say."

"Don Orsati . . ."

The don waved his hand dismissively.

"Is that what this is about? Money?'

"No," the don admitted. "It's about Keller."

A gust of wind beat against the French doors leading to Don Orsati's garden. It was the libeccio, a wind from the southeast. Usually, it brought rain in winter, but for now the sky was clear.

"Here on Corsica," the don said after a moment's silence, "our traditions are very old. For example, a young man would never dream of proposing marriage to a woman without first asking her father for permission. Do you see my point, Gabriel?"

"I believe I do, Don Orsati."

"You should have spoken to me before talking to Christopher about going back to England."

"It was a mistake on my part."

Orsati's expression softened. Outside the libeccio overturned a table and chair in the don's garden. He shouted something at the ceiling in the Corsican dialect, and a few seconds later a mustachioed man with a shotgun slung over his shoulder came scampering into the garden to put it back in order.

"You don't know what your friend Christopher was like when he arrived here after leaving Iraq," Orsati was saying. "He was a mess. I gave him a home. A family. A woman."

"And then you gave him a job," said Gabriel. "Many jobs."

"He's very good at it."

"Yes, I know."

"Better than you."

"Who said that?"

The don smiled. A silence fell between them, which Gabriel allowed to linger while he chose his next words with great care.

"It's not a proper way for a man like Christopher to earn a living," he said at last.

"People in glass houses, Allon."

"I never realized that was a Corsican proverb."

"All things wise come from Corsica." The don pushed his plate away and rested his heavy forearms on the tabletop. "There's something you don't seem to understand," he said. "Christopher is more than just my best *taddunaghiu*. I love him like a son. And if he ever left . . ." The don's voice trailed off. "I would be heartbroken."

"His real father thinks he's dead."

"There was no other way."

"How would you feel if the roles were reversed?"

Orsati had no answer. He changed the subject.

"Do you really think this friend of yours from British intelligence would be interested in bringing Christopher back to England?"

"He'd be a fool not to."

"But he might say no," the don pointed out. "And by raising the matter with him, you might endanger Christopher's position here on Corsica."

"I'll do it in a way that poses no threat to him."

"He is a man of trust, this friend of yours?"

"I'd trust him with my life. In fact," said Gabriel, "I've done it many times before."

The don exhaled heavily in resignation. He was about to give Gabriel's unusual proposition his blessing when his mobile phone rang again. This time he answered it. He listened in silence for a moment, spoke a few words in Italian, and then returned the phone to the tabletop.

"Who was that?" asked Gabriel.

"Your wife," replied the don.

"Is something wrong?"

"She wants to take a walk into the village."

Gabriel started to rise.

"Stay and finish your lunch," said Orsati. "I'll send a couple of my boys to keep an eye on her."

Gabriel sat down again. The libeccio was wreaking havoc in Orsati's garden. The don watched it sadly for a moment.

"I'm still glad we didn't kill you, Allon."

"I can assure you, Don Orsati, the feeling is mutual."

The wind chased Chiara down the narrow track, past the shuttered houses and the cats, and finally to the main square, where it swirled in the arcades and vandalized the display tables of the shopkeepers. She went to the market and filled her straw basket with a few things for dinner. Then she took a table at one of the cafés and ordered a coffee. In the center of the square, a few old men were playing *boules* amid tiny cyclones of dust, and on the steps of the church an old woman in black was handing a slip of blue paper to a young boy. The boy had long, curly hair and was very pretty. Looking at him,

Chiara smiled sadly. She imagined that Gabriel's son Dani might have looked like the boy if he had lived to be ten years of age.

The woman descended the church steps and disappeared through the doorway of a crooked little house. Then the boy started across the square with the slip of blue paper in his hand. Much to Chiara's surprise, he entered the café where she was seated and placed the paper on her table without a word. She waited until the boy was gone before reading the single line. *I must see you at once . . .*

The old *signadora* was waiting in the door of her house when Chiara arrived. She smiled, touched Chiara's cheek softly, and then drew her inside.

"Do you know who I am?" the old woman asked.

"I have a good idea," answered Chiara.

"Your husband mentioned me?"

Chiara nodded.

"I warned him not to go to the city of heretics," the *signadora* said, "but he didn't listen. He's lucky to be alive."

"He's hard to kill."

"Perhaps he is an angel after all." The old woman touched Chiara's face again. "And you went, too, didn't you?"

"Who told you I went to Russia?"

"You went without telling your husband," the *signadora* went on, as though she hadn't heard the question. "You were together for a few hours in a hotel room in the city of night. Do you remember?"

The old woman smiled. Her hand was still touching Chiara's face. It moved to her hair.

"Shall I go on?" she asked.

"I don't believe you can see the past."

"Your husband was married to another woman before you," the old woman said, as if to prove Chiara wrong. "There was a child. A fire. The child died but the wife lived. She lives still."

Chiara drew away sharply.

"You were in love with him for a long time," the old woman continued, "but he wouldn't marry you because he was grieving. He sent you away once, but he came back to you in a city of water."

"How do you know that?"

"He painted a picture of you wrapped in white bedding."

"It was a sketch," said Chiara.

The old woman shrugged, as if to say it made no difference. Then she nodded toward her table, where a plate of water and a vessel of olive oil stood next to a pair of burning candles.

"Won't you sit down?" she asked.

"I'd rather not."

"Please," said the old woman. "It will only take a moment or two. Then I'll know for certain."

"Know what?"

"Please," she said again.

Chiara sat down. The old woman sat opposite.

"Dip your forefinger in the oil, my child. And then allow three drops to fall into the water."

Chiara reluctantly did as she was told. The oil, upon striking the surface of the water, gathered into a single drop. The old woman gasped, and a tear spilled onto her powdery white cheek.

"What do you see?" asked Chiara.

The old woman held Chiara's hand. "Your husband is waiting for you at the villa," she said. "Go home and tell him he's going to be a father again."

"Boy or girl?"

The old woman smiled and said, "One of each."

AUTHOR'S NOTE

The English Girl IS A work of entertainment and should be read as nothing more. The names, characters, places, and incidents portrayed in the story are the product of the author's imagination or have been used fictitiously. Any resemblance to actual persons, living or dead, businesses, companies, events, or locales is entirely coincidental.

The version of *Susanna and the Elders* by Jacopo Bassano that appears in the novel does not exist. If it did, it would look a great deal like the one that hangs in the Musée des Beaux-Arts in Reims. There is indeed a small limestone apartment house on Narkiss Street in Jerusalem—several, in fact—but an Israeli intelligence officer named Gabriel Allon does not actually reside there. The headquarters of the Israeli secret service are no longer located on King Saul Boulevard in Tel Aviv; I have chosen to keep the headquarters of my fictitious service there in part because I have always liked the name of the street. The bombing of the King David Hotel in 1946 is historical fact, though Arthur Seymour, the father of my fictitious MI5 officer Graham Seymour, did not actually witness it. There is no exhibit at the Israel Museum featuring the pillars of Solomon's Temple of Jerusalem, for no ruins from the Temple have ever been discovered.

There is in fact a restaurant called Les Palmiers on the Quai Adolphe Landry in Calvi, but, to the best of my knowledge, it has never been used as a rendezvous point for two Russian spies. The

Orsati Olive Oil Company was invented by the author, as was the friendly-fire incident that led Christopher Keller, who first appeared in *The English Assassin*, to desert the Special Air Service and become a Corsican-based professional killer. Those familiar with the island and its rich traditions will know that I have given my fictitious *signadora* powers that most of her colleagues do not profess to have.

The Russian energy company known as Volgatek Oil & Gas does not exist. Nor is there a trade group called the International Association of Petroleum Producers, though there are many just like it. I tinkered with the times of El Al's flights between Tel Aviv and St. Petersburg to meet the needs of my operation. Those brave souls who visit St. Petersburg in the depths of winter should not attempt to scale the glorious dome of St. Isaac's Cathedral, for it is closed in cold weather. For the record, I am quite fond of the Café Nero on London's Bridge Street. Deepest apologies to the Hotel Metropol, the Astoria Hotel, and the Ritz-Carlton for running intelligence operations from their premises, but I'm sure I was not the first.

I did my utmost to describe the atmosphere inside 10 Downing Street accurately, though I admit that, unlike Gabriel Allon, I have never set foot beyond the security barrier along Whitehall. When creating Jeremy Fallon, my fictitious chief of staff, I gave him the broad authority that Prime Minister Tony Blair gave to his real chief of staff, Jonathan Powell. I am quite confident that, had the brilliant and scrupulous Powell been at the side of Jonathan Lancaster, the entire sordid affair portrayed in *The English Girl* would not have occurred.

The increased spying on the part of Russia's intelligence services against Western targets has been well documented. The KGB defector Oleg Gordievsky recently told the *Guardian* newspaper that the size of the SVR's London *rezidentura* has reached Cold War levels. Gordievsky is in a unique position to make such a claim because he worked for the KGB in London from 1982 to 1985. Furthermore, he is not alone in his assessment; MI5 has come to the same conclusion. "It is a matter of some disappointment to me," said MI5 Director General Jonathan Evans, "that I still have to devote significant amounts of equipment, money, and staff to countering this threat. They are resources which I would far rather devote to countering the threat from international terrorism."

While London is clearly an important hub of Russian intelligence activity, the United States remains the primary focus of Moscow Center. The FBI provided ample proof of this fact in June 2010, when it arrested ten Russian spies who had been living in the United States under non-official illegal cover for several years. Fearful of jeopardizing its much-touted "reset" in relations with the Kremlin, the Obama administration quickly agreed to return all the spies to Russia as part of a prisoner exchange, the largest between the United States and Russia since the Cold War. The most notorious of the Russian spies was Anna Chapman, a comely femme fatale who lived in London for several years before settling in New York as a real estate agent and party girl. Since returning to Russia, Chapman has hosted a television program, written a newspaper column, and posed for a magazine cover in French lingerie. She was also appointed to the guiding council of the Young Guard of United Russia, a pro-Kremlin organization affiliated with the country's ruling party. Critics of the Young Guard often refer to it darkly as the "Putin Youth."

Much of Russia's spying against the United States is industrial and economic in nature. The reasons are painfully obvious. Nearly a quarter of a century after the collapse of the Soviet Union, Russia remains largely an economic basket case, heavily dependent on raw materials and, of course, oil and gas. President Vladimir Putin has made no secret of what energy means to the new Russia. Indeed, the Kremlin spelled it out clearly in a 2003 strategy paper that declared the "role of the country in the global energy markets largely determines its geopolitical influence." Wisely, the Kremlin has softened its language when talking about the importance of Russia's energy sector, but the goals remain the same. Stripped of its empire and militarily feeble, Russia now intends to wield power on the world stage with oil and gas rather than nuclear weapons and Marxist-Leninist ideology. What's more, the Kremlin's state-owned energy giants are no longer content to operate only within the boundaries of Russia, where production of oil and gas has leveled off. They are now acquiring both "upstream" and "downstream" assets as part of their stratagem to become truly global energy players. In short, the Russian Federation is attempting to become a Eurasian Saudi Arabia.

Gazprom, the state-owned Russian behemoth, is the world's largest gas company, and its revenues are the source of much of the Kremlin's annual federal budget. Several former Soviet Republics receive *all* their natural gas from Russia, as does tiny Finland. Austria receives more than 80 percent of its gas from Russia; Germany, about 40 percent. While advances in drilling technology are bringing more gas to the international marketplace, the pipelines linking Europe and Russia will help to ensure Gazprom's dominant position for years to come. Its many European customers should bear in mind that Gazprom operated as an instrument of political repression in 2001, when it purchased NTV, Russia's only independent national broadcast outlet and a harsh critic of Vladimir Putin and his United Russia party. NTV's editorial outlook is now reliably pro-Kremlin.

After a brief stint as prime minister, Putin was elected to a third term as Russia's president in March 2012. A former officer of the KGB, he is now in a position to rule until at least 2024, longer than Leonid Brezhnev and nearly as long as Joseph Stalin. Needless to say, not all Russians support Putin's dictatorial hold on power, but increasingly the voices of opposition are being silenced, sometimes harshly. In November 2009, Sergei Magnitsky, a Moscow lawyer and accountant who accused tax officials and police officers of embezzlement, died suddenly in a Russian jail at the age of thirty-seven, provoking international condemnation and sanctions from the United States. Now it appears the Kremlin has set its sights on Alexei Navalny, Russia's most prominent dissident and a leader of the protest movement that swept the country after Putin's return to the presidency. At the time of this writing, Navalny is awaiting trial on embezzlement charges—charges he and his legion of supporters have denounced as politically motivated. If convicted, he faces the prospect of spending ten years in prison, where he would be no threat to Putin and his fellow *siloviki* in the Kremlin.

All too often, a prison sentence of any length in the new Russia of Vladimir Putin is tantamount to a death sentence. According to Russian officials, 4,121 people died in custody in 2012 alone, though pro-democracy advocates say the actual figure is likely far higher. Which might help to explain why Alexander Dolmatov, a Russian pro-democracy activist, chose to take his own life in a Rotterdam detention center in January 2013. Fearing arrest and prosecution in Russia, Dolmatov had fled to the Netherlands in search of political asylum; and when his application was denied, he hanged himself in his cell. The Dutch government has said the denial of asylum had nothing to do with Dolmatov's suicide. His friends from the opposition movement believe otherwise.

Magnitsky, Navalny, Dolmatov: their names are known in the West. But there are many others who already languish in Russian prison cells because they dared to carry a sign, or write an Internet blog, critical of Vladimir Putin. In Russia, the steady descent into authoritarianism continues. And the Kremlin's oil and gas giants are footing the bill.

ACKNOWLEDGMENTS

THIS NOVEL, LIKE THE PREVIOUS books in the Gabriel Allon series, could not have been written without the assistance of David Bull, who truly is among the finest art restorers in the world. Each year, David gives up many hours of his valuable time to advise me on technical matters related to the craft of restoration and to review my manuscript for accuracy. His knowledge of art history is exceeded only by the pleasure of his company, and his friendship has enriched our family in ways large and small.

I spoke to numerous Israeli and American intelligence officers and policy makers while preparing this manuscript, and I thank them now in anonymity, which is how they would prefer it. My dear friend Gerald Malone, the former Conservative member of Parliament and minister of state for health, served as my guide to British politics and shared many fascinating stories about life inside the pressure-cooker atmosphere of 10 Downing Street. It goes without saying that the expertise is all his and that the mistakes and dramatic license are all mine.

I consulted hundreds of books, newspaper and magazine articles, and Web sites while preparing this manuscript, far too many to name here. I would be remiss, however, if I did not mention the extraordinary scholarship and reporting of Daniel Yergin, Edward Lucas, Pete Earley, Allan S. Cowell, William Prochnau, and Clint Van Zandt. Additionally, the memoirs of former prime ministers Tony

Blair, John Major, and Margaret Thatcher were invaluable sources of information and background.

Louis Toscano, my dear friend and longtime personal editor, made countless improvements to my manuscript, as did my copy editor, Kathy Crosby. Obviously, responsibility for any mistakes or typographical errors that find their way into the finished book falls on my shoulders, not theirs.

We are blessed with many friends who fill our lives with love and laughter at critical junctures during the writing year, especially Andrea and Tim Collins, Enola and Stephen Carter, Stacey and Henry Winkler, Joy and Jim Zorn, and Margarita and Andrew Pate.

A heartfelt thanks to Robert B. Barnett, Michael Gendler, and Linda Rappaport for all their support and wise counsel. Also, to the remarkable team of professionals at HarperCollins, especially Jonathan Burnham, Brian Murray, Michael Morrison, Jennifer Barth, Josh Marwell, Tina Andreadis, Leslie Cohen, Leah Wasielewski, Mark Ferguson, Kathy Schneider, Brenda Segel, Carolyn Robson, Doug Jones, Karen Dziekonski, Archie Ferguson, David Watson, David Koral, and Leah Carlson-Stanisic.

I wish to extend my deepest gratitude and love to my children, Nicholas and Lily. Not only did they assist me with the final preparation of my manuscript, but they kept me company while I did my research and were a source of love and comfort while I worked. Finally, I must thank my wife, the brilliant NBC News journalist Jamie Gangel, who listened with remarkable forbearance as I worked through the twists and turns of the story and then skillfully edited my early drafts. Were it not for her patience and attention to detail, *The English Girl* would not have been completed by its deadline. My debt to her is immeasurable, as is my love.

ABOUT THE AUTHOR

D ANIEL SILVA IS THE NUMBER ONE *New York Times* best-selling author of *The Unlikely Spy, The Mark of the Assassin, The Marching Season, The Kill Artist, The English Assassin, The Confessor, A Death in Vienna, Prince of Fire, The Messenger, The Secret Servant, Moscow Rules, The Defector, The Rembrandt Affair, Portrait of a Spy,* and *The Fallen Angel.* He is married to NBC News *Today* correspondent Jamie Gangel, and they live in Washington, DC, with their two children, Lily and Nicholas. In 2009 Silva was appointed to the United States Holocaust Memorial Museum Council.

www.danielsilvabooks.com